the Sweetest Spell

Also by Suzanne Selfors

Saving Juliet
Coffeehouse Angel
Mad Love

the Sweetest Spell

SUZANNE SELFORS

WALKER & COMPANY
NEW YORK

First published in the United States of America in August 2012
by Walker Publishing Company, Inc., a division of Bloomsbury Publishing, Inc.
www.bloomsburyteens.com

For information about permission to reproduce selections from this book, write to
Permissions, Walker BFYR, 175 Fifth Avenue, New York, New York 10010

Library of Congress Cataloging-in-Publication Data
Selfors, Suzanne.
The sweetest spell / by Suzanne Selfors.
p. cm.
Summary: Scorned in her Flatlands village because of a deformed foot, Emmeline Thistle's life changes when she is taken in by Wanderlands' dairy farmers and discovers her magical ability to make chocolate, which is more precious and rare than gold or jewels in the kingdom of Anglund.
ISBN 978-0-8027-2376-5 (hardback)
[1. Fantasy. 2. People with disabilities—Fiction. 3. Prejudices—Fiction.
4. Chocolate—Fiction. 5. Magic—Fiction.] I. Title.
PZ7.S456922Swe 2012 [Fic]—dc23 2011034591

Book design by Regina Roff
Typeset by Westchester Book Composition
Printed in the U.S.A. by Quad/Graphics, Fairfield, Pennsylvania
2 4 6 8 10 9 7 5 3 1

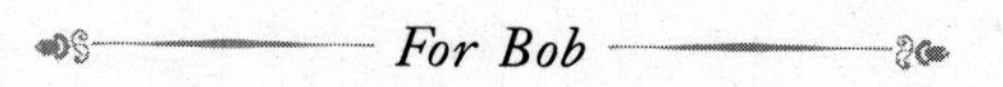

For Bob

the Sweetest Spell

Part One
Dirt-Scratcher Girl

Chapter One

I was born a dirt-scratcher's daughter.

I had no say in the matter. No one asked, "Wouldn't you rather be born to a cobbler or a bard? How about a nobleman or a king? Are you certain that dirt-scratching is the right job for you?"

If someone had asked, I'm pretty sure I wouldn't have answered, "My heart is set on being a dirt-scratcher. I'm really looking forward to a life soured by hunger, backbreaking work, and ignorance. That sounds delightful. Sign me up."

Oh, and I'm absolutely certain I wouldn't have added, "Could you also give me some sort of deformity? Just to make things *interesting*."

The midwife told me the full story of my birth, as much as she could remember. She said nothing out of the ordinary happened that evening. No blinding star appeared on the horizon, the world wasn't darkened by an eclipse, time didn't stand still—the sort of thing that heralds the birth of someone really important. But the midwife boiled the water and counted the beats between my mother's screams, and after I'd been pushed from the womb, the midwife wrapped me in a rag and carried me outside.

"She's no good," the midwife told my father.

"No good?" My father bowed his head and stared at the cracked leather of his boots.

"She's not a keeper." The midwife didn't hesitate. In this time and place, decisions of life and death had to be made. "You must cast her aside, Murl Thistle."

My father ran his callused hand over his face as if trying to wipe away the truth.

"She's got a curled foot," the midwife whispered. She'd whisked me out of the cottage before my exhausted mother could catch a glimpse of me.

Reaching ever so hesitantly, my father slowly peeled back the stained rag. Peering at my misshapen foot, sadness settled in his eyes. Learning your babe is not a keeper has to be the worst feeling in the world. He'd seen the deformity before and it sealed my fate. A dirt-scratcher's daughter needed two strong feet. A curled foot would slow me down, would keep me from doing my fair share of work in the fields. I would be a burden, a gaping mouth to feed. I would never earn enough coin to buy myself a husband. No man would want me.

"Go tell your wife the babe was stillborn." The midwife's tone was matter-of-fact, for she'd learned that it was always best to lie to the mother. A mother, once she's laid eyes on her child, will always beg to keep it despite its defects. "I will take her to the forest, Murl Thistle."

A quiet sound, like a wood dove's coo, floated from my mouth. My father didn't look at my face. Perhaps he figured that if he looked into my eyes, he would see that they were exactly like his eyes, and he'd want to claim me as his own. My father didn't hold me. Perhaps he knew that if he felt the warmth that ebbed from my tiny body and if he felt the beating of my heart, I would become a keeper. I would become his daughter.

He turned away. "Do what you must," he said. "I will tell my wife." Then, with heavy footsteps, as if his legs were felled trees, he stepped into the cottage and closed the door.

My mother's sobs seeped between the cottage stones as the midwife carried me away. The sun was setting, and she wanted to get some distance between the cottage and my fate. She didn't want my parents to hear me cry out. Nor did she want them to accidently stumble upon my tiny bones one day.

Toward the forest the midwife hurried, keeping between the ruts worn into the road by the dirt-scratchers' carts. The day's heat was fading, but I was as warm as a stone taken from a fire. Images flooded the midwife's mind of her own warm children tucked beside her at night. She pushed those images away as she passed the first tilled field, then the next. I wiggled in her arms but she offered no soothing words—what would be the point? Death was coming. In the best of circumstances it would be swift and merciful.

She turned off the road and started across a meadow, her skirt swooshing through tall grass. The forest hugged the edge of the field like a dark curtain, hiding the creatures that lived within its depths. The midwife stopped. She didn't dare go closer. She gently set me on the ground. The predators would come. They always did. And it would be as if I'd never been born.

Finding a clean spot on her bloodied apron, the midwife wiped sweat from her neck. Twilight would soon caress the sky and she needed to get home. She slid the rag free, exposing me so my scent would mix with the evening breeze. A brief twinge of pity pulled at her but she stopped herself from looking into my eyes. Pity wouldn't help me.

The rag tucked under her arm, she left me to my fate. That was the end of her story.

The milkman told how he'd found me the next morning. But the in-between comes from my remembering. I know it sounds strange that a newborn babe could remember, but I do. I swear I do. To this day, it's the brightest memory I have.

Four brown milk cows, having grazed in the field for most of the day, were on their way back to their barn when they caught my scent in the air. Usually wary of the forest's edge, they moseyed up to me, their tails flicking with curiosity. Ignoring their instinct to return home, they stood over me, even as twilight descended. Even as the predators began to stir.

And so it was that four pairs of large, brown eyes were the first to look directly at me, and I met their gazes with an unblinking fascination. Four pairs of eyes, framed with thick lashes, were the first to acknowledge me, and I cooed with appreciation. One cow gently nudged me from side to side while the others licked me clean. As night crept into the meadow, the cows settled in the grass, forming a protective circle. The ground absorbed their heat the way it had absorbed the sun's heat, and warmth spread beneath me. I found a nipple and warmth spread throughout my little body.

And I, the babe who'd been cast aside, lived.

Chapter Two

The only thing on my mind that morning was the upcoming husband market. It never failed to be the most exciting day of the year, promising passion, heartbreak, comedy, even murder. Aye, murder, because on a few occasions, disappointed women had turned on the highest bidder. Nothing else could compare to the husband market for sheer entertainment. My head swirled with excitement. That's why I didn't notice the cows until Father said something.

"Those creatures are at the window again."

It wasn't a fancy window for it had no glass, but it was a hole in the side of our cottage and I'd drawn the ragged curtain aside to let in some fresh air. Clearly the cows thought this was an invitation, for they stuck their noses through the hole and flared their wet nostrils. One white-faced, the other brown, they snorted for attention.

"I'll take them back," I said, scraping the last mouthful of mashed potato from my bowl. When the cows showed up, which they did now and then, I always walked them home. It was the only way to get them to leave. They'd come to see me, after all.

After licking my spoon clean, I pushed back my stool and waited for Father's permission.

"Go on then," he grumbled, hunching over his bowl. His sharp shoulders pressed at the seams of his threadbare shirt. I hoped he'd look up and offer a reassuring nod, but he didn't. He rarely looked directly at me. But I'd caught him a few times, staring as I stumbled across the field, sadness dripping off him like rain.

Everyone in the village of Root knew that my father had rejected me at birth. But he'd simply done what any other dirt-scratcher would have done. Food and shelter were precious and not to be wasted on those who couldn't contribute. This was the way of my people. Over the generations, countless deformed babes had been fed to the forest. When the milkman found me, he knew I was Murl Thistle's babe because my mother was the only woman who'd gone into labor that week. The villagers said my survival was a bad omen. Some kind of black magic had influenced the cows. It was unnatural. *I was unnatural.* That's why villagers always kept a wary distance.

"I'll be as quick as I can," I said, pulling my shawl from its peg. There were kitchen chores to get to. Socks to wash. A donkey's stall to be mucked out. The sun never stayed around long enough for all the work to get done. The precious time it would take for me to walk the cows back to the milkman's land was sacrificed because my father didn't want to face the milkman's temper.

"I got no time to chase after my cows," the milkman had hollered at my father one day. "They stray, Murl Thistle, because that daughter of yours has unnatural power over them. If she doesn't bring them back, I'll complain to the tax-collector!"

As I hurried from the cottage, the white-faced cow stepped away from the window and greeted me with a soft moo.

"Hello," I answered. The cow dipped her head and I kissed her wide brow. She smelled like grass and dirt and wind. I'd known this cow my entire life, and though the milkman never named his cows, I secretly called her Snow. Snow was the only cow left of the original four that had saved me.

A nudge to my elbow drew my attention to the other cow, Snow's daughter. "Hello," I said, running my hand down her back. Five more cows, brown as freshly hoed dirt, waited on the road just below our cottage. "Oh, you brought your friends." I wrapped the shawl around my shoulders. "Well, I'd best get you home. The milkman will be missing you."

Planting season had come to the village of Root. Having finished their noon meal, villagers were at work sprinkling seed into furrows and setting potato tubers into holes. Men and women, boys and girls, young and old—if you breathed and you lived here, you worked the fields. This part of Anglund's kingdom was called the Flatlands, a wide valley wedged between River Time and the Gray Mountains. My ancestors, the red-haired Kell, came to the Kingdom of Anglund as invaders many generations ago but were brutally defeated. The Queen of Anglund took pity on the survivors, mostly women and children. Though we were forbidden to ever again call ourselves Kell, or make or carry weapons, we were given the right to farm the Flatlands. Honestly, no one else wanted the land, which is parched in the summer and soggy in the winter. But after a single generation, the villages of Root, Seed, and Furrow arose, and we have lived there ever since.

No one stared at me as I hobbled down the road. They'd gotten used to the sight of me leading the cows, just as they'd gotten used to the strange way I walked, my right side dipping with each step of my right foot. I walked that way because my right foot was shrunken and curved inward so that I bore my weight on its side. A long trek, such as the distance between my father's cottage and the milkman's land, was difficult and painful. But the cows never seemed to mind my slow pace.

My thoughts drifted to tomorrow's husband market. The boys who'd turned eighteen since the last husband market would be up for bid, joined by the men who had yet to find wives or who had been widowed. Flatlander girls saved all their coins for the occasion. The highest bidder got the best husband. Usually.

There was no law forcing a girl to marry, but most did. A husband provided a house. A husband meant that a girl was no longer a child and could speak for herself. A husband meant other things too—things I'd heard girls whisper about.

Everyone knew my fate was to remain unmarried, thanks to my *unnatural* status. I suppose, out of desperation, I could bid on an "unwanted." The unwanteds were the men who rarely got bids, usually because they had frightful tempers or because they had a flock of nasty, bad-mannered children from previous marriages. Or because they were hideous.

No thank you.

The cows' hooves clomped along the road. Soft clouds drifted lazily over the fields. Two robins circled each other in a spring dance of love. I could pretend that my pride would keep me from bidding on an unwanted, but the truth was this—I was also an *unwanted*.

The pain began at the next bend in the road. It started in my curled foot, then shot up the outside of my leg. It would worsen throughout the afternoon as I followed Father around the field, dropping the potato tubers into the holes he'd dug. I fought the urge to slow down, maybe take a rest beside the river. Daylight was precious. Father needed my help. We had a lot to get done if we wanted to take tomorrow off for the husband market.

No way was I going to miss it. Not this year. Not with Root's most popular boy stepping onto that stage. Every girl in the village of Root dreamed of marrying Griffin Boar.

Including me.

And that's why I gasped when he appeared around the bend.

Chapter Three

Who was this boy who consumed the thoughts of the village girls?

Griffin Boar was the milkman's only son. Because the Boars were rich by Flatlander measure, Griffin's future wife would never want for food. She'd never want for shelter either, because for the past three years, Griffin had been building a cottage. Girls often gathered at the river's edge to watch the progress as, shirtless, he stripped the bark off timbers and set them into place. Other young men were building their cottages, but Griffin's effort drew the most attention. His cottage was double the size of anyone else's.

This would have been enough to explain his popularity. But Griffin Boar had more going for him than security.

He was beautiful.

Even after casting aside the deformed babies, most Flatlanders didn't make it to the age of eighteen without some sort of disfigurement—a crooked nose from a break, an arm scarred from a burn, cheeks pockmarked by disease. Missing teeth, split lips, boils, and bruises were the markings of village life. But somehow Griffin had been spared.

And that is why so much female time in the village of Root was spent thinking about Griffin Boar. Security *and* beauty came along once in a generation, if at all.

Griffin didn't notice me as he appeared around the bend, his horse cantering at a steady pace. One hand on the reins, the other hand holding a small mirror, Griffin stared, transfixed by his own reflection, his red locks bouncing at his shoulders. I froze as the horse headed straight at me and the cows. Surely it would veer around us. Surely Griffin would look up in time. Oblivious, he held the mirror closer and inspected his smile. He smiled with teeth, then without teeth. Then with teeth again.

"Watch out!" I cried, trying to limp out of the way. The horse neighed as it skidded to a stop. Griffin looked up just before he flew over the horse's head and landed on the road, right between two cows.

I stumbled, then caught my balance. Holding my breath, I stared at Griffin. He wasn't moving. Was he dead? Was the most beautiful boy in Root Village *dead*? I reached cautiously, my fingers floating just above his shoulder. "Hello? Are you . . . hurt?"

Squinting into the sun, he turned his face toward me. "Who's there? Emmeline?" His eyes widened. "Get away," he said, waving a hand. "Don't touch me."

"I wasn't going to touch you," I snapped.

I stepped back. Griffin may have looked better than the other boys in Root, but he shared the same stupid superstitions. He didn't want to get too close lest my black magic taint him in some way.

Griffin and I had lived in the same village all our lives, but I could count on one hand the times he'd spoken to me. I could remember exactly what he'd said on each occasion:

"Move out of the way. I've got somewhere important to go."

"Move out of the way. I'm in a hurry."

"Move out of the way, now."

"Move out of the way."

"Move."

So this encounter was a bit unusual. He'd said "get away" instead of "move." After being on the receiving end of such poetic tenderness, how could a girl not fall in love with Griffin Boar?

After scrambling to his feet, he brushed dirt from his woven shirt and pants. "Why are you walking in the middle of the road?" he asked angrily. "Are you stupid? The middle of the road is for horses."

"I'm not the stupid one. I was walking in the middle of the road because the middle of the road has fewer ruts," I said, equally angry. "And I'm walking your father's cows home. Maybe *you're* too stupid to notice a road full of cows."

He glared at the cows, then pushed one out of his way. "Stupid cows," he grumbled. A thin line of blood appeared at the edge of his chin. It glistened in the sunlight. A sudden pang of sadness struck me. It was as if a beloved piece of pottery had cracked.

Griffin frowned. "What are you looking at?"

I pointed at his chin.

His fingers found the wound. Then he stared at the blood on his fingertips. "I'm hurt," he said, his face slack with surprise. He felt the wound again. "It's a cut. On my face. My *face*."

"It's a small scratch," I said. "It'll heal."

But Griffin wasn't listening. He whirled around, scanning the ground. "Where's my mirror?" He shoved another cow out of the way. As he desperately searched, his horse wandered to the side of the road and helped itself to spring clover.

Light flashed at my feet. While Griffin's back was to me, I reached down and picked up the oval mirror. A crack ran through it, dividing it into two equal pieces. Though distorted by the crack, my reflection revealed a dirt-smudged face. I ran my hand over my hair, tangled and matted, as red as river clay. When my mother was alive, she'd combed and braided it. But I never learned to braid it on my own and the teeth in my comb had broken long ago. No wonder Griffin never paid me much mind. I was nothing to look at. I held out the mirror. "Here it is."

He yanked the mirror from my hand. He'd never stood so close to me. A musky scent floated around him, born from sweat and horse. "It's broken," he snapped. "Do you know how expensive a mirror is?"

I shook my head. We didn't have a mirror in our cottage, but I bet Griffin owned more than one.

He held up the cracked glass and examined his face. "I'm going to have a scar," he said, running a finger over the wound. "You've ruined my face. This was your doing."

I was used to being blamed. The villagers often pointed fingers at me and said, "It's her doing. She brought this bad luck." I couldn't prove that I had nothing to do with the amount of snow that fell in winter or the size of the crops at harvest time. That I had nothing to do with last year's infestation of caterpillars or with the fever that had killed many of the roosters. I couldn't prove my innocence in those matters so I'd stopped trying. But this was ridiculous.

"It wasn't my doing," I said.

Though still inspecting the scratch, he quickly glanced at me from the corner of his eye. "You made me fall."

"I didn't." My leg was really hurting. I relaxed it, my right side dipping lower. "You did this to yourself because you weren't paying attention."

He looked into my eyes, his gaze burning. "Are you saying I don't know how to ride?" He stomped over to his horse, opened the saddlebag, and shoved the mirror inside. "I've been riding since I could walk. I know how to ride a horse. You're too stupid to know anything about it."

My cheeks burned. "I'm smart enough to know you shouldn't look in a mirror while riding. You should look where you're going."

"Smart? You?" He grabbed his horse's mane. "You talk to cows, that's how smart you are." He hoisted himself upward, swung his long leg, and settled onto the saddle. "Do you know how many girls have been waiting their whole lives to bid on me? I wouldn't go to the husband market if I were you. When they find out you caused this wound, they'll eat you alive."

"It's just a scratch," I said. "You're still . . ." But I stopped myself from finishing that sentence. He was still beautiful, and despite his arrogance and lack of manners, I still wondered what it would be like to kiss him.

"It's true what they say. You're bad luck, Emmeline Thistle." He tucked his hair behind his ears, then seized the reins. "Now, move out of the way."

I stepped aside.

With a sharp kick to his horse, Griffin Boar rode away at full gallop, his hair rising and falling with the horse's graceful stride.

He'd warned me not to go to the husband market. But I wasn't afraid. So what if the hopeful brides blamed me for the scratch? They already treated me like a flea-infested dog. How much worse could it get?

Maybe no one would bid on Griffin and his scarred face. Maybe people would point at him the way they pointed at me. Maybe he'd feel, for the first time in his life, like an unwanted.

But I wouldn't wish that on anyone. Not even a rude boy like Griffin Boar.

Chapter Four

The sound of wheels and donkey hooves woke me. I pulled my blanket around my shoulders and walked to the kitchen window. By foot and by cart, villagers were traveling the road, heading to the village square. Some of the families I recognized but many were unfamiliar, come from the nearby villages of Seed and Furrow. Excitement darted up my spine. The morning of the husband market had arrived.

I mashed some cold boiled turnips for Father's breakfast and set a half loaf of oat bread onto the table. Back in my bedroom, I tossed the blanket over my hay-filled mattress and washed my face in the washing bowl. Then I stood in my nightfrock, staring at the two dresses that hung from pegs. One dress was for home, the other for town. There wasn't much difference between the two. Both were made of a coarse handspun weave, both had wooden buttons, and neither was dyed. The town dress, however, had less wear. As I pulled it over my head, I wondered if I was making a mistake. Word would have already spread about Griffin's tumble off his horse. In the Flatlands, gossip traveled faster than plague thanks to Lull Trog, the gravedigger's wife. All the lovesick girls would be cursing me for scarring Griffin's face. The glaring would be worse than usual.

On the other hand, my day wouldn't be complete without all those glares.

"Time to go," Father called.

I fastened the buttons, then sat at the edge of the bed and pulled on my good pair of wool socks. I'd long ago figured out how to make my curled foot fit into a boot by stuffing the boot with fabric scraps. The boot's seam was beginning to give way. I'd make do as long as I could before asking Father for a new one.

He was outside, hitching our only donkey to the cart. He wore his best shirt, which I'd scrubbed with well water and dried by the fire. I'd patched the hole at the elbow with a bit of fabric from another shirt that he'd worn to shreds. "Get on in," he told me, tipping his head toward the cart. I climbed in.

Father walked alongside the donkey. A few carts rolled ahead of us. As we neared the milkman's field, the cows ambled across the pasture and stood by the side of the road, watching us pass by. Snow's white muzzle glowed next to the browns of the other cows. I leaned over the side of the cart, but as I did so, Father cast a warning glance over his shoulder. With so many families within earshot, my talking to the cows would bring shame to him. I sighed and said nothing. Snow smiled at me. I imagined her voice. *One day, Emmeline, the husband market will be for you, too.*

As we neared our village square, I broke into a huge grin. So many people! Carts were lined up along the road, some turned into little houses for those who'd traveled from Seed and Furrow. Father unhitched the cart, then led our donkey to a communal pasture to join other donkeys. There'd be no confusion when we went to retrieve the creature because it had been branded with Father's symbol. As I climbed out of the cart, villagers walked past, also dressed in their best town clothes. They gave me a wide berth. The children whispered.

Without a word to me, Father headed straight for the tavern, as did most of the men. They'd drink throughout the day, breaking into boisterous song as the ale numbed their minds. Singing was good for my father. He'd changed so much since my mother's death, curling into himself like a snail into its shell, keeping all his feelings inside. Since her passing, Father had never once stood on the husband market's stage. He told me he didn't want another wife. But I knew the truth. No one would want to marry the father of Emmeline, the unnatural girl. My mere existence had doomed both Father and me to solitude.

As Father stepped into the tavern and disappeared behind its heavy door, a pebble bounced off my leg. I spun around. Maude Boar, the milkman's daughter, hurried past, two friends by her side. "You shouldn't have gotten in Griffin's way," she snapped just before throwing another pebble, which stung my arm.

"I didn't," I snapped back.

"Are you calling my brother a liar?" Her crooked tooth caught on her lower lip. Despite the sneer, Maude looked pretty, a painted comb tucked into her braid.

Fortunately I didn't have to answer her question because a hopeful bride hurried past Maude and her friends, catching their attention. A chorus of squeals filled the air as the girls surrounded the bride. I hobbled away.

Our village square wasn't much to look at—just a big open space between the tax-collector's house and the tavern. The gravedigger and the blacksmith lived in the other buildings. No merchants lived in the Flatlands. We were forbidden from obtaining merchant licenses, so we relied on a few traveling peddlers to bring in goods.

A wooden stage sat in the middle of the square. The few benches had already been claimed. Everyone else sat in the dirt or stood. The eager brides, all wearing floral wreaths in their hair, began to gather in front of the stage, chattering among themselves. A boy selling bags of roasted walnuts wandered throughout the crowd, as did a girl selling bunches of baby spring carrots. Milkman Boar had brought some rounds of cheese and was selling wedges. My mouth watered. I'd forgotten to pack a lunch and I had no coin to spare. I took a long drink from the town fountain.

"Emmeline!" Lull Trog, the gravedigger's wife, hurried up, nearly knocking me over. Clearly her need to spread gossip was greater than her fear of my unnaturalness. As she adjusted her black apron, many heads turned to watch. "Tell me what happened."

"I don't know what you mean," I said coldly, then took another sip of water.

Lull Trog frowned. "Of course you know what I mean, girl. Tell me how Griffin got that wound on his face."

"It's not a wound. It's a scratch." As I wiped my mouth with the back of my hand, a devilish thought crept into my mind. I lowered my voice to a whisper. "Do you want to know the truth? Even if you find it *shocking*?"

She widened her eyes and nodded. "Aye."

I leaned closer. Lull Trog's entire body stiffened and I stifled a wicked smile. "Griffin Boar got that scratch on his face because he tried to kiss me."

"He didn't," she said with a gasp.

"He wanted to have some fun before he got married." I raised my eyebrows. "I had to protect myself."

Lull Trog held her breath. Then she spun on her heels and dashed off, her arms pumping madly. She grabbed another woman by the arm and whispered into her ear. They both turned to look at me. I smiled and waved. What would life in Root be like without some new gossip about Emmeline Thistle? I didn't want to disappoint.

Villagers stepped aside as I found a spot in front of the blacksmith's. Leaning against a post I had a clear view. Rousing applause filled the air as our tax-collector, Mister Todd, walked up the steps and onto the stage. He nodded as if the applause was meant for him. It wasn't. Villagers tolerated him because they had no other choice. All tax-collectors worked for the king. Because the collection of taxes was the most important job in the kingdom, tax-collectors wielded the power of life and death. Todd had hanged more than one tax evader. But he made no attempt to hide the fact that he hated his job. Being assigned to the Flatlands was the lowest rung on the tax-collector ladder. Living with us lowly dirt-scratchers was punishment for something he'd done. He was constantly trying to get reassigned.

Todd's three men stood nearby, each carrying a sword. They acted as his enforcers and bodyguards.

As Todd walked to the middle of the stage, his steps stiff and bowlegged, the applause grew louder and louder, joined by whistles and cheers. The husband market was about to begin. He cleared his throat, his floppy black tax-collector's hat drooping over one eye. A flagon of ale in one hand, he punched the air with the other hand. "Shut your traps!" he hollered. The cheering continued. The hopeful brides pushed closer to the stage. After a long drink, he turned the flagon upside down. Finding it empty, he tossed it aside. It flew across the stage and slammed into a guard's chest. Laughter arose. Todd wiped his mouth with his sleeve. "Shut your traps, you stupid dirt-scratchers, or I'll double the ale tax!"

Immediate silence fell over the square. "That's better." He tightened his belt, pulling his gut up a few inches. "Let's get to it. Calling all unmarried men. Get up here, you doomed fools."

Cheers and whistles erupted again as the men made their way onto the stage. Some took eager steps, rubbing their hands in anticipation of a bride. A few, mostly the young ones, had to be pushed onstage by their fathers like sheep to the slaughter. Twenty-three men in all, a good number—unlike that year long ago when plague wiped out an entire season of husbands. The hopeful brides pressed close together. It's one thing to imagine a husband. It's another thing to look into his eyes and face your future.

Griffin Boar was the last to take his place onstage. His hair bounced with each of his confident steps. His mother, Finny Boar, and his sister, Maude, sat together, waving excitedly. On the other side of the square, men emerged from the tavern to watch the event unfold. While most smiled and cheered, a dark expression covered my father's face. *He's thinking of the time he stood on that stage*, I guessed. *When my mother bid on him and won.* I wanted to tell him how deeply I missed her.

As the husbands-to-be lined up, tax-collector Todd stumbled to the side of the stage and grabbed another flagon from one of his guards. Once he'd emptied it, he returned to his duties. "All right, ladies, feast your eyes on this loathsome group of losers." He pointed to the first man, an old guy named Gus who flashed a toothless grin. "This one's a real beauty," Todd said. Everyone laughed, including Gus. "Don't waste your coin on him, ladies. All you need to win Gus is an old rooster or a lame donkey." More laughter. "How many years you've been widowed, Gus?"

"Three," Gus said.

"And how old are you?"

"Sixty-one," Gus replied. "But I've got a nice cottage with a deep well and a good roof."

"Sixty-one?" Todd slapped Gus on the back, nearly knocking him over. "Ladies, bid on Gus if you want to get a good night's sleep. He's too old to *bother* you, if you know what I mean." This comment brought on raucous jeers from the tavern crowd.

Tax-collector Todd stopped at the next in line, a young man wearing a fur vest. "I don't know you. What's your name?"

"I'm from Furrow." Furrow lay on the very edge of the Flatlands, where the forest was thickest. "I'm Boris, son of a huntsman."

The crowd ooohed.

"A huntsman's son is a good catch," Todd shouted. "He's not much to look at, but he's got nice breath." Then, after adjusting his floppy hat, he moved to the next man and the crowd quieted. There stood an *unwanted.*

The unwanted had been widowed, with five young mouths to feed. If he'd been a nice man, my heart would have ached for him. But he was cruel, known to beat his children. He deserved his unwanted status, though his children didn't deserve a house without a mother. "No pretty girl's gonna bid on you, that's for sure," Todd said. "Any of you ladies desperate enough to want this dirt-scratcher?"

The brides huddled closer, fearful that such a fate might befall them. For some families, it was better to get rid of a daughter, even if it meant sending her to live with a horrible man. One less mouth to feed. Would this be my fate next year when I turned seventeen?

The sheriff made his way down the line, prodding the men with insults. One was as skinny as a rat's tail. Another was as ugly as a toad. One was so shy that he turned beet-red and tried to run off the stage. "Virgin!" the tavern men cried. But then the crowd fell silent again. Todd took a long pause as he stepped up to the next candidate.

"Well, well, well," he said. "You've been counting the years waiting for this one, haven't you, ladies?"

If gold coins had suddenly rained from the sky, the excitement wouldn't have matched that moment. The screams were heavy with agony. The tears held as much hope as dread. Years of dreaming of this moment could be dashed in an instant—or the prize could be won. The brides jumped up and down, daisies falling from their hair. "Griffin!" they yelled. "Griffin!"

The parents of the hopeful brides rushed toward Griffin's parents, surrounding them with gifts—a basket of eggs, a chicken in a crate, a skinned rabbit carcass, a clay bowl. Griffin's parents would naturally want their son to marry into a family that could provide lots of gifts, and they'd try to influence his choice. But Griffin could choose to ignore his parents' wishes. He could accept the highest bidder or not. He could even refuse all bids and wait until next year. There was no predicting the outcome of the market.

"What's this?" tax-collector Todd asked, pointing at Griffin's chin. "Is this the tragic wound we've heard so much about? Did our very own Emmeline do this to you?" Heads whipped around. Glares shot my way. "From what your mother was saying, I thought you'd be unrecognizable. But this? Someone get me a magnifying glass so I can see it." The tavern men burst into laughter. Griffin scowled.

I hadn't told my father about the encounter with Griffin. But he didn't react to the uproar. Still standing with the tavern men, he'd turned away from the stage and was looking down the road that led from the village square.

Todd took another drink from his flagon, then stomped his

boot. "We'd best bid on Griffin Boar first. None of these other wretched oafs will get a single coin until Griffin's out of the way."

The brides started pushing again. One scrambled onto the stage and shoved her coin bag at Griffin. "He's mine," she said as one of the guards pulled her away. "Mine!"

"No, he's mine!" another bride hollered, and a fight broke out. One bride punched another in the face. Two brides fell onto the ground, wrestling like mad women. Griffin folded his arms and smiled. I cringed. It wasn't their fault they were acting like idiots. What else did a girl have to look forward to? A village girl was supposed to marry and have children. She was supposed to serve her husband. Nothing more was expected. Nothing more could be achieved.

"I love a good fight!" Todd hollered.

Father didn't appear to notice the fighting. He walked a few paces down the road, his steps cautious, his head cocked as if listening for something. Had the donkey gotten loose? I held tight to the post, leaning forward to watch him. Suddenly he spun around and looked through the crowd, right at me, his gaze filled with fear.

My heart skipped a beat as the sound of horse hooves thundered in the distance.

Chapter Five

Villagers scrambled to their feet and parted as fourteen horses and fourteen soldiers rode into the village square. The crest of Anglund, a white swan in a sea of yellow, hung over each horse's flank and covered the front of each soldier's tunic. It was rare to see royal soldiers in the Flatlands. They occasionally brought messages to the tax-collector, but never more than two or three soldiers at a time. Why would the king send so many?

A stunned expression swept over tax-collector Todd's face as the soldiers spread out along the edge of the square. Their yellow tunics shone brightly against the drab browns of Flatlander clothing. Three wagons came to a halt outside the square. The drivers jumped out, then led their horses in a half circle, turning the wagons around to face away from the square. The drivers waited, reins in hand, as if to make a quick exit.

The lead soldier maneuvered his horse right up the staircase and onto the stage, which creaked beneath the creature's weight.

My gaze darted between the stage and my father. I could tell by his clenched expression that he was worried. Something serious was about to happen.

The lead soldier dismounted, then handed the flag to the huntsman's son, who looked as bewildered as everyone else. "I'm Captain Finch." That seemed a fitting name since his nose was small and sharp like a beak. "You are the local tax-collector?" Todd nodded. Captain Finch opened a saddlebag and removed a scroll. "This proclamation is sent from His Royal Majesty, King Elmer. You are ordered to read it immediately."

Murmurs arose as Todd unrolled the scroll and read to himself. His shoulders slumped. My father began to push through the crowd. "Emmeline," he called. He wanted to tell me something. I squeezed between two little boys who were sharing a bag of walnuts. This time, villagers did not step aside to let me pass. They were transfixed on the scroll.

Todd and Captain Finch turned their backs to the crowd for a muffled conversation. The captain nodded his head, confirming whatever news had been delivered. Shouts arose from the crowd. "Tell us!"

Todd wore a stiff expression when he faced the crowd. "Listen," he demanded, waving the scroll. "Listen." The crowd quieted. "The news is bad. Very bad." The scroll dropped to his side. "Anglund is at war."

I stopped in my tracks. Father, now only halfway across the square from me, also stopped. No one moved as the word slithered though the crowd like a poisonous serpent. *War?* I'd heard stories of war, but they were of generations long dead. The kingdom had been at peace all of my life.

War.

Captain Finch tucked his feathered helmet under his arm and cleared his throat. His sword handle caught the sunlight as he stepped to the edge of the stage. "The war wages in the east where the barbarians are trying to lay claim to our mineral fields. King Elmer needs more soldiers. All unmarried men must accompany me to Londwin City immediately."

"What?"

"What did he say?"

"Did you say all unmarried men?" Nather Trog, the gravedigger, shouted.

"All unmarried men," Todd confirmed. "That's the order."

Villagers murmured and shook their heads. "Why should our sons fight this war?" a man cried. "We pay our taxes but the king gives us nothing."

"We are forbidden to own our land."

"We are forbidden to leave."

"We have no rights as citizens. Why should we sacrifice our sons?"

"That is treason," Todd said, waving a fist at the crowd. "The king allows you to live here, you ungrateful dirt-scratchers."

Captain Finch scowled. "You'll fight this war because King Elmer has ordered you to fight. You must obey your king."

"But what about the law?" The question came from my own mouth. I'm sure I wasn't the only one shocked by my act. Captain

Finch stared at me. I nearly choked on my next words as I forced myself to speak. "It's against the law for a Flatlander to carry a weapon. How can our men fight without weapons?"

Silence fell as we looked to the captain for an answer.

"The king *is* the law," Captain Finch said. Then he pointed to the waiting wagons. "All unmarried men will prepare for immediate departure."

Griffin Boar tried to run off the stage, but his escape route was blocked by one of Todd's guards. "You can't take away our young men," a woman called. "It's planting season."

"I have children to feed," said the unwanted man who still stood on the stage. "Who will take care of them?"

Beneath my boots, tremors of unrest rippled. Villagers began to push, panic blanching their faces. "Hide," mothers told their young sons. "Go, quickly. Hide."

Three of the soldiers dismounted and marched onto the stage. Captain Finch pulled his sword from its sheath and pointed at the line of men who'd thought the day would end with a bride and a wedding bed. "Into the wagons. Now!" As one of the soldiers pointed his sword at Griffin, Missus Boar fainted in her husband's arms.

"No!" a desperate bride screamed, climbing onto the stage. She grabbed Griffin's arm. "You can't take him away. He's supposed to get married today. I've got the coin right here. Marry us now. Marry us now!" She shook her coin purse in the soldier's face. He grabbed the purse, then pushed her off the stage. She landed on two other girls, her elbow jabbing one in the face. The soldier's gaze was cold and without regret.

That's when chaos erupted.

As villagers tried to escape the square, the soldiers and guards drew their swords. In the uproar, I lost sight of my father. "Don't panic!" tax-collector Todd hollered, but no one listened. "Stupid dirt-scratchers. I'll hang every last one of you if you disobey the royal command."

Mothers burst into tears as their unmarried sons were rounded up. Only the youngest boys, the ones still scrawny and smooth-faced, were spared. A few men tried to dart into the blacksmith's house to escape but were dragged out by soldiers. "Father!" I called, tripping between villagers. Then suddenly, he stood before me.

He clutched my shoulders, his eyes wild. "What will you do? What will become of you?"

"Father . . ." I had no idea what to say. My legs felt as if they were melting. Soldiers' shouts and women's wails swirled around us. "Father . . ."

"You can't take care of the farm by yourself."

"I can. I can do it."

"You're not strong enough," he said as a soldier grabbed his arm.

"You got a wife?" the soldier asked. It was the same soldier who'd pushed the bride off the stage.

"Aye," I said, stepping in front of my father. I clenched my jaw, trying to keep my chin from quivering. "I'm his wife."

The soldier motioned, and tax-collector Todd, who'd found another flagon of ale, staggered over. "Is this one married?" the soldier asked.

"Please," I begged our tax-collector. "Please tell him that this is my husband."

Todd ignored my plea. He glared at my father. "This one is named Murl Thistle. He tried to lead a revolt last year against the potato tax. Caused me some trouble." He narrowed his bloodshot eyes. "He's not married."

The soldier shoved my father toward the waiting wagons.

"No," I cried, holding tight to my father's thin arm.

"You'll have to find work," he said to me. "Leave the farm and find work."

"I can't leave the farm." My eyes filled with tears. Why was he saying such a thing?

"Listen to me," he said as we reached the first wagon. The huntsman's son staggered past. He'd put up a fight. His nose dripped with blood as he cursed the soldier who shoved him into the wagon. "You must find work. It's your only chance." Father grabbed my hand and pressed two coins into my palm. "It's all I have."

I closed my fingers around the coins. "I will work the farm and keep it for you. For when you come back."

He grimaced, the truth making its painful way to the surface. "I will not be back."

The soldier pushed me aside, then forced my father into the wagon, next to a trembling boy from the village of Seed.

"Make way," the driver hollered as the first wagon, the one carrying my father, started down the road. Hot tears in my eyes, I followed, ignoring my pain to run alongside as mothers screamed their sons' names. Fathers froze, as still as trees, as if life had drained from their limbs.

"Father," I called again.

"Out of the way," another driver ordered as the second wagon began its journey.

"Find work," were the last words I heard before the second wagon caught up to me. Milkman Boar tried to steady his wife as the second wagon gathered speed and headed down the road, carrying Root's most desired son to war.

Griffin Boar met my gaze as he passed by, his eyes also filled with tears.

For the first time in my life, I felt equal to my fellow Flatlanders. A curled foot or a handsome face made no difference—in the end, each of us was at the mercy of fate.

And that's when the rain began to fall.

Chapter Six

Clouds rolled in. The sky let loose as if it, too, were grieving. Villagers gathered around the tax-collector, bombarding him with questions.

"Will we ever see them again?"

"I can't do the planting without my son."

"Who will we marry?"

Shivering, I stood at the edge of the crowd, rain dripping off my eyelashes.

"They're gone," Todd grumbled, his words slurred from drink. "There's nothing I can do. Now leave me be." He staggered toward his home, his guards following. His heartlessness was no surprise.

Only a few families were untouched by the royal proclamation. With Todd and his guards drinking behind locked doors, Fin Bitter, the blacksmith, took over. He was one of the oldest men in Root, and we looked up to him as a sort of elder. "Gather the orphaned children," he said. "We must take care of them." The unwanted's five were rounded up, their faces streaked with tears and rain. I was too old to be considered an orphan. Not that anyone would take me. "Those of you who've suffered no loss today, I urge you to take one of these orphans," Fin said. Then he split up the children. It had to be that way. No family could afford to take on two additional mouths. Fin himself took the smallest boy. "I could use some help stoking the fire," he said, patting the boy's head.

Soon after, the village square cleared. Villagers hitched their donkeys and headed for home. Griffin Boar's parents and sister climbed into their cart. Maude curled into an angry ball on the back seat. Milkman Boar put an arm around his wife, comforting her.

Floral wreaths, once adorning the heads of dream-filled brides, lay abandoned on the ground. I crushed one as I hobbled toward the donkey field. What would become of me? What would happen to my father? Panic swept over me as I hitched our donkey to our cart. The creature knew the way home without guidance, so I climbed into the back and lay on the wet wooden planks. The rumble of wheels and hooves hid the sound of my sobbing.

The rain fell hard, soaking through my dress. When we reached the cottage, I put the donkey in his shed, then sat at the table. War had come to Anglund. The unmarried men were gone, carted off like beasts. Father was gone. I stared at his empty chair. How could he fight in a war? He'd been born a Flatlander. A seed-sower. He'd never used a sword in his life.

What if he never came back?

There were chores to be done yet I had no desire to do anything but sit. I didn't eat, didn't drink, didn't move. The two coins Father had given me now lay on the table. How long would they keep me from going hungry? Get a job, my father had said. But who would employ me, a dirt-scratcher girl with a curled foot? A dirt-scratcher girl who was supposedly unnatural?

The sky darkened until day looked like night. Exhausted by grief, I fell asleep at the table only to awake to something dripping on my face. The rain had broken through a patch in the roof. Not bothering to light a candle, I stumbled to Father's bedroom, and for the first time since my mother's death, I lay on their bed. Mother's scent was long gone. But Father's scent of dirt and sweat wrapped around me and eased me back to sleep.

All night long and all the next day it rained—the kind of angry rain that stings the skin. A stream of water ran alongside the cottage and into the road, where huge puddles formed. On the third day of rain, the field turned to mud. The potato tubers that Father had planted lay exposed as the soil around them washed away. I sank to my ankles in the muck as I tried to replant, but the next day they lay exposed again. And on the fifth day of nonstop rain, a current of water ran through the field, carrying the tubers toward the river. I was in serious trouble. The village itself was in trouble, for all the fields were suffering the same fate. A season without planting meant starvation.

On the seventh day of rain, a cart rode by carrying a family, their belongings stuffed into the back. Soon after, another family rode past, then another. I threw my shawl over my head and hurried through the mud to the edge of the road. "Why are you leaving?" I called.

The man and his wife ignored me, but their little girl, whose wet hair hung in her eyes, said, "The river ate our cottage."

The river?

As the cart rode away, I looked down at my boots. The water on the road was ankle-deep. My soaked skirt clinging to my legs, I climbed up our ladder and stood on the donkey shed's roof. River Time lay at the edge of the neighbor's farm. I took a deep, worried breath. After seven straight days of rain, the usually gentle river rushed with rage—white, churning water overflowed its banks and poured into the neighbor's field. My mother once told me a story of a terrible spring, long ago, when too much rain had made the river rise and flood the village. Many people had died in the rising water, but those who'd gone into the hills above the Flatlands had survived.

Back inside the cottage I grabbed a few belongings—Mother's rocking chair, the rug woven by Mother's mother, the wooden bowl that Father had carved. I loaded these into the cart, along with a bag of potatoes and turnips. Water seeped beneath the cottage door. I tucked the two coins into my dress pocket. By the time I'd pulled the last bunch of winter carrots from the sand barrel, water covered our stone floor. The stones had been taken from the river long before my birth, but now the river had come to reclaim them with its icy fingers.

Offering a carrot as a bribe, I managed to get the donkey out of the shed and hitched to the cart. The creature didn't like walking through water. It snorted and flattened its ears. "It's okay," I cooed, trying to keep my voice steady and calm. But even with another carrot to entice, the donkey couldn't pull the cart from the mud. I pushed but the wheels sank deeper. "Please," I begged. "Please." It was no use. Neither the old donkey nor I had the strength. I collapsed against the cart and closed my eyes. Fear wanted to consume me. But if I gave in, I might crumple to the ground and never get up again.

After a long, deep breath, I wiped rain from my eyes and looked toward the distant hills. I'd have to leave the belongings and go on foot. As I unhitched the donkey, another cart approached carrying Milkman Boar and his family. Six brown cows trailed behind. Not one had a white face.

I dropped the donkey's reins and sloshed through the water. "Where's Snow?" I asked, blocking the way. "Where's the white-faced cow?"

"She's old," Milkman Boar said as his cart rolled to a stop. Maude and her mother, who sat on a wheel of cheese, peered out from beneath a soaked blanket.

"I know she's old but where is she?"

"I don't know," he grumbled. "I couldn't find her. Now move out of the way. There's not much time."

"Where are you going?" I asked.

"Wife's got family in Furrow, in the foothills. It'll be dry in the foothills."

I made a quick decision. "Please take my donkey," I said. "If you take him to safety, you can keep him. He's a good donkey."

The milkman jumped out of the cart. He grabbed a rope then waited as I bribed my donkey with the last carrot. As Milkman Boar tied the donkey to the cart, I gave the creature a reassuring scratch. Maude said nothing to me. She pulled the blanket over her face and huddled against her mother. Even if the Boars had offered to take me to safety, I wouldn't have gone. Not without Snow.

As the milkman's cart headed down the road toward Furrow, I waded up the road. My feet grew numb in the cold water, as did my calves. Rain pelted my aching face. The rough fabric of my farm dress clung to my skin. I clenched my jaw, forcing my legs to run. Pain shot up my right leg. I stumbled, falling twice before reaching the milkman's farm.

The pasture had been swallowed. Water flowed through the barn. Chickens perched in the barn's rafters, clucking unhappily. Snow was not inside. If I could find her, I could lead her into the hills to wait out the rain. She'd follow me anywhere. But where was she? "Snow!" I called. "Snow!"

A soft moo sounded. I pushed through the water, around to the back of the milkman's cottage. My heart nearly stopped. Snow lay on the ground, water running over her back. She kicked her front legs, struggling to keep her head above water. "SNOW!"

I tried, summoning strength from the deepest places in my body, but I couldn't get her onto her hooves. "Get up," I pleaded. "Please get up." She groaned. Her body felt as cold as the river itself. I pushed and pushed. "Snow," I whispered. Shivering, I wrapped my arms around her neck and held her head as the water flowed past. "Please don't die, Snow. Please don't die."

There was no feeling left in my arms or hands. My body, like

Snow's, had become river. The only part of me not numb was my heart, which ached as if being squeezed. I moved my hands to either side of Snow's face. A tiny bit of life remained in those warm brown eyes—the first eyes to have looked directly at me. "You saved my life," I said, tears mixing with rain. "Why can't I save yours? Please, please get up. Please don't leave me. I have no one." I kissed her muzzle, then pressed my forehead against her white forehead. "Please stay."

Snow released a long last breath, and as she did, her final surge of life blew over me. I stopped shivering as warmth filled my entire body. The warmth spread down my spine, out to my fingertips, into my boots, wrapping around my curled foot. There, soaked to the bone, I was suddenly as warm as a griddle cake. As we locked gazes, I knew that Snow would be with me forever.

I held her head for as long as I could after she died, even as the water rose up to my waist. The current took on a merciless speed, carrying furniture and trees, collecting everything in its path.

As I was swept away, Snow disappeared beneath the churning water.

PART TWO

Dairyman's Son

Chapter Seven

I was born a dairyman's son.

It's not too bad. Lots of work, but that's life, right? My father says that if you work hard, treat others with respect, and give your heart to a good woman, then life will reward you. He's always telling me things like that. But it's not entirely true. Life doesn't always reward those who follow the rules. Sometimes you have to make your own rules.

Which is why I got home late last night. I'm not supposed to compete in the barefist fights, but I did. I couldn't resist. The challenger was a one-eyed oaf twice my size, bragging about how he'd been a champion back in his village. I watched him for a while. He wasn't drunk, but he lumbered like a bear, tripping over his feet as if he'd forgotten they were attached to his legs. His reaction time was slow too. When I called out "Hey, Oaf!" he circled around twice before he saw me. Smaller, faster, I knew I could beat him. Besides, the prize was a snakeskin belt all the way from Londwin City.

I won. In the last fight of the night. Now it was morning, and I stood in my bedroom cinching my britches with the new belt. Maybe snakeskin was too fancy for a dairyman's son, but I was going to wear it anyway. If Mother asked where I got it, I'd tell her I bought it from Peddler. She'd lose sleep if she knew I was fighting again.

Dawn felt extra early that morning. I wished I could have slept a bit longer, floating lazily between dreams—girls with long hair, a plump fish pulled from the river, another victory won with my fists. But Father had stuck his head into my room. "One of the cows is missing."

We owned one hundred and twenty-two milk cows and two bulls. The Oak Dairy Farm, my father's dairy, was the largest in the Wanderlands. It was rare for a cow to go missing. Coyotes were no concern because they kept themselves fat on a plentiful supply of rabbits and mice. Thieves were no concern either. Wander was a prosperous town of merchants, the kind of people who could afford to buy the best cheese and butter. No one had ever stolen a cow. Most likely the cow had gone missing due to its own stupidity. They're not the smartest creatures.

I slipped my arms through my vest and started down the hall toward the kitchen. Six generations of Oak men had walked that very hallway. I learned to shovel manure at age four, the sharp fumes stinging my eyes. At age six I learned to clean the milk buckets and the water troughs. At age eight I learned the art of churning butter, and at age ten I learned to milk. I remember how strange it felt to pull the teats. How difficult it was to aim the milk stream into the bucket. Milking's the hardest job on the farm. Sitting on that stool all morning makes your back ache something fierce. But I liked the company, surrounded by the milkmaids who tousled my hair and kissed my cheeks, their breasts spilling over the tops of their aprons. But on the eve of my fifteenth birthday, when Mother caught me and one of the milkmaids half-naked, she decided it was time for me to leave the milking barn and join her in the shop. Now my main duty was to load our wagon with milk, cheese, and butter, drive into town, open the shop, then sell our wares to the people of Wander.

The snakeskin belt in place, I tiptoed past Mother's room. She was always the last to rise. Our shop didn't open until noon, after the morning milking, so Mother liked to get a few hours of extra sleep. But Nan, our cook, who constantly complained about lack of sleep, was already working up a sweat in the kitchen. "Morning," she grumbled as she set a bowl of hard-boiled brown eggs onto the table.

"Morning," I replied, grabbing one of the eggs. I cracked it on the table's edge, then slid the shell away with my thumbs. "Morning, Father."

"Morning, Owen." Father sat at the head of the table, his hands wrapped around a large mug of hot broth. We shared the same brown curly hair, but Father wore his in a tail, tied at the back of his neck. I kept mine short. Long hair is too easy to grab during a bare-fist fight. "It's one of the brown woollies," Father told me. "She didn't come back to the barn yesterday. By the time we did the counting, it was too dark to go looking."

"She probably got stuck in the mud," I said, stuffing the entire egg into my mouth. I grabbed another egg and sat next to Father. "I'll go find her. Just need something to eat first."

Father raised his eyebrows and gave me a knowing look. "You got home late last night."

My mouth full, I said nothing.

"You sure you want to wear that belt? Your mother will notice."

I glanced sideways. No use lying to him. "You're not going to tell her, are you?"

"Stupid boy," Nan hissed as she set a platter of sliced cheese on the table. "I don't know what's wrong with men, getting into fights on purpose."

"You won't tell her, will you, Nan?" I smiled sweetly. She was a difficult one to charm.

"I don't want no part of this," Nan said, cinching her apron tighter. "I don't approve."

Father took a sip of broth, then nudged my arm. "Lay off the fighting for a while, just until spring has passed. You know how difficult spring is for your mother."

"I know," I mumbled.

I'd tried, many times, to explain to Nan and Mother why I liked the barefist fights. The thrill when everyone cheered. The rush just before the final blow when I knew I'd be victorious. The look of respect in my opponent's eyes when I helped him to his feet. But Nan and Mother only considered the dangers of fighting, not the glories.

A knock on the front door called Nan from the kitchen, but she soon returned with a familiar face. “Peddler,” Father greeted, motioning for the morning guest to join us at the table.

“Morning, Mister Oak. Morning, young Mister Oak,” he said, lifting the hem of his coat as he settled in the chair across from me. His coat hung down to his knees and was covered in patches and pockets. As a little boy, I was fascinated by the treasures that emerged from those pockets—marbles made from polished stones, seashells from distant shores, a shiny green beetle.

“Mornin’,” I said, cramming three slices of cheese into my mouth. I didn’t know Peddler’s age—just seemed as if he’d always been old with his crinkled skin and those deep grooves. But he moved nimbly and his eyes flashed as if a young man was trapped behind the old skin.

Nan set a mug of broth in front of Peddler, a shy smile flashing across her wide face. “Thank you,” he said with a wink. “You have the prettiest cook in all of Wanderland, Mister Oak.”

Nan snorted, then ripped a loaf of bread from my hand and offered it to Peddler. “Glad to see the rain’s stopped,” Peddler said, tearing off the end of the bread.

“That it has. That it has,” Father said.

“You’re lucky,” Peddler said. “You only got three days of rain. It’s been much worse upriver.”

Father scratched his beard. “Is that so?”

“Loganberry jam?” Nan asked, shoving a small jar in Peddler’s face.

“Don’t mind if I do,” he said, dipping a spoon into the jam, then spreading it on his bread. “Rain’s been real bad up north.

Heard tell it rained for seven straight days and nights. Heard tell the Flatlands flooded."

"Flooded?" Father leaned on his elbows. "The river's high, that's for sure, but we haven't had any flooding down here."

Peddler licked jam from his fingers. "The river's lazy up that way. Meanders and turns like a snake. And the land is as flat as parchment. With that much rain, the water rose quick."

"Have you ever been to the Flatlands?" I asked my father.

"Never," he said.

"No reason to go there," Peddler said. "Dirt-scratchers don't have the coin to buy nice butter and cheese like you folks make."

I knew about dirt-scratchers but had never met one. They had hair the color of fire. They were fierce and primitive and couldn't be trusted. That's what I'd heard.

"Heard tell from another peddler that the road into the Flatlands has been washed away," Peddler said. "A village is gone. I don't do business with the dirt-scratchers so it's no loss for me. There's too many of them anyway. Stupid, filthy people, those dirt-scratchers." He smiled with jam-covered teeth. "A few less won't make much difference."

"Dirt-scratchers don't bathe like the rest of us," Nan said as she kneaded dough. "And they don't send their children to school. They don't love their children the way we do. They live like animals. They—"

"Did you say an entire village is gone?" I interrupted.

"Washed away. Buildings, livestock, people, all of it gone. Those dirt-scratchers never belonged in this kingdom," Peddler said, picking up the broth bowl. "I say good riddance to all of them."

Father and I shared a long look. No one in our family would call Peddler a friend. He was a businessman who stopped by now and then, bringing news and trinkets. As a boy, I'd looked up to him as a magical sort of figure with his pockets of surprises, but at that moment I realized he was full of ugliness. "You think it's good that an entire village has been destroyed?"

Father set his hand on my arm. "You'd best go see to our missing cow. If she's injured, we don't want her to suffer."

"Right." No use getting into an argument with Peddler. The river's damage had been done. I grabbed another egg and started peeling it on the way out the door, leaving flecks of shell in my wake.

"That's a fine snakeskin belt," Peddler called after me. "You interested in selling?"

"Not a chance."

The clear morning sky promised a break in the rain. Peddler's horse snorted as I walked past Peddler's tented wagon. Blue flashed at the corner of my eye. The milkmaids in their blue dresses and white aprons were just arriving. Town dwellers, they walked to our dairy each morning, rain or shine. They smiled and waved at me.

In order to be a milkmaid at the Oak Dairy, a girl had to be unmarried. That was my mother's rule and the reason was simple. A milkmaid worked every single day because the cows needed to be milked every single day. A maid could make this commitment, but a married woman with children had too many distractions. So once a girl got married, she left the dairy. Mother hired all the maids. Ever since that day when she found me half-naked in the barn, she'd done her best to hire only ugly girls. This preference was well-known throughout the town of Wander, so the girls who wanted jobs would make themselves look ugly for the interview. One girl painted her teeth black. She was hired immediately. But as the months passed, the girls would slowly transform back into their true selves, and by that time they'd be expert milkers and Mother couldn't bring herself to fire them just because they were pretty.

"You stay away from those girls," she always told me. "I don't need them falling in love. They get no work done when they fall in love."

I wasn't the least bit interested in falling in love. My friend, Barley, had already made that mistake. Barley had lost himself to love, like a wagon rolling downhill then crashing into a tree. With one babe just born and another on the way, Barley rarely had time to attend the barefist fights or go fishing. He complained about his wife's expensive tastes and about her parents, who always needed money. Falling in love had ruined Barley.

I waved at the milkmaids but didn't stick around to talk. Hurrying into the stables, I threw a saddle over my horse. Then I hung two coils of rope from the saddle's horn. If the missing cow had gotten stuck somewhere, fallen into a ditch or ravine, I'd have to pull her clear. But if she'd been injured and there was no saving her, I'd have to put her out of her misery, which is why I slid a knife under my snakeskin belt.

No fences marked our farm. Grazing land was shared and plentiful in the Wanderlands. The cows grazed one field in the spring where the clover was tender, and another field in the heat of summer where the alfalfa was plentiful. But the missing cow was not in either field.

Our cows liked to drink from a nearby stream. I rode up and down the stream, expecting to find that the creature had fallen in and broken a leg, but she wasn't there. I let the horse graze as I tried to guess which direction she might have traveled. My gaze settled on the distant river.

It was rare for one of our cows to amble all the way to River Time. When it had happened in the past, it had been a sick cow, confused by fever. Cows are particular about the terrain they cross, and river rocks are unsteady beneath their hooves. There was no reason for the cow to wander that far.

I shaded my eyes. Though not much more than a speck, I could tell from the wingspan that a vulture circled on the horizon, just above the river. Another vulture approached from the north. If the cow had wandered all the way to the river and if the vultures were circling, then surely the cow had drowned. Or worse—the vultures were waiting for her to die. They'd go for the eyes first, then the belly. I shuddered. There was a place for vultures in the world, but the way they waited for death gave me the creeps.

I kicked the horse and we galloped across the low, rolling hills. The horse seemed to sense my urgency for it kept a steady pace and did not slow until we reached the riverbank. Strange objects littered the bank—a wooden chair, a waterlogged basket, and a wooden bowl. *They must be from the drowned village*, I thought, remembering Peddler's story. I turned the horse upriver toward the circling vultures, passing more bits and pieces of village life. Not long after, I sighed with relief at the sight of the brown cow.

Brown woollies were unique to the Wanderlands. Their long, wavy hair kept them warm during winter. Their short stumpy horns, found on both the females and males, were prized for knife handles. If the cow had died, I would have carefully removed the horns to sell in town. But there she stood on the riverbank, her coat rippling in the breeze. She didn't appear to be injured so why had the vultures gathered?

Something was lying on the ground in front of the cow. More rubbish that had floated downriver, perhaps. I pulled on the reins, slowing the horse, then took a quick, sharp breath.

The rubbish was a girl!

Chapter Eight

The girl lay on her back, her eyes closed, her face turned toward the sky. I slid off my horse and rushed to her side, wincing as my knees hit river rock.

Her long red hair fanned across the rocks. Her drenched dress clung to her small frame, her hipbones protruding. The cow lowered its head and nuzzled the girl's neck. She lay perfectly still, even as the cow licked her face. Was she dead? I pushed the cow away, then touched the girl's cheek, which was as cold as the river itself. Then I held my hand over her mouth and nostrils. There it was, a slight tickle as she exhaled, barely felt but there. I pressed my ear to her chest. The cow snorted. "Quiet," I told the cow, but I couldn't tell the river to be quiet. Straining to hear, I pressed my ear closer and there it was—a faint *thump thump*.

"She's alive," I announced. The cow flicked its tail. "She's not dead," I hollered at the three vultures who'd settled on a nearby boulder. They stared at me with their disgusting red eyes. "Get outta here. She's not dead." I rushed at them, waving my arms. They took off.

Is this why the cow hadn't returned home? That seemed a ridiculous thought. Why would an animal that only cares about grazing stand guard over a half-drowned girl?

She was a dirt-scratcher, no doubt about it. Even though her hair was wet, it was redder than any hair I'd ever seen. She must have been washed downriver by the flood, just like the other things. But how had she survived such a long journey? I looked down at her pale face. She was pretty in a strange way. I had to fight the urge to simply stand there and stare. Kneeling, I sat her upright, but she didn't open her eyes. Sliding an arm beneath her knees, I lifted her. She was limp. There was no meat on her, as if nothing existed beneath the dress but a hollow skeleton. The only weight came from her boots, which dripped with river water.

Getting her home would be tricky. I laid her facedown across the saddle. She still didn't move. Once I'd hoisted myself onto the horse, I turned the girl onto her back, then lifted her into a sitting position so that her legs draped over one side. As I held her against my chest, her drenched dress soaked through my vest.

I'd come to find our missing cow, but there was no way to get the girl home quickly with the cow in tow. I'd have to return later. Kicking the horse into a gallop, I held the girl tight, trying to keep her head against my shoulder so it wouldn't flop about. She felt frail. I worried she might break along the way. As her wet hair pressed against my neck I shivered. I could have been holding a girl made of ice.

The horse was foaming by the time we reached the farm. My back and arms ached. Father, who'd been leaning against the fence enjoying a pipe smoke, hurried over. "What's this?" he said, holding the girl steady as I dismounted.

"She was lying on the riverbank," I told him. "She's half-dead."

"And nearly frozen." Father helped slide her off the horse and into my arms. "Nan!" he hollered as we hurried toward the house. The milkmaids were busy inside the milking barn so they took no notice of the commotion. Peddler's wagon was gone. Father opened the front door. "Nan!"

"Don't be bothering me," Nan hollered back. "It's not yet time for noon meal."

I stepped into the sitting room, but Father grabbed my arm. "It's warmest in the kitchen," he said, motioning me to follow. "No time to waste."

Nan stood at the washbasin, scrubbing a cooking pot. Her mouth fell open as we rushed inside. Father grabbed a vase of flowers off the table. "Put her here," he told me.

"What are you . . . ?" Nan gasped as I gently laid the girl on the table. "God have mercy, what have you brought into this house?"

"She's half-dead. Go get the missus," Father ordered, setting the vase aside.

"But . . ." Nan pointed a sudsy finger at the girl. "Half-dead or half-alive, that girl's a dirt-scratcher. You've put a dirt-scratcher on my table, where we eat."

"It doesn't matter who or what she is," I said. Had she stopped breathing? She lay dead still, a faint tint of blue coloring her lips. "She's going to die if we don't help her."

Nan looked imploringly at my father, who nodded his head and repeated, "Go get the missus."

"What do we do?" I asked as Nan rushed out of the room.

"If the cold gets into her organs she'll never recover," Father said. He was right about that. Once, when I was much younger, we had a winter the likes of which no one had ever seen. The field grasses froze and branches fell from trees, shattering into pieces. One of our cows slipped on a patch of ice, and by the time we found it, it was cold all over, just like the dirt-scratcher girl. The cow never woke up. Father said the cold had spread into the cow's organs, freezing them. "We'll warm her. Get those boots off."

While Father soaked Nan's kitchen rags in hot kettle water, I untied the girl's boots. They were pathetic things, poorly stitched, and both heels had almost worn through. As I pulled off the left one, river water dribbled onto the floor. I peeled off the drenched, thick wool sock. The skin on her foot was as pale as moonlight and as puckered as an old apple skin. Clearly she'd been in the water a long time.

Father wrapped a warm rag around the exposed foot. Then he pushed up the girl's sleeve and draped another warm rag over her forearm. "This might do the trick," he said.

The right boot was in worse condition, with its outer seam giving way and a hole worn through at the outer ankle. It took a bit of a tug to get the boot off because it was stuffed with bits of drenched fabric. Something didn't look right. This foot was smaller than the other. I peeled off the sock and gasped. The skin on the left foot was just as pale and puckered as the other, but the foot itself was curled up like a fern's frond before it opens. "How can she walk?"

My father shook his head. "Poor creature," he murmured as he placed a warm rag over the curled foot.

Nan hurried back into the kitchen with my mother at her heels. Mother froze in the doorway for a moment, her eyes wide with shock. Then she pushed her sleeping bonnet off her head and pressed her fingertips against the girl's neck. "Her pulse is weak. We need tea. Strong tea. As black as you can make it," she told Nan. "But cool enough to drink."

"But, Missus," Nan said. "That's a dirt-scratcher. As sure as I'm standing here, that girl's a dirt-scratcher."

"I can see that," Mother said, exchanging a worried look with Father. "We'll sort that out later. Now make the tea."

As Nan strained tea leaves, Mother took a small vial from the cupboard. "Sit her up," she told me.

With Father's help, I lifted the girl into a sitting position. Then I sat at the edge of the table, supporting her head against my chest. Mother opened the vial and waved it beneath the girl's nose. When the strong scent reached my own nostrils, I flinched. The girl, however, had no reaction to the disgusting odor. Mother waved the vial three more times until finally, the girl moaned and turned away. "That's a good sign," Mother said. "Very good indeed."

On the first try, the tea simply pooled at the corner of the girl's mouth, dribbling onto the front of her dress. On the second try, some trickled down her throat. She coughed, her eyelids fluttering.

Her lungs rattled with water. Mother tipped the cup again and this time the girl swallowed. The blue tinge to her lips disappeared. With focused determination, Mother managed to get an entire cup of tea into the girl. As Nan refilled the cup, Mother said, "Now, someone best tell me how this girl got onto my kitchen table." She turned to me, not to Father, immediately suspecting my hand in the situation.

"I went looking for a missing cow and I found this girl lying on the riverbank," I said. "Well, the cow found her first. It was standing over her . . ." I hesitated because it was going to sound crazy. "I think the cow was protecting her from the vultures."

Nan snorted. "I don't see why a cow would do such a thing."

"I agree," Father said as he set a warm rag over the girl's shin. "The cow was simply curious. Cows can be very curious creatures."

"But the cow didn't come home," I said. "Don't you think that's odd? It stayed at the river. It stayed with her."

No one said anything, watching as the girl swallowed the second cup of tea. Mother handed the empty cup to Nan, then pressed her fingers to the girl's neck again. "Her pulse is stronger. Much stronger. Now, we must get her out of those wet clothes and into bed."

"Bed?" Nan asked, her cheeks flushing. "You want to put that girl into one of your *beds*?"

"Do you have a better idea?" Mother asked.

"Put her in the barn. That's where she should go," Nan said, pointing out the window. "Dirt-scratchers are filthy creatures."

"In the barn?" I said. The girl still leaned against my chest, her breathing steady but wheezy. "She's not an animal."

"Then put her in the bunkhouse," Nan said.

We waited for Mother's decision. After all, matters of the house fell into her jurisdiction. She said nothing, simply reached out and ran her finger down the girl's pale cheek. I'm sure I'm not the only one in the kitchen who noticed the sadness that spread across my mother's face. My older sister had died four years ago, and she was about the same age as this girl. "She is not a creature," Mother whispered, her lower lids glistening with tears. "She is someone's daughter. She does not belong in the barn, and the bunkhouse is for men only."

"You can put her in my bed," I said. "I can sleep in the bunkhouse. I don't mind."

Nan began to protest, but Father silenced her with a steely look.

I lifted the girl from the table and carried her to my room. Father had once carried my sister in much the same way. He'd let her sit by the window for a bit each morning to watch the birds, then he'd take her back to bed. I well remembered the spring morning when he carried her for the last time to the gravedigger's wagon.

I stood in my room, unsure if I should set the girl on the bed, what with her wet clothes and all. Mother hurried in, carrying a nightfrock that had once belonged to my sister. "Strip the bed," she told Nan, who pulled the blankets and pillows off. After I'd set the girl on the mattress, Mother gently pushed me into the hallway.

"Nan and I don't need your help undressing her, thank you very much."

Father and I waited outside the closed bedroom door. He pulled his pipe from his pocket and set it at the corner of his mouth, unlit. My sleeves were soaked, as was the front of my shirt. I could still feel the girl's body pressed against my chest.

"No doubt the flood washed her downriver," Father said, chewing on the pipe as he often did while deep in thought. "No doubt others will wash downriver as well."

"Do you think she'll live?" I asked.

Father set his hand on my shoulder. "Even though Nan doesn't approve, she won't let the girl die. Now, how bout I go fetch our wandering cow while you load up the wagon and tend to the shop."

The door to the bedroom flew open and Mother stepped out, her face pinched with worry. "Husband, you'd best fetch the surgeon," she said, a kitchen rag in her hand.

"Are you certain you need the surgeon?" Father asked. "Don't you think we should keep this a secret? Dirt-scratchers aren't permitted to leave the Flatlands. We might get fined for helping her."

"Is it her foot?" I asked. "Is that why you want the surgeon?"

"No, it's not her foot. It's much worse than her curled foot."

From my vantage point I could see the end of my bed and two pale naked legs, skinny as saplings. A large gash had opened the right leg, just above the knee.

"The wound is corrupted," Mother said. "I fear we are too late."

Chapter Nine

It was a short ride from Oak Dairy to the surgeon's shop in the town of Wander. I took Father's horse since mine was still cooling after the morning rescue. Wander was a walled town. Its only entrance was at the northern end where the gates, kept closed many generations ago when barbarians ran amok, were now kept open throughout the day. As I rode beneath the stone archway, the town greeted me in its usual cheerful manner. Ladies in colorful bonnets bustled between shops, men gathered in groups to discuss the latest news, merchants stood at their doors greeting passersby.

Our shop, Oak and Son's Milk, Cheese, and Butter, sat at the corner of the main square, next to the clockmaker's shop and right across from the town hall where our tax-collector lived. When the clock tower struck noon, a line always formed outside our shop. But this line wasn't made up of the bonneted ladies, wives of the merchants and tradesmen. It was their cooks and maidservants, people like Nan, who bought the fresh milk, butter, and cheese for the households. As I neared the surgeon's, the clock's hand struck eleven. Looked like we'd be late opening the doors today.

I rode through the square, around the golden fountain, and dismounted outside the surgeon's—Surgeon and Apothecary for Matters Pertaining to Both Sexes. Father had given unconditional instructions. "Do not tell the surgeon that she's a dirt-scratcher or he might not come." But the concern stretched beyond the surgeon. If word spread around town, which tended to happen faster than a fox circling a chicken coop, there'd be a whole mess of judgment thrust our way and that wouldn't be good for business.

As I tied the horse to a post, someone called my name. Bartholomew Raisin scurried across the square, his thick thighs making a swooshing sound as they rubbed together. Bartholomew's business was the promotion and management of the local barefist fights. We stood toe to toe as he looked up at me. That was Bartholomew's way—to get right in your face when talking. "Got news for you."

"It'll have to wait," I said.

"It can't wait. I got news." Bartholomew nodded eagerly. He shuffled from side to side. His fingers twitched as if the news was eating him from the inside out.

"I got something to do," I said, turning away and heading for the surgeon's door. Bartholomew had made a lot of coin from the fights over the years, and he doled out a meager percentage to the fighters. He was a rat bastard.

The scent of chopped herbs freshened the stuffy air of the surgeon's shop. The surgeon's assistant stood in the back, mixing green paste. Frightful instruments for cutting, piercing, probing, and stitching hung on the back wall. My heart kicked up its pace as I looked around. I'd face an opponent's fists in the circle any day, but the surgeon's hands, well, I tried to stay away from them.

A stranger lay on a table, moaning, his eyes shut tight. A traveling knapsack sat on the floor. The surgeon, a tall, thin man with a flat nose and a head of wiry black hair, leaned over his patient, tying the ends of thread that he'd sewn through the patient's finger. "Hello, Owen," he said, glancing up briefly. "What brings you here? Have your fists loosened a tooth or blackened an eye?"

"No, it's not like that," I said.

The surgeon tugged on the thread, then severed the ends with a knife. "You're done," he told the man, who slowly opened his eyes and sat up. "Keep the finger dry or it won't heal."

The man looked at his swollen finger. The surgeon's assistant held out a silver platter, onto which the man set a coin. Then he grabbed his knapsack and staggered from the shop. As he did, Bartholomew Raisin stuck his sweaty head inside. "You done yet?" he asked me. "Cause I still got news. News doesn't just disappear."

"I'm busy," I grumbled. "Wait outside."

"You're not sick, are you?" Bartholomew asked. "You can fight, can't you?"

"I said wait *outside*." I shut the door in Bartholomew's face. It was no one's business why I'd come to the surgeon's.

As the surgeon wiped his hands on his stained apron, I pictured the girl's naked legs. There was no time to waste. "One of the milkmaids gashed her leg and it's corrupted. Mother needs your help right away."

"Corrupted?" The surgeon picked something out from under his fingernail. "How corrupted?"

"I'm not sure," I said. "I didn't get a good look. But Mother says it's bad. She wants you right away."

The assistant had already begun to collect the surgeon's things, which he arranged in a small wooden case. "I'll head straight over," the surgeon said. Then he winked at me. "Don't want you losing one of your pretty milkmaids."

As I followed the surgeon outside, Bartholomew Raisin jumped in front of me like an overgrown frog. "Where are you going?" he asked.

"Got to get home and load the wagon. It's almost time to open the shop."

"Hold up there. You'll listen to me, Owen Oak. You got to hear this. It concerns you."

As the surgeon climbed into his wagon and headed down the street, I folded my arms and looked down into Bartholomew's puffy eyes. There'd be no getting rid of him. He'd follow me around like a tail. "I'm listening."

Bartholomew smiled. "You remember the guy with the missing eye, the one you fought? The win that got you that pretty prize?" He pointed to my belt.

"Course I remember. It was only last night. I didn't get punched in the head."

"He said he was leaving, right? You remember him saying he was leaving?"

"Yeah. He said he was just passing through."

Bartholomew rubbed his hands together. "Well, he never did leave. He's still here and he wants to fight you again. Surgeon stitched up his forehead good and tight and he says he's ready. Tonight."

"Tonight?" Surprised by this news, I took a long breath. I'd hit the one-eyed man hard. He was a big lout, a laborer of some kind so his thick arms were used to lifting and hauling, not throwing swift punches. My hand still ached. "I already fought him," I said, heading for my horse. "It's done."

"But I'm collecting the wagers," Bartholomew said, keeping close to my heels. His pockets jiggled, heavy with coin.

"I never agreed to the fight. The wagers aren't my problem." I untied Father's horse.

"Listen to me, Owen Oak." Bartholomew grabbed the reins. "The wagers are mostly *against* you."

I narrowed my eyes. "Why would they be against me? I beat him. I won."

"Sure, you beat him. You won. But he's bigger than you. And he's mad this time. Real mad. He's not the kind to take to losing." Bartholomew held his tongue for a moment, watching while I considered this news. Then, knowing exactly how to goad his best fighter, Bartholomew stood on tiptoe and said, "He says it was luck that brought your victory. Said you don't deserve that belt. Said you need to be taught a lesson."

I clenched my jaw. Father had told me not to fight until spring had passed so as not to bring more sorrow to my mother. Spring days might have been blessed by gentle sunshine, but they were also tainted by the memory of a daughter's death.

"You'll fight him, won't you?" Bartholomew asked. "You can't let him say you won because of luck. You can't let him say you don't deserve that belt. You'll fight him? Tonight?"

Even knowing that Bartholomew only wanted to make a profit, I couldn't ignore the challenge. "Yeah," I said. "I'll fight him."

Chapter Ten

I worked the shop all afternoon. Mother never joined me, staying home to tend to the dirt-scratcher girl. Between filling crocks with butter and jugs with milk, I wondered how the girl was doing. But honestly, I thought more about the upcoming fight. It didn't help that Bartholomew kept stopping by, reminding me of the event, his irises pulsating with greed. I wanted to get it over with, wanted to defend my reputation. I'd avoid any hits to my face and Mother would be none the wiser.

So right after closing, I stood barefoot on the dirt floor. My vest, shirt, and boots lay outside the fight circle. But I kept the snakeskin belt around my britches, a reminder of my previous victory. The circle had been raked and its perimeter marked by a thick line of flour—an expensive boundary, but cost was no issue to Bartholomew Raisin. He offered the best barefist fights in all the Wanderlands. His building had been erected solely for that purpose.

The crowd grew by the minute as men pushed inside the building. No women, though. It wasn't that women weren't allowed, but if one should happen to step inside, she would risk irreparable damage to her reputation. But Bartholomew had long ago discovered that many of the merchants' wives loved to gamble, so he'd visit them and take their wagers in secret.

It was normal for my stomach to tighten just before a fight. No win was guaranteed. A scrawny man could surprise everyone with unexpected strength. A short man could possess an unnerving ability to soar through the air. But landing face-first in the dirt wasn't something the one-eyed man had expected. And now he was furious enough to demand a rematch even though his forehead was being held together by the surgeon's stitches.

I stretched my fingers, trying to ignore their bruises. I liked to wait at least a week between fights so my hands could heal from the blows they'd delivered. But this time I'd broken my own rule.

When the one-eyed man stepped into the circle, anger boiled in his good eye. Sweat glistened on his broad, hairy chest. It didn't worry me that my chest was half the size and hairless. Advantage came not from size or age, but from nimble feet and quick reflexes. The anger worried me though. Fighting an angry man was tricky. Angry men tended to ignore rules, their only intent to inflict pain.

He cracked his knuckles and glared at me. I took a deep breath and scanned the crowd. Bartholomew Raisin was collecting the final wagers. "Owen, Owen," a few men called. I grinned and nodded at them, trying to push away the doubts about my sore hands. The drummer pounded three times—the signal that the fight would begin.

"You're gonna lose," the one-eyed man called from across the circle. His words were slurred. He wobbled, as if about to fall over. Was he drunk? He staggered forward, pointing. "I'm gonna . . ." He staggered from side to side. "I'm gonna . . ."

My father had fought in his youth, before marrying my mother. He'd always told me, "Never fight a man who's clouded by drink. He's as likely as an assassin to pull a knife on you."

"I'm not fighting him," I called. "He's drunk. I'm not fighting him!"

"What's this?" Bartholomew asked as the crowd quieted. He hurried into the circle.

"He's drunk," I repeated. "I'm not fighting a drunk."

"Coward," the one-eyed man said, spittle dribbling on his chin.

"Look at him. He can barely stand up." I motioned with disgust.

Bartholomew grabbed my arm and whispered in my ear. "Do you know how much coin I've collected? Do you know what I stand to lose?"

"I don't care about your profit." I pulled my arm from his grip. "I want a fair fight."

Bartholomew grabbed my belt buckle and pulled me close. "Who cares about a fair fight?" he hissed between clenched teeth. He looked over his shoulder, smiled, and waved at the restless crowd. Then he turned back to me. "You agreed. You accepted the fight. One punch and you'll knock him right off his stupid drunk feet."

"Quit talking and fight," the one-eyed man bellowed. Then he lumbered across the circle, pushed Bartholomew aside, and swung at me. I darted out of the way. The man growled. "Running away, are ya? Too scared to fight me?" He swung again, a slow awkward punch that I easily sidestepped. This would be no match. On the third swing, the man tripped over his own feet and landed face-first into the crowd. A roar of laughter filled the air.

Humiliation bloomed in the man's reddening face. Twice he'd ended up on the ground, twice he'd been laughed at. This humiliation would fester and feed his anger. I needed to calm the situation. "Sober up and I'll fight you tomorrow," I told him, loud enough so everyone could hear. "You're a worthy opponent when sober." I was about to reach out my hand to help him up, but changed my mind. It was too much of a risk. The crowd made way as I left the fight circle.

"Owen!" someone yelled. "Watch out!"

I swung around. The one-eyed man lunged like a bull, his head ramming into my chest. Something cracked and pain shot up my side. I tumbled backward, the man landing on top of me, pinning me to the ground. I couldn't breathe as he grabbed my throat. Looking into eyes reddened by drink and fury, I tried to pry the man's fingers loose, knowing it was only moments before my windpipe would snap. As his fingers tightened, an odd sense of calm came over me. This was how I was going to die.

"Help him!"

Voices rose and the crowd rushed into the circle. Onlookers pulled the man off and held him as he flailed and clawed the air. I should have jumped to my feet, should have made my exit. But I couldn't move. With each shallow breath, pain shot across my chest and down my legs.

"He broke the rules. He attacked when his opponent's back was turned. Get him outta here," Bartholomew ordered, and the one-eyed man was dragged from the building. Then Bartholomew leaned over me. "You want me to reschedule the match?" he asked. "We don't want to miss out on this opportunity. I think we could make double the coin if we reschedule."

"Shut up," I snapped. "And get me the damn surgeon."

As shouts for the surgeon rang across the building, I stared up at the wide timbers that supported the ceiling. It wasn't the broken rib or the surgeon's instruments of torture that worried me at that moment. It was the pain my mother would feel when she learned I'd been fighting.

Chapter Eleven

Voices drifted in and out. Light pierced my eyelids, then faded. Sleep kept a tight hold on me, like a cocoon around a caterpillar. Warm. Cozy. Safe.

I opened my eyes.

I'd never slept on anything so soft. The bed was wider than my outstretched arms, and my body melted into the mattress. I slid my hands over the blanket. No moth holes, no itchy fibers. Where had such a smooth blanket come from?

I turned my face toward the light. From the gentle way it streamed through the window, I guessed it was morning. As my eyes adjusted, the outline of the window came into focus, as did the plaster wall, the corner chair, the little table with a vase of honeysuckle.

This was not my room. This was not our cottage.

I sat up. Pain shot down my leg. My lungs burned when I breathed. My head felt heavy, my thoughts as thick as mud. I raised the blanket and peered beneath. The white nightfrock did not belong to me. Where was my work dress? Someone had stolen my clothes. Who would want a stained dress in exchange for this beautiful frock? I raised the blanket higher and gasped. My boots were gone. My feet, bare.

Both feet.

My heart fluttered. What was going on? Where was I?

I tried to scoot to the edge of the bed, but the pain in my leg was unbearable. I pushed off the blanket and pulled up the nightfrock. A strip of fabric wound around my right leg, knotted just above the knee. The flesh beneath ached. I untied the knot, then unwound the fabric. A jagged wound, held together with black thread, crossed my thigh. That's when I noticed the bruises on my other leg. More bruises dotted my forearms.

A wave of dizziness pushed me back onto the pillows. I almost called for my father, but then I remembered.

My gaze raced back and forth across the beamed ceiling as the events played out. Father had been taken away to fight in a war. The farm had flooded. Snow had died. The river had grabbed hold of me, pulling me away from Root. I'd fought but the current wouldn't release its grip. My body had turned numb as I'd struggled to keep my head above water that rushed into my ears and eyes and up my nose. Then a plank had crashed into me, come loose from someone's barn or shed. I'd managed to pull myself onto the plank, holding tight as the current carried me on and on and on until the memory faded, replaced by darkness.

But how did I get here?

A creaking sound caught my attention. The door opened and a man entered the room. I slid low, pulling the blanket up to my eyes, my heart pounding like a rabbit's. The man didn't look at me as he tiptoed, his gaze set on the table at the far end of the room. His long-sleeved white shirt hung over the top of his britches, and his vest was unbuttoned. Brown curly hair fell just below his ears.

He reached for a book that lay on the table. "Oh," he moaned, grabbing his side. Then, as if realizing he'd made a sound, he turned quickly and looked at the bed.

I snapped my eyes shut. He wasn't a man after all. Well, he was a *man*, just not old like my father. He was closer to my age. I held my breath, my heart pounding in my ears. As he cleared his throat, I held perfectly still, hoping he'd go away. "Uh, I saw you close your eyes. I know you're awake. I'm Owen. Owen Oak."

With a shaky exhale, I opened my eyes, peering over the edge of the blanket. He stood at the foot of the bed, his hands behind his back. I'm not entirely sure why, but I immediately compared him to Griffin Boar. Maybe it was because they looked the exact same age, with the same soft stubble of beard along the edge of their jaws. But unlike Griffin, this guy wasn't tall and broad-chested. He wasn't short, either, just medium-sized and lean. Unlike Griffin, he wasn't heart-stoppingly handsome. He was nice-looking in an entirely different way, with his dark eyes and high cheekbones. He didn't sound like Griffin, either. The way he spoke was different, an accent that sounded a bit like Mister Todd, our tax-collector.

"You've been asleep for three days," he said.

I frowned. Three days? How was that possible?

"I didn't mean to wake you. I just wanted to get my book." He held it up as proof. "This is my room, you see. That's my bed."

His room? His bed? Had he been the one who'd taken off my dress? My face burned.

"No, it's not like that," he said. "You've got it all wrong. You're in my bed because you needed a place to sleep. Not because . . ." He shuffled. "Well, I'm the one who put you in my bed, that's true, but only because . . ." He shuffled again. "Look, I didn't take your clothes off so don't worry about that. I mean, I took your boots off, that's all."

I cringed. What was that look on his face? Was it disgust because he'd seen my curled foot? Or was it pity? I wanted no one's pity. Slowly I sat up, holding the blanket beneath my chin. "You had no right to take off my boots," I said. Even though my leg ached, I pulled up my knees, tucking my feet as close as possible. "Go away!"

He scratched the back of his head, looking like a boy who'd been scolded. "Look, I didn't mean to offend you. I was just trying to help. I—" He turned toward the window.

A cow pressed its nostrils against the pane. Owen opened the window and pushed the cow away. "Go on," he said. "Go out to the field." As soon as the cow moseyed away, Owen closed the window. "They've been doing that since you got here. I don't know why they keep coming to the window," he said. "They've never done that before. It's almost as if they're checking on you."

I shrugged, as if it were the oddest thing that a cow should pay attention to me.

"Owen Oak, what are you doing in here?" An old woman stood holding a tray in the doorway. Her gray dress hung to her ankles, and a wooden spoon stuck out of her apron pocket. Her gaze darted up the blanket and stopped on my face. She took a sharp breath. "You know this room is off-limits, Owen."

"I came to get my book. Father won't let me work so what else am I supposed to do?" He held a hand against his rib cage.

"I'll tell you what you're supposed to do. You're supposed to let that rib heal. Now get out of here before I tell your mother that you broke another one of her rules." Still holding the tray, she jabbed Owen with an elbow. "First you break her heart with all that fighting and now you sneak into this room."

"How's a guy supposed to have fun if he can't break a few rules?" he said with a grin.

"Out with you," she said, cocking her head toward the door. "And tell your mother that the dirt-scratcher is awake." She frowned, tossing another glance my way. Just before leaving, Owen nodded at me. I pretended not to have noticed.

The old woman crossed the room and set the tray on the bedside table with a loud *clunk.* Then she tucked a loose strand of silver-streaked hair into the tight knot at the back of her head. "Guess you can feed yourself now that you're awake." She grabbed a small jug from the tray and held it out. "Go on, take it. I've got better things to do." She pursed her lips and shook her head—her disapproval as visible as a black sheep in a snowy field. I held tight to the blanket. "Drink. The sooner you get better, the sooner you can go back to where you belong."

My arms trembled slightly as I took the jug. A sweet, warm scent rose from the clay. My insides felt hollow. I knew hunger, but this was worse than normal. If I'd been asleep for three days, then I hadn't eaten for as long. Putting the jug to my mouth, I sipped.

"That's the best milk you'll ever taste," the woman said, folding her arms. It was true. I gulped as fast as I could, not caring that she watched, her foot tapping all the while. With each swallow, my insides warmed. Strength flowed down my limbs. I took the final drink, then held out the jug. The woman snatched it from my hands.

"Thank you," I said.

Another woman hurried into the room and stood at the end of the bed, her arms spread wide. Her brown hair tumbled out from her lacy white bonnet. "Oh, my dear girl, you're awake." A big smile burst across her face. "Get her something to eat, Nan. Get her some eggs and porridge. Bring yogurt with dewberries and cheese. Lots and lots of cheese. We need to fatten her up."

"Yes, Missus Oak."

Like night and day were these two women—the old one with her pinched thin face, the middle-aged one soft and dimpled. As Nan left the room, Missus Oak sat close to the bed. Her nightfrock and robe draped over the sides of the chair. "Can you speak? The surgeon wasn't sure if you'd be able to speak. He wasn't sure how the cold water might have affected your brain. But you're looking at me and your eyes are alert. I think you can understand me. Oh, you're trembling." She reached out and took my hand. "Don't be frightened. You're in a safe place."

Though the act surprised me, I didn't draw back. No one had taken my hand since my mother's death. This woman's hand was warm and soft, not covered in calluses like mine. Her nails were short and filed, not jagged like mine. It was such a simple gesture to take someone's hand, but it almost took my breath away. *Why was she being so nice to me?* I wondered, as two fat tears rolled down my cheeks.

"My dear, dear girl," Missus Oak whispered. "There, there. Whatever is the matter?"

"I don't know where I am," I said.

She pulled her hand away and clapped. "Wonderful! You can speak." She leaned forward. "How do you feel? Oh dear, that's a very big question, isn't it? How does your leg feel? Let's start there." She pointed to my right leg, hidden beneath the blanket. "You gashed it on a rock, that's what the surgeon said. He cleaned and stitched it. Does it hurt?"

"A little," I said, wiping away the tears.

"What about the rest of you? Is there any pain?"

"A few aches, but no real pain."

"Very good. The bruises will go away. The surgeon said they were from your trip downriver. That must have been very frightening."

I nodded, then asked again. "Where am I?"

"You're in the Wanderlands, just down the road from the town of Wander. This is the Oak Dairy. I'm Missus Trudence Oak. My husband owns this dairy."

So many questions swirled in my head. "How . . . ?" My voice felt waterlogged and weak. "How . . . ?"

"How did you get here?" Missus Oak asked. "Is that what you want to know?" I nodded. "You were lying on the riverbank, almost dead. Then you were found and brought here. You've been resting for three days. Do you remember what happened?"

"The river grabbed me."

"That's what we thought," Missus Oak said. "We heard about the flooding."

"My village," I said with a sudden surge of panic. "My father's farm. I need to get back."

"You can't go anywhere, not in your condition. You've been through a terrible ordeal and you need to recover." She paused, then folded her hands on her lap. "Besides, the road into the Flatlands was washed away. You must wait for the king's troops to repair it."

"Oh." I sank against the pillows. "How long will that take?"

Missus Oak shrugged. "No way to know."

I dreaded the answer to my next question. "What about my village? The village of Root?"

"I'm sure your family is fine. As soon as the road is clear, we'll send a scroll telling them of your recovery." She smiled weakly, obviously gentling the truth. I'd seen the destruction with my own eyes. I already knew the truth.

Missus Oak fiddled with the ribbons that dangled from her sleeping bonnet. "I'm sorry, dear girl, I've neglected to ask your name. How rude of me. What is it?"

"Emmeline. Emmeline Thistle."

"Emmeline Thistle," she repeated. "You have such a strange manner of speech. Does everyone in the Flatlands sound like you?"

"Aye," I said. "Does everyone in the Wanderlands sound like you?"

"No, not everyone. We get lots of travelers. They come through here on their way to the coast or on their way to Londwin City."

The older woman, Nan, marched into the room and set a new tray on the table. "Don't have any dewberries," she grumbled. "And I don't have time to pick any." Without so much as a glance at me, she left.

Missus Oak lifted a plate from the tray, then sat on the edge of the bed. "You must eat," she said. She set the plate on my lap, then fluffed my pillows.

I'd never seen so much food on a single plate. I'd never eaten so much food in an entire day. Was all this for me? "There are two coins in my dress pocket," I told her. "I can pay for this."

"There were no coins in your pocket. They must have fallen into the river."

"Then I can't pay." My stomach ached as I pushed the plate away. But she pushed it back. Then she handed me an eating knife, its handle made from some sort of horn.

"This is not an inn, Emmeline. We do not charge for meals or for the bed. This is my home and you are my guest." Missus Oak waved her hand. "Eat."

And so I ate—thick slices of soft buttered bread, wedges of white cheese, some strips of salty meat. "Thank you," I said between bites.

"You're most welcome." She watched as I stuffed food into my mouth. Then, gathering her robe close, she walked toward the door. "I must go and get dressed. I have a shop to run. But when I get to town, I'll send the surgeon to check on you. Nan will be here if you need anything."

"Could I have my boots?" I asked.

"I'm afraid your boots were ruined, as was your clothing." Her eyes darted to the end of the bed where my feet hid beneath the blanket. She paused, as if carefully considering what to say. "I'll bring you a pair of my husband's socks until we can get you a new pair of boots. In the meantime, if that son of mine steps foot in here again while you're recovering, you can tell him that I'll be most displeased."

"Do you mean Owen?"

"Yes. Owen is my son. My son who brings me constant grief." Her voice softened. "He's a good boy, though. He's the one who found you at the river and brought you here. He's the one who saved your life."

I dropped a piece of cheese. Owen Oak, the boy I'd been rude to, the boy I'd told "Go away," had saved my life?

Chapter Twelve

Three more days passed lazily. I slept curled up like a cat, waking only to eat and use the chamber pot. Missus Oak and Nan took turns tying clean rags around my wounded leg. I didn't speak much. More than food or drink, my body craved rest. At first I tried to fight it, but then I sank into the soft mattress and drifted away. It was easier to sleep than to think about the terrible fate of my village. And of my father.

On the fourth day, I awoke to voices in the hallway. Two men were speaking.

"Surgeon, may I have a word with you?"

"Certainly. I was just going to check on the girl."

"This concerns the girl."

"What is it, Mister Oak?"

I hadn't yet met Mister Oak or the surgeon. Besides Nan, Missus Oak, and the brief encounter with Owen, no one else had entered the room. At least not while I was awake. I'd never met a surgeon, for none lived in Root. When our tax-collector got ill, he'd leave the Flatlands to seek help. When Flatlanders got sick, we turned to the village midwife because she knew how to mix medicines and how to splint broken bones.

"Our cook is worried. She's heard that dirt-scratchers carry diseases," Mister Oak said.

"I've heard that as well," the surgeon said. "But other than malnourishment, she appears healthy."

"What about her foot? Was that caused by disease?"

"She was born that way. Not enough room in the womb."

"Ah, I see." Another pause. "We are most grateful to you for keeping our secret. If it got out that we had a dirt-scratcher here, in my son's bedroom, well, there'd be much talk." The surgeon didn't reply. "You are keeping this in confidence, aren't you?" Still the surgeon said nothing. "How is your wife enjoying that basket of cheese I sent?"

"Very much," the surgeon said after a long clearing of the throat. "Very much indeed. But I'm sorry to say there is no more. She shared it with her relatives."

"Then I shall send over another basket immediately."

"That would be a most hospitable gesture, Mister Oak. And do not fret. I will continue to keep a tight seal on your *situation*. No one need know you've helped a dirt-scratcher."

"Most appreciated."

"I've met a few in my time," the surgeon said. "They are a stupid lot. You can't educate them. They fear modern medicine and from what I understand, they only bathe in moonlight. Missus Oak has a heart of gold to allow a dirt-scratcher into your home."

"My wife is a good woman."

"She has shown mercy to the lowest of God's creatures, even though they've done nothing deserving of mercy," the surgeon said. "That red hair comes from the devil himself. She may have been better off if the river had swallowed her."

Sickness welled in my stomach. I was used to people aiming their fear at me, but the surgeon was talking about Flatlanders as if we were animals. Stupid disease-carrying animals.

Loathing filled me, prickly and hot. I hated this man.

When the surgeon entered the bedroom, I pretended to be asleep. "Wake up," he said. If I kept my eyes closed, maybe he'd go away. But he cleared his throat and insisted. "Wake up, wake up. I'm here to look at your leg."

I opened my eyes and slowly sat up. He set his tall black hat on the table, then opened a wooden case and pulled out some sort of tool. "I'm here to remove the stitches." He pointed the tool at me. It looked sharp.

"Stitches?" My hand reached under the blanket and touched my wounded leg. He was going to poke more holes into me with that thing. "No," I said, shaking my head. "Leave me alone."

"The stitches must be removed or they'll fester."

I shook my head harder. When he reached for the blanket, I scooted away. "Don't touch me."

The surgeon scowled, his bushy brow nearly covering his eyes. "You are most disagreeable and I have other patients to see this afternoon. I don't expect you to understand medical procedure, or even common courtesy, but I do expect you to yield to my authority."

Authority? This man was nothing to me. I detested him for

what he'd said about Flatlanders. Maybe I shouldn't have felt so loyal to people who'd shunned me since birth, but I was one of them. We shared the same blood. I had no one else.

When he reached again, I swung my arm at him. The tool flew through the air and landed in the corner. "Go away," I spat.

He took a deep, frustrated breath, retrieved his tool, then stuck his head into the hallway. "Mister Oak?" he called. "I require assistance. Hello? Can anyone assist me with this girl? Oh, Owen, could you give me a hand?"

"I'm not supposed to enter that room," Owen said from somewhere down the hall. "Mother's orders."

"I will explain the circumstances to your mother. I require an assistant to hold her still. She is consumed with hysteria."

I didn't know what hysteria was, but I cringed at the thought of Owen holding me still. Aye, he'd saved my life, but he'd also looked at me with pity. He'd seen my ugly, deformed foot. *Please*, I thought. *Please refuse.* But suddenly there he was, standing at the end of the bed. He must have been in the act of dressing for he wore his britches but no shirt. A long strip of fabric wound tightly around his rib cage. A dark bruise spread beyond the fabric's edges. I remembered that Nan had mentioned a broken rib. My gaze lingered on his chest—smooth, hairless, so different from the men of Root.

"She attacked me," the surgeon said. "We must approach with caution."

"She attacked you?" One side of Owen's mouth turned up.

"There is wildness in her blood. Her kind knows not the social graces." The surgeon tapped the blunt end of the tool against his palm. "If she doesn't lie perfectly still while I perform the procedure, the wound could reopen."

Owen raised his eyebrows and looked at me. "You'll lie still, won't you, Emmeline?"

I clenched my jaw. "He's not touching me."

"But he has to take out the stitches. It's for your own good."

"No!" Spit flew from my mouth. My instinct was to run from that room, but they were blocking my exit. It wasn't the potential pain that terrified me—it was the surgeon himself. I didn't trust him. He was just like the old woman Nan. He hated me. He hated my people.

"Restrain her," the surgeon ordered. "She is a creature of instinct, not intellect. Restrain her so she cannot flee."

"Emmeline?" Owen said gently. "There's no need to be frightened. Do you understand what the surgeon is going to do?"

"He's going to hurt me. He thinks I'd be better off dead."

The surgeon snorted. "Stupid girl."

Owen pushed his hair off his forehead, revealing a thin silver scar. "See this? I had stitches just like the stitches in your leg. But after a while the surgeon took the stitches out. See, my skin has healed." He leaned closer, running his finger across the scar. "It didn't hurt. I promise it didn't hurt. There was a little bit of tugging, that's all." Then he straightened. "Your leg will heal, but only if the surgeon takes out the stitches."

I wanted to believe him. He spoke so kindly.

The surgeon peered over Owen's shoulder. "Get the blanket from her," he whispered. "Quickly, before she lashes out again."

"I won't fight," I told Owen. "Please go." I didn't want him to see my foot again. I didn't want his pity. "Please."

With a quick nod, he left the room.

I gripped a pillow and looked away as the surgeon settled next to me. The tugging was strange, but the pain was bearable. Once he'd pulled all the stitches from my skin, he dabbed the scabs with some tonic, which stung for a moment. I suppose I should have been grateful, but I couldn't bring myself to thank him. Then he wrapped a strip of fabric over the wound. As he began to repack his wooden case, I remembered Owen's words—*He's a good surgeon. He can fix most everything.*

"Can you fix my foot?" I asked.

He closed his case and set his tall hat on his head. "If a surgeon had been consulted when you were born, your foot could have been remedied. It's a painful procedure, the uncurling, and it takes many years." He shook his head. "But now it is too late. You are too old. Nothing can be done."

"Nothing?" I whispered.

"Such ignorance," the surgeon said, his wooden case gripped in his hand. "When you return to the Flatlands, tell your people that modern medicine is nothing to fear. And that it's idiotic to believe that a bath should be taken only in moonlight."

"Moonlight is good for the skin," I told him. "It cures things."

"Moonlight cures nothing. If you want to cure skin ailments, you must use garlic, horse urine, and leeches." He started toward the door. "You're a very fortunate girl," he said just before leaving. "Most people would have left you to die on that riverbank."

I had no doubt he spoke the truth. "We don't fear modern

medicine," I said. "We would welcome a surgeon, but none of you will live in the Flatlands."

"Why would we want to live in the Flatlands?"

I had no answer.

"How odd," he said before leaving. "There's a cow at the window."

I smiled at her. She smiled back.

Chapter Thirteen

I believe you are well enough to join us for supper," Missus Oak declared a few days later.

I did feel better. I'd been walking around the bedroom in the borrowed nightfrock and wool socks, strength returning to my legs. My lungs no longer burned and the bruises on my arms were fading. But since I wasn't sleeping as much, the days had begun to feel endless. I'd never spent so much time in bed, not even when I'd come down with spotted fever. "I can leave the bedroom?" I asked excitedly, wrapping the blanket around my shoulders.

"Yes, but . . ." Missus Oak pursed her lips. "We can't have you going to supper looking like that. We must clean you up." She took my arm and led me to the doorway. As I took my lopsided steps, Missus Oak gave me a reassuring smile. We walked a short distance down the hall, then turned into another room. Nan stood in the center of the room, pouring a bucket of steaming water into what looked like a giant wooden bowl.

"First thing is a nice bath," Missus Oak said, dipping her fingertips into the water. "The surgeon said your wound has healed well enough. We'll help you climb in."

"Climb in? You want me to sit in that thing?" I looked nervously at the strange contraption.

"Of course," Missus Oak said. "How else would you take a bath?"

As I peered into the water's depths, steam drifted onto my face. In the Flatlands, we always bathed in the river. The current carried away our filth and any bad luck we might have picked up.

"I bet she's never seen a bathtub," Nan said.

I stepped away from the tub and looked pleadingly at Missus Oak.

"Don't you worry," Missus Oak said sweetly. "We'll wash you with rose petal soap. You'll smell like a vase of flowers."

They had their minds set. I didn't want to offend the family who'd been so kind to me. They'd saved my life, after all. The least I could do was to partake in their strange custom. Besides, it would be nice to smell like a vase of flowers rather than the way I currently smelled, which was as if I'd been sweating out in the fields.

I'd never stood naked in front of anyone but my mother. Missus Oak seemed to sense my embarrassment for she gently patted my shoulder. "Modesty is an important virtue for a girl, but there is nothing shameful about bathing in our presence. Nan and I have the same body parts that you have." She smiled. "And remember, we are the ones who removed your soiled clothing and put you into that nightfrock."

Missus Oak had the gentlest voice I'd ever heard, somewhere between a whisper and soft singing. She could convince me to do anything. I pulled the nightfrock over my head and handed it to Nan, along with one of the socks. But no matter what Missus Oak said, I was not going to take off the other sock. Nan raised her eyebrows, waiting, but I shook my head. With a *humph*, she carried the clothes from the room.

Gripping the edge of the tub, I carefully stepped into the water with my good foot. When I sat, the water reached to my shoulders. Easing into the cold river always took my breath away, and getting out as fast as possible was always the goal. But this was very, very nice. Flower petals floated by as the warm water caressed me. I took a long, deep breath. Nothing had ever felt so good.

The bathwater quickly turned gray. My face was scrubbed, along with my neck, face, back, arms, and scalp. The soap did smell like roses—the ones that grew wild on the riverbank. I closed my eyes as warm water was poured over my head. Once I'd stepped out of the tub, I was dried with soft fabric, then wrapped in a blanket.

"Sit here," Missus Oak said, gently pushing me into a chair.

"Ow," I said as Nan tried to run a brush through my hair.

"Hold still," Nan grumbled, yanking. "I've never seen so many knots and tangles. It's the devil's hair. We'll have to cut it off."

"No," I pleaded, pulling away from the brush. "You can't cut it off. I won't let you cut it off."

"I know what we can do," Missus Oak said. She hurried from the bathing room and was back a few moments later with a small bottle. "When my daughter was little, she used to cry when I combed her hair. So we used this to smooth out the tangles." She opened the bottle, poured some sort of oil into her palms, and rubbed her hands together. Then she ran them over my hair, working the oil from scalp to ends. She and Nan each took a side of my head and worked their brushes. My eyes teared up, but the pain was worth not having my hair cut.

After the brushing, I was left alone, to put on a yellow dress that had once belonged to Owen's sister. From the sad look on Missus Oak's face when she handed me the dress, I guessed the girl had died. But I didn't ask. Like my father, Missus Oak might prefer not to talk about loved ones who'd gone into the everafter.

When I opened the door, Missus Oak's mouth gaped with surprise. "My dear girl, take a look at yourself," she said, leading me to a mirror.

The girl staring back at me from the depths of the mirror, with her clean glowing face and long, shiny hair, was someone I'd never seen before.

"You're a beauty," Missus Oak whispered. "A true beauty."

Chapter Fourteen

My stomach growled. Who came up with the idiotic idea that only three meals a day should be eaten? I'd eat ten meals if given the chance.

Nan set a bowl of buttered carrots on the table, next to a loaf of bread. I wanted to rip the loaf in half and shove it in my mouth. I tried to sneak a carrot but Nan slapped my hand. "You wait for your mother." I folded my arms and sat back in the chair, my rib aching from the movement. Nan always treated me like a child.

"Wife!" Father hollered. "You want a man to starve to death?" He strummed his fingers on the table, his gaze set on a platter of sliced roasted hen. As soon as Nan left the room, we each grabbed a slice and ate as fast as humanly possible, wiping the grease from our lips before Nan returned with a pitcher of milk and a platter of beef ribs.

"Missus Oak is tending to the dirt-scratcher," Nan said. "I don't know how long . . ." She looked beyond my shoulder to the other side of the room and gasped. Father and I turned around.

Mother stepped into the supper room, followed by a beautiful girl. Even though the red hair hinted that she was the same girl I'd found at the river, I wasn't certain until our eyes locked. What had happened to the waterlogged creature I'd carried home? Where was the terrified girl with the messy hair who'd kicked at the surgeon? I scrambled to my feet, knocking my chair backward. My father also stood.

"Do I finally get to meet our guest?" he asked after clearing his throat.

"Husband," Mother said. "This is Emmeline Thistle."

"We are happy to see that you've recovered," Father said. He pulled out a chair on the opposite side of the table from me. "Please sit down."

"You've already met my son," Mother said, narrowing her eyes at me. "He was not supposed to enter his bedroom while you were recovering, but he has a habit of breaking my rules."

"Hi," I said. Emmeline nodded but didn't smile. Then she walked around the table, her steps uneven. That's when I remembered her curled foot. It was amazing she could walk at all. As she sat in the chair, my gaze swept over her. She was stunning! The red hair had looked like tangled yarn when I'd found her at the river. Now it fell in sheets that looked as soft as silk. I wanted to reach across the table and touch her hair. I wanted to bury my face in it. I wanted—

"Owen?" Father poked my arm. He and Mother were seated, both looking at me. "Why don't you pick up your chair, son?"

I did. As I sat, Nan headed back to the kitchen, grumbling

about a dirt-scratcher sitting at the supper table. Emmeline gripped the armrests of her chair, her knuckles turning white.

"Blessings upon this family," Father said with a quick bow of his head. Then he grabbed the platter of roasted hen. "Let's eat."

Mother spooned food onto Emmeline's plate. "You need to eat," she encouraged. "Eat as much as you can, then eat some more. You're not much more than skin and bones." It was true. I remembered Emmeline's thin ankles when I'd taken off her boots, the way her hip bones had protruded from her skirt. The yellow dress she wore was loose, even though my sister, the previous owner of the dress, had been a rail of a thing.

"Why aren't you eating?" Father asked, handing me a slice of bread. I started to shove it into my mouth, then remembered all those lectures about table manners. I chewed with my mouth closed, then thought how ridiculous it was to be worried about impressing a dirt-scratcher. Did her people even eat at tables? They probably ate everything with their fingers.

"Eat," Mother insisted, pointing her fork at Emmeline's plate.

Emmeline picked up the fork and stabbed a carrot. She chewed slowly. We watched her chew, then swallow. Her mouth turned up slightly. "It's good," she said.

I held out the platter of ribs. She frowned. "What kind of meat is that?"

"Cow," I said.

"My people don't eat meat that comes from cows."

"Oh." I put the platter on the table. "What about hen?"

"Aye," she said. "I'll eat that." And so we ate our supper. Emmeline ate everything put on her plate.

"There's color in her cheeks," Father said, waving a hen's leg. "You've done well, wife. She looks ready to travel."

Emmeline stopped eating. "I can travel?" Her voice was stronger, which made her unusual accent easier to understand. The way she rolled some of her letters was strange and took a bit of time to get used to. "Does that mean I can go home?"

Father shared a long, worried look with Mother and me. We knew things that Emmeline did not yet know, news that had come to us that very morning by way of the civil engineer. "You should tell her," I said.

"It's too soon," Mother whispered. She reached out and placed a protective hand over Emmeline's. "She's still very frail."

"Tell me what?" Emmeline asked, her eyes widening.

Father set the hen leg onto his plate and folded his hands, a serious pose for the delivery of serious news. "The road is destroyed. No one has ridden in or out of the Flatlands since the flood. But a small raft came downriver, carrying a tax-collector and two of his guards." He paused.

"She needs to know," I quietly urged. As horrid as it was, she had the right to know what had happened.

Father unfolded, then folded his hands. "The news is not good. The flood swallowed one of the villages. I think it was called Root."

"Root is my village." Emmeline's shoulders sank. She seemed to shrink within the dress itself. "Swallowed?" she repeated, her lower lip trembling.

"I'm afraid so. No buildings were spared. The river took everything." There was more to be told, but I knew from his tender expression that he would save the details for later, when Emmeline had regained her strength. For it wasn't only a raft that had made its way downstream. Over the past few days, planking and household goods had piled up along the distant riverbank, as had ten bodies—all red-haired. Because rotting corpses spread disease, our tax-collector had ordered the bodies to be buried in a mass grave outside of town.

Panic surged in Emmeline's eyes. I'd seen the same look in a calf's eyes when it had been separated from the herd during a windstorm. I shifted in my chair. "I'm sure your family survived and are waiting for you," I said.

Emmeline stared at her plate. "My father is not waiting for me." We had to lean close to hear her words, her voice soft, her lips barely moving. "He was taken away to fight in the war."

"War?" Father and I asked at the same time.

Emmeline's eyes sparkled with tears. "The war in the mineral fields," she said.

"War in the mineral fields?" Father rubbed the back of his neck. "I don't know of any such war."

"But the soldiers came," Emmeline said. "They came on horseback with a scroll from the king."

"When?" I asked.

She wiped at a rolling tear. "Just before the rain. The king needed men to fight. That's what the scroll said. So they took all the unmarried men."

"Are you sure they were the king's soldiers?" I asked. "Did they wear yellow tunics with the white swan crest?"

She nodded.

"But why did they take your father?" Mother asked.

"My mother died when I was ten and my father never took another wife."

Father sat back in his chair and ran his fingers through his beard. "This is very strange. If a war raged in the mineral fields, surely we would have heard of it."

"Why would there be a war in the mineral fields?" I asked. "I thought that place was long abandoned because of the deadly gases."

While Father and I sat perplexed, Mother turned her attention to Emmeline. "Have you no one else?" she asked. "An aunt or uncle? Cousins, perhaps?" Nan walked into the supper room and began to clear the table.

"I have no one," Emmeline said.

"What about friends? Surely there will be someone you can stay with."

Emmeline sat very straight. "I can take care of myself. You've helped me more than I can repay. Since I'm well enough to travel, I'll leave in the morning." How beautiful she looked, her hair draping over her small shoulders, her lips the same color as the jam we ate at breakfast.

"You can't leave," I blurted. "I mean, not yet. The road isn't repaired. You'll have to stay until the road is repaired."

"Stay here?" Nan balanced an armful of dishes. "Dirt-scratchers are supposed to stay in the Flatlands. It's against the king's law for them to leave. It's against the king's law for her to be here."

"She didn't leave," I said. "She was pushed out. There's a huge difference. And besides, how could the king expect Emmeline to stay in the Flatlands when her village is gone?"

Mother began pouring tea. "Owen is right, husband. We can't send Emmeline back to nothing. We should keep her."

"Keep her?" Father pulled his pipe from his pocket and tapped its contents onto his plate. "She's not a stray cat, wife. What would we do with her?"

"Why not give her a job?" I said with a shrug.

"A job?" Emmeline's eyes brightened. "Yes. I will work for you, to pay back my debt."

"She could help Nan in the kitchen," Mother suggested, though her tone was half-hearted. We all knew Nan's reaction before it burst from her lips.

"I don't want anyone messing with my kitchen," she insisted, her cheeks turning red. "I do the kitchen work, no one else."

"Why not make her a milkmaid?" I said.

Nan gasped. "You're going to let a dirt-scratcher milk your cows? What will the townsfolk say?"

Father frowned. "We can't make her a milkmaid."

"Why not?" I asked. "The cows seem to like her. They never looked in my bedroom window before. And that cow at the river—"

"The cows aren't the issue," Father said. "The law is the issue. It's against the law for a dirt-scratcher to live outside the Flatlands.

It's been that way ever since they came to this land as invaders. Ever since they cursed our queen and the chocolate disappeared."

In my schoolhouse years, I'd learned all about the terrible dark day when the chocolate had disappeared. Everyone knew the story. That's why I couldn't believe my ears when Emmeline, her lips glistening with butter from the carrots, innocently asked, "What is chocolate?"

Chapter Fifteen

Father sputtered, his pipe dangling from his lower lip. "Surely you jest."

Emmeline frowned. "Jest?"

"Emmeline?" I asked. "You really don't know about chocolate?" She shook her head. "But that's the reason your people were sent to the Flatlands. Don't they teach you history in . . . ?" Then I remembered that Nan had said dirt-scratchers don't send their children to school.

I reached into my vest pocket and pulled out the book I'd been carrying around. Normally I wouldn't have spent so much time reading, but what else was I supposed to do with a broken rib and Mother's orders to rest? The days moved slower than a caterpillar across a field. "This book contains the famous legends of Anglund," I said. "There's a chapter on chocolate if you'd like to borrow it."

Emmeline's frown deepened. "I can't read."

"Oh." I should have guessed that. As I opened the book and

shuffled through its pages, Nan brought a platter of honey cakes to the table. "One of us can read it to you, if you'd like," I said.

"Do you think that's wise?" Mother asked. "It's a most upsetting story and Emmeline is still frail."

"I'm not frail," Emmeline insisted. "I want to know why we can't leave the Flatlands. I want to know why . . ." Her gaze darted to Nan. "I want to know why people hate us."

"Are you going to read *The Sweetest Spell*?" Nan asked. "That's a real good story." She pulled a chair from the corner and sat behind Mother.

Back when my sister was alive, we used to do this all the time—read from one of our favorite books, right there at the supper table. But those days seemed so long ago.

Though there were no windows in the supper room, night had crept in, seeping around the furniture. Mother lit two candles and set them close to me. "You sure you want to hear this?" I asked after finding the page. "It's about your people and it's not a nice story."

"My life has never been a nice story," Emmeline said.

And so I read.

The Sweetest Spell: The Story of Chocolate

As recorded by Filibus Minor, Royal Secretary to Queen Margaret, divinely bequested ruler of the Kingdom of Anglund.

In the reign of Her Royal and Rightful Majesty Queen Margaret, there was great prosperity and peace. This era, known as the

Years of Happiness, was brought about by the magnificence of the Queen Herself. A renowned scholar and philosopher, Queen Margaret understood that trade could be a more powerful purveyor of peace than the sword. Thusly, in accordance with Her grand plan, She withdrew Her warships from the Southern Sea. Merchant ships could now sail the waters between our island kingdom and our enemies' distant shores, enriching our land with silk, porcelain, and oil in exchange for the one commodity our enemies desired more than anything else—chocolate.

During my reign as Royal Secretary, Queen Margaret possessed the magic for making chocolate. The secret was delivered to Her in a divine dream. The most delicious food ever known, chocolate was a sweet delicacy that melted on the tongue and filled its host with desire. Though its dark, muddy brown color was unappealing, the taste was pure ecstasy. Queen Margaret shared the magic with Her royal chefs. In the vast underbelly of the palace, where the royal kitchens spread like a labyrinth, chocolate was made every day. The scent wafted out the palace windows and drifted down the streets and was almost impossible to resist. Anglunders with coin were never without the precious treat. During the annual Festival of the Swan, the Queen supplied a piece of chocolate to everyone in the kingdom, even the poorest families. Such was Her generous nature.

With the trade routes open and word of chocolate spreading, dignitaries began to arrive from all over the world to taste the delicacy. They laid treasures at Queen Margaret's feet, in the hopes that She would trade chocolate. More chefs were hired and trained to meet the demand. Another wing of the palace was converted into an enormous kitchen. The royal barn, which housed the royal cows, quadrupled in size. Cream, a main ingredient in the chocolate-making process, became highly sought after. Anglund's dairymen grew wealthy. And Queen Margaret grew more beloved each year of Her reign as her power to create chocolate gave the country wealth and influence.

Then tragedy struck. In the thirtieth year of Queen Margaret's reign, a wild wind invaded our kingdom. A cloud of dust descended over the land, choking those who couldn't find shelter. The dust cloud stayed for three long days, blocking out the sun. On the fourth day, it blew away as quickly as it had appeared, but in its wake came a strange tribe of invaders, a red-haired people who . . .

I stopped reading and glanced up at Emmeline. She stared intently at my lips, as if trying to see the story as it emerged from my mouth. Mother and Nan munched honey cakes. Father smoked his pipe. I continued reading.

. . . a red-haired people who called themselves the Kell. Their chieftain, whose fiery hair fell to his knees, claimed they'd been forced from their land by the dust storm, which had strangled most of their people, animals, and crops. Queen Margaret, in Her benevolence, made the following decree. "We shall grant the Kell sanctuary in our land. They are welcome here." Because they came without belongings, the Queen offered them food, shelter, and clothing in exchange for their work in the mineral fields.

"The mineral fields?" Emmeline interrupted. "My ancestors used to work in the mineral fields?"

"Yes," Father said. "The very same place where your father has been taken."

"Shall I keep reading?" I asked her.

"Aye," she said.

It was Queen Margaret's kind heart that blinded Her to the true nature of the Kell chieftain. He was not satisfied with the work given to his people in the mineral fields. A greedy spirit hid beneath his fur pelts. "Why should my people live as slaves?" he demanded. "The Kell are proud. The Kell are strong. Give us land and we will take care of ourselves."

"Why should We give you land?" Queen Margaret asked. "We have granted you sanctuary and work. That is enough."

But the chieftain wanted more. He wanted to rule Anglund. He wanted to share the Queen's bed. He wanted to share Her wealth. When She refused, he led an uprising of his strongest men, and they invaded the palace kitchens, where they murdered most of the royal chefs. Only two chefs survived and these the chieftain held as hostages. "Give me the magic of chocolate or I will slit their throats," he threatened the Queen.

Soldiers of the royal army stormed the kitchen and valiantly fought the devil-haired barbarians. The scent of chocolate mixed with the scent of fresh blood, rivers of which ran along the corridors. The chieftain was eventually captured, but only after he'd murdered the last two chefs.

When the chieftain stood on the execution platform, he made the following declaration: "I am the chieftain of the Kell. She who takes my life will be forever cursed. I take from Her what She most cherishes, and I give it to one of my own."

At the stroke of the blade, when the chieftain's head rolled from his neck, his curse flew through the air and pierced Queen Margaret's heart. Her magic disappeared. Never again could She make chocolate. Sadness fell over the entire kingdom. The merchant ships left our ports, never to return.

Despite the brutality to Her Person and Her people, Queen Margaret's heart remained pure and kind. The remaining Kell, mostly women and children, were sent to the uninhabited region known as the Flatlands and left there to take care of themselves. But never again would they be allowed to wander the kingdom. Never again would they be trusted to be full citizens of the realm.

As I, the Royal Secretary, record this history, our beloved, beautiful Queen has locked Herself inside Her chamber, seeking slumber, hoping for the divine dream to return. Hoping, once again, to possess the magic of chocolate.

I closed the book, wondering what Emmeline's reaction would be. But she said nothing, lost in thought. Mother broke the silence. "Have a honey cake," she said, holding the platter out. "They are delicious. I'm sure they are even better than chocolate."

Emmeline took one of the cakes but set it on her plate without taking a bite. Her hair had fallen over her shoulders, gently framing her oval face. "Is it true?" she asked.

"Of course it's true," Nan mumbled.

"It is legend," Father said, moving his pipe to the other side of his mouth. "Legend is part truth and part story."

"Husband, we still have the matter at hand." Mother wiped the corners of her mouth with a napkin. "How are we breaking the law if there is no way for Emmeline to return to the Flatlands? The road is closed. No boat can go up that part of the river. What is she supposed to do? Fly?"

"Well . . ." Father strummed his fingers on the tabletop. "I wanted to keep Emmeline a secret until she could return home. But seeing as sending her home isn't possible, I suppose there's no harm in discussing the situation with our tax-collector. If we can get his approval, then we'll have no worries about the law. If he agrees, then Emmeline can work as a milkmaid. Temporarily, of course."

"A milkmaid?" Nan asked. "A dirt-scratcher as a milkmaid?"

"It's the only job we have around here," Father said.

Nan stomped out of the room. Emmeline and Mother shared a happy smile while Father refilled his pipe with the brown leaf that he bought from the spice merchant. And I sat back in my chair, once again staring at the girl who'd washed up on our riverbank. As I breathed deeply, my lungs pressing against the surgeon's wrap that held my rib in place, I realized I was glad to have Emmeline stay a bit longer.

More than glad.

Part Three

Milkmaid

Chapter Sixteen

Over the next few days my broken rib stopped aching, but I didn't tell my parents. A healed rib meant I'd have to go back to work at our shop. An unhealed rib meant I was expected to stay home.

With Emmeline.

I felt a twinge of guilt, but only a twinge. Polly, our eldest milkmaid, was happy to take my place in the shop. She liked dealing with the customers because they always brought a hearty helping of town gossip. Mother didn't seem to mind my absence. "The longer you stay away from the temptations of town, the better," she'd said.

But the temptations of town came looking for me in the form of Bartholomew Raisin. It was early morning. Father and I were walking toward the barn when Bartholomew rode up on his horse. "Good day, Mister Oak," he said. His stirrups were cinched high so his short legs could reach them. "Hello, Owen."

I grunted a response. Father narrowed his eyes. "What do you want, Mister Raisin?"

Bartholomew slid off the horse, landing on wobbly legs. "Just passing by," he said. "Out for a bit of fresh air and exercise." He rubbed his fat hands together and peered up at me. "How's that rib of yours? Is it almost healed? Never knew a rib could take so long to mend."

"You're wasting your time," Father said. "Owen's not going to fight in your circle. He's promised his mother."

"But Mister Oak," Bartholomew said, his swollen fingers twitching. "Barefist fighting is what your son does. He's the best I've ever seen. It's in his blood."

We headed toward the barn, Bartholomew scuttling alongside. "I know it's in his blood," Father said. "But you'll have to find yourself another fighter. My boy's done with it."

I said nothing. I simply shrugged—a gesture of surrender that sent Bartholomew twitching at greater speed. I'd made the promise, but how long I could keep it was another matter. The fighting circle beckoned me the way trickling water beckons a thirsty animal.

"But the king has issued a new tax on barefist fighting. He's going to take a 20 percent cut of my profits. I need Owen to—"

"Good day, Mister Raisin," Father said, shutting the barn door in Bartholomew's round face. Then he placed a hand on my shoulder, his expression serious. "Don't tell your mother I said this, but you need to get yourself a wife. That will take your mind off fighting." He walked down the steep steps that led into the underground cheese cellar.

Get myself a wife? I hesitated on the top step. I hated the cheese cellar. My chest always tightened down there, deep beneath the barn, with thoughts of the ceiling caving in. "I don't want a wife," I hollered down.

"You don't know what you want," Father hollered back. "Take my word for it. A good wife will tame that fighting urge. A wife's what you need. But not Emmeline. She's not the one for you."

"Emmeline?" With a deep breath I forced myself down the stairs, my heart pounding with each step. The cellar's cool air mixed with the sour scent of aging cheese. Slowly my eyes adjusted to the dim light. "Why would you bring up Emmeline?"

"I've seen the way you look at her. I know that look."

"What look?"

He heaved a wheel of cheese from the shelf. "She's a nice girl, but she's not your kind. Chasing her would bring you both a world of unhappiness." With a grunt he set the wheel on a table.

"I'm not *chasing* her," I said.

"We don't have permission from the tax-collector yet, so don't go getting your hopes set on Emmeline staying. As soon as he gets back from his visit to Londwin City, I'll be discussing the situation with him. But I'm thinking, maybe it's not such a good idea to have her stay. Not with you following her around."

I held up my palms, defending myself from this crazy notion. "I'm not following her around. I don't know where you got that idea."

Father snickered. "I've got two eyes. That's where I got that idea. So don't you go getting her with child."

"What?" I forgot all about the ceiling caving in. "That's crazy."

As Father wiped dust from the wheel of cheese, I leaned against the cellar wall. Eleven days had passed since that supper when Emmeline had joined us at the table, transformed. And for eleven days I'd conjured excuse after excuse to be near her. At first she'd kept to the house, her fiery hair always tucked into a bonnet. When she swept the floors, I moved furniture out of her way. While she dusted the shelves, I read to her. When she went outside for the first time to hang the laundry on the line, I lowered the cord so she could reach it without having to stand on a bucket.

"Owen Oak, you leave that girl alone," Nan had scolded, shooing me away. "That rib of yours is never going to heal if you keep following her around."

Even Nan had noticed. What was the matter with me? A knot formed in my stomach as I pushed the embarrassment away. I took a deep breath of the cellar's cold air. "It's not what you think," I told my father. "She's pretty. That's all it is. I just like looking at her. Nothing more."

"Well, *that* I do understand. A pretty girl is hard to ignore." Father glanced over at me. "Look, son, your mother's taken a liking to the girl. Ever since your sister's passing, there's been a terrible ache inside her. She's giving all that unused love to Emmeline. But Emmeline will have to go back to her own people one day. Dirt-scratchers belong in the Flatlands." He stabbed the wheel with a knife, then cut it in half. "It's going to be difficult enough for your mother to let her go. I don't need you getting attached too."

"I'm not getting *attached*. I don't even know what you mean by that." I trudged up the stairs and out of the cellar.

So what if I helped Emmeline with the chores? Who else did she have to talk to? Why not me? I'm the one who found her. Well, the cow found her, but I carried her to safety. It was good manners to help her. That was all.

And there she was, standing inside the front door, a feather duster in her hand. She'd taken to wearing a blue milkmaid's dress and white apron, on Mother's orders. Better to wear a work dress while doing household chores than one of my sister's fancy getups. "Hello, Owen," she said as I walked into the house. "There's something I wanted to ask you."

"I don't have time," I grumbled, moving quickly past her, holding my breath so I wouldn't smell the rose soap on her skin. Too much time spent with one girl was not good. If Father had gotten the wrong idea, then maybe Emmeline had gotten the wrong idea as well. And if Emmeline thought I had feelings for her, then I needed to put an end to that. I wasn't going to follow in Barley's footsteps—fall in love, get married, have babies, the whole nightmare. I'd admit that my rib was better and get back to work at the shop.

"Owen?" Emmeline called softly. I stopped but, rather than looking at her, looked down at my boots. "Would you take me to see the cow?"

"Huh? What cow?"

"The one who found me by the river. I want to thank her."

I scratched the back of my neck. "Well . . ." I couldn't help it. My gaze traveled up her skirt, up her bodice, and up her neck until it locked on to those green eyes that seemed to be made of dew-speckled moss. "Sure, I guess."

Who was I kidding? I was lying to myself, just as I'd lied to Mother when I'd promised I'd never fight again. At night, alone in the bunkhouse, I could still feel Emmeline's head against my shoulder. When I closed my eyes, I could still feel my arm around her tiny waist, holding her as the horse galloped across the pasture.

I was *attached*.

Chapter Seventeen

Emmeline wasn't supposed to leave the house, so I waited until Father, Mother, and Polly drove into town to open the shop. And because no one outside my family, except the surgeon, knew about Emmeline, I waited until the milkmaids finished the morning milking and walked back to their homes for midday meal, their blue dresses disappearing around the fence. Only then, with the coast clear, did I lead Emmeline from the house, keeping the pace slow as we crossed the yard. I'd gotten used to the way she dipped to one side when she walked. Many times I'd wanted to ask about her foot, but I remembered the embarrassment in her eyes when I'd told her that I'd been the one who'd removed her river-soaked boots.

With the morning milking done, the cows were grazing in the nearby pasture. They raised their horned heads as we approached. Maybe they thought she was one of their regular milkmaids, seeing as she was dressed in a milkmaid's dress. I had no idea which cow had found Emmeline. They all looked exactly alike. But Emmeline seemed to have her heart set on thanking the creature. "We don't have cows like this in the Flatlands," she told me as we stood at the pasture's edge.

"How many cows did you have on your farm?"

"We never had cows. Only Milkman Boar had cows." She frowned and I sensed she was thinking about her village. I'd tried to imagine what it would feel like to lose everything. I'd tried to picture Wander washing away in a flood. What would it be like to walk through empty streets? To look for buildings that no longer stood? To look for people who had simply vanished?

We stood in silence for a few moments. Then she closed her eyes briefly and shook her head, probably pushing the images away. "Where is she?" she asked. Midday sunlight spread across her cheeks as she looked into the field. "The cow who found me. Where is she?"

I was about to choose a random cow when one of the creatures began a slow mosey toward us. Emmeline smiled and held out her hand. The cow sniffed, then stuck out a grass-stained tongue and licked her hand. Emmeline pressed her forehead against its cheek. "Thank you," she whispered. It mooed, as if answering.

"The cows really seem to like you," I said.

"It's always been that way."

At Emmeline's request, I showed her the rest of the farm. I didn't mind that the going was slow. If it took twice as long to get from one end of the farm to the other end of the farm, that meant I had twice as long to look at her. Did all dirt-scratcher girls look like this? If so, the king should open the Flatlands and let them run free.

We ended the tour in the butter room. "These are full of fresh cream," I said, pointing to two large barrels. "The milkmaids will churn the cream into butter this afternoon."

"Butter?" Emmeline peered into one of the barrels. It had not escaped my attention that she loved the stuff. She smothered it on everything. But all that eating had done her good. The hollows beneath her eyes and at the base of her neck had filled in. And her wrists no longer looked like they might snap as easily as dried twigs.

"We never had butter at home. How do you make it? Will you show me?"

"I guess we could make a small batch," I said, motioning her to sit on one of the stools. Then I poured cream into a churning bucket. "This is the paddle," I told her, pressing it into the top of the bucket. I pulled another stool close, set the bucket at my feet, and began to turn the handle. "This moves the paddle from side to side and stirs the cream. You do this until it thickens."

"Doesn't your rib hurt when you do that?" she asked, pointing to my side.

I stopped churning. "Uh, it's getting better." As my hand slipped from the handle, it bumped into her hand. "Sorry," I said, pulling away. Then I pushed the bucket closer to her. "Why don't you give it a try?"

She turned the handle until she found a steady rhythm. She relaxed her shoulders, easing into the motion as if she'd been churning her whole life. "I'll stay here and work long enough to repay your mother and father for the food and lodging. But I can never repay you."

"Repay me?"

"You saved my life."

"You'd have to churn that butter into gold if you want to repay me." She stopped churning, her eyebrows arched with surprise. "I'm teasing," I said with a gentle laugh. "Just teasing. You owe me nothing. I did what any man would have done if he'd found you on the riverbank."

"That's not true." She looked away. "I know what most men would have done. They would have left me there to die. A Flatlander girl is less than an animal."

I said nothing. I wanted to tell her it wasn't true. But it was true.

She began turning the handle again. "I will repay you one day. I will."

"Where will you go?" I asked. "When you leave here?"

"I want to find my father so I can bring him home. If there is no war then the king should let him go. How far away are the mineral fields?"

"Very far," I said. "They lie on the northeastern corner of the kingdom." Resting my forearms on my knees, I stared at the floor as I delivered the bad news. "Look, Emmeline, there are only three ways to get out of the king's army. If a soldier is wounded, he's sent home. If he comes from a rich family, he can buy his way out."

"What is the third way?"

"Death."

We sat in silence. The room seemed to darken with the mood. I tried to change the subject.

"We have this peddler who comes and visits. He said that you buy yourselves husbands in the Flatlands."

"Aye. At the husband market," Emmeline said. She must have noticed my pained grin because her cheeks flushed. "Don't you have a husband market?" I shook my head. "Then how do you get a wife in the Wanderlands?"

"I don't know," I said with a shrug. "You meet someone and fall in love. Or your parents find someone for you. Are you going to buy a husband at this market when you go home?"

"No one would marry me," she said quietly.

"What are you talking about?" I asked. "You must be one of the most popular girls in your village. Even with your . . ." I didn't say it, but both our gazes darted to her right boot. "You're beautiful," I said softly. It had slipped out without my even thinking about it.

She stopped churning and looked at me, her eyes as round as the moon itself, as if I'd just told her a secret or had found something she'd lost. I wanted to kiss her. I wanted to pull the bonnet from her head and run my hand through her hair. I leaned forward. She held her breath, unblinking as I inched closer. Then someone cleared her throat.

Emmeline tightened her bonnet, hiding the edges of her hair. A girl stood in the doorway to the butter room. I jumped to my feet and stepped in front of Emmeline. This was not going to be good. "Hello, Fee," I said.

Fee, a milkmaid who'd been at the Oak Dairy for three years, stood with her feet planted wide, her arms folded. She narrowed her eyes. Everyone knew she wanted to be the next Missus Oak. She'd told this to my family, to her family, and even to me. I'd never asked Fee to get married. I'd never even told her I loved her. She had no reason to glare at me like that.

But it was possible that all those hours spent kissing behind the toolshed had given her the wrong idea.

"Who's that?" Fee asked, pushing her bonnet to the back of her neck, her corkscrew curls bouncing free.

"What are you doing here?" I asked. "You're supposed to be at midday meal."

"I came back early to see you." She took a side step, trying to peer around me. I mirrored her side step, blocking her view of Emmeline. "How come no one told me we had a new milkmaid?"

"We don't," I said. Then I took Fee's arm and led her away from the butter room and deep into the barn.

"Who is she?"

"She's . . . she's nobody. Why'd you come back to see me? What do you want?"

Fee slid from my grip, then wrapped her arms around my waist, pulling me close. "You want to go out to the shed?" A devilish smile spread across her round face.

Kissing Fee had been fun at first. She was warm and eager. I enjoyed and encouraged it, I won't lie. But after a while it lost its charm and started to feel like all we were doing was pressing our lips together. I could have been kissing a fence post for all the passion I'd felt. This happened before Emmeline's arrival, so it wasn't on account of my head swimming with thoughts of another girl. I just didn't feel anything for Fee. And I'd been avoiding her, unsure of what to say. But now I had to tell her. "I don't think we should meet anymore," I said quietly.

Fee pulled away. "Why?" Her gaze darted toward the butter room. "Because of her? Is she your new girl?"

"I don't have a girl," I said. "New or old. I don't have one."

"I thought I was your girl," Fee snapped. Then her eyes misted and she sniffled.

"Fee, it's never been like that." I shrugged. "I've told you over and over, we're not getting married." She blinked watery eyes, sniffling again. What an idiot I'd been. She was a sweet girl who hadn't paid any attention to my words, only to my actions. "I'm sorry. It's over." What else could be said?

A sudden burst of anger flashed in her eyes. "I despise you," she hissed. Then she kicked me hard in the shin. Clutching the sides of her skirt, she ran from the barn. I called after her but she screamed at me to drop dead.

There'd be no keeping this secret. Fee would tell the other milkmaids that I'd hurt her. She'd probably tell Mother. That was not a scene I was looking forward to. *Owen Oak, I told you to stay away from the milkmaids!*

I would. I would stay away from them from now on. It always ended badly, anyway. I rubbed my shin, then walked back to the butter room.

Emmeline stood over the churning bucket, wringing her hands, her face clenched in a worried sort of way. Had she overheard me and Fee? "I'm so sorry," she said. "I've ruined it. I've ruined the butter."

"What do you mean?" I pulled the paddle from the bucket. Peaks of soft butter clung to the paddle's sides but instead of the usual creamy yellow hue, the butter had turned dark brown.

Emmeline whimpered. "I'm sorry," she repeated. "I've ruined it."

Had she ruined it? I'd watched her and she'd done everything properly. "There must have been dirt in the bucket," I said. "I didn't check to make sure it was clean." I carried the bucket to the back of the room and left it on the counter. It was a waste of cream, but there was plenty more. Then I grabbed a new churning bucket, cleaned it with a burlap rag, poured in cream, and set the paddle into place. "Let's try again."

"But—"

"You love butter, right? So let's make some and we can give it to Nan."

She nodded.

We both sat, side by side, our knees almost touching. I tried not to think about Fee running home in tears. Her father would surely pay my father a visit. At least I'd been smart enough not to go beyond kissing.

Emmeline churned and right before my eyes the yellowish cream began to take on a light brown hue. "It's happening again," she said.

I leaned over the bucket. "Huh? But I cleaned it."

"Maybe it will go away," she said, desperately turning the handle.

But it didn't go away. The light brown cream changed into dark brown cream. Emmeline hesitated. "Keep going," I whispered, amazed by the transformation—like watching the sky slowly darken at night. The cream thickened as she churned until it was the consistency of butter. I stuck in my finger and scooped some out.

"What are you doing?" Emmeline asked, grabbing my arm as I tasted the discolored butter. "You'll get sick."

Smooth, creamy, just like the usual Oak Dairy butter, but what was that flavor? I tasted again. "My God, it's delicious. I've never tasted anything like it. Try it."

Hesitantly, Emmeline stuck her fingertip into the muddy concoction. Then she took a small taste. A smile broke across her face. "It's amazing. But it doesn't taste like butter."

I scooped more into my mouth. "It's not butter." Nothing made sense. "The bucket was clean, the cream was fresh. And yet somehow the butter changed into whatever this is. It's the most delicious thing I've ever eaten. It's sweet and . . ." I froze, a realization gripping me hard, almost squeezing my breath out. "No, it can't be."

"What can't be?" Emmeline asked.

I hurried to the other churning bucket. The first batch of dirty butter had hardened. I turned the bucket upside down and knocked a few times until the hardened, dirty butter cracked and fell out in pieces. Then I bit into one of the pieces. It melted on my tongue, creamy and sweet. I wanted to eat more. I wanted to eat all of it. It filled me with . . . desire.

The most delicious food ever known, chocolate was a sweet delicacy that melted on the tongue and filled its host with desire. Though its dark, muddy brown color was unappealing, the taste was pure ecstasy.

"Emmeline?" I said, wiping my mouth on my sleeve. "Do you think . . . ?" I could barely contain myself. It was the same powerful feeling I got when I stepped into the fight circle. "Do you think . . . ?"

Wide-eyed, Emmeline took the piece from my hand. She stood so close I caught the scent of rose soap that clung to her hair. A few dots of perspiration sat on the bridge of her nose.

"Remember the legend I read?"

Emmeline slid the piece between her lips and took a small bite. She closed her eyes as she chewed. Upon swallowing, her eyes flew open and a smile burst across her face.

"Owen," she said. "Did I make chocolate?"

Chapter Eighteen

I liked the Oaks' kitchen, which was so much bigger than the kitchen we had in our cottage in Root, before the flood took it away. It was always warm in there because Nan never seemed to stop cooking. And it was full of food. No empty shelves, no empty baskets. The Oaks had plenty. Was this the way Owen's life had always been? Had he never known hunger?

I sat at the table watching Nan pace. She stopped to peer into the bucket of brown butter, then paced some more. Maybe it was chocolate. I didn't really know. I'd never heard the word until Owen read from that book. But he seemed to think I'd made chocolate. And he'd rushed off to town to get his parents from the shop. So there I sat, waiting for them to come back.

Waiting for Owen.

He was being nice to me because he felt sorry for me. I knew that. It was nothing more than the same kind of pity he'd feel for a half-drowned dog. But in his bedroom at night, I liked to imagine pity had nothing to do with it. I was a different girl, a girl from Wander. My red hair was brown just like theirs. I was a whole girl with two perfect feet. And I was his.

Nan glared at me. "I don't know what you're smiling about," she said. She'd refused to taste the brown butter. Refused to touch it. "Don't know what that is," she said, pointing to the churning bucket. "Don't know what young Owen is thinking. Dirty butter is nothing to get excited about."

"He says it's chocolate," I reminded her.

"I know what he said, dirt-scratcher girl." She put her hands on her hips. "You don't have to tell me what he said. I heard it with my own two ears."

We'd been waiting a long time. I didn't like being alone with Nan. It wasn't because of the wary looks she gave me; that was nothing new in my life. It was because she always called me "dirt-scratcher" in a way that made the word sound like it was made from cow dung, or worse.

At the sound of horse hooves and wheels, Nan rushed to the kitchen window. Soon after, Mister and Missus Oak, led by Owen, hurried into the kitchen. I scrambled to my feet, reassured by Owen's beaming smile. Missus Oak's bonnet was askew and she wrung her hands. "You know I don't like to leave Polly alone in the shop. She'll eat her weight in cheese."

"I'm losing patience," Mister Oak sternly told his son. "Tell us what has happened."

Owen's smile disappeared and he cleared his throat. "Sit down," he said as if about to tell them that someone had died. Mister Oak grumbled, then plunked into a chair.

"Oh dear," Missus Oak said as she sat next to her husband. "Owen? What have you done?"

Owen folded his arms. "What did *I* do?"

"Yes, what did *you* do?" Missus Oak asked.

"This time I am innocent, Mother. It's Emmeline you should be asking." He raised his eyebrows at me.

Missus Oak grabbed her husband's hand, as if to steady herself for whatever news was coming her way. "What has happened? Did someone see her hair? Do they know we've been housing a dirt-scratcher girl?"

"No one saw her hair," Owen said. He grabbed the bucket of dirty butter and set it on the table. "This is why I brought you home. This is what I wanted you to see." He turned the bucket upside down, thumped his hands against its sides until the contents slid onto the table. Then he set the bucket aside. We all stared at the circle of hardened brown butter.

"What is that?" Mister Oak asked.

"Emmeline made it," Owen said. He pulled his knife from his pocket and plunged it again and again, breaking the circle into smaller pieces. Then he picked up one of the pieces and held it out to his father. "Taste it."

"Emmeline made it?" Missus Oak asked. "Nan let Emmeline cook?"

"Never," Nan insisted. "That mess has nothing to do with me. It looks like something a cow left behind."

I almost laughed. It was a pretty good description.

"Father," Owen insisted. "Try it. Let it melt on your tongue. I promise you won't regret it."

Mister Oak took the piece, sniffed it, then popped it into his mouth. We all leaned closer, waiting for his reaction. At first it was hard to tell if he was disgusted or if he liked it because he closed his eyes and just stood there. It was melting, that I knew. It was filling his mouth with the most amazing flavor ever. He swallowed, then opened his eyes. "Delightful!" he exclaimed. "I shall have another." And he did.

"Mother?" Owen said, offering her a piece.

Missus Oak carefully pinched the piece between her fingertips. Like her husband, she sniffed it. Then she delicately nibbled the corner. "Oh my," she said, her other hand pressing to her chest. "Oh my, oh my." She popped the rest of the piece into her mouth. Nan inched forward, watching Missus Oak chew. Satisfied sounds of "oh" and "ooh" escaped her lips. Her eyes rolled back. "That is the best thing I've ever tasted." She grabbed another piece. "What is this, Emmeline? However did you make it?"

"I really don't know," I said with a shrug.

"From our cream," Owen said. "She churned our cream and it turned into this."

"But what did she add to the cream?" Mister Oak asked, his lips glistening as he chewed. "We must have the recipe."

"I didn't add anything," I said. "It just . . . happened."

"I watched it happen," Owen said. "I watched her churn. When the cream thickened, it changed color. It was like some kind of magic."

"Dirt-scratcher magic," Nan whispered, her eyes widening fearfully. "Black magic. Don't eat it. It'll cast a spell over you."

"Now, Nan, calm down," Mister Oak said. "There's no such thing as magic."

"I'd usually agree with you," Owen said. "But now I'm not so sure." He turned to me. "Shall we show them?"

A new churning bucket was brought into the kitchen. And so, as the afternoon passed, I churned cream until my arms went numb. And each time, without fail, the cream thickened and turned dark brown. They tasted it when it was still soft. Then they tasted it after it hardened. "I could eat this every day," Mister Oak said.

"Me too," Missus Oak said.

Nan finally tried a piece and, like the rest of us, ate until her stomach ached. I stopped churning. My arms felt like deadwood.

"Now do you finally believe me?" Owen asked, leaning back in his chair and opening his book. He read, "*I am the chieftain of the Kell. She who takes my life will be forever cursed. I take from Her what She most cherishes, and I give it to one of my own.*" He closed the book. "It's chocolate. It has to be."

"Emmeline," Missus Oak said, wrapping an arm around my waist and giving me a gentle squeeze. "You've been blessed."

"And we've been blessed too," Mister Oak said. "Our customers will love it. We could sell enough to make up for all the coin we're losing to the king's new butter tax."

"But, Father," Owen said. "The chocolate is not ours to sell."

"Not ours to sell?" Mister Oak scratched his beard. "It's made from our cream."

"But it's Emmeline's magic."

All eyes turned to me. My cheeks began to burn. My magic?

How was it possible that I possessed this magic? "You can have the chocolate," I said. "I will happily give it to you for all you have done for me."

Mister and Missus Oak shared a long look. Then Mister Oak cleared his throat. "That is very generous, but my son is correct. We Oaks did not make the chocolate so it is not ours to sell." He stood at the kitchen window, his arms folded behind his back. A pair of cows stood outside, their noses pressed to the glass. "Emmeline, do you realize what this means? No one has seen or tasted chocolate for many generations. But you alone can make it."

"You'll be rich," Owen said.

"But she's a dirt-scratcher," Nan said.

"No one's going to care where Emmeline comes from once they've tasted the chocolate," Owen said. "They'll line up for days just to get a piece. She'll be very rich. Maybe the richest woman in the kingdom."

A shiver ran down my spine. Then it felt as if someone was squeezing the breath out of me. "Rich?" The word sputtered from my mouth. "Me?"

Owen smiled.

My head filled with a million thoughts. No Flatlander had ever been rich. "Do you think I could make enough coin to buy my father's freedom from the king's army?"

"It's possible," Mister Oak said.

"Do you think I could make enough coin to build my father a new cottage?"

"I bet you could build a hundred cottages," Owen said, smacking his palm on the table.

Do you think I could buy a husband? Someone like you? But this I didn't ask.

How could I ever leave this wonderful place? "I would like to stay here and be one of your milkmaids," I said. "I'll make the chocolate, and if you'll sell it in your shop, then we can split the coin." It was a bold suggestion. I tried to keep my voice from wavering. I might have asked too much. I waited, as did everyone else, for Mister Oak's reaction.

"So be it," he said, eagerly shaking my hand. "So be it."

Chapter Nineteen

Poor Emmeline. She fell fast asleep at the kitchen table. Father swept her into his arms and carried her to my room, where he tucked her into bed. When he returned, an amused smile crinkled his face.

"Who would have thought," he said, shaking his head. "Who would have thought a tiny little creature could hold such a big secret."

While Father finished the chores, Mother, Nan, and I spent the late afternoon working with the chocolate. In its soft form it was easy to cut into perfect squares. Nan pressed our seal into the top of each square, leaving an oak leaf imprint. The squares hardened quickly, a glossy sheen forming at the surface. Mother discovered she could roll the soft chocolate into little balls. Then she dipped each ball in lavender sugar. They were delicious.

As evening fell, Father returned to the kitchen. I expected him to start hollering about the fact that Nan hadn't made supper, but instead he grabbed a bowl. "Give me some of that chocolate."

"What for?" Mother asked.

"Might as well start spreading the news." With his forearm, he swept some of the chocolate squares into the bowl, then hurried outside. "Girls," he hollered. The milkmaids were heading toward the road, their day's work done. Fee glared at me, as did a few of the others. I'd clearly been the subject of conversation that afternoon. "Girls," Father called again. "Wait until you see what I have for you."

I watched from the doorway as he dumped a handful of chocolate squares into each girl's basket. "Take these home and share them with your friends and family. Tell everyone that the Oaks will be selling these tomorrow at Oak and Son's."

"What are they?" Fee asked.

"Chocolate," Father said. "Tell everyone you meet that the Oak Dairy will be selling chocolate."

The girls laughed with disbelief, but quickly ate every piece so that Father had to get more from the kitchen. Fee's anger vanished. She pushed to the front of the pack to get more. "Save some for your families," Father said. "If you spread the news, I'll give you more tomorrow." Their baskets refilled, the girls hurried off.

Emmeline slept past supper. We didn't wake her. I'm sure she was overwhelmed by everything that had happened. After a long conversation with Father about how much we should charge for the chocolate and how we might advertise, I walked to the bunkhouse as I had every night since Emmeline's arrival. The bunkhouse had been built for calving season, when the calves came so quickly it was necessary to bring in hired hands. But the season had come and gone so I was out there alone.

Maybe it was a stomach full of chocolate that caused my unsettled feeling. I stretched my arms behind my head and stared up through the darkness at the pine beams of the bunkhouse ceiling. The day had been filled with wonder, so why did an anxious sensation bite at me like an insect?

When I'd found Emmeline at the river, she seemed frail enough to break. With each passing day she'd grown stronger. At first she'd seemed to despise me, the way she glared up at me from my bed. But lately she'd begun to smile, sometimes when I spoke to her, sometimes simply because I'd walked into the room. She enjoyed it when I read to her, asking all sorts of questions and wanting me to read more. And that day, in the butter room, she'd blushed when our hands touched. Could she feel something for me?

Time spent thinking about her flowed without measure. When I wasn't with her, I wanted to be with her. Even when I was thinking about other things, she lingered between those thoughts. When I woke, I wondered what she was doing. When I went to bed, I imagined her beside me. An ache filled my body.

On the other side of the bunkhouse wall, the cows stirred, then broke into a chorus of agitated mooing. A fox or rat had probably dug its way inside the barn. Cows are easily disturbed so I wasn't too worried. Still, I rolled off the bunk and grabbed a lantern, lighting it with a box of matches we'd bought from Peddler.

Moonlight filtered through the cracks in the barn, illuminating the cows' shaggy backs like a landscape of rolling brown hills. Suddenly the cows began to stomp and shift, worked up about something. I held the lantern high, watching for scurrying movement along the floor. Then I heard it—a muffled cry from outside. I raced into the yard.

All was still. I cocked my head, listening for any unusual sounds. But even the crickets had quieted. Then the muffled cry came again. I ran around the barn. A tented wagon stood in the roadway, just outside our dairy. Even in the dim moonlight I recognized the wagon that carried Peddler's trinkets.

Peddler's silhouette was unmistakable, his skinny leg propping up his long, pocketed coat. He was shoving something into the back of the wagon.

Not something—*someone.*

"Emmeline!" I cried, running as fast as I could.

Peddler closed the tent's flaps and turned on his heels. My heart pounded at my temples. Peddler was taking Emmeline! I didn't stop to ask why. And there was no time to call for help. Fists clenched, I ran straight at him. An odd smile spread across his face. If I'd been in the fighting circle, I might have taken a moment to evaluate that smile. I might have approached my opponent with caution.

But Emmeline was my only thought.

Just as I swung my arm, the blade appeared, glinting in the moonlight. I gasped at its sting. I couldn't breathe. Another muffled cry came from the wagon. The curtains ruffled. "Emmeline," I said, the word lost in a blur of pain. Falling backward, my head hit the ground.

Horse hooves and rolling wheels were the last sounds I heard before darkness sucked me into its depths.

Part Four
Peddler Man

Chapter Twenty

It happened so quickly. One minute I was fast asleep, safe and warm beneath Owen's blanket. The next I was awakened by something moving on the bed. I turned and saw a man kneeling next to me, outlined in faint moonlight. At first I thought it was Owen, but he didn't smell like Owen. The man had the sour smell of unwashed clothes.

Was this the Thief of Sleep? When I was very little, my mother had told me the story about the old man who comes into the house and steals sleep from children who have been disobedient during the day. If too much sleep is stolen, the disobedient child dies, for no one can live without sleep.

I opened my mouth to ask who he was, and that's when he rolled me onto my stomach and pressed his knees into my back. Confusion turned to sheer terror. As I started to scream, he tied something around my mouth, muffling any sound I made. I tried to roll away, tried to kick him, hit him—*anything* to get him off me—but he was too strong. He tied my hands together and then my ankles before lifting me off the bed and flinging me over his shoulder.

He'd come through the window, I realized, as he carried me past the open shutters. He carried me down the hallway, past the room where I'd taken my first warm bath, past the room that had once belonged to Owen's sister, past Mister and Missus Oak's room, and out the front door, tiptoeing with long, jerky steps.

Where was he taking me? I kicked my bound feet. I pounded his back with my hands, but his grip was strong. As we crossed the yard I screamed desperately but the rough fabric held my tongue. The worst had happened. Wander's tax-collector must have heard that a Flatlander girl was living at the Oaks. He must have ordered my arrest. I'd be hanged for breaking the king's law.

Just before the man dumped me into a tented wagon, someone called my name. My face hit the wagon floor but I paid no mind to the pain. The voice had been Owen's. He was out there. "Help," I gurgled. Struggling to my knees, I shoved my head through the tent's flaps.

The man's back was to me. Moonlight shone upon his head, weaving between strands of thinning, greasy white hair. Then he lunged forward and as he did, Owen's face came into view. I rocked back and forth, desperately trying to catch Owen's attention. But he stood, oddly frozen, staring into nothingness. Then his hand darted to his chest and he fell backward, hitting the ground like a sack of grain. He didn't move. I called to him, the edges of the handkerchief pinching the sides of my mouth. Why wasn't he moving? That's when I noticed the knife in the man's hand. The man reached down and fiddled with Owen's clothing, pulling free Owen's snakeskin belt. "This will fetch a pretty price," he said.

Then the man spun around and shoved me into the tent's depths. He climbed inside and dragged me between crates and baskets. "He's not going to rescue you," he hissed as he tied me to a corner post. "He's dead." Leaving those words to echo in my head, he climbed out the tent's flaps. Moments later, the wagon began to move.

Cold sweat broke across my forehead and chest.

Dead?

Deep, uncontrollable trembling rolled across me the way a storm rolls across the sky. Then the tears came, slinking down my face and pooling in the soft spot behind my collarbone.

Owen Oak was dead.

Chapter Twenty-one

I huddled in the corner of the wagon, my knees pulled close to my chest. Wearing only my underclothes, a nightfrock, and socks, I shivered as cool morning air found its way through the cracks in the wooden floor.

A cord wound around my ankles, another around my wrists. A rope wrapped around my waist, holding me tight against the corner post. I'd kicked and twisted, trying to free myself. I'd fought, even as the cords dug into my skin.

But I couldn't get loose. Now the slightest movement brought pain, as if someone held a flame to my bound flesh. The post pushed against my spine, leaving it raw and bruised.

I sobbed until my gut burned. The trembling continued, long after the tears had dried up. Why was this happening? Why did Owen have to die? I'm the one who broke the law. I left the Flatlands. Owen helped me, but he didn't take me from the Flatlands. He'd done nothing wrong.

An eternity passed before my body finally quieted. The wagon rumbled along the road. Squeezing my eyes shut, I tried to erase the image of Owen lying dead on the ground. The man had stabbed him, had murdered him. Why? If he'd come to arrest me, why would he kill Owen? It made no sense.

In an instant, I'd been taken from a dream and thrust into a nightmare. For that is how it had seemed at the Oak Dairy—a dream come true. Such kindness and happiness I hadn't known since my mother's death. The Oaks had saved my life. They'd sheltered me. They'd paid a surgeon to tend to me. The wound on my leg was healed. I hadn't felt hungry, not even for a moment. Never once had they called me unnatural. Even Nan, who despised dirt-scratchers, had looked after me.

And then there was Owen.

At first I'd hated him. I'd thought he was another Griffin Boar, the way he'd stood at the base of the bed staring at me as if I were some sort of odd creature he'd dug out of the river's muck. I'd felt small beneath his gaze. But the days had passed with Owen stuck at home with a broken rib. Forbidden to work, he'd paced with boredom like a caged animal. Maybe that's why he'd turned to me for company. Maybe that's why he'd followed me around while I did chores, asking me all sorts of questions about life in the Flatlands. I'd been a distraction, nothing more.

But time spent with Owen was more than a distraction for me. No boy had ever asked me questions. No boy had ever read to me. No boy had ever paid me any attention other than to call me names or tease me. When I heard his footsteps, I got this tickled feeling in my stomach. When he said my name, I longed to hear him say it again. I wanted to throw my arms around him. I wanted him to be mine.

Of course, a Flatlander girl could never marry a boy who lived beyond the Flatlands, but there was no stopping my feelings. They grew so quickly I thought I might burst with love. Sitting at the Oak's supper table, I began to imagine myself as Owen's wife. And when I lay in his bed at night, I imagined that he lay beside me, his legs wrapped around mine, his arms holding me close.

If it hadn't been for Owen, I would have never known I could make chocolate. I would have never known the wondrous gift I possessed.

Now Owen was dead, murdered because he'd tried to keep this man from arresting me. I squeezed my eyes tighter but the lifeless image floated in the blackness behind my eyelids.

It was mid-morning before the wagon finally stopped. Sunlight warmed the sides of the tent. Rattling sounded as the horse was unhitched. The man said something to the creature, and the soft clip-clop of hooves passed by the wagon. Then footsteps neared. Fear gripped my stomach.

The tent's flaps opened and a head, backlit by sunlight, poked inside. "You're awake," he said. My heart pounded in my throat. The man rolled a tent flap to the side and secured it with a cord. As light filled the wagon, I got my first good look at Owen's murderer.

He was an old man. The grooves in his weathered face were so deep you could store seeds in them. Thinning white hair hung to his shoulders. Wild hairs sprouted from his eyebrows, reaching for the sky as if they longed to be free of such an ugly face. There was nothing old about his eyes, however. Flashing with energy, they nearly burned a hole through me.

I stared back. I would memorize his face, take in every inch of it. I'd never forget it as long as I lived. Hatred ignited and spread through me. I'd never forgive him for what he'd done. If I lived through this, he would be punished. Even if by my own hands, he'd be punished.

"You're a dirt-scratcher," he said, not bothering to hide his disgust. "Well, dirt-scratcher, you're a long way from home."

With a grunt, he climbed into the wagon, pushing aside some crates to make room. Still gagged, I growled like a cornered animal. "Stop squirming," he said as he reached behind my head. As soon as he pulled the handkerchief free, I screamed.

"Help! Help!"

"No use in doing that. No one will hear you."

"HELP!"

He dangled the spit-soaked handkerchief in my face. "You want to keep wearing this?"

My mouth snapped shut. Blood oozed from the corners where the handkerchief had rubbed the skin raw. My tongue dry, my throat parched, I shook my head.

To my surprise, he untied my ankles. I resisted the urge to fight, waiting to see if he'd untie my wrists. With my hands free, I might be able to get away.

"If you don't try to run, you won't have to wear the ropes." He untied me from the post but, to my disappointment, left my wrists bound. A tight grip on my arm, he dragged me to the end of the wagon, past Owen's snakeskin belt. Then he climbed out. With his hands around my waist, he lifted me and set me on the ground. I wanted to kick him, but my moment of escape needed to be perfectly timed. I'd have only one chance.

Dizziness washed over me as I wobbled on my feet. Leaning against the wagon, I waiting for my sight to clear. Then I looked around.

We'd pulled into a sunlit clearing. Woods surrounded us, of pine and spruce. A narrow trail, barely wide enough for the wagon, disappeared into the woods. *That must be the way to the road*, I thought. But how far would I have to run to reach it?

A shallow creek trickled along the edge of the clearing. A black horse raised its head for a moment to glance at me, then resumed drinking. I took a long steadying breath as the man walked to the center of the clearing and crouched, his coat fanning out across the dirt. He began to collect twigs.

Fear overcame me. I had no plan, only the hope that an old man wouldn't be able to move as fast as a girl with a curled foot. I took another deep breath, then ran.

The trail would be the easiest route, but he could follow on horseback. So I turned toward the trees, hoping to escape among the thick trunks. But with my hands bound in front, my steps were clumsier than usual and I couldn't pick up speed. I winced as something cut into my heel, the wool socks providing no protection against roots and rocks. Despite the pain, only one thought hammered in my head—escape.

I'd barely made it across the clearing when a hand grabbed my shoulder and spun me around. Yellow tinged the whites of the man's eyes. I kicked out with my good foot, but he easily overpowered me. His were not brittle old man's arms, but arms as strong as a Flatlander's. Wrapping a rope around my waist, he pulled me toward the wagon. "NO!" I yelled, falling to my knees. "I won't go with you!"

He yanked me to my feet, but I fell to my knees again. "You want me to drag you?" he asked, glaring down at me.

"I want you to let me go," I said, my voice hoarse. "Please don't take me to the tax-collector. He'll hang me."

"Tax-collector? What are you talking about?" With a grunt, he dragged me until we reached the wagon where he knotted the rope around my waist, then tied the other end to one of the wagon's rear wheels. "I told you, if you don't run you won't have to wear the ropes. But you ran." Then he went back to collecting twigs into a pile.

"You're not arresting me for leaving the Flatlands?"

He frowned. "Do I look like a tax-collector's grunt?"

I could barely hold back the tears. Every inch of me hurt, inside and out. "I hate you!" I screamed. "I hate you for killing Owen!"

"Why do you care so much about the Oak boy?" he asked. "Are you sweet on him?" I said nothing. "Well, it doesn't matter now, does it?" He pointed past the wagon. "You can do your business behind that tree. The rope's long enough." He broke a stick and threw it onto the pile.

My bladder nearly bursting, I struggled to my feet. Then I

limped as far as the rope would take me, behind a pine tree and a patch of shrubs. If he wasn't working for Wander's tax-collector, then what was his reason for taking me? Was he going to force himself on me? My stomach clenched. A girl in our village had been raped by a royal soldier. She'd drowned herself in the river.

After checking to make sure my kidnapper hadn't followed, I wrestled with the nightfrock and undergarments. Once I'd finished, I tried to loosen the rope from my waist, but with my wrists still tied together it was hopelessly impossible. Holding my wrists to my face, I tried chewing through the thick cord.

"Hurry up!" the man shouted.

Dropping my hands, I leaned against the tree. How could I get away from him? How could I get back to the Oaks's farm? But would I be welcome there? They'd rightfully blame me for Owen's death. If I'd never washed downriver, Owen would still be alive. Surely the Oaks would forever hate me the way I now hated the man who'd killed their only son.

Owen, I whispered to the bark. *I'm so sorry.*

The scent of smoke drifted around the trunk. "Get over here so I can keep an eye on you," the man hollered.

Rage pulsed with each footstep as I hobbled back toward the wagon. A small fire now burned in the clearing, the smoke vanishing into the sunlit air. The horse had waded across the creek to graze on a patch of grass. Rummaging in the wagon, the man pulled out a basket, then set it next to the fire.

"Why did you kill him?" I demanded. "Why?"

From the basket he pulled a green apple. When he yanked a

knife from one of his coat's many pockets, I recognized the knife's handle, made from the horn of a brown woolly. I cringed as he used the hem of his coat to wipe blood from the blade. Was it Owen's blood? Then he crouched, his knees poking out from under his coat. As if he could feel my gaze burning hotter than the flames, he stopped peeling and said, without looking at me, "He got in the way." He slid an apple slice between his thin lips and chewed. "I regret killing him." The tone was casual, as if regretting not wearing a hat on a rainy day.

"Regret?" My legs trembled. I could barely get the words out. "What do you want from me?"

He cut another slice and held it between the knife and his thumb. "I want what everyone will want from you." He chewed the slice with his mouth open, his crooked teeth glistening with bits of apple. "I want you to make me rich."

"I don't know what you're talking about."

"You don't know what I'm talking about?" He smiled wickedly, then tossed the rest of the apple to the horse. "Imagine my surprise when I rode into Wander last night, thinking I'd just be passing through on my way to Briar. But the tavern talk wasn't about the price of mutton or the barefist fights. Everyone was talking about *chocolate*."

I held still.

"I thought it was just a bunch of drunk men talking nonsense. But all of them claimed they'd tasted a piece. They said Oak's milkmaids had handed them out. They said the chocolate had come from Oak's dairy." He slid the knife into one of his pockets.

Then he opened the basket and took out a small iron grate that he laid over the fire. He pulled an iron kettle from the basket, filled it at the stream, then set it on the grate. "One man said he'd pay double the price if it meant his daughters could have a piece of chocolate every day. I asked him if he'd pay triple and he said to me, 'I might, Peddler. I might pay triple.'"

I clenched my jaw. *Peddler* was his name.

As Peddler poked the fire with a stick, flames licked the kettle. "Mister Oak never mentioned chocolate, and I've spent many mornings at his breakfast table. If he's got the only known recipe for chocolate, why wait until now to make it?" He dropped the stick. Then he crouched again and stared into the flames. "I was pondering this question when one of Oak's milkmaids walked into the tavern, looking for her father. When she couldn't find him, I followed her outside. A pink seashell necklace was all it took. She told me about a new milkmaid who didn't come and go with the others, but she'd seen her in the butter room."

I remembered the girl's round face, her yellow curly hair, and her angry look when she'd found me with Owen.

"When I gave her another seashell necklace, she told me that she'd seen the new milkmaid through Owen's bedroom window. The Oaks were keeping her inside the house." He picked a bit of apple from his teeth. "For a ten-piece coin, the little milkmaid sold me the last six pieces of chocolate she had in her basket. That's more coin than she makes in a month. I would have paid double. Triple, even. I've never tasted anything like it." He flicked the apple bit into the air. "But now I won't have to pay because I own the chocolate-maker herself."

The horse waded back across the creek. Keeping its distance from the fire, it lay on the ground and closed its eyes. Weariness tugged at me too. But though the rope was heavy around my waist, and though my curled foot throbbed, I chose to stand, defiantly facing this evil man. "I'll never make chocolate for you," I hissed. "You killed Owen."

Peddler took a loaf of bread from the basket and tore off a heel, which he tossed to me. It landed at my feet. Despite my hunger, I didn't reach for it. "Don't be stupid," he grumbled. "Eat. We've got a long journey ahead of us."

"Where are you taking me?"

He stuck the remaining loaf on a stick and held it over the fire. "Word will spread quick like fever. It won't take long for the Oaks to figure out I'm the one who took you and killed their boy. There'll be a price on my head. We'll have to hide until the time is right to sell you."

"Sell me?"

"A dirt-scratcher girl is worthless," he said, a curl to his lip. "No one wants anything to do with a dirt-scratcher. That's why the Oaks were keeping you hidden. But that'll change. I'm risking my life on the wager that you're gonna be famous. And I'm gonna be the one who sells you to the highest bidder. I won't have to peddle no more."

"I'll never make chocolate for you or for anyone who tries to buy me," I said. "I'd rather die."

Peddler slowly turned the bread. The warm, toasted scent filled the air. "You don't want to die. Even though you got that bad foot, you tried to run away. You want to live just like everyone else." Then he smiled wickedly. "You'll make chocolate. You make it and you'll live."

Silence filled the clearing, broken only by the crackle of the fire and the horse's deep breathing. Through all the hardships I'd faced, I'd never wanted to die. I'd never thought of ending my life just to escape the melancholy of the Flatlands or the ridicule of being *unnatural*. But I wasn't about to help Owen's murderer get rich.

Peddler pointed to the bread that lay at my feet. "Sit down and eat. It's the only meal you'll have today."

I could barely control the hatred that filled my entire being. I wanted to lunge at him. I wanted to scratch his face, wrap the rope around his neck, and . . .

I took a deep breath. Then I settled on the ground, wiped pine needles from the chunk of bread, and ate.

I'd need strength to kill this man.

Chapter Twenty-two

Four days passed on the road with me gagged and bound. Four days stuffed inside the tented wagon like the other objects Peddler would sell. Each day carried me farther away from Oak Dairy.

If I'd died the way I was supposed to, an unwanted babe at the edge of the field, Owen would still be alive.

The days dragged on, filled with tormented thoughts and restless sleep. Early in the journey, Peddler hid the wagon deep in the woods. With Owen's belt in hand and a basket of trinkets, he abandoned me for a few hours while he rode to a nearby town for supplies. I listened hopefully for the sound of someone. Anyone. A small creature climbed up the side of the tent and sat on the roof for a while, but no rescuer came.

When Peddler returned, he brought a cloak that he threw over me. I was happy to have it because the cool night air seeped through my thin nightfrock. Unfortunately he didn't buy me boots. Boots would have helped my hoped-for escape.

Peddler spoke little when we sat around the fire in the evenings, but when he did, the same question was asked. "How do you make chocolate?"

"I'll never make it for you. Never."

On the morning of the fifth day, I sat on the ground next to the wagon eating a wedge of cheese. As I watched Peddler from the corner of my eye, an idea took root. I ran the idea over and over in my mind. If he had no proof of the chocolate's existence, he'd have nothing. No one would believe him when he claimed he'd found a girl who could make the legendary treat.

I waited as patiently as an owl for the right moment to strike. It presented itself when Peddler left the fireside and wandered over to feed a handful of grain to the horse. I struggled to my feet. Then I lunged for the wagon and with my bound hands, reached inside and grabbed the box that hid the six pieces of chocolate, each imprinted with an oak leaf.

I crammed two into my mouth. There was no time to savor the deliciousness. The man who'd killed Owen would never profit from my chocolate. I needed to chew faster. Two more made it in before Peddler bellowed, "Stop!" He ran toward me, waving his hands. "You stupid girl!" I shoved in the final two pieces just as he seized the empty box. "What have you done?" he cried, his face contorted. He flung the box aside and grabbed my shoulders, furiously shaking me. I chewed faster. He tried to pry open my mouth, but the chocolate disappeared in a final swallow. His eyes blazing with rage, he slapped my cheek. I stumbled backward, then fell to the ground. He clenched his fists. My eyes closed, I waited for the blow that would end it all. For the thrusting blade that would stop the nightmare.

But no blow came. Instead, cold laughter drifted toward me.

I opened my eyes. Peddler picked up the empty box, then tossed it onto the fire, his laughter subsiding as the flames consumed that which had once held his treasure.

My cheek stinging, I struggled to my feet. "You have no chocolate and I will never make it for you," I said, summoning my last dregs of courage. "Let me go."

"Quiet!" He stood close to the fire, the smoke disappearing into his white hair.

"No one will believe you. You have no proof." I wiped the sweet remains from my lips. "Let me go."

"Not another word!" He reached inside his coat and pulled out the horn-handled knife.

This was it. I balanced on the tip of my curled foot, trying to stand as straight as possible to face death. But with another wicked laugh, he dug the knife into a shank of smoked ham and ate his breakfast.

On the seventh day, Peddler did something different. Instead of tying me to the post in a sitting position, he wound a rope around my entire body. He gagged me again, then rolled me into a carpet. I couldn't move an inch. The opening at the top of the carpet let in air. I knew I wouldn't smother to death, but that gave me little comfort. Peddler arranged the crates around me, then took his seat at the front of the wagon and whistled at the horse. The steady clip-clop resumed.

A lot of traffic passed by that day. We must have been on a main road. Peddler stopped the caravan twice to sell something. Try as I might, I couldn't move. Each grunt and groan was swallowed by the layers of carpet. Memories, stirred up by the pain of my imprisonment, tormented me—images of my father being carted away, of Snow disappearing beneath the water, of Owen lying motionless. I tried to cling to good memories—of my mother, of Nan's dumplings, of Owen's smiling face—but they slipped away just as Root had in the raging river.

"Stop in the name of King Elmer."

My breath caught. My heart doubled its beat. The gruff voice belonged to a man. The wagon slowed, then stopped.

"I'm just a lowly peddler making my way from town to town," Peddler said innocently. "What can I do for you fine soldiers?"

Soldiers? I pushed against the ropes. *I'm in here!*

"We're tracking a deserter from the king's army," one of the soldiers said.

"When we find him he'll be hanged," the other soldier said.

Owen had mentioned three ways to get out of the king's army—buying one's way out, injury, or death. He'd never mentioned desertion.

"I commend you for upholding the king's laws," Peddler told the soldiers. "A man who leaves the king's army is a coward who deserves no mercy."

I'd seen a hanging. Everyone in Root had watched the guilty man swing from the noose, his eyes bulging, his tongue dripping blood, his britches soiled. He'd stolen food from the tax-collector. I stopped fighting the ropes so I could hear what was being said.

"We'll need to search your caravan," the first soldier said.

Aye, search the caravan! They might find me. If only I could move. I tried rolling back and forth, but the rug was wedged tightly between crates.

A pair of horses walked the length of the wagon. Then the tent rustled. "All I carry are crates filled with trinkets," Peddler said, his words hurried. "But I do believe there are a couple of gifts back here, just for you gentlemen." The wagon shifted as Peddler climbed inside. "How about two lovely necklaces made of pink seashells? And two bottles of rose water? I'm sure you have special ladies who would appreciate such gifts." The wagon shifted again as he handed the bribes to the soldiers.

Search the wagon. Please search the wagon.

But the bribes worked their magic. The soldiers rode away.

Peddler patted the rolled carpet. "You should be pleased they didn't find you," he said. "They'd have had their way with you, no doubt about that."

Did he expect gratitude? I closed my eyes. It was the only way to dismiss him.

On the afternoon of the tenth day, I sat on the ground outside the wagon, tied to a wheel as usual. I could smell my own stink. Fear changes the scent of sweat, like sickness.

"What is that?" I asked, pointing to a rolled parchment that lay at Peddler's feet.

"That?" he grunted, then reached out and grabbed it. "Found

it nailed to a tree. Might as well show you." He unrolled the parchment and held it out. I rose onto my knees, staring at the drawing.

"That's me," I said with a gasp. A drawing of my face, framed by a milkmaid's bonnet, took up half the parchment. I got to my feet. The rope trailed behind as I walked cautiously toward Peddler, just far enough to take the poster from his knobby fingers.

It wasn't a perfect likeness, but it was very close. I'd stared at my reflection every morning in Owen's bedroom mirror. At the way my newly brushed hair fell, at the way my face had filled out from all the food I'd eaten. Though I couldn't read, I recognized one word: *Wanted.* Tax-collector Todd tacked WANTED posters to the oak tree in the village square. Thieves and murderers sometimes tried to hide in the Flatlands. Now I was the criminal. I'd broken the law by leaving the Flatlands. I pressed my bound hands against my neck, imagining the noose.

There were more words on the poster. "What does it say?"

Peddler yanked the poster from me and pointed to the biggest words. "It says, *Wanted: The Milkmaid. A one hundred coin reward is offered but only if she is delivered, alive and unscathed, to the tax-collector of Wander.*"

"What does unscathed mean?"

"It means they don't want anyone to hurt you."

If my fate was to be hanged, what did it matter if I was hurt?

He continued reading. "*The Milkmaid was kidnapped by a white-haired old man who drives a tented wagon and goes by the name Peddler.*" He crumpled the poster and threw it onto the fire. The parchment curled and blackened. Turning away from the sudden burst of heat, I wondered if the Oaks had told their tax-collector about me. Or if it had been the other milkmaid, the one who'd seen me in the butter room.

Peddler climbed into the wagon, shuffled around, then emerged a few minutes later with a small wooden crate, which he carried to the far edge of the clearing. "The only reason the tax-collector of Wander would offer a hundred coin reward for you is because he knows you made the chocolate." He led the horse away from the wagon and tied it to a tree next to the crate. He untied me from the wagon wheel, then tied me to the same tree. Why was he rearranging things? And why had he pulled a burning stick from the fire?

My fate was not to be hanged? Hope flickered.

"If you take me back to Wander, you can collect the one hundred coin reward," I told him. "That's the most coin you'll ever get because I'll never make chocolate for you. Never. So take the reward." And when he handed me over, I'd tell the tax-collector that he'd killed Owen. I'd stand in the front row and watch him hang.

"You might not make chocolate for me, but I'd have to be an idiot to give you up," Peddler said, pointing the glowing stick at me. "Once word spreads beyond Wander, the reward will double. Then it will triple and triple again. I just have to keep you hidden until the price is right." I gasped as he touched the end of the burning stick to the wagon's tent. The fabric smoldered. The horse stomped nervously as flames fanned out across the wagon's roof.

All his trinkets would burn, including the carpet. Where would he hide me?

With his knife's blade, Peddler sawed at the ends of his hair until all that remained were short tufts. After scraping charcoal from a burned log, he pulverized it between his palms, then rubbed the black powder all over his scalp. Gone was the white hair. Gone was the tented wagon. Gone was that flicker of hope.

Now, no one would recognize him as the kidnapper of the Milkmaid.

We rode the rest of the day on horseback, following a narrow path through sparse woodlands. No towns, no houses, no people. The end of my rope was tied to the horse's neck, making escape impossible. My cloak provided a thin barrier between my body and Peddler's. It sickened me to sit so close to Owen's murderer. His stale breath coated my neck, his bony fingers held my waist. I hated every inch of him.

At twilight, the woods opened to a lonely landscape of rustling grasses. The air held a new scent, something I didn't recognize. When the horse stopped at the edge of a cliff, I realized what I was smelling.

The sea.

It lay before me, a choppy expanse of blue and white. On and on it spread until it met the edge of the sky. Until that moment, the river was the only water I'd known, and it was mysterious in itself, winding to places I thought I'd never see. But the sea was huge. Endless. Amazing.

"We walk now," Peddler said as he dismounted. He grabbed

the crate that had balanced on my lap during our ride. I slid off the horse, my legs aching as they straightened. He removed the rope from my waist but left my wrists bound. Leaving the horse to graze, Peddler pointed to a trail that led from the clifftop to the beach far below. "Go on," he said.

A sign, with one word painted across it, marked the trailhead. A skull perched atop the sign, the empty eye sockets collecting wind-blown dirt. "What does that say?" I asked.

"Never you mind," Peddler said, pushing me down the trail. Even without knowing the word, the warning was clear. Danger waited. The deadly kind.

I stumbled as the path steepened, the holes in my wool socks collecting small stones. Three dwellings stood on the highest section of beach, built of wood that had washed ashore. The dwellings looked abandoned with their gaping roofs and caved-in walls. A ring of stones that had once held fire lay half-buried in sand. Who had lived here and where had they gone? Then I spotted the answer. Built from piled-up rock, nine graves lay in a row at the base of the cliff. In the Flatlands, it was often said that the wind carried the souls of the dead. As a breeze tickled my neck I shivered, imagining ghostly fingers reaching for me.

The trail flattened, and we stepped onto the beach where a massive tree trunk had washed up on the shore. It must have been part of a building for its ends were cut square and four holes had been drilled into it. Peddler opened the crate and pulled out a long chain. Then he threaded the chain through one of the holes and secured it with a padlock. My heart nearly stopped beating. "No," I begged.

"Please, no." He was going to chain me to this haunted place. I grabbed a rock. "No! I won't let you. You can't leave me here." I threw the rock, hitting his shoulder. He spun around and pushed me to the sand where he quickly slid the chain around my waist and locked it in place with another padlock.

"I hate you!" I screamed. "I swear I'll kill you. Do you hear me, old man? I swear to God that one day I will kill you for what you've done!"

He wasn't paying any attention. He'd stepped away and was looking down the beach. I wiped sand from my face, then squinted into the distance.

A woman stood where the beach curled around a rocky outcropping. Her skirt hung to her ankles. A knit scarf covered her head and wound around her neck, hiding her mouth. Had she seen Peddler chain me to the log? If so, she was in danger.

Peddler picked up the crate and headed toward her. "Run!" I screamed, trying to warn her. "RUN!" But the woman stayed put. What would he do to her? Would he chain her, too? Kill her? Why wasn't she running away?

When Peddler reached the woman, he dropped the crate. They spoke, words too far away to catch. They never touched, keeping a few feet between them as they spoke, but it seemed as if . . . *they knew each other*. The woman nodded her head many times. Then she picked up the crate and left, disappearing around the rocky point.

"She'll look after you," Peddler told me as he returned. I lay in the sand, my entire body betraying me with its exhaustion. "But

you must never get close to her. And you must never touch her."
Then he knelt and removed the cord from my wrists. Before I could ask any questions, he walked back up the trail.

Leaving me alone, chained to a log, as the sun set at the edge of the sea.

Chapter Twenty-three

Mother didn't leave my side. She sat in the chair beside my bed, clutching my hand, her voice ragged as she begged the surgeon to save me. Peddler's blade had slid between two ribs, narrowly missing my heart. The blood had pulsed from the wound, warm and sticky, running down my side as I lay in the dirt. Luckily Father had been woken by the horse and wagon and had rushed to my side. If he hadn't been such a light sleeper, I'd have bled to death.

The surgeon assured my parents that no internal organs had been pierced. "But we must hope that no fever appears," he said. "If fever comes with the morning, then the wound is corrupted."

"I've got to go," I murmured through a haze of pain.

"Steady," Father said, as if gentling an injured horse. "Steady."

"Keep him still," the surgeon said. Father sat on the bed and held me down. With his assistant at his side, the surgeon mixed up some sort of paste and smothered my wound. The stinging was unbearable. Then he wrapped it tightly, just as he had wrapped my once broken rib.

"Emmeline," I whispered. "I need to find Emmeline."

Something bitter was poured into my mouth. "Brew this tea three times a day," the surgeon told Nan. "Give it to him each time you change the poultice." Then he leaned over me, his dark eyes piercing with concern. "You stay in bed, Owen Oak. Those are my orders. I can't cure you if you don't follow my orders."

I closed my eyes against the pain. Stay in bed. My bed, which still smelled like her.

Chapter Twenty-four

I'm not sure how many days passed. It was the surgeon's voice that woke me. "There's no fever. His color's good. Continue the poultice three times a day, along with the three cups of tea."

The edges of the room blurred. I tried to sit up but Mother stopped me. Her hair hung loose and uncombed. Dark circles had settled beneath her eyes as if they'd been painted there. "Have they found her?" I asked.

"No," Father said, chewing on the end of his pipe.

"How long?"

"It's been ten days. Tax-collector Pinch has printed posters. He's offered a reward for Emmeline's return."

"What?" I pushed away Mother's hand and sat up. "He knows about Emmeline? Who told?" I glared at the surgeon.

"Pinch came to the house," Father said. "He brought the town council. They demanded to know where the chocolate had come from. Pinch threatened me with an importation tax. He threatened to double our pasture tax if I didn't tell. The council was willing to evict us from our shop." Father sat on the edge of the bed. "I had to tell him the truth about Emmeline. Now everyone knows she made the chocolate."

"Are they going to arrest her?" I asked. "For not staying in the Flatlands?"

"On the contrary," the surgeon said, closing his wooden case. "They want her to make more chocolate. Our tax-collector knows an excellent investment opportunity when he sees one."

"As does Peddler," I said, grimacing as I leaned against the pillows. "I'm sure that's why he took her."

"But how did Peddler know about Emmeline?" Mother asked. "Your father didn't tell the tax-collector until well after Emmeline's disappearance."

Who would have told Peddler about Emmeline? A round face popped into my head.

"It's my fault. I took Emmeline to the butter room and Fee saw her. Peddler must have bribed the information from Fee with one of his trinkets." I grimaced again. "How much reward is being offered for Peddler?"

"There's no law against kidnapping a dirt-scratcher," Father said. Then he raised his voice and it echoed off the walls. "But there is a law against attempted murder, and when we find him he shall stand trial for trying to kill my only son." His cheeks burst with color and he waved a fist. "I'll hang him myself."

Mother took my hand again, fear swimming in her gentle eyes. I knew her thoughts. To lose one child was more than she could bear. To have almost lost the other . . .

I squeezed back. "I'm fine," I told her.

Peddler hadn't killed me. But if he'd hurt Emmeline in any way, he'd wish he'd never been born.

I waited until nightfall. Mother had finally left me alone, falling into a deep sleep in her own bed. I slipped into my britches, shirt, and vest. Peddler had taken my snakeskin belt, so I grabbed a corded belt. I tucked my knife into my boot, then tiptoed down the hall. The pain wasn't so bad, as long as I didn't cough.

This was my fault entirely. Without me, Emmeline would never have made chocolate. And Fee would never have seen her. And she'd still be here, safe in my bed.

Hold on, Emmeline. I'll find you.

Part Five
Daughter

Chapter Twenty-five

Time presses as heavy as armor when one sits alone, chained to a log.

Everything was a blur of sameness. In the evenings I took shelter in one of the crumbling dwellings, sleeping on the sand-covered floor. Though the roof had partially rotted and the gaping holes offered little protection from the elements, I felt safer with walls around me. Who knew what might crawl from the depths of the sea when night fell? How many ghosts lingered in this lonely place?

In the mornings I awoke to the shriek of gulls. As the sun rose above the cliff, the woman would appear carrying a basket of food, which she'd set on the beach, never getting too close to me. Then she'd retreat to a nearby boulder and watch while I ate the basket's contents. The food was always the same. Smoked silver fish, the size of fingers. A bowl of chopped sea plants, red and green, salty and strange. And water in a jug. The first morning I ate everything, then discovered there was only one meal a day so I started saving some of the fish for evening.

The woman never spoke, nor did she remove the scarf that hid her hair and most of her face. I guessed she was in her middle years only because of the occasional wisp of graying hair that stuck out from the scarf. At first I tried to reason with her. "If you free me, you can get the one hundred coin reward." But she never spoke. "Who are you? Why won't you talk to me? Why are you helping Peddler? He's a thief and a murderer." Still, she said nothing. She never stayed long, eventually walking down the beach and disappearing around the rocky outcropping.

I spent hours trying to break the chain, pounding it with a rock, sawing at it with a sharp shell, but the iron held fast around my waist. I tried jamming small sticks into the padlock, but they'd only break. I tried moving the log but it would have taken a group of men to move such an enormous timber.

The chain was long enough that when the tide rose I could wade into the sea to bathe. The seawater wasn't as cold as the river, and the wind quickly dried my clothes and skin. Though I was clean, the seawater left my skin feeling tight and scratchy.

Ships passed by, some with tall white sails, some just specks amid the blue and white. I waved but they never came close, staying well beyond a reef where the waves crashed.

At times I screamed in desperation. Surely someone would hear me. Craning my neck and pointing my face at the clifftop, I screamed until my throat burned. But no one ever answered. Nothing moved up there except the grasses. Hatred grew with each passing day. *I'll never make chocolate for you*, I whispered as if Peddler sat next to me. *I'll never make chocolate for him*, I whispered to the tiny white crabs that scuttled over my socks.

Why me? I wondered countless times. Why could I make chocolate? Was it possible that other Flatlanders could make it but didn't know? If my mother or father had been given a churning bucket, could they have changed the course of their lives? But I'd never be able to answer these questions as long as I was chained to this sorrowful place.

Ten days, twelve days—what was Peddler doing?

The woman was the answer, the only hope of escape.

"You must never get close to her," Peddler had ordered. "You must never touch her."

"What's your name?" I asked each time she appeared. "Where are you from?"

But she never answered.

It seemed forever since I'd heard another voice. Even with my outcast status back in Root, I'd never felt completely alone. Father had always been there, asleep in the next room or sitting at the table—a beating heart just an arm's reach away. But the long days on the beach were eating at me. There was nothing to do but mourn Owen and try to think of ways to escape.

So when the woman finally spoke one morning, tears filled my eyes.

"My name is Lara." Her voice was surprisingly sweet—not cold the way I thought it would be.

"Where are you from?" I asked, wiping away the tears. "Are you from here?"

Lara said nothing. She sat on the boulder and folded her hands, which were always wrapped in shreds of cloth. Did she keep her face hidden behind the scarf so I wouldn't know her true identity?

But why would she hide her hands? Lara probably wasn't her real name.

"Do you live over there?" I asked, pointing down the beach. She must have a house, a husband, maybe even a family around that bend. Surely she was not alone here. She didn't answer.

"How do you catch the fish?" I asked, desperate for conversation. If I could gain her trust, maybe she would help me.

"I catch them with a net."

"You catch them yourself?" She nodded. "Do you live out here alone?" She looked over at the gravestones. "Did you know those people?" No reply. "What does the sign say? The one at the top of the hill?"

She pulled the scarf closer, her eyes nearly disappearing behind the fabric. Then she folded her arms, tucking her hands away. Was she hiding them the way I hid my foot?

"Is there something wrong with your hands?" With the chain trailing behind like a monster's tail, I took a few steps toward the boulder. Lara tensed, preparing to flee. "No, don't go, please. I won't get any closer." I winced as a piece of shell pierced my left heel. I sank onto the sand and peeled off the left sock. Cuts and scrapes covered my good foot. I couldn't control the anger that burst forth. "Why are you helping Peddler?" I cried. "Why? Why would you help him? Is he paying you? Is that it? Can't you see I'm miserable? Don't you care?" I didn't even look at her, knowing she wouldn't answer. "He's a murderer," I yelled. "Peddler's a murderer. Did you know that? He murdered Owen Oak. You're working for a murderer!"

Heartless about my plight, she slid off the boulder and walked away.

That same day, Peddler finally returned with a bulging burlap sack slung over his shoulder. He'd kept his hair short and smothered in soot. He'd traded his long, pocketed coat for a green merchant's jacket with shiny buttons. I was actually happy to see him. Since Lara had proven impossible to win over, Peddler was my last hope.

"What do you think of my new coat?" he asked as he stepped off the trail. His tone was matter-of-fact, as if it were completely normal for a girl to be chained to a log. "Can't let anyone know who I am. Peddler's still wanted for kidnapping the famous Milkmaid."

I held a rock in my hand. The plan was to throw it at his head, knock him out, then take the key and unchain myself. But I faltered. "Famous?"

"*Very* famous." He set down the bag, then handed another poster to me. As I unrolled the parchment, my face appeared. "The reward has increased to one thousand coin," he said, a grin spreading across his wrinkled face. What dreams swirled in his mind? What was it that he hoped to buy? He did an odd jig in the sand. "One thousand coin."

"Then let's go," I said, tossing the poster aside. "Take me to Wander's tax-collector. I'm ready." *Just get me off this chain.*

"Wander's tax-collector?" Peddler stopped dancing. "I'm not selling you to him. He was outbid the moment word spread beyond Wander. It's the Baroness of Salt who wants you."

"The Baroness of Salt? Who's that?"

"Nobility." He picked up the bag and looked down the beach. Lara appeared around the bluff, walking slowly toward us. "Looks like my daughter's been taking good care of you."

"Your *daughter*?"

I would never have guessed. He carried the bag down the beach and laid it a few feet away from Lara. He didn't embrace her, didn't touch her as they spoke, the gap between them wide enough to fit three men. She kept the scarf over her face. Why would she keep her face hidden from her father? Amid the hatred, a new emotion took hold—pity.

Lara wasn't helping Peddler for coin. She was being a dutiful daughter.

Their conversation was short. He left the burlap bag with her. "Where are you going?" I demanded as he walked past. "Please," I begged. "Take me away from this place. Sell me to the Baroness of Salt."

"If the baroness is offering one thousand coin, then someone will offer two thousand. It's just a matter of time."

"But you can't leave me here!" I cried. The rock still clutched in my hand, I threw it at him. He ducked as it whizzed past his head. "What if someone finds me? Then I'll be rescued and you'll never make any coin."

He straightened and smoothed his green collar. "No one would dare come here," he said, glancing down the beach. Lara and the bag were gone. "Remember, you must never go near her. And you must *never* touch her." He started up the trail.

Was he afraid I'd hurt his daughter? "If you leave me I'll go near her," I cried. "I swear I will!" He quickened his pace, my freedom disappearing with each jerky step.

A scream, from the depths of my gut, pierced the air. Not even the hearts of those buried nearby could be unmoved by such a sound. But Peddler didn't miss a beat of his long-legged strides.

Chapter Twenty-six

No one had seen her. She'd vanished like a dream.

I sat on a bench outside a butcher's shop, gnawing on a roasted pheasant leg. The town was called Moonshire, a four-day ride from our dairy. I'd been there twice before. When rotting disease attacked our cows' hooves, Father and I rode to Moonshire in search of a rumored cure, which we found at the herbalist's shop. During another visit, we attended a secret meeting of dairymen to discuss the new milk taxes imposed by King Elmer. But this time I was on my own.

Because Peddler had taken Emmeline in the middle of the night, no one in Wander had witnessed his escape. So when I reached the fork in the road, just beyond the town, I had to guess his direction. He'd taken Emmeline for one reason—to sell her. Why else would he steal a girl who can make chocolate? The right fork led toward the coast. There was nothing in that direction but fishing villages. It made better sense that he'd take the left fork and travel east to Londwin City, the largest and richest city in our kingdom. If only I had the nose of a bloodhound to follow Emmeline's sweet scent. Or the eyes of a hawk to spot her from the treetops. In the end, I had to rely on instinct. Instinct led me east.

I dug my teeth into the pheasant leg. Fury rushed through me as I remembered how Peddler had dumped Emmeline into the wagon as if she were a piece of cargo. As if she were nothing more than a carcass to be sold at market. That morning at our kitchen table, he'd called dirt-scratchers stupid and filthy. This particular dirt-scratcher, however, could make him rich so he'd be a fool not to treat her right. But if he hurt her, I'd rip through him like a lightning bolt.

The stab wound no longer burned or itched, but it seemed to have a memory of its own, conjuring the sting of the blade over and over. I'd wake at night, sure that the knife was piercing my skin, reaching in the dark to find nothing. The stitches had held tight during the four-day ride. A blessing. Last thing I needed was for my guts to fall out so far from home. I would never forget that Peddler had tried to kill me. I would never forget that he'd spat upon my parents' trust and hospitality. Revenge would go hand in hand with freeing Emmeline.

But no one in Moonshire had seen the wretch. They knew him, for he often came to sell his trinkets. "It's been at least two moons since he was last here," the tavernkeep told me.

"More than two moons," the cobbler said.

I knew he hadn't sold her yet because posters still hung everywhere. If the Milkmaid had been found, news would have spread faster than butter in a hot frying pan. She was all anyone talked about. While some doubted and some believed, most everyone had ideas about how they'd spend the coin.

What I knew was this—Peddler was hiding in the shadows like a rat, drooling, flicking his greedy tail, waiting for the reward to increase.

A *WANTED* poster hung across the road outside the candlemaker's shop. As I ate, I stared at Emmeline's sketched face. The drawing was a good likeness but the bonnet hid her wild red hair. And the artist hadn't captured the sparkle in her eyes. The pheasant suddenly tasted sour. I swallowed, my stomach knotting. She was just a girl. Just a girl who'd never been outside the Flatlands, who had no idea what the world was like. She couldn't run fast, even if she had the chance to get away. I should have seen Peddler's knife, should have blocked it with my left arm. I should have saved her.

She was probably scared out of her mind.

Emmeline, where are you?

What more could I do but travel the roads, asking questions of everyone? Someone had to have seen them. They'd need food and water. Someone had to know something.

"Hey, you there," a man shouted. I wiped grease from my mouth and looked down the street. The tavernkeep strode toward me, an ale-drenched rag hanging from his belt. "You the boy what was asking questions about Peddler?"

"That's me," I said, tossing the bone to a scraggly cat.

The tavernkeep stopped a few paces away. "I just remembered something. He's got a daughter."

"Really?" I scrambled to my feet, my heart kicking up its rhythm. Maybe he'd hidden Emmeline at his daughter's house. If not, there was a good chance the daughter would know Peddler's whereabouts. "Where does she live?"

The tavernkeep held out his hand, palm up. I fished in my pocket for a half-coin and tossed it. He caught it in midair, then tucked it away. "She used to live in Lime, but she don't live there no more. Heard tell she got sick so he moved her to the leper colony out on the coast."

"Leper colony?"

"No use going out there. You can catch leprosy just by looking at a leper." Then, with a twirl of his rag, he moseyed back to the tavern, his thick thighs scraping together.

I sighed. What a waste of a half-coin. Peddler wouldn't risk taking Emmeline to a leper colony. So I was back to knowing nothing. I balled up my fists. All I could do was keep looking and keep asking.

Chapter Twenty-seven

Spring was turning toward summer. The days were growing longer, and purple flowers had burst open along the trail. Swallows tended their nests in the cliff's crevices. Even with the constant breeze from the sea, I could feel change in the air.

Something had changed in Lara, too. As I ate my breakfast of fish and sea-plant salad, she doubled over, a thick, wet cough rattling her lungs.

"You need a surgeon," I said. She shook her head. The small patch of face that I'd grown used to, her eyes and the top of her cheeks, looked paler than usual. "How long have you been sick?"

"Many years." Then she asked me a question, something she rarely did. "How long has your foot been curled?"

"I was born like this."

"It could be worse. At least you have your magic." She coughed again. I'd told her the truth about my life. "Your magic will give you great power. Usually a woman only has power if she has beauty or if she has a keen sense of business. Father taught me about business. He trained me in the art of negotiation."

"What's that?" I asked.

"It's the art of getting what you want." She wrapped her scarf tight around her shoulder. "You have something that is very valuable. No one else has what you have. So, if you are wise, you can get whatever you want."

"I want my freedom."

"You will get your freedom, one day."

"I want my father's freedom and my people's freedom, too."

"You can get that."

"How?" I asked. It was unusual for Lara to speak this much. Would she keep talking? *Please keep talking.*

"There are two things to remember when you are about to negotiate. First, if you want something, you must ask for it. You rarely get what you don't ask for. Second, you must always include something that you're willing to give up. That makes the buyer feel like he's won."

A sudden gust of wind pushed across the beach. It caught an edge of Lara's scarf and for a moment, she was revealed. I gasped. Some sort of creature had eaten her face. The tip of her nose was gone, as were chunks of her chin. Her lips were blackened and covered in sores.

Shame widened her eyes and she grabbed the scarf. I remembered the moment when I'd realized Owen had seen my foot. How I couldn't bear his pity and disgust. But a disfigured face was a far worse plight for a woman than a disfigured foot. This was why she

lived in this lonely place where no one would stare or cry in horror.
"Don't go," I called as she hurried away. "I don't care about your face."

Though she wore no chain around her waist, she was as much a prisoner on this beach as I.

"I'm sorry," I said when Lara appeared the next day. "I'm sorry I looked at you. I know you didn't want me to. Please forgive me." Her walk was slower than normal and she stumbled a few times. The sea plants hadn't been chopped and there was no fish. But the water jug was full. Leaning on the boulder, she coughed, gasping for breath. "I can help you," I told her. It wasn't a lie. "If you'll unchain me, I'll hurry to the nearest town and get a surgeon."

She coughed again. "No surgeon will help a leper."

Leper? My mind raced to the top of the cliff, to the skull that sat atop the little sign. The word painted on the sign must have been *Leper.*

It was a word that turned even the bravest man into a trembling coward. Lepers who wandered into villages were to be burned. That was the law. I'd never seen one but I'd heard stories.

"But you need medicine."

"There is no medicine for me." She stared at the stone graves. Then she stumbled away.

"Lara!"

Just as I feared, no food or water was delivered the next morning. Standing at the base of the cliff, I screamed for help. The sea wind caught my cries like a gull catching fish, carrying them far away. Something had happened to Lara. She was too sick to tend to me. Or worse, she'd died. Without Lara's food I'd die too, if Peddler didn't return. I set clam shells around the hut. If rain came, it would collect in the hollow bowls.

A day passed. No rain fell.

My throat burning with thirst, I stumbled to the salty shallows. While days of hunger were well known in the Flatlands, never were we without water. In the hot summer months when the wells ran dry, we simply drank from the river. I knelt at the sea's edge, waiting for the next wave to fill my cupped hands. Then I took a gulp.

The salt water raged down my throat like poison. I vomited.

When the sun trickled through the hut the next morning, I rushed outside, hoping to find Lara standing down the beach. Though she was nowhere to be seen, a new basket sat on the log. No food lay inside. But she'd delivered something better.

A key.

My hands trembling, I dropped the key a dozen times before it finally slipped into the lock, releasing its iron grip with a quiet click. The chain immediately loosened and fell to the sand. I felt so light I thought I might float away. I grabbed the padlock and threw it into the ocean.

There was no time to waste. Though freedom had been delivered, Peddler could appear at any moment. I grabbed my cloak and started up the trail. But halfway up, dizziness washed over me. My prison lay below. Escape had been what I most craved, but something tugged at me. There was only one reason why Lara would give me my freedom—only one reason why she'd betray her father.

She knew she was going to die.

The decision didn't come easily. Freedom tasted sweeter than anything, even chocolate. But I imagined Lara, with no one to hear her last words. I'd feared I would die alone on that beach, and that thought had terrified me.

I'd long wondered where Lara lived. My question was answered as I rounded the bluff where a cave cut into the towering cliff. Lara's fishing net hung from a tree that jutted from the embankment. Two jugs sat next to a steady trickle of fresh water that snaked down the cliff. I threw myself at the water, filling my cupped hands and drinking until I could drink no more.

"Lara," I called. No reply came. Slowly, knowing what I'd find but hoping not, I entered the cave. Morning light flooded the interior.

Lara lay crumpled on the cave floor as if she'd been washed ashore. Her scarf lay at her side. Her mangled face was turned up. I knelt beside her. The blueness of her skin told me that she was long gone. Her last act had been to deliver me my freedom.

I wept for my captor. I wept for the woman who'd been ravaged by disease. Who'd died alone in the silence of that place. Who'd served her father as all daughters were taught to do. I think I was weeping for myself, as well. All that I'd lost came rushing back. My parents. My village. My love.

Something glittered in the corner of the cave. The burlap sack Peddler had brought on his last visit lay open. A necklace with bright blue beads peeked out. A white dress, a pair of dainty boots, handkerchiefs, undergarments, and a bonnet lay inside. More gifts lay in the corner of the cave—dresses, combs, ribbons, hairpins. Beautiful things to help a girl feel beautiful. This is where Peddler had hidden his daughter to keep her safe. Was this why he wanted to be rich? So he could hide her in a better place?

At any moment, I expected Peddler to rush into the cave, grab me, and wrap another chain around my waist. The urge to flee was overwhelming. But in our village, even murderers and thieves were granted the right of burial. And if anyone found this cave, they'd take all of Lara's treasures—the only things she had.

I didn't move her, fearful of the disease. I covered her face with a new scarf, then set all her treasures around her—save for a few things I needed from the burlap bag. The nightfrock I'd worn since being kidnapped was torn and ragged. The white dress fit well, as did the soft boots. I used the handkerchiefs to cradle my curled foot. Lastly came the bonnet, which was loose enough to hide all my hair.

I piled beach rocks around and over Lara's body and her treasures. The grave would do for a while. Hopefully Peddler would return and bury her with a proper gravestone. I'd done my best.

I decided not to take the steep path. Knowing my luck I'd walk right into Peddler's gnarled hands. So I said a final good-bye to Lara—a daughter like me, who only wanted to help her father. I would hold no grudge against her for her part in my captivity. I hoped the Thief of Sleep had found her and was escorting her to the hereafter, where her body would heal. With the cliff on my left, the sea to my right, I headed down the beach.

I soon passed two more signs painted with the same word, each guarded by a human skull. *Leper*. I didn't expect to find a village or even a house nearby. Peddler would have chosen this place for its seclusion.

While I wanted desperately to return to Wander and make chocolate for the Oaks, I knew the only way to free my father and my people was to find someone powerful, someone who could talk to the king on my behalf. My plan was this—to get myself to the Baroness of Salt. I possessed what she wanted, so therefore I'd be able to negotiate for what I wanted. I would make chocolate for her if she bought my father's freedom, my people's freedom—and if she found Peddler. All those days and nights imagining him swinging at the end of a noose for what he'd done to Owen, for what he'd done to me, and it turned out he'd only been trying to make his daughter's life better.

But he'd killed Owen, and for that, he'd earned my eternal hatred.

As I walked into the late afternoon, I came to a place where the cliffs gradually dipped down to meet the beach, stretching into a field of tall grasses. My stomach clenched with hunger and my right leg throbbed, but I didn't stop to rest. Freedom was a powerful force, as if hands were pushing me from behind. A ship sailed in the distance, its three sails looking like clouds that had been captured and tied to posts. When the ship turned toward the shore, I smiled hopefully. Maybe there was a town nearby.

I froze at the sound of shouts in the distance. A man with a knit cap pulled over his ears was running through the field, followed by two more men—soldiers. I dropped to my stomach, peering over a tuft of grass. They looked exactly like the soldiers who had come to the Flatlands, with their white swan crests and yellow tunics. "Stop in the name of King Elmer," the lead soldier cried.

I felt sorry for the man they were chasing. The poor guy looked terrified, his legs pumping wildly as he tried to outrun them. But they were gaining fast. I pressed close to the ground, my heart pounding. The last thing I needed was to be caught by soldiers. I'd stay right there, wouldn't move an inch until they'd passed by.

But suddenly the man turned toward me. *Go the other way!* I wanted to scream. His face clenched, his arms swinging, he stumbled. The lead soldier reached out and grabbed the man by his hat, pulling it off just before the man ducked out of reach. A mass of red hair tumbled free, falling to the man's shoulders.

My heart nearly stopped beating. As the soldier unsheathed his sword, the red-haired man stumbled again. He was going to die. The soldier clutched the sword in both hands, raised it above his head. I cupped my hands around my mouth. "Griffin! Watch out!"

Griffin Boar darted just as the blade swooshed through the air, missing his shoulder by mere inches. Then he spun around, kicked out his leg, and tripped the soldier. The sword flew from the soldier's hands. Griffin grabbed it and, with a swift motion, plunged the sword into the soldier's chest. I grimaced as Griffin pulled the sword free, its blade glistening with blood. The soldier lay motionless.

The other soldier, slower and fatter than his dead friend, stopped in his tracks. He held his sword but did not approach. His gaze darted fearfully from Griffin to the blood-streaked sword. Then, with a whimper, he turned and ran in the opposite direction. I sighed with relief. It was over. But Griffin, who'd seemed so desperate to escape these men, followed, and when he caught up to the second soldier, he took him down with a slice to the man's neck.

I nearly vomited, closing my eyes against the horror of the spraying blood.

"Emmeline?" I looked up from my hiding place in the grass. Griffin Boar stood over me, breathing like a man who'd outrun death. "What are you doing here?"

Part Six
Soldier

Chapter Twenty-eight

For the second time that day, I found myself making a grave—this time for two bodies.

We dragged the bodies into the woods beyond the field. Before digging the shallow pit with pieces of driftwood, Griffin stripped the soldiers down to their undergarments. Then he hurriedly removed his own clothes—the same ones he'd worn at the husband market. They were supposed to have been his wedding day clothes. Now they were torn and stained with filth. That day at the market felt like a lifetime ago.

I had a million questions for him. "Griffin—"

"Not now. There's no time."

Kneeling next to me, he smelled like sweat, the sour kind that comes from fear. Rummaging through the pile of soldiers' belongings, he picked out usable pieces. One of the soldiers was tall like Griffin, so he pulled on that soldier's pants. They were made of some sort of animal hide that had been pounded soft and thin. Both of the soldiers' jackets were stained with blood so Griffin threw them into the grave, keeping one of the scabbards and one of the swords. The second soldier's tunic was still mostly clean so Griffin put it on. After searching through all pockets and finding a single coin and a purse, which he hung around his neck, he dumped the rest of their belongings into the grave.

The soldiers had been young men. I tried not to think of their families, tried not to imagine their mothers or sisters as we rolled them, side by side, into their final resting place. We didn't speak, the horror of the moment slithering around us. I looked away as dirt fell onto their faces, into their open mouths. Did they have wives? Children? Girls who were waiting?

"Griffin," I tried again.

"Not now," he said gruffly.

Once everything was covered with soil, he replanted the upturned ferns and tossed leaves and branches around to hide the grave.

We washed our hands at the beach. He crouched at the water's edge and scrubbed the sword's blade with sand until the blood disappeared.

"Griffin," I said, drying my hands on my dress, once clean and white, now stained with forest dirt. "I won't be quiet any longer. I want you to answer my questions and I want you to answer them now." I could barely believe I was demanding something of Griffin Boar. But I wasn't the same girl I'd been. I wouldn't accept silence when there was so much at stake.

A chill spread through the air as the sun lowered on the horizon.

Griffin slid the sword into its scabbard. Standing with his hands on his hips, he'd transformed himself into a soldier of the realm. The only thing that would give him away was his Flatlander hair. He stared out over the water, ignoring me.

"How did you get here?" I asked, stepping in front of him. "You're supposed to be fighting in the mineral fields."

"I escaped," he said, still looking past me like he always did. Then he strode back to the field and grabbed the knit hat that had been yanked from his head. He pulled it over his hair, tucking the ends beneath.

"You mean you *deserted*?" I asked, catching up to him.

"Something like that."

"What about my father? Where is he?"

"He's still there," he grumbled.

"He's alive?"

"He was when I left. Look, Emmeline, it's not safe out here. I need to hide for a while. Where are you staying?"

"Nowhere," I said. "I have nowhere to stay."

His gaze drifted to the marks on my wrists. Though the wounds had healed since the days in Peddler's wagon, two thick red scars remained. "Who did that to you?"

"A man," I said. "A dangerous man."

"Is he looking for you?" he asked, still staring at the scars.

"He will be," I said. "When he finds out I've escaped."

"Did you steal that dress and bonnet?"

"No. Not exactly."

For the first time since our bloody reunion, Griffin looked me in the eyes. His were green, like mine, and ringed with thick red lashes. I could practically hear his thoughts. *I should leave her here. She's got someone after her.* I imagined myself curled up in the woods, sleeping beneath a shrub or hidden in the corner of someone's barn. I wouldn't get a wink of sleep, thinking each sound was Peddler coming to get me. I'd definitely feel safer with Griffin by my side.

"We're both in trouble," I said quietly. "You're a deserter and I'm . . ." It wasn't the right time to tell him about the chocolate. Besides, I didn't trust him. Not in that way. We shared the same ancestors, the same homeland, traditions, and red hair, but nothing more. He'd always treated me like the unnatural, unwanted girl. What would keep him, once he learned the truth, from selling me to the highest bidder? "I left the Flatlands and you deserted the king's army. We've both broken the law."

He turned and started across the field.

"Where are you going?" I called.

"To find a place to spend the night."

I did my best to keep up with his hurried steps. His stride was long and determined. "Griffin," I called. "Tell me about—"

He whipped around and pointed a finger at me. "Don't speak my name! Not out here. Not ever again." Then his hand dropped to his side. For a moment, his face softened. "Look, Emmeline, we need to get someplace safe for the night. There's a village nearby. This uniform should open some doors."

He'd said "we." He wasn't going to leave me out there alone. It was perhaps one of the most surprising things that had happened. Griffin Boar was being nice to me. Maybe I shouldn't have been shocked. We'd become two totally different people. Griffin, who'd spent his life working the land, wielding nothing more dangerous than a rake and hoe, had killed two soldiers. And me, well, I'd caused a boy's death—the boy I loved. We were forever changed.

Not far into our walk, the field ended at the edge of a bay where the ocean water left its powerful currents behind and turned gentle. The sailing ship I'd seen in the distance had tied up at one of the many docks that jutted from the shore. Smaller boats lined the other docks. Villagers hauled baskets and barrels, ropes and nets. "Come on," Griffin said.

"My hair," I asked, tightening my bonnet. "Is it hidden?"

He glanced at me. "Aye. Mine?"

"Aye," I said.

"Say nothing," he warned. "Just follow my lead."

A pebbled road ran the length of the bay. Wooden buildings, two and three stories tall, lined one side, the docks lined the other. Griffin's stride changed. He slowed down, puffed out his chest, held out his chin. I was happy for the slower pace, but watched nervously from the corner of my eye as we passed the first dock. Would he be able to fool everyone? What if we ran into other soldiers? Murdering two soldiers of the realm was treason and would be punished by death, but I'd helped hide the evidence so I was equally guilty. Maybe I shouldn't have stayed with him. But since he was the only person who could tell me about my father, the risk was worth it.

My stomach growled as we walked past baskets of fish. The little silver ones, the kind Lara had cooked for me, lay alongside large orange ones with bulging eyes. There were other creatures for sale, bigger versions of the sand crabs that had shared the beach with me and creatures with long necks that squirted water. Gulls flew over the docks, circling and swooping as they tried to steal a feast. Crusty fishermen gutted and cleaned their catch, while merchants in green coats argued prices. No one spoke to Griffin as he strode past, his hand on his sword's hilt, but they cast ugly glares. Some whispered, their eyes narrowed as they stepped aside. Others simply chose to ignore him. Clearly there was no love for the king's soldiers in this village. Perhaps they had come, just as they had in the Flatlands, to take away the unmarried men.

From beneath the rim of my bonnet, I kept a look out for Peddler. My heart fluttered at the sight of each green jacket. An old man sitting on a bench caught my eye. When he turned and faced me, I took a relieved breath.

I hobbled across the street, following Griffin. My curled foot had gone numb, as if it had died sometime during the day's long walk. One of my WANTED posters hung from a lamppost. Griffin walked right past without so much as a glance at it. We stopped beneath a hanging sign that had no words, just a bed painted on it. "Remember, say nothing," Griffin hissed. Then he wrapped his fingers around my arm and led me inside.

The place was dark, the scent of cooked meat heavy in the air. A man sat behind a counter eating some sort of stew. Voices, boisterous and slurred, tumbled from a room nearby.

"Who do I talk to about getting a room?" Griffin asked.

"I'm the innkeeper," the man said, wiping his mouth on his sleeve. His face was pale, unlike the weathered, sunburned faces of the fishermen outside. "Welcome to the Gull's Breath Inn. Soldiers of the realm are always welcome here." His nose, shaped like a malformed turnip, took up too much of his face. His thick yellow beard held bits of his meal. "This your first visit to Fishport?"

"I want a room," Griffin said keeping a tight grip on my arm. Was he worried I was going to run off?

"Are you wanting a bed for one or two?"

Griffin hesitated, then wrapped his arm around my waist and pulled me close. My face burned as the innkeeper raised an eyebrow and nodded knowingly. Griffin set the soldier's coin on the counter.

The innkeeper shook his head, pushing the coin toward Griffin. "Soldiers don't pay," he said. "You must be a new recruit if you don't know that. The king's men never pay for nothing."

It was Griffin's first mistake, but he recovered instantly. "I was testing you," he said, retrieving the coin. "I was testing your loyalty to the king."

"I'm as loyal to the king as any man," the innkeeper insisted with a scowl.

"Prove it," Griffin said. "Give us your best room." His courage impressed me. But after all, he was used to getting his way.

After grabbing a ring of keys from a hook, the innkeeper led us past a crowded room where men sat drinking and eating at long tables. The smell of cooked meat was stronger here, and I caught a glimpse of a creature roasting over a fire. I'd never been inside our village tavern, but this is probably what it looked like—flagons overflowing with ale, men with reddened cheeks and noses. Laughter arose as one man fell off his stool.

"You're not from these parts," the innkeeper said as we followed up a creaky staircase to the second floor. "I don't recognize your accent. Where are you from?"

"I'm from all over," Griffin said, darting a glance at me. "Here and there, wherever the king sends me."

"Here it is," the innkeeper said, fiddling with the keys and opening a door. "Our best room. It comes with a view of Lonely Bay and a tub for washing."

"What about food?" Griffin asked.

"Meals are served in the main room downstairs."

"I'll be too busy to go downstairs," Griffin said, pushing me into the room and onto the bed. "Bring us some food immediately, and I'll tell the king that the Gull's Breath Inn knows how to treat royal soldiers."

The innkeeper nodded, then started down the hall. I scrambled off the bed and pushed past Griffin. "Excuse me," I called, stepping into the hall. "How do I find the Baroness of Salt?"

"The Baroness of Salt?" The innkeeper twirled his ring of keys. "She lives in Salt, of course. Everyone knows that." His curious gaze crawled across my face like a wandering insect. I looked down at my boots.

"Could you please tell me where I can find . . . Salt?"

"It's just down the bay, not far from here. But if you want to see her, all you have to do is wait. She always rides into Fishport on market morning, which is tomorrow."

I couldn't believe it. Was luck shining upon me? The Baroness of Salt would be here tomorrow. As the innkeeper's footsteps faded, Griffin pulled me into the room, closed and bolted the door.

"I told you not to say anything," he grumbled. "Who is this . . . salt person?"

"Someone who will help me." I sat on the edge of the bed, smiling at this ray of hope. "Someone who can free my father."

Griffin yanked off his knit cap, his blazing locks falling onto his shoulders. Then he unclasped his belt and let it slide from his hands. The sword clanged as it hit the floor. He pulled off the soldier's tunic and threw it aside, groaning as if it had burned his skin. Then his face went slack, and I could practically see the confidence melt away as he sank to the floor. He brought his knees to his bare chest and held his face in his hands. The tears were silent. To think I'd ever see Griffin Boar scared, that I'd ever see him cry. It never occurred to me back in Root, in the days before all this hell, that he was . . . human.

"Please, Griffin," I said, pulling the bonnet from my head. "Please tell me about my father."

He kept his face hidden for a long while, then dropped his hands. A flash of anger lit up his eyes. "The king is a liar," he hissed. "There's no war in the mineral fields. Our people have been turned into slaves."

Chapter Twenty-nine

Slaves?" I whispered the word.

"Aye. Slaves. The king has turned our men into slaves."

I fell back against the pillow. The Oaks were right. They hadn't heard of a war in the mineral fields because there was no war. It was a lie. "I don't understand." My gaze flew across the ceiling. "How can my father be a slave? He's a citizen of Anglund."

"We're dirt-scratchers," Griffin said. "We're scum."

"I hate that word," I snapped. "Don't use it. We're Flatlanders."

"To everyone else we're filthy stinking dirt-scratchers."

I took a long, controlled breath. Lashing out at Griffin would solve nothing. "Why does the king need slaves?"

"Because he wants gold and silver and the last place in Anglund to get gold and silver is the mineral fields. But it's a death trap. No citizen will willingly work there." As Griffin lowered his voice, a shiver rolled down my back. "The mineral fields are the ugliest places I've ever seen. No trees, no animals, no river. Just a wasteland of holes. Piles of rock and dirt in every direction. And you can see the air."

I sat up. "What do you mean you can see the air?"

"It's so full of dust and poison you can see it. You can run your fingers through it. And there's a yellow fog that clings to everything and takes your breath away. It comes out of the holes." He shuddered. "The place smells like death."

I scooted to the edge of the bed, pressing the tips of my boots on the floor. "Father can't stay there. He'll die."

"All our men will die," he said, slumping against the wall. "There are others who came before us. Convicts who were sent there instead of the noose. They looked like walking skeletons. And many were coughing up blood. They said it was from the yellow fog. That's why the king took us dirt-scratchers. Because he doesn't have enough convicts."

"My father would never work as a slave. You're lying. He's a proud man."

"Pride be damned, Emmeline!" He pounded his fist on the floor. "If your father refuses to dig, they'll whip him. If he still refuses, he'll be hanged from a rafter by his ankles and left to die in the burning sun. They toss the corpses into a pit." Griffin's breathing quickened, his eyes widening as he recalled the horror of the place. "I knew that if I didn't escape on that first night, I'd never escape."

I gripped the blanket, picturing my father breathing poison, imagining him cringing beneath the blows of a whip. "Why didn't you take him with you?"

"I couldn't take anyone," he snapped. "One man could slip away, but more would have drawn attention. I had one chance and I took it."

There was no time to waste. I needed to turn myself over to the Baroness of Salt as soon as possible so I could buy my father's freedom. Morning couldn't arrive fast enough.

Laughter arose from below, followed by singing. The muscles in my right leg cramped with each step as I walked to the window. Night had fallen over the bay. A boy made his way down the road, lighting lanterns that hung from wooden posts. I found a candle and flint on the room's only table. As flame took hold of the wick, soft light bounced off Griffin's face. The little scar on his chin would always remind me of the day when he'd been so enchanted by his own reflection that he'd almost run me over. He'd be shocked if he could see himself now. Greasy hair, reddened eyes, hollowed cheeks—his handsomeness covered with grime.

He stared into space. Was he thinking of home? Of our green pastures and sweet air? Of the crops that needed tending and the girl who might have become his wife? He still hadn't asked how I'd gotten there, but that was no surprise. I was still unimportant—an odd creature of no interest to him. I took a deep breath. "Griffin, there's something you need to know." Though I spoke the next words softly, they pierced the air like poisoned darts. "Root is gone."

He furrowed his brow. "What are you talking about?"

The story poured forth, as if pushed by the floodwaters themselves and no matter how I tried to slow my words, they came fast and furious. Griffin's gaze never left my face as I spoke of the days and nights of endless rain. How the fields turned to mud, how the river rose. How the villagers fled and how his family piled their belongings onto their cart. I told him that I gave my donkey to his father and his family left for higher ground. I skipped the part where I tried to save Snow. I still couldn't say her name without tears.

"Wait," he interrupted. He got to his feet and walked toward me, pointing his finger at my face. "If you were washed away, then how do you know everything's gone?" His arrogance had returned in full force. Why should he believe me, the girl he'd looked upon with scorn his entire life? "Maybe it's not as bad as you say."

"Griffin," I said gently, "you must believe me. A boy . . . a family saved me. The Oak family. They didn't care that I was from the Flatlands. They fed and clothed me. They paid a surgeon to stitch my leg. They told me Root was gone."

"They helped you even though you were a dirt-scratcher?" Griffin folded his arms. "Show me the stitches. Then I'll believe you."

I looked down at my hem, hanging just above the top of my boots. To show Griffin my leg would have shamed me in my old life. But he needed to accept the truth, otherwise he wouldn't be prepared for the disaster that waited back in Root. Slowly, I rolled up the hem, stopping mid-thigh. "The stitches are gone but you can still see the marks on my skin." His gaze lingered on the scar. I dropped the hem and walked back to the window.

"Okay, so these Oaks took care of you. But how could they possibly know about Root?"

"Tax-collector Todd came downriver on a raft. He said everything had washed away in the flood."

"Did you talk to Todd?"

"No. But—"

"But nothing. These Oaks lied to you."

"Why would they lie to me?"

"Because they wanted to keep you from leaving. Were you working for them?"

"Aye. I agreed to work to pay my debt for what they'd done for me."

"I thought so." He smacked his palm on the table. "They told you a lie to keep you there. Just like a slave. They want us to be their slaves! We can't trust anyone. Not outside the Flatlands."

At the sound of knocking, Griffin grabbed the sword off the floor. "Who's there?" he demanded, his face pressed to the crack in the door.

"Food," replied the innkeeper.

"Leave it outside," Griffin ordered. "I'm . . . *busy*."

Pottery rattled, then the innkeeper's footsteps faded. Griffin tucked his hair back into his cap and slowly opened the door. After peering down the hallway, he pulled the wooden tray inside and closed and bolted the door once again. My stomach knotted as the scent of cooked meat filled the small room. "They treat soldiers like gods," he said as he set the tray on the table. I could barely control myself, having eaten nothing but fish and sea plants for an eternity. But there sat a loaf of dark bread, a roasted hen, and a bowl of boiled potatoes—a feast in the Flatlands.

We ate as if it were our last meal, stuffing our cheeks between swallows. I tried to keep up with Griffin. He didn't care one bit about sharing. Without bothering to divide the food, he started shoveling it into his mouth. My jaw ached I chewed so quickly. But even though he ate twice as much, I was nearly full. When he'd gnawed the last piece of poultry from its bone, he sat back, his lips glistening with grease. He wiped his hands on his bare chest. Then after a long burp, he went into the water closet to do his business.

When he returned, he rubbed his neck wearily, then fell face-down upon the bed. The *only* bed. His feet hung over the edge and his outstretched arms took up the width. Before I could ask him where I was supposed to sleep, snoring filled the room.

The singing downstairs had stopped. I looked out the window into the inky darkness. Ugly images filled my mind. My father working between the lashes of a whip, breathing thick yellow air. Lara's scarred body in its lonely rocky grave. Owen on his back, moonlight settling on his lifeless face.

Then I looked across the room to where Griffin lay. I couldn't bear sleeping alone, not with those memories haunting my dreams. But there was only one man whose bed I wanted to share.

That would never happen now.

Chapter Thirty

It was warm beneath the quilt. At first I thought I was back on the beach because the sound of crying gulls woke me. But the pillow was soft and someone's arm was draped over my side.

How many Flatlander girls would have given everything for a night with Griffin Boar? And there I was, curled against him, his chest as warm as a riverbank that had baked all day in the sun. Sure, he'd be disgusted if he woke and realized I was there. But after so many nights alone on that beach, half-frozen in that crumbling shack, these few hours in bed had felt like paradise.

Owen. Why couldn't he be Owen?

I carefully lifted his arm and slipped out from beneath. Perched at the edge of the bed, I gazed upon his sleeping face. His hair, the exact color as mine, fanned across the white pillow. He was badly in need of a shave but the stubble helped hide the little scar, which was barely visible unless you leaned in real close and knew exactly where to find it.

His eyes flew open. "What are you doing?"

I leaned back. "Nothing."

He looked around. "Where?" Then he scratched the back of his head. "Right. Now I remember. We'd better get going. We can't hide here all day. It's a long way back to Root."

He was right. I did need to get going. I wanted to be at the market the moment the Baroness of Salt arrived. "I'm not going to Root."

He wasn't listening. He sat up, mumbling to himself about getting a horse and water—listing things he'd need for the journey. He stopped mid-mumble and stared at me. Reaching out, he touched a lock of my hair, looking at it as if he'd never seen red hair before. Then he lunged off the bed and grabbed the soldier's purse that lay on the floor. He shuffled through its contents and pulled out a small blade. "Griffin," I asked nervously. "What are you doing?"

"Take it," he insisted, holding the knife at arm's length. "Go on, take it!" I took it. Then he sat on the stool and folded his arms. "Do it."

"Do what?"

"Cut my hair."

I winced, drawing away as if he'd asked me to cut his wrists. "No," I said. "I can't do that. I won't." How could Griffin Boar, the guy who loved looking at his own reflection, who'd been surrounded by lovesick girls his entire life, ask me to do such a thing?

He tightened his arms. "Don't argue, Emmeline. I'm an escaped dirt-scratcher. The hair will give me away. Cut it short. Cut it to the scalp."

It was an enormous sacrifice, but he was right. I didn't know how many days it would take him to reach the Flatlands, but trying to keep every lock of his long hair hidden would be difficult.

Gripping the knife's handle, I stood at Griffin's shoulder. With a trembling hand, I grabbed a clump of his thick hair and pulled it taut. Tears pooled on my lower lids as I sawed with the blade. As the locks fell, Griffin moaned. Flatlander men grew their hair long as a symbol of pride. Power and beauty shone in Griffin's hair. Our people's history wove through each strand.

"Stop looking at me like that," he grumbled.

Clenching my jaw and pushing away the tears, I sawed the knife back and forth, back and forth. It was a terrible mess, as if an animal had been grazing on his head. I worked as fast as I could, the pile of hair growing around my feet. As the sun rose outside, fishermen shouted on the docks. Surely the market wouldn't begin this early. Surely I still had time.

"Who's Owen?" Griffin asked as I worked my way behind his ear.

"Owen?" My face went hot.

"You called out his name in your sleep."

I hesitated for a moment, then grabbed another clump, pulling extra hard. "Never mind who he is." It wasn't a story I wanted to share, not with Griffin, not with anyone. Then, realizing I had him in a sort of headlock, I decided to test my luck. "Griffin, I need your help this morning."

His shoulders slumped as he stared at the fallen locks. "What are you talking about?"

"I need to find the Baroness of Salt. The innkeeper said she'd be at the morning market. I need you to stay with me until I find her." He'd keep me safe. Peddler wouldn't dare take me away from a soldier of the realm. "As soon as I find her, you can leave for home."

"Why do you need to find her?" he grumbled.

"It's a long story." Another lock fell away. "But if you take me to her, she will pay you one thousand coin."

He snorted. "Why would someone pay one thousand coin for a dirt-scratcher? You're crazy."

"I'm not crazy."

"That's what everyone says about you. The way you talk to the cows. They say you're crazy."

I stepped back and waved the knife at him. "I'm not crazy!"

"Watch it with that thing."

"Fine! Don't help me. You've never helped me. All you've ever done is ignore me, Griffin Boar. You ignore me or you tell me to move out of your way."

In a flash, he yanked the knife from my hand. "Give me that. You're taking too long." He sawed through the last clumps of hair, then stood. He looked so strange, so vulnerable without the mane. I held my breath. It was almost as if I'd witnessed the dethroning of a prince.

After rummaging through the soldier's purse, Griffin found a straight razor. I watched from the water closet's doorway as he pumped water into a basin and, with a bit of hard soap, began to shave his face. Then he stomped back into the room. "Move it," he said, pushing me out of the way. He put on the tunic, then the scabbard, sword, purse, and knit cap. He crouched and swept the hair clippings under the worn rug. Then he took a long breath and unbolted the door.

"Griffin, listen to me," I said, following him into the hallway. I pulled my bonnet over my head, tucking my hair beneath and tying it tight. "If you help me find the baroness, you'll be rich. You can take all that coin back to Root and use it to rebuild."

"I think you bumped your head during that ride downriver." He started down the stairs. "Stay if you want. I don't care."

It was no use. He was as stubborn as my old donkey. I imagined trying to lead Griffin with a carrot and, despite my worries, nearly laughed at the thought. I couldn't compete with the force that tugged at his heart—a desperate need to see his family.

When he suddenly stopped on the bottom stair, I bumped into him. "What—?" He raised his hand to silence me. Voices drifted around the corner.

"Where are those two soldiers that always hang out here?" a man asked.

"Igor and Burl? Haven't seen those two rat turds this morning." I recognized the innkeeper's voice. "Why are you asking?"

"They're always interested in the WANTED posters. Just got a new one for the Milkmaid. Says she's a dirt-scratcher. Can you believe that?"

"A dirt-scratcher? But their sort is not supposed to leave the Flatlands."

"Says here she's got a bad foot."

"A bad foot?" the innkeeper repeated.

Griffin's entire body stiffened.

"That's right," the man said. "Says she walks with a limp. And look what else it says. The Baroness of Salt has been outbid. By the king himself!"

"The king?"

"That's right. Says here King Elmer is offering five thousand coin. Says here the Milkmaid is to be turned over to the palace and to no one else, on penalty of death."

"Five thousand coin?" The innkeeper coughed. "I could retire on that much coin."

"Who would have thought a dirt-scratcher girl could be worth so much coin?" the man asked.

Griffin whipped around, but I silenced him by pressing my palm to his mouth. He narrowed his eyes as the conversation around the corner continued.

"Wait a minute," the innkeeper said, his tone turning serious. "Did you say she's got a limp? A girl come in here last evening. She's got a limp. And she's still upstairs."

"Is her hair red?" the man asked.

"I'm not sure," the innkeeper said. "But we could easily find out." He lowered his voice. "She's got a soldier with her, but we could take him. I've got no problem killing a soldier. They're all thugs and rapists. Got a good blade right here."

Griffin grabbed my shoulder, turned me around, then shoved me back up the stairs. I tripped. His arm around my waist, he lifted and whisked me back to our room. After bolting the door, he spun to face me. "Emmeline?"

"I told you about the reward, but you wouldn't listen," I said.

He backed me toward the window, his teeth clenched. "Tell me again."

"I'm wanted. They call me the Milkmaid because . . ." The walls trembled as boots stomped down the hallway. Griffin grabbed the sword's hilt as the door rattled.

"Open up. It's the innkeeper. I have business with you."

"We have to get out of here," I said, grabbing his sleeve. "They'll kill you so they can get the reward."

"Move it!" he ordered, pushing me aside. As he darted toward the window, his boot caught on the little rug. The edges rolled over, revealing the locks of cut hair. With a grunt, Griffin opened the window. Cool morning air and the shrieks of hungry gulls drifted into the room. "We'll have to jump," he said. "I'll go first, then I'll catch you."

The door rattled again as the innkeeper turned the key. But the deadbolt held tight. "We've got important business," he called. "Open up."

Griffin climbed onto the windowsill. After a curse, he jumped. The bedroom door nearly split as one of the men threw himself against it. I scrambled onto the sill. Luckily our room was on the second floor, not much higher than the donkey shed back home. Griffin stood in the road. "Come on," he quietly insisted, trying not to draw attention. I gripped the sides of the window frame. I might have hesitated, might have worried about landing on my curled foot or breaking my leg or neck, but that's when the innkeeper crashed through the bedroom door. So I jumped.

Griffin caught me. He didn't even stumble. All those days chopping trees for his cottage, when he'd worked shirtless and the girls had watched, me included, had turned his arms into timbers. He set me on the ground, then looked around. "Hey there!" he yelled, dashing into the road and waving his arms at an approaching carriage. The driver pulled the reins and the horses, a pair of glossy black beauties, skidded to a stop. "I'm taking this carriage in the name of the king," Griffin told the driver, his sword drawn. The driver released the reins and hopped onto the street.

"Stop!" the innkeeper hollered from the window. "Stop that girl." He clutched a handful of Griffin's hair. "They're dirt-scratchers. Stop them!"

Griffin yanked open the carriage door. Then he reached inside and pulled out its only occupant, a woman in a checkered cape. "How dare you?" she said. "Do you know who I am?"

"Get in!" Griffin yelled at me.

Thanks to another push, I landed facedown inside the carriage. The carriage door slammed shut. I peered out as Griffin leaped into the driver's seat. The woman waved her arms, screaming as we rode away in her carriage. As the horses picked up speed, the innkeeper ran from the Gull's Breath Inn, waving a poster. Curious bystanders gathered around. The carriage owner grabbed the poster. They knew who I was. They'd come after me.

Scooting deeper into the carriage, my hand bumped into two small bags. I opened one. It was filled with white crystals. As I tasted a crystal, I knew what we'd done. We'd stolen the carriage of the Baroness of Salt. But according to the latest WANTED poster, the baroness was no longer the highest bidder. King Elmer wanted me. He wanted my magic. And I knew what I wanted.

"Griffin?" I called out the window. "We need to go to Londwin City."

"I know," he called back.

I leaned against the seat, my heart racing along with the horses' hooves. I was going to meet the king of Anglund. And free my people.

Chapter Thirty-one

Trying to find Peddler was getting me nowhere. He'd been seen here and there, but each time I followed the lead I was always a day or two behind. So, instead of trying to follow him, I decided it would be better to wait for him. And I'd wait in the place he'd be sure to turn up. Salt was the place because the latest poster listed a one thousand coin reward from the Baroness of Salt. Peddler wouldn't be able to ignore that.

But my brilliant plan was dashed soon after I arrived in Salt, where I spied a new WANTED poster, listing a five thousand coin reward from the king himself.

So I was off to Londwin City.

My current location was a town called Lime, a main stop along the Merchant's Highway on the way to Londwin City. I'd left my horse at a public stable, paying generously for oats and alfalfa. After a flavorless but filling meal at the tavern, I headed back to collect my horse. Town life moved around me. Women washed clothing in the fountain, a group of children kicked a sheepskin ball. Singing bled from the tavern as patrons came and went. Homesickness tugged at my heart. Was Mother worried sick? Probably. I'd sent scrolls so she'd know I was well, but I didn't tell her that I wouldn't return without Peddler. Nor would I return until I'd made sure Emmeline was safe. Now that the king wanted her, there was little hope she'd return to Wander with me. But if I could see her one more time . . .

What was that?

I stopped in my tracks and narrowed my eyes. Villagers crossed between shops, baskets in hands as they went about their daily errands. Nothing appeared out of the ordinary, but a feeling crept over me—like the way the air tingles just before a storm. Or the way skin prickles just before a shiver.

I drew a quick breath. A lone figure darted across the street, something tucked beneath his arm. It was his long, jerky stride that distinguished him from everyone else. He disappeared so quickly between two buildings, I thought he might have been an illusion.

Only one person ran like that.

"Peddler!" I screamed.

In a heartbeat, I was after him. Maybe I was mistaken. The man had black hair and wore a green merchant's coat. But he shared Peddler's odd way of moving, his long legs bending awkwardly like a stickbug's. I raced around two chatting men, then turned into an alley. At the far end, the flaps of the merchant coat disappeared around the corner. Pumping my legs, I flew down the alley, bumping into a man who was carrying a crate of kindling. "Watch it!" the man hollered as the crate fell to the ground.

"Sorry," I called, turning sharply on my heels. The narrow dirt road twisted between buildings like a snake. The merchant's coat, green as Emmeline's eyes, darted around the first bend. Following, I caught sight, then lost it, then caught sight again. He was fast, but not fast enough. Narrow timber houses lined this part of the road, pressed together so tightly that the roofs overlapped. At the next bend I gained on him, close enough to hear his terrified breathing. Clutching a loaf of bread, he darted a quick look over his shoulder—a mistake, for in doing so he stumbled. The loaf of bread fell from his grip. With a leap, I was on him.

We landed facedown on the packed dirt, me on top. He broke the fall with his hands, but the jolt sent a sharp pain through my newly healed rib. He hissed and clawed at the road. I rolled him onto his back, pinning him. The face I'd last seen at our dairy, beneath the half moon, stared up at me. His eyes widened. "It's . . . *you*," he whispered with thin, trembling lips.

"That's right, old man, I'm alive!" I wanted to wring his neck. "Where is she?" I demanded, spit flying onto his face. He kicked, trying to free himself. I dug a knee into his thigh and pressed my thumbs into his wrists.

"Get off and I'll tell you," he said with a groan.

"Tell me now."

"She's with my daughter," he said between clenched teeth.

I pulled my knife from my boot and held the tip to his throat. A droplet of blood seeped between the folds of his wrinkled neck. "You're a liar. You will die, here and now, if you don't tell me."

"I'm telling you." A ridge of black ran along his forehead

where the hair dye had seeped into his skin. "I left her with my daughter."

"Your daughter has leprosy. Why would you leave Emmeline with a leper?" I pressed the knife's tip deeper.

"No one would look for her there. I knew she'd be left alone."

Could it be true? It made sense. How could I have overlooked such a brilliant plan?

Peddler's jaw relaxed. He stopped struggling, surrendering the moment. "You can't blame me for taking her. I needed the coin to help my daughter. You understand, don't you? You'd do anything for your family, wouldn't you, young Mister Oak?"

He was trying to trick me. "I don't believe a word you've said. You've hidden her somewhere nearby. Otherwise, why would you be here?"

"I'm here because I've been spreading the word about the Milkmaid who can make chocolate. That's what I've been doing. And it worked because the news traveled all the way to the king." He lifted his head, staring desperately into my eyes. "You got a horse, young Mister Oak? If you'll give me your horse, we can work together."

"Work together?"

"We'd be helping each other." He smiled sheepishly. "After we take her to the king, we can split the reward. Think of all the nice things you could buy for your parents."

I wanted to pound his head into the ground. "Where is she?"

"It's a robbery!" someone shouted. "A merchant's being robbed!" Footsteps sounded. A pair of boots appeared at the corner of my eye, then another pair.

"Call the soldiers!" a woman cried.

Ignoring the gathering crowd, I wrapped a hand around Peddler's neck. "Don't forget that you're still a wanted man. I can turn you over to Wander's tax-collector, and he'll *hang* you for attempted murder." I realized I no longer cared about Peddler's fate. He was scum—pure scum. I wanted only one thing. "Listen to me. I can get you out of here. But only if you tell me *where . . . she . . . is*."

Something sharp pressed into my back. "Drop the knife," a man ordered.

"This isn't a robbery," I said, looking up just before a rake hit the side of my head. Someone yanked the knife from my grip. Two hands grabbed me and pulled me to my feet. For a moment my vision blurred. When it cleared I found myself surrounded by villagers—a rake, a knife, and an ax pointed at my chest. "Wait," I said. "You've got it all wrong."

"We saw it," the ax-holder said. "You were trying to rob this merchant."

Someone helped Peddler to his feet. "Thank you," he said as he brushed dirt from his jacket, his eyes darting wildly.

"I wasn't trying to rob him," I said. "He's not a merchant. That's a disguise. He's a wanted man."

"Shut up, you," the knife-holder said.

My mind raced. The man wielding the knife was small. I could easily fell him with one swift punch to the throat. Then I could whip around and take the ax-holder down with a kick to the groin. But the man holding the rake, two heads taller and built like a bull, was going to be a tough match. My head throbbed where he'd hit it with the rake's flat edge. "Listen to me. He's a wanted man. He's the man who kidnapped the Milkmaid."

The knife-holder's eyebrows raised and everyone turned to look at Peddler.

But Peddler was gone.

Chapter Thirty-two

I stood in the tax-collector's office, my wrists shackled. I'd tried to plead my case, but each word was met with a punch to the jaw by one of the guards.

Lime's tax-collector was like an exact replica of Wander's tax-collector—a well-fed, soft sort of fellow who grunted when he moved across the room, his feet sliding lazily, his enormous belly sagging to his knees. The kind of fellow who gave no thought to anything but coin. Maybe all tax-collectors were born from the same parents. When not stealing coin from citizen's hands, they sat on their cushioned stools counting coin, stacking coin, plunging their hands into chests filled with coin. They probably slept beneath coin blankets.

King Elmer was of the same cloth. Nothing was more important than the collection of coin. He decreed long ago that tax-collectors, having the most important jobs in the kingdom, would wield the utmost authority. So he got rid of sheriffs and magistrates. No need for judges or juries either. Even town councils were beginning to disappear.

"You are hereby sentenced to hard labor in the mineral fields," the tax-collector said.

"You're wasting time," I insisted. "If you send your men after Peddler, you'll find the Milkmaid." At this point I didn't care who found Emmeline, as long as she was rescued from Peddler's clutches. She was close by. I could feel it.

"Shut up!" the soldier ordered with a slap to the side of my head.

I glared at him. "Unshackle me and then try to hit me, you—"

Whack! Again to the side of my head. I stumbled sideways, crashing into the wall.

The tax-collector rested his swollen hands on his table. His floppy black hat drooped over one eye. "I have read the WANTED posters. The man accused of stealing the Milkmaid has long white hair. Today's witnesses claim that the merchant you accosted has short black hair. Your defense has no merit."

"If you'll just listen to me—"

"You want me to listen to you? So that you can claim innocence?" He curled his lip. "Innocence comes with a price." He tapped his fingers, waiting for me to offer a bribe. I could have, if the soldiers hadn't taken all my coin. Of course that's what it came down to. Facts were of no concern. Truth was a mere trifle.

"Peddler dyed his hair, you stupid—" I ducked and the soldier's hand slammed into the wall.

"Enough!" the tax-collector shouted as the soldier growled. "We'll get paid less if he's injured. And we certainly won't get paid if he's dead." He smiled at me, then heaved himself onto his feet. "Lucky for you, the king is offering fifty coin for each criminal we send to the mineral fields. Otherwise, you'd be hanging by a rope."

He took his black tax-collector's coat off a hook and put it on. White swans of the realm swam along the wide collar. He buttoned it over his substantial gut, then pushed his floppy hat from his greedy eyes. "Those dirt-scratchers are proving to be good workers, from what I hear. Too bad there aren't more of them. Slavery is a very lucrative business."

"Slavery?" I grimaced. "Is that why they were taken from the Flatlands?"

"You're very lucky I'm such a gracious person," the tax-collector said. The soldier loomed next to me, his fists balled and ready. I held back my curse. "Take him away."

A wagon waited outside, its bed converted into a cage. Two men sat inside. My friendly soldier opened the cage door, then shoved me. I landed on the chain that wound around the other men's ankles. Pain shot through my hip. "If my hands were untied, I'd kill you, you louse!"

The soldier reached inside. The next blow was the one that knocked me out.

I don't know how much time passed before I came to but the wagon was rumbling down a road. I sat up. My hands were free but a chain wound around my ankles. The chain snaked across the cage floor, linking me to the other two unfortunate passengers, one of whom was staring at me with his eye.

His only eye.

“Oh crud,” I said, recognizing him from the barefist fight. “It’s you.”

“That’s right.” He growled like a wolverine. “You don’t have to worry about the mineral fields. I’m going to kill you before we get there.”

Chapter Thirty-three

The baroness's carriage was like a hollowed-out gourd, hard on the outside but soft on the inside. The seats were lined with white rabbit pelts. The black walls and ceiling curved around me like night. Sunshine trickled in through two windows. Such a beautiful carriage might have belonged to a goddess or a queen. I imagined that one day I might own such a beautiful thing. I wouldn't have to hobble down the street ever again.

Once we'd covered some distance, we turned onto a path made by grazing animals. As soon as the main road disappeared from sight, Griffin stopped the carriage and leaped off the driver's bench. "I want to know what's going on," he said, yanking open the carriage door. "Why is there a reward for you? And why is everyone calling you a milkmaid? You don't milk cows. You talk to them, but you don't milk them."

I took a deep breath, gathered the hem of my skirt, then climbed out. I left the bonnet inside. It felt good to free my hair. "They call me the Milkmaid because the girl who saw me in the barn and told everyone about me thought I was a milkmaid."

"Why would she think that?"

"Because I was dressed in a milkmaid's dress and bonnet."

He folded his arms. "And so . . . ?"

"Chocolate. I can make chocolate." His expression didn't change. Of course not. Like me, he'd never heard of the stuff. "It's this delicious treat that is prized above all else. It's part of the legend about our people. It's in a book."

"A book? Since when do you read books?"

"I don't. Owen read it to me." His name escaped. Let loose from where I'd held it, deep inside, it floated among the grasses like a whisper. *Owen.*

Before Griffin could ask about Owen, I launched into the story. I told him the legend as well as I could remember it. About Queen Margaret. About how the people loved her because she had a magical gift for making chocolate, this amazing food that tastes unlike anything else. I told him how merchants traveled from all over the world to get this chocolate and how it had made Anglund and its queen very rich. But then the invaders came, our people, the Kell. Griffin nodded, for he recognized this part of the story. Our people tried to conquer the land but were defeated. I told him how the chieftain had cursed Queen Margaret, taking away her magic. And chocolate disappeared, never to be seen or tasted again.

He tightened his arms. "I still don't understand."

"While I was at the Oak Dairy, I tried to churn cream into butter. But instead it turned into chocolate."

He snorted. "This all sounds crazy."

The narrow path that we'd taken from the road led across a field. Cows grazed in the distance. A cottage and barn sat on a gentle hill. Weeks had passed since I'd sat in the butter room with Owen. During all that time I'd wondered—what if it had been some sort of mistake? A once-in-a-lifetime happening? What if the cream had come from a special cow and had nothing to do with me? Doubt hung over me like a waterlogged roof. We couldn't go to the king unless I knew for sure. That would be suicide.

"I'll show you," I said. Reaching into the carriage, I grabbed one of the salt bags. "Go get some cream and a churning bucket. Give this to the farmer in exchange."

Clearly Griffin needed proof as much as I for he bolted across that field, his long legs crossing the distance quickly. The cows had noticed our arrival for they began to mosey toward the carriage. Griffin passed them on his return. "Here you go," he said, setting a churning bucket at my feet. The cream was already inside.

Finding a clean spot on the ground, I sat, the bucket between my knees. A warm breeze tickled my face and arms. Griffin chewed on a strip of dried meat. He'd also managed to get a wedge of cheese, a loaf of bread, and some apples. Whether the salt bag had covered the cost or whether Griffin, still wearing the soldier's uniform, had bullied the food from the farmer, I didn't know. Nor did I care. At that moment my father's future lay in my hands. Could I make the magic happen again?

"Get away," Griffin said when the first cow arrived and nudged him with a wet nose. A few cows wandered around the carriage, a few gathered around me. "Move it!" Griffin hollered as a cow nibbled his boot.

"Leave them alone," I said. "They're just curious." I wrapped my fingers around the churning handle.

"They're stupid, that's what they are. Now hurry up."

"Stop pestering me," I told him. I was trying to focus my thoughts—trying to remember exactly what I'd done in the butter room.

"Pestering *you*?" he snapped. "I'd be halfway to Root by now if I hadn't run into you."

"You should be grateful you ran into me," I snapped right back.

"Grateful?" He grabbed another strip of meat and pointed it at my face. "Why should I be grateful? You almost got me killed at that inn. My family needs my help and I'm stuck here with you."

"Your family's fine. I told you, they had the cows and they got out of the valley before the flood. Anyway, you should be grateful you ran into me because I saved your life." I glared up at him. "Or have you already forgotten that little fact?"

"Saved my life?" His face turned red. "You're crazy. You never saved my life."

"That soldier was going to stab you. But I yelled *watch out* just before . . ." I closed my mouth, swallowing the words. The flash in Griffin's eyes told me that he did indeed remember. He looked away, as did I. We would always share the memory of the two men in their shallow grave.

Without another word from either of us, I began to churn. As the blade pushed through, the white cream swirled, twisting into graceful waves. I could hear Owen's voice as if he sat next to me. As if we were back in the butter room. "You're beautiful," he'd said.

I turned the handle faster. Griffin knelt, watching over my shoulder. The cows watched too. They even stopped flicking their tails. If this didn't work, all would be lost. I wouldn't be able to negotiate with King Elmer for my people's freedom. Griffin would have no reward coin to take back to Root. I closed my eyes, churning, churning, churning. Griffin grunted impatiently. One of the cows mooed. I squeezed my eyelids tighter, churning, churning, churning. *Please*, I thought. *Please let the magic work*. Then a warm feeling took hold, deep inside, spreading all over my body like sunshine. The warmth traveled down my arms and into my fingertips.

"It's changing color," Griffin said.

With a huge relieved sigh, I opened my eyes and watched as chocolate formed where cream had once been. Griffin didn't hesitate. Crouching beside the bucket, he dipped his finger and tasted. "How?" He tasted again. "But . . ." And again. "Nothing can taste this good." His eyes sparkled. "I feel different. I feel . . . happy. I want more." Then his eyes widened. "Is this some kind of spell? Is this black magic? Everyone in Root says you have black magic."

For the first time in my life, that didn't make me angry.

"I guess I do." I scooped out a bit and ate it. "But it's not black. It's brown."

Chapter Thirty-four

The one-eyed man didn't talk much during the journey, except to remind me numerous times that he was still planning on killing me. "Thanks for the advance notice," I grumbled. "Very considerate of you."

A chain still wound around our ankles, linking us together. Fortunately, the third member of our entourage sat between us—a human shield of sorts. The boy was a dirt-scratcher who'd lost his family in the flood. His hair was lighter than Emmeline's and streaked with copper strands, but still red enough to mark him from the Flatlands. I'd managed to get a few sentences from him. After the flood he'd left the Flatlands on foot, foraging for mushrooms and roots. Too young to fend for himself, he'd been arrested for stealing smoked pig's feet from a butcher. He cried the first day of our journey, then settled into quiet submission.

The one-eyed man, however, seethed like a caged bull. Listening to his threats was unpleasant enough, but looking at him was worse. Steady seepage from the hollow socket coated the lashes of his missing eye, gluing the lid shut. I tried to be friendly. I had enough on my mind without having to worry about being strangled in my sleep. "So, what brought you to this cage?" I asked, forcing a chipper tone to my words.

"Murder," he said. The response didn't surprise me, though I'd hoped it might be something tame like pickpocketing or littering. I didn't really want to know who he'd killed. And asking might piss him off. The dirt-scratcher boy pressed closer to me. Poor kid. Just like Emmeline, he'd been cast into a world he didn't know. And now he was chained to a murderer. And poor me. I'd started off trying to rescue a girl and now I was headed for hard labor in the deadly mineral fields.

Fortunately, my rib was fully healed and the knife wound had also healed. Days ago, I'd worked a blade beneath the stitches, pulling them free. But I couldn't pull free from the feeling of helplessness that descended over me. So I tried to distract myself with conversation. Asking about the Flatlands, I gradually coaxed the boy from his silence. "When the soldiers came, they took all the unmarried men to the mineral fields to fight in a war. They took my older brother. And now they're taking me. I don't know how to fight."

The way he rolled some of his letters brought Emmeline's voice to mind. "You won't have to fight," I told him. "There's no war."

"But the soldiers said—"

"They lied to you. We haven't been at war since my great-grandfather's generation. They took your people to work in the mineral fields, not to fight."

"I know how to work," he said with a relieved grin. "If we only have to work, then maybe I'll see my brother again."

"I hope so," I said, patting his bony shoulder. "Work is definitely better than war. And how bad can it be? We'll dig a bit, get some gold, dig a bit more." I didn't use the word "slave." Nor did I mention our impending death if we stayed in that poisonous place. Instead, I ventured into the subject that consumed me. "Do you come from the same village as Emmeline?" The boy shrugged. "She has a curled foot and walks with a limp."

"Oh, her. She lives in Root," he said. "I live in Seed. But everyone knows her. She's the unnatural girl. That's what people say. She has black magic."

"Why do they say that?"

"Because she was cast aside and she didn't die."

The one-eyed man turned his head toward us, the oozing hole glistening in the daylight. He sat quietly, listening.

"What do you mean she was cast aside?" I asked.

"When a babe is unwanted, it's left at the edge of the forest to die. My younger brother was unwanted because he was born too early. He died in the forest like he was supposed to."

"Wolves," the one-eyed man grumbled.

"Sometimes it's a spirit who takes the babe away," the boy said. It was the first time he'd spoken to our murdering companion. "Forest spirits eat human flesh."

I grimaced. Forest spirit or predator, it was a horrid way to die. "How did Emmeline survive?"

"Some cows saved her," the boy said. "That's why everyone calls her unnatural. She talks to cows. And they talk to her."

The images flashed in my mind—the riverbank, Emmeline's

half-drowned body, our missing cow standing over her as if guarding her from the vultures. Then there'd been the cows with their noses pressed against my bedroom window as if checking on Emmeline's recovery. And I'd never forget the moment when the cow who'd found her moseyed from the field to greet her and she'd thanked it. Could she have more magic in her besides the magic of chocolate? Why hadn't there been more time to talk to her? More time to get to know her?

I asked more questions about the Flatlands and its people. But our conversation was not appreciated by everyone. "Shut up!" the one-eyed man bellowed. As he stomped his foot, the chain tightened, burning my ankles. The boy pressed close to me again. "Or I'll shut you up!"

Enough said.

Chapter Thirty-five

I tossed the churning bucket and its chocolaty contents into a pond, hiding the evidence that the Milkmaid herself had traveled this way. Griffin unhitched the horses, leaving the baroness's carriage on the path. He lifted me onto one of the horses, then mounted the other. Twice since my journey downriver I'd sat on a horse's back, but each time there'd been someone with me. First when Owen brought me to his house, but that ride I didn't remember. Then with Peddler. I shuddered, recalling his bony arms wrapped around my waist and his sour breath on my neck.

"What's the problem?" Griffin asked. "Why are you just sitting there?"

"I can't ride like this," I complained. Because of my long dress, I had to sit with my legs draping over one side of the horse.

"Try." He slapped my horse's flank.

"I'm going to fall off!" I yelled, holding tight to the reins as the horse picked up speed and headed into the field. Griffin shouted instructions. But each gallop jostled me and I nearly slid off. How was I supposed to hang on? I yanked the reins until the horse stopped. "It's impossible to ride this way."

Pulling up alongside, Griffin glowered from beneath the rim of his knit hat. "It's not impossible. You're not trying."

"I am trying." But how pathetic was I? I couldn't run. I couldn't ride. Angry at myself, I lashed out. "If you're so smart, you try to ride in this dress!"

"Then take off the stupid dress," he said.

"What? You want me to ride in my underclothes?" He raised his eyebrows. "Forget that."

Eventually I got the feel for it, but only at a slow pace. Griffin didn't want to go back to the road so we cut across pastures, getting directions to the nearest village from a farmer. Griffin fumed with impatience, constantly looking over his shoulder and hollering at me to go faster. When we reached the village, I hid in the forest while he rode off to play the part of the soldier. It wasn't long before he returned with a bag full of stuff. "These are boy's clothes," he said, shoving the bag at me. "They should fit. Then you can ride like me."

I changed behind a tree. The shirt and vest fit fine. I'd never worn pants before. No girl in the Flatlands ever wore pants. My legs felt so light. "These are great," I said. It was easier to hide my limp under a skirt, but I didn't care about that. The freedom was wonderful. I spun around. "What do you think? Do I look like a boy?"

He reached into the bag and pulled out a knit hat. "Better get rid of that bonnet."

"Oh. Right."

While I tucked my hair into the hat, Griffin changed out of the soldier's clothing. He told me it was too dangerous to keep playing the part since everyone in Fishport now knew I was traveling with a soldier. "We can pretend we're brothers," I said when he'd finished.

"You still look like a girl," he said, staring at my bottom.

We hid our old clothing, including the soldier's sword and scabbard, beneath some shrubs deep in the forest. I felt terrible leaving Lara's dress behind. It was such a beautiful dress, meant to help her forget her disease. But it had served me well and for a brief moment I felt a sense of gratitude to Peddler. I tied the cloak he'd given me around my shoulders.

"Let's get out of here," Griffin said.

We rode the rest of the day, stopping occasionally to talk to other travelers. The road was called the Merchant's Highway and would lead us straight to Londwin City. The town ahead was called Lime. My face was plastered everywhere. WANTED: THE MILKMAID. Without the soldier's uniform, I wasn't sure how we were going to get food and a place to sleep. Griffin had only one coin—the same one he'd taken from the dead soldier. But Griffin could easily turn on the charm when he needed to. Even with the tight knit cap covering what remained of his hair, he was incredibly handsome. So once he'd spent the coin, a smile got us a loaf of bread from a baker's daughter. A kiss got us a ham shank from a butcher's wife. I'm not sure what got us the jug of ale, but the tavern girl was grinning like an idiot. Flirtation was Griffin's skill, no doubt about it. I admired his ability. It came so easily to him. He was the opposite of me. I'd never flirted in my life.

We ate our feast just outside the town wall. Small fires flickered down the Merchant's Highway as travelers set up their camps for the night.

"Why you?" Griffin asked, wiping his mouth on his sleeve.

I'd asked myself the same question over and over. Only one answer had ever come to mind. "Why not me?"

He could have listed all the reasons. But he didn't. "Can you do anything else magical?" he asked, looking into my eyes. I'd had ample opportunity to stare into those mossy green eyes on this journey. I'd seen fear, anger, even resentment in them. But at that moment I saw something new—admiration. "Can you cast other spells?"

"If I could cast spells, do you think I'd have this foot?" I shook my right foot, which I'd kept hidden in its boot during our entire time together.

He grabbed the last of the ham. After a long chew, he asked, "Does your foot hurt?"

"Aye," I said. "Almost all the time."

He chewed some more, then leaned against a tree trunk. "Do you ever think about what might have been?"

This question took me by surprise and my face went hot. *All of the time* would have been the honest answer. "It doesn't matter. What might have been doesn't matter."

"I've been doing a lot of thinking about what might have been," Griffin said. "If the soldiers hadn't come to Root, I'd be married. If the river hadn't flooded, I'd be living in my cottage with my new wife."

"Aye, you would." I reached under my knit cap and scratched my scalp. If only I could free my hair, just for a moment. All of Missus

Oak's hard work washing and brushing had gone to waste. My hair was once again a wild, knotted mess. "Who would it be?"

He shrugged. "I didn't have my heart set on anyone in particular."

"Really?"

"I wanted to wait, actually. But Mother insisted. I know they were all in love with me, but I didn't feel that way about any of them." He stared at me. "You know, I never really looked at you. I never noticed . . ." His sudden serious expression made me uncomfortable. His gaze traveled over my body.

I shifted my weight. "Did you know that no one else in Anglund has a husband market? It's another reason why they hate us. They think buying a husband is primitive."

"They can call us primitive all they want," he said with a sudden burst of anger. "But at least we don't enslave people. I hate them right back."

I felt Griffin's anger. They'd taken him against his will, just as Peddler had taken me. "Not everyone hates us," I said quietly.

"Oh really?" He pushed his knit cap off his forehead. "And who doesn't hate us dirt-scratchers?"

"Well, the Oak family. They helped me, didn't they?"

"That's one family in the whole of Anglund. That means nothing." He stretched out his legs. "This Owen, the one who read you the book. Is he their son?"

I glanced away.

"Look, Emmeline, you can ignore my questions all you want, but I'm not an idiot. I heard the way you said his name in your sleep. You've got your sights set on this fellow, don't you?" I looked down at my boots. "Put that idea out of your head right now, Emmeline Thistle. You hear what I'm telling you? Dirt-scratchers marry dirt-scratchers."

"Stop calling us that," I snapped. "That's their word for us. And it's ugly."

He slowly nodded. "You're right. But it's true what I'm saying. Flatlanders should marry Flatlanders. That's the way it's always been."

"Have you forgotten that no one back home would have married me?"

"Well, maybe not the *old* you."

"Doesn't matter," I told him. "Owen's dead."

Griffin offered no soothing words, but I expected none. Instead, he tossed the ham bone aside and stood. Then, rubbing his chin, he spoke calmly. "If you want to get married, you should bid on me at the next husband market."

I cringed, expecting him to burst out laughing at his joke. But there'd been no hint of humor or sarcasm in his words.

He looked down at me. "I'm serious, Emmeline. If you keep making chocolate, you're going to be the richest girl in the Flatlands. You'll be able to bid the most coin. That will make my parents very happy."

"Your parents? But they despise me. Your father yells at me every time the cows wander to my house."

He stuck his hands into his pockets. "So?"

"So?" I scrambled to my feet. "Maybe you haven't noticed,

Griffin, but your sister throws rocks at me, and you, well, you were never nice to me, either."

"Aye, but now you're going to be rich." He smiled. "You'd be foolish not to bid on me. Every girl wants to bid on me. I'm the handsomest man in all the Flatlands. Maybe in all of Anglund."

I rolled my eyes.

"Think about it. With your chocolate and my good looks, we could launch our own empire. Forget about King Elmer. We don't need him."

"But we do need him. He's got our people, remember?"

"Oh. Right." His chest deflated. Then he pulled his hat back down his forehead.

I thought my life couldn't get any more amazing. Now something else unbelievable had happened. For a brief moment, Griffin Boar had imagined me as his wife. I couldn't help the satisfied smirk that spread across my face. He glared at me. "By the way," he grumbled, "you reek."

"So do you."

We decided not to journey any farther that evening. The horses were tired and my legs ached from the ride. Griffin set the saddles on the ground. We could have hidden deep in the woods but Griffin thought it would be more dangerous in there, what with wild animals and thieves. Sleeping near the road, where other weary travelers had set up camp, seemed best since there was protection in numbers. Besides, no one was looking for a pair of brothers so we felt relatively safe in the open.

As I was about to lay my head on the saddle, a wagon rolled

past. I might not have paid any attention except that the wagon carried an enormous cage. Two men sat inside the cage, their shoulders slumped. Another man lay facedown on the floor, his brown curly hair catching my eye. Owen's hair looked like that. *Stop thinking about Owen*! I told myself. *It does you no good.*

One of the caged men raised his head, and when he did so, long red locks cascaded over his shoulders. I was about to cry out when Griffin said, "Hold your tongue." He'd noticed the boy, too.

A humpbacked man and a soldier sat on the driver's bench. They paid no notice, but we couldn't tear our gaze away from the wagon as it rolled down the road with one of our own. "Did you recognize him?"

"No," Griffin said.

"Where are they taking him?"

"Same place as the others. But we can't help him. Not yet."

Just like the day at the husband market, I felt totally helpless, watching as they carted another one of my people away. Griffin was right. This was not yet the time.

But it soon would be.

Part Seven

Queen

Chapter Thirty-six

We smelled Londwin City long before it came into view. The scent reminded me of autumn days in Root when spawning fish were caught in the river and hung over the fire to cure. The smoky scent grew stronger as we neared, and a dark cloud bloomed in the sky. I wondered if the city was on fire. But no fiery glow appeared.

Then the chimneys came into view, hundreds of them, standing on the horizon like a metal forest. Streams of smoke spouted from the chimney tops like dragon's breath, blocking the sunlight. I slowed my horse, hesitation grabbing hold of me and squeezing hard. We'd come so far, but the thought of actually facing King Elmer sent my heart racing. Griffin also slowed, staring slack-jawed at the massive stone wall that surrounded the city. "We're here," he said. Was that fear in his voice?

"We're here," I echoed, wiping my sweating palms on my pants. I pulled my hat low, as did Griffin, making sure every bit of hair was hidden.

Soldiers stood along the top of the wall, yellow stalks in a world of gray. A pair stood guard at the massive iron gate. "Where you from?" one asked as he stepped in front of our horses.

"We're from Fishport." Griffin did a pretty good job hiding his accent. He pointed at me. "That's my brother."

"You here for the Bestowing of Coal?" The soldier scratched beneath his feathered helmet.

"Yeah," Griffin said. "That's why we're here."

"You'll have to pay the horse tax if you want to ride inside the gates. Covers the cost of cleaning up their dung."

"We can't pay," Griffin said.

"Then leave the horses or go away. The choice is yours."

At this point I could have made my true identity known. But Griffin and I had discussed this. What would keep one of these soldiers from claiming the reward, leaving Griffin in the cold? We had to get closer to the king before I revealed myself. Griffin would take the reward back to Root.

"These horses belong to the Baroness of Salt," I told the soldier. "Can you make sure she gets them?"

"The king takes ownership of all horses," he said. "That's the law."

So we left the horses. Someday I'd pay the baroness back. The soldier led them to a fenced yard where others had also left their horses. Then Griffin and I walked through the open gates into Londwin City.

We entered a world of stone. Narrow gray buildings lined the cobblestone road, their chimneys hard at work. Strange stone creatures with pointed ears and forked tongues stared down at us from the roofs. It felt as if their carved eyes followed our every move. With each hesitant step we kicked up soot. It covered everything and didn't take long to settle onto Griffin's hat and face. I wiped some from my lips. My eyes watered as we passed through drifts of smoke. Though I knew it was mid-morning, the looming darkness gave the city a feeling of doom, as if the storm of the century was on its way.

A ditch, filled with thick brown sludge, stretched alongside the road. I plugged my nose. In Root we buried our sewage in deep holes. Here they let it run through the city. Disgusting. Seemed odd that they collected a tax to clean up horse dung. Why not clean up the rest of the gunk?

"Where is everyone?" Griffin asked. "Why is this place so quiet?"

Except for the soldiers back at the gates we hadn't seen a soul. Soot blackened the windows so we couldn't see inside any of the buildings. A shiver ran down my spine as I looked up and into the glaring eyes of a stone creature. Its sharp teeth protruded from its chiseled mouth, and it looked like it might leap from the roof and bite me. I picked up the pace, with Griffin, for the first time, at my heels.

When we turned a corner, the cobblestone street branched in three directions. Fortunately a signpost, with a painting of a golden crown and arrow pointing to the center road, marked our destination. As we passed more gray buildings, the road gradually widened and another scent greeted us—the stench of unwashed people. Griffin and I would fit right in. As we turned the next corner, the stench rushed at us like a bull in heat. I breathed through my mouth, which helped a bit.

A crowd had gathered—more people than I could ever count. They faced away from us, looking toward a golden fence that, even in the dusky light, gleamed like the rising sun. "What's going on?" I asked a woman.

"Bestowing of Coal," she said, clutching a reed basket. Soot had settled into her wrinkles so it looked as if someone had drawn all over her face. A thick line of soot ran down the center part in her hair. She didn't look at me, her gaze fixed beyond the fence where the golden towers of the royal palace disappeared into the smoky sky.

"Follow me," Griffin said. Then, in classic Griffin Boar style, he told the people who blocked our path, "Move out of my way!"

As he pushed through, I followed. With bodies pressed so closely together, no one seemed to notice my limp, the only part of my identity I couldn't hide. No one complained as Griffin elbowed and shoved his way deeper into the crowd. The people stared at the fence with blank expressions, like owlettes dazed by a full moon. I plugged my nose. Didn't anyone in this city take a bath?

The people of Londwin were oddly dressed. I'd expected that those who lived in the royal city would wear fancy clothes. But they were as ragged as anyone from the Flatlands, maybe more so, with loose hems and ripped sleeves. Dark stains covered their clothes, which were made from cheap, coarse, colorless fabrics. Worse, though, was the hunger that revealed itself in their hollowed cheeks and dark circled eyes. We Flatlanders were familiar with bouts of famine, but we looked robust in comparison. Griffin was twice as wide as any man here and a good head taller. How could people who lived this close to the king know hunger? And why were they all holding empty baskets?

When we finally reached the edge of the crowd, I took a deep breath. The fence was only an arm's length away. And just beyond, across a golden courtyard, stood the palace.

A man scurried along the fence, wiping soot from the golden posts with a rag. Another man stood at the top of a ladder, polishing the posts. Back at the dairy, Missus Oak showed me a bowl that was plated in gold. She said it had been handed down through her family and was one of her most precious possessions. But here was an entire fence made of gold. Though the royal palace was built of stone, the windowsills and balcony railings were golden, as were the towers and roofs. Two golden swan-shaped sculptures stood on either side of a massive golden door. As an old man with a hunched spine polished one of the swans, a bitter taste filled my mouth and it wasn't from the soot-filled air. Is this why my people were slaving in the mineral fields? So King Elmer could live in a golden world?

"How do you want to do this?" Griffin asked. A line of soldiers blocked the entrance to the palace courtyard.

He was asking my advice? *Everything* in my world had changed.

"Tell them we're here to see the king," I said.

We held each other's gaze for a moment. I couldn't hide all my fear, but neither could he. He had deserted the king's "army." If his true identity were discovered, he'd be hanged. When I reached out and squeezed his hand, he didn't pull away. "You can still leave."

"No. We're the only hope for our families." Then his eyes flashed and he spun around. "Hey," he called to one of the soldiers. "We're here to see the king." The closest soldier stepped forward.

"No one sees the king."

"It's important," Griffin said. "We need to—"

The soldier pointed his sword at Griffin's throat. "No one sees the king without a royal invitation."

"You don't understand," I said. I smiled sweetly, even though I was so scared I felt like I might vomit. "The king will want to see me. I'm—"

A horn blasted, startling me silent. Murmuring arose, the crowd waking from its daze. "Coal, coal, coal," voices whispered. The people raised their baskets above their soot-coated heads. "Coal, coal, coal."

I pressed against Griffin, watching over his shoulder as a wagon, pulled by a glossy black horse, appeared around the side of the palace. Five men, dressed head to toe in black and carrying shovels, ran behind the wagon. The horse stopped in the center of the courtyard. A hill of small black rocks filled the wagon's bed. "Bestow the coal, bestow the coal," the crowd chanted, voices rising with excitement. They began to push forward. "Bestow the coal."

I tried to stand my ground but the crowd's momentum swept me up and moved me into the courtyard. Memories of being carried away by the river washed over me and I panicked. "Griffin!" I yelled. He grabbed me around the waist and pulled me from the current.

As the people of Londwin City held out their baskets, the

black-clad men filled them with shovelfuls of coal. Children grabbed stray bits that tumbled from the shovels. But the coal quickly disappeared and most still held empty baskets. "There's not enough for everyone!" someone shouted.

"We need more!" another voice yelled.

One of the black-clad men stood in the wagon, his hands cupped around his mouth as he hollered at the crowd. "There's no more! Go home!"

"We paid our coal tax."

"How can we cook without coal?"

"There's no more!" the man repeated.

Fights broke out as those without coal tried to take baskets away from those who'd been lucky enough to be first to the wagon. Soldiers tried to stop the fighting, but it spread as quickly as smoke.

"They won't notice us," Griffin said. "Let's go." We crept around the wagon. Though the palace door waited just across the courtyard, the distance felt like a vast chasm. I cursed my foot for slowing us down.

"Halt!" A soldier leaped in front of us, his sword drawn, his helmet askew.

"I need to see the king," I pleaded. "It's very important." Screams and shouts erupted behind us as more people joined the fighting.

"No one from the outside gets to see the king without a royal invitation," the soldier said. "Now get back to where you belong."

We'd come all this way. With each passing moment, time was running out for my father. Each moment in the mineral field meant another breath of the poisonous yellow air Griffin had told me about. The guard pressed the sword's tip against the soft spot at the base of Griffin's neck. "Get back!"

I knew no words would convince the soldier. So, with a sweeping gesture, I pulled the cap off my head. As my hair fell free, the soldier's eyes widened. He gasped. Silence descended over the courtyard. I knew, without turning around, that everyone was looking at me.

"You're—"

"That's right," I said, holding myself as straight as possible. "I'm the Milkmaid and . . ." I tried to remember exactly what the new poster said. "The king is expecting me."

Griffin smirked as the soldier lowered his sword.

Chapter Thirty-seven

In the Flatlands we are told that after death the Thief of Sleep leads us to the everafter where all is peaceful and beautiful. As Griffin and I walked down a grand hallway, I could have sworn we'd entered the everafter, even though I didn't remember dying and even though our guide was dressed as a royal soldier. But still, the place felt not of this world.

The white marble floor was perfectly clean, which is probably why a servant had washed the soot from our boots before entering. Our footsteps echoed off a ceiling painted like the sky, complete with puffy white clouds. Two more golden swans waited at the end of the hallway, a golden door set between then. The soldier whispered to another soldier who stood outside the door. They both pointed to my hair. Then, after gawking at me, the new soldier opened the door. I squinted as beams of dazzling light shot out, as if they'd been held prisoner in the room beyond and were eager to fly away.

The room we stepped into was so big and so crowded I couldn't see where it ended. Golden wheels, each holding dozens of lighted candles, hung from a domed ceiling. Spicy perfume replaced the smoky, unwashed stench of the city. I wanted to plug my nose but didn't, since that might offend the people who'd stopped dancing and were now staring at me.

These were not the tattered, hungry masses like those in the courtyard fighting for chunks of coal. The people inside this sparkling room were an entirely different sort. White powder covered the faces of both men and women. Red stain colored their lips as if they'd all just gorged on strawberries. The women had painted red circles on each of their cheeks and wore feathered hats. Their long dresses dipped so low their breasts nearly spilled out. And the dresses were cinched so tightly at the waist I don't know how they were able to breathe. The men had thick sideburns, trimmed in different shapes. Their shirts were covered in ruffles and their pants reached to their nipples. How did they walk in those long pointed shoes?

The music stopped and the musicians, who sat in a balcony, leaned over the golden railing to stare at me. "Red hair," people whispered to one another. The soldier who'd led us inside cleared his throat. Then he raised his hand, and as he did so, the crowd parted down the middle, revealing a checkered path. I gulped. The path ended at a little stage where two golden chairs perched. In those chairs, candlelight bouncing off their jeweled crowns, sat King Elmer and Queen Beatrice.

The soldier whispered to me. "Call them Your Majesties."

Then he motioned for me to walk down the path. But he blocked Griffin with his sword. "Hey," Griffin said. "I'm with her." The soldier shook his head.

"I'll be okay," I whispered to Griffin. The deafening silence caught my whisper and carried it around the hall like a whirlpool carries a fish.

"She'll be okay," people whispered.

"Stay here," I told Griffin. "Don't go anywhere."

"Who's that?" a voice bellowed. The question shot down the checkered path. All eyes, including mine, darted to the end of the path where King Elmer stomped his foot. "What's happening down there? Come closer, boy, so we can hear you."

Powdered faces turned back to me. Painted eyebrows raised, reddened lips pursed. I ran my hand over my tangled hair, my only evidence that I was the wanted Milkmaid. Then a sudden rush of excitement made me smile. It felt good to not hide myself. *It's me, Emmeline*, I wanted to shout. My fingers wiggling with anticipation, I began the long trek down the checkered path, my boots echoing with my uneven steps. Gazes dropped immediately from my face to my right foot. No one said a word. *Breathe*, I told myself. Wave after wave of perfume tickled my nostrils. After what seemed the longest walk of my life, I stood before the king and queen of Anglund.

I'd seen a painting of King Elmer in our tax-collector's office. I'd gone there many times to deliver our land tax. But the king who sat on this throne looked nothing like the king in the painting. In person he was not as . . . well, not as handsome.

King Elmer's nose took up most of his face. His bottom

drooped over the sides of his throne, and his belly was as bloated as a pregnant donkey's. His crown sat on his nearly bald head, a single patch of white hair sprouting in the center. He was a man of many chins and grayish, doughy skin.

It surprised me how different the queen was from the king. I'd never seen a portrait of her, nor had I ever heard anyone speak of her. She was the most beautiful woman I'd ever seen, even with the white face powder and painted cheeks. Flickers of candlelight caught in her black hair, which draped over her shoulders. She pressed her long fingertips together and watched me from beneath black eyelashes.

Not knowing what to do, I bowed. Then I bowed again. King Elmer squinted at me over the top of his bulbous nose. "What is the matter with your foot?" he asked.

Fabric crinkled as people pressed closer to the stage. "Your Majesty," I said. "My foot is curled."

"Curled?" the king asked. Then he slapped the back of the man standing closest to him. "This stupid boy curled his foot." As the king laughed, the crowd broke into laughter, which stopped at the exact moment the king's laughter stopped.

The queen cleared her throat. "He is not a boy," she said, her voice soft and sweet.

"Not a boy?" the king asked. He drummed his fingers on his belly. "He's wearing pants."

The queen slipped her fingers into her bodice and pulled out a pair of spectacles. Holding the lenses to her eyes, she peered at me, her gaze traveling from my scalp to the tips of my hair. A slight upturn of her mouth was her only reaction. With a wave of her hand, a soldier scurried to her side. "Take her to my chambers," she ordered. "Immediately."

"But I need to speak to King Elmer," I said as the soldier grabbed my arm. "He's offered a reward for me." The king paid me no mind. A platter of honey cakes now balanced on his belly, and he licked his fingers happily. "I'm the Milkmaid," I told him. "Your Majesty, I'm the Milkmaid."

"What's happened to the music?" the king asked, his mouth full of cake.

The queen snapped her fingers at the soldier, who tightened his grip on my arm. This was not going the way I'd planned. I twisted around, searching for Griffin. But the crowd had closed the gap and I couldn't see over the tops of the feathered hats. "Griffin!" I called. The soldier pulled me behind the little stage. "Griffin!"

"Emmeline!" he called from the other end of the throne room. Murmurs arose. "Move out of my way. Take your hands off me! Emmeline!"

The queen rose from her throne and clapped her hands. "Resume the music," she said. "Resume the dancing."

Strings plucked, drums thumped, a horn's melancholy notes filled the air. Griffin's voice disappeared. I called out to him again and again but knew he couldn't hear. As I was whisked into another hallway, a terrible feeling overtook me.

That I'd seen the last of Griffin Boar.

Chapter Thirty-eight

"Why can't my friend come with me?" I asked. The soldier followed behind me as the queen took the lead, her skirt dragging along the floor. Strands of jewels hanging from her belt swung back and forth. She walked with confident steps, holding herself straight and tall. Though I'd only been in the king's presence a few moments, I'd already figured out who was really in power.

"Do not worry about your friend. He shall be treated well," she said.

The hallway turned right, then right again. We passed two people who were dressed in black, like the men who'd been shoveling coal. One carried a tray of food, another carried a bucket and mop. They stepped aside and bowed as the queen strode by.

The hallway opened onto a golden bridge, which crossed another enormous room. A woman dressed in black polished the bridge with a rag. Midway across the bridge, the queen stopped and peered over the railing. "What is that contraption?" she called out.

I hadn't realized we were so high above the floor until I looked over the railing. Far below, two men tinkered with something I'd never seen before. It was some kind of enormous woven basket. Ropes connected the basket to a pile of fabric.

"It's a surprise," one of the men replied as he tugged on a rope. His black hair was tied back with a bow, but I couldn't get a good look at his face. Neither man was dressed like the people in the throne room or like the servants. They wore normal pants and billowy white shirts.

Queen Beatrice made a *humph* sound, then resumed our walk. The bridge led to another hallway where, after a few more twists and turns, a servant opened another golden door, and I followed the queen into her chambers. I knew it was her chambers because paintings of her hung on all the walls. With a clap of her royal hands, a group of servants scuttled from the room. The queen bolted the door.

I took a long breath. I was alone with the queen of Anglund.

She placed her crown on a glass table. Smoothing her skirt as she did so, she sat at the end of a long yellow couch. Motioning with a graceful wave of her hand, she said, "Sit."

I sank into the soft cushions at the other end of the couch. Griffin was probably worried. What if the soldier had sent him back into the city streets? "What about my friend?" I asked, but the queen held up her hand. I closed my mouth, waiting, wondering.

She folded her hands on her lap and cocked her head, her

expression as serious as the expressions in her portraits. I found myself looking into eyes as green as Griffin's. "Do tell us about yourself."

The queen's perfume smelled like the honeysuckle that wound around the willow trees back home—a comforting scent that helped calm my pounding heart. "Your Majesty," I said. "My name is Emmeline Thistle. I'm from . . ." I hesitated. "I'm from the Flatlands. I know it's against the law to leave the Flatlands, but I didn't want to leave. The river flooded and carried me out."

She raised her eyebrows. "Continue."

"I came to see the king because he offered a reward for the Milkmaid." I pushed back my shoulders and sat as straight as I could. "I'm the Milkmaid. And the man who brought me here is waiting to claim the reward."

As Queen Beatrice took a quick, excited breath, her small chest squeezed against the dress's stiff bodice. "If you are lying to us, you will be executed."

"I'm not lying, Your Majesty. I can make chocolate. All I need is some fresh cream and a churning bucket."

A cluster of eavesdropping servants scurried away from the door when the queen threw it open. "Bring us a churning bucket and cream!" she called. I waited on the couch. Gone was the fear that I wouldn't be able to make chocolate. I'd make it and I'd win her over. And then I'd begin my negotiations, the way Lara had taught me. "And bring us the Royal Secretary!"

As the queen's orders echoed down the hallway, gold and silver objects glinted around me—vases, statues, candleholders. Each of these objects was a reminder of my father's enslavement. Soon, very soon, he'd be freed.

The Royal Secretary quickly arrived, along with the bucket and cream. A man of middle years, his ruffled shirt collar reached to his powdered chin. He'd tucked a white quill behind his ear.

I sat on the marble floor of the queen's chamber and churned as fast as I could. How easy it was to sit in a pair of pants. I never wanted to wear a skirt again. Even with the threat of execution hanging in the air, I knew the magic would enter the churning bucket and the chocolate would appear. I closed my eyes, willing the warmth to work its way down my arms. It did, tingling as it hit the tips of my fingers. At the sound of the secretary's gasp, I opened my eyes. Then I pushed the bucket until it rested at his yellow shoes. He peered down at the brown sludge as if looking at the sewage that ran alongside the city streets.

"Taste it," Queen Beatrice ordered.

Pulling a silver spoon from the pocket of his high-waisted pants, the secretary bent over, scooped a bit of chocolate, and tasted. The reaction was as expected—soft, satisfied sounds followed by another bite, then another.

"Well?" the queen asked.

The Royal Secretary straightened himself and said, "Your Majesty, I do believe, without a doubt, that this is the most delicious concoction I have ever tasted."

"We shall be the judge of what is or isn't most delicious." The queen had her own silver spoon. She tasted the chocolate, then ate five spoonfuls in a row, her serious expression unwavering. Without a word, the queen slowly crossed the room and stood before a window, looking out at the horizon of gray buildings. I got to my feet, waiting for her reaction. Why wasn't she speaking? Was it possible she didn't like chocolate? Just when I couldn't hold my tongue any longer, she spoke.

"We knew this would happen one day," she said, clasping her hands behind her back. "We knew the chocolate would once again take its rightful place."

"Rightful place?" I stepped forward.

She spun on her heels, her jeweled chains clinking. "This is where chocolate belongs, here in the royal palace. It is our family, our bloodline that created chocolate. Our great-great-great-great-grandmother, Her Majesty Queen Margaret, possessed the magic, granted to her in a sacred dream." She pointed to a portrait of a woman whose black hair hung in two thick braids. I'd mistaken it as a portrait of a young Queen Beatrice. "But the magic was taken away by a Kell curse."

I took a sharp breath. No one ever called us Kell. We weren't allowed to speak the word.

The queen's voice turned shrill. "A Kell took the magic away and now a Kell has brought the magic back. It is the just end to an unjust history, is it not, Royal Secretary?"

He'd been gorging on the chocolate. He nodded and said, with a full mouth, "You are always correct, Your Majesty."

She tossed the spoon aside and stood before me, a good head taller. Her eyes flashed, her breathing quickened. "You will live here for the rest of your life, dirt-scratcher girl. You will make chocolate for us. You will make chocolate for no one else."

It wasn't an invitation, but I already knew I'd never leave this place. She wanted my magic. This was it. "I will happily make chocolate for you, Your Majesty," I said, trying to hide the quaver in my voice. "But the chocolate comes with a price."

"A *price*?" When she repeated that word, the Royal Secretary's hand flitted to his mouth and he gasped. The queen folded her arms. "You are referring to the reward promised by our husband, the king?"

"Aye, Your Majesty. My friend is waiting to be rewarded the five thousand coin. He brought me to Londwin City. His name is Griffin Boar and he is the reason I arrived here safely."

Queen Beatrice nodded. "Very well. Let it never be said that our husband keeps not his promises. Make it so," she said, waving a hand at her secretary.

"Your Majesty?" He fiddled with his collar, leaving a chocolate stain along one of the ruffled edges. "Surely not *five thousand* coin?"

She raised a single eyebrow. "Are you questioning our husband's judgment?"

"Never would I do so." He bowed apologetically. "But—"

"Pay the friend in the . . . *usual* manner," the queen told him.

"Ah, yes." He nodded. "I shall do so immediately." And with that, the Royal Secretary hurried from the room, disrupting the growing group of eavesdroppers huddling outside the door.

"Now, dirt-scratcher girl," the queen said as the door closed. "Exactly how much chocolate can you make in one day?"

I couldn't believe I was about to say what I was about to say. I gripped the armrest of a golden chair to hold myself steady. Lara's instructions flowed through my mind. *You never get what you don't ask for.* "The price is not paid in full. There are a few more things I want."

A red blotch appeared beneath the queen's powdered chest. "Want?" she sputtered. "*You* want something from *us*?" Her green gaze burned as hot as dragon's blood.

Though I wanted to with all my heart, I did not step back. "The unmarried men in my village were taken against their will to fight in the king's army. My father, Murl Thistle, was with them. But I have learned there is no war. My people are working as slaves in the mineral fields."

The queen returned to the yellow couch, once again arranging her skirt as she sat. "There are no slaves in Anglund. Slavery is against our husband's law."

"They were taken. I saw them taken," I insisted. "And I know they are being forced to work."

"We don't see how they are being forced." She fiddled with one of her rings. "But if what you say is true, then there has been an unfortunate breakdown in communication."

"I want them freed," I said. "I want them sent home."

"This is a simple matter. We shall issue a proclamation immediately that any dirt-scratcher who wishes to leave the mineral fields may do so."

"I'd like my father brought here so he can live with me."

She curled her stained lip. "Another dirt-scratcher living here? Is this necessary?"

"It is."

"Very well. We shall send for him." She leaned back against

the couch cushions, tapping her pointed shoe on the floor. "Is there anything else?"

I slid my hands into my pants pockets and considered for a moment whether I was pushing this too far. I had taken her patience to the brink and wouldn't have been surprised if she ordered my immediate execution. Surely the Oaks would do everything they could to find Peddler. But then Owen's face filled my mind. Before I made my final request, I remembered Lara's instructions. *Always include something you're willing to give up. That makes them believe they've won something.*

"There are two more things."

She clenched her jaw. "We wait with bated breath."

"There is a murderer by the name of Peddler. He killed a Wander boy named Owen Oak. I want you to send soldiers to find him and, once he's found, take him to Wander so he will hang for his crime."

She cocked her head. "Who was this Owen Oak to you?"

"A friend," I said, looking away. "Just a friend."

"And the last demand, dirt-scratcher girl?"

"That you stop calling me dirt-scratcher girl. My name is Emmeline."

She darted to her feet. "You expect us to call a dirt-scratcher by name?"

This time I retreated, stepping back with a submissive bow of my head. "I did not mean to upset Your Majesty. I am willing to drop my last demand."

She strode up to me, then reached out and brushed a finger

over my cheek. Her voice returned to its sweeter tone. "Who would have guessed that a dirt-scratcher girl would prove to be a good negotiator? We admire your determination. Except for your name, you shall have everything you've asked for. But in return, you must swear your loyalty to us. You will become our Royal Chocolatier until the day you die. Do you swear your service and loyalty?"

"I swear," I said.

She gently touched a lock of my hair, then pulled her hand away quickly as if she'd touched poison. "Never again make demands of us," she warned. "We can make your life pleasant or we can make your life unpleasant. Never forget this."

Suddenly I felt as if a carpet had been rolled around me and I was back in Peddler's wagon.

Chapter Thirty-nine

The road to the mineral fields perched high above the sea and was barely wide enough for the wagon to maneuver. Sheer mountain walls rose on one side, while a steep cliff dropped to the ocean on the other side. Dizziness rippled over me as I clutched the bars of the cage and looked down at the crashing waves. The wagon's wheels rolled close to the cliff's edge. We'd meet certain death if the horse lost its footing. Why hadn't I ever learned to swim?

"How much farther?" I asked our driver, a hunchback with a sour odor. The soldier who sat next to the driver delivered a sharp jab with the end of his sword through the cage bars, right between my shoulder blades. I expected a laugh from my one-eyed companion, but he glared at the soldier.

"Leave him be," he growled. "He's mine to kill."

Why the one-eyed man hadn't killed me yet was beyond me. He'd had plenty of opportunity. He could reach across and wrap those gargantuan fingers around my neck and I'd have no way to escape.

"You know," I said, thinking maybe I could defuse the situation. "Instead of killing me, could you teach me some of your barefist maneuvers?"

He raised his huge head. "You trying to be funny?"

"No," I insisted. "I'm serious. You're a great fighter. The only reason you . . ." It would be best to avoid the word *lost*. "Only reason you *tripped* was because you'd been drinking. I know you would have beaten me. Look at the size of your hands. I'd have no chance against fists that size." I didn't point out the scar that glowed on his forehead—a result of our first fight. The flattery did its job and the man's scowl softened.

"You were lucky I was drunk," he said.

"Agreed."

He leaned across the dirt-scratcher boy, who whimpered as if he feared being crushed. "You and me, we can work together," the one-eyed man whispered. "That's what I've been thinking. As soon as they let us out of this cage, you take the driver and I'll take the soldier."

Escape was part of my plan too. I'd thought about waiting until I'd found Emmeline's father. I'd tell him how his daughter had become the most famous girl in all of Anglund and that she had her mind set on buying his freedom. But now that the king himself wanted Emmeline, she'd have no problem negotiating her father's freedom. So if my opportunity to escape came before I met him, well, then so be it. No one was negotiating my freedom.

"We can't escape with these chains around us," I told the one-eyed man.

He leaned closer, his breath as rank as his personality. "After we kill them, we'll get the key."

"There's no key," the boy said, his voice muffled by the one-eyed man's back.

"What are you talking about?" I asked.

He peered around the gigantic shoulder. "I heard the soldier say he doesn't have the key. It's to keep us from escaping. Someone at the mineral fields has it."

"We'll have to wait until we get to the mineral fields," I told the one-eyed man. He grunted, then nodded. I'd made a deal to help him, so that probably meant he wouldn't be killing me anytime soon. Nice to know.

The road took a sharp turn away from the sea, and soon after, the wagon rolled to a stop. The soldier leaped off the driver's bench and unlocked the cage. "Out," he ordered as the gate swung open. With the chain dragging between us, we three shuffled through the gate and jumped onto the ground.

"Look," the dirt-scratcher boy whispered.

Fear gripped my gut. What stretched before us was born from a nightmare.

We stood at the edge of a vast and deep chasm, within which the entire town of Wander could have fit six times over. Mountains ringed the chasm. Yellow air hovered within. No trees grew here, no shrubs or grasses. Rock and dirt ruled this place. Far below, a few buildings stood in a cluster. Movement caught my eye. I squinted into the haze. Was that a line of people? From this far up they looked like insects. I couldn't tell the color of their hair. Maybe Emmeline's father was in that line.

"Walk," the soldier ordered, pointing to a trail.

"If you want us to walk, shouldn't you take off these chains?" I asked, just in case the boy was wrong and the soldier did possess a key.

"Chains don't come off until you're in the pit." The end of his sword greeted me just behind the knee. "Walk!"

The trail was deadly steep, just a series of narrow switchbacks cut into the mountain wall. Having the one-eyed man take the lead didn't give me much confidence. His footsteps were clumsy, his center of balance somewhere in his chest. At each sharp switchback I feared the top-heavy oaf would topple over. If the half-starved dirt-scratcher boy fell, we could easily pull him back to safety. But if the one-eyed man fell, we'd all meet our end at the bottom of the pit.

"What's your name?" I asked the boy, trying to take my mind off the danger.

"Billy. My name is Billy Weed." A quaver broke his voice.

"Don't worry, Billy Weed. We're not going to fall." Had I managed to sound confident? Because I wasn't.

With cautious footsteps, I followed. Rocks broke free beneath my steps, tumbling into the void. At the fourth turn I looked back. The soldier and driver watched our progress from the top of the trail. Guess they weren't going to visit the lovely land that lay below. The soldier, who was drinking from a jug, didn't seem too concerned that we'd escape. There was nowhere to go but down.

That's when I stumbled. Distracted by my thoughts, I'd stepped off the trail. Teetering at the edge, I waved my arms, desperately trying to regain my balance. "Hey!" Billy cried out. "He's gonna fall!" The yellow air waited to welcome me into its stagnant folds. So this was how it was going to end? I cursed and just as the ground beneath my feet gave way, a hand reached out and pulled me to safety.

"Thanks," I said, looking up at the soggy lid of the one-eyed man. I wasn't stupid enough to believe he'd saved me for any altruistic reason. By saving me, he'd saved himself. But I was still grateful.

We trudged our way downward. I never looked over my shoulder again, my gaze focused on my feet. Every muscle in my legs ached, the chain heavy around my ankles. As we descended the air thickened with floating specks. A bitter taste invaded my mouth. Billy coughed. The world had turned yellow. Even the one-eyed man, paces ahead of me, took on a yellowish tint through the hazy air. Switchback after switchback we hiked and then, finally, we stepped onto flat ground.

"Only three of you?" a soldier asked as he walked toward us. He was bare-chested, his swan-crested tunic tied around his waist. His skin glistened with grime and sweat. Who could blame him for the relaxed appearance? It was hot as hell down there. The yellow air seemed to catch the sun and amplify it. "Don't know how they expect to find gold if they don't send more men," he complained, rubbing the back of his neck. He looked Billy up and down. "What am I supposed to do with you? You're too scrawny to dig."

"If he can't dig, then why not let him go?" I asked.

The soldier laughed. "That's a good one." Then he furrowed

his brow. "You two ain't dirt-scratchers. What'd you do to get sent to this hole?"

"I met the wrong tax-collector," I said.

He nodded. "And you?" he asked the one-eyed man. "What'd you do?"

"I killed a man in a barefist fight," he answered between clenched teeth.

So that's what happened. A punch to the windpipe could have done it, or a neck that snapped on impact. But the question lingered—had it been an accident?

"Barefist?" The soldier's eyes widened. "We got a fight circle here. The winner gets extra food. You interested?"

The one-eyed man spat onto the dusty ground. "I'm always interested in fighting."

I didn't volunteer my services. Not yet. Best to wait and check out the situation.

A cart rolled by, pulled by a man who had lost patches of his black hair. The man's gaze was downcast, his steps slow and heavy. Four bodies lay in the cart, none red-haired. "How'd they die?" I asked the soldier.

"Don't live long working in a place like this. Wet lung gets them eventually. It'll get us all."

I could already feel the floating particles working their way down my throat. I tried spitting them out, but they returned with each new breath. "How long does it take to get wet lung?"

"Depends. Some men live a few months, others a year or two." He held out his hand to me. "Name's Wolf. That's what you call

me. We got no formalities down here in the mineral fields. What're your names?"

I shook his hand. He seemed a friendly fellow, though I don't see how anyone could be cheerful in this wretched place. "Owen."

"Billy."

The one-eyed man hesitated. Then he grunted, "Henry."

"Didn't have you pegged as a Henry," Soldier Wolf said with a laugh. "Well, better get you started on your work. Come with me."

The chain dragged across the rocks as we followed. Steam rose from holes in the ground. The scent of boiled eggs stank up the air. My gaze darted here and there, looking for any possible means of escape. The path we'd taken appeared to be the only entrance and exit. That would prove problematic. But no one stood guard at the path so that was in my favor.

Six soldiers, all shirtless, stood at the side of a building in a patch of shade. They paid no attention to us, their shoulders slumped with weary surrender. I wiped a bead of sweat as it rolled down my neck. "Why are you here?" I asked Wolf.

"I got reassigned cause I broke some laws." He shot me a wicked smile. "I let a few people get away with not paying the king's taxes. Well, maybe it was more than a few." He spat out a wad of phlegm. "They'll be tossing my dead body into the pit just like those other poor bastards, unless I can figure a way to get back into the king's favor."

We headed toward another building, its walls made from thin sheets of pounded metal. Another group of soldiers mingled at the door. Armed with swords and whips, they watched us warily from beneath sweaty brows. Soldier Wolf led us to a pile of shovels. Then he reached into his pant pocket and pulled out a ring of keys. "I'm going to unlock the chain. But you see those men?" He tilted his head at the soldiers. "They're so bored, they'll kill you for no reason at all. Take my advice and don't tempt them by trying to escape." Then he knelt at our feet and unlocked the padlocks. The chain fell away, leaving my ankles feeling suddenly weightless. Henry, the one-eyed man, caught my gaze. His fists clenched and I knew he was thinking of escape. I shook my head. This was not the time. Not in daylight. Not with that group of bloodthirsty thugs eyeing us. Henry seemed to read my thoughts. His fists relaxed.

"The dirt-scratcher will work in the caverns with the others," Soldier Wolf said. He picked up a shovel from a pile and handed it to Billy. Then he folded his arms and stared at Henry. "If you'll fight tonight, I'll keep you out of the caverns. You can work in the kitchen." Henry agreed with a grunt.

"What about you?" Wolf asked. "I can keep you out of the caverns too if you'll fight in the circle." A grin spread across his face. "You probably won't last long against one-eyed Henry here, but at least my men would have some entertainment."

A barefist fight versus working in a cavern? At any other time I would have chosen the fight circle—even knowing that my opponent had killed a man. My stomach tightened at the thought of being belowground. Of the smothering darkness. Of the unstable rock walls. "Are all the dirt-scratchers in the cavern?" I asked.

"Every dirty one of them."

Since I'd have to wait until dark to escape and there was still a half day of daylight left, I figured there was time to see Emmeline's father. "I'm better at digging than fighting," I lied, holding out my hand.

"Too bad," Wolf said as he tossed a shovel at me. Then he and one-eyed Henry walked away. A pair of soldiers led Billy and me across the doomed landscape to an opening in a rock wall. "See you in a few weeks," one of the soldiers said.

"Wait. What? A few weeks?" I nearly choked on my surprise. "I'm going to be in a cavern for a few *weeks*?"

"Yeah. We can't be bringing you back to the surface too often. You got a lot of digging to do. And we never know when we're going to lose you to a cave-in or to wet lung. We got to get as much work out of you as we can." He shoved Billy at the opening.

"Wait," I said again. "I've changed my mind. I'll go fight in Wolf's circle."

The soldiers laughed. "Get in," one said. Then he cracked his whip, stinging Billy's leg. Billy cried out. The soldier raised his whip again. "Both of you get in or I'll kill the boy."

Gripping the shovel so tightly my hands ached, I was ready to swing it at the soldier's head, but another pair had left the building and were walking toward us. I released my grip and grabbed Billy's arm. "Come on," I said. Then I ducked into the tunnel.

Chapter Forty

We crawled like dogs. The tunnel was barely wide enough to fit through, and not even a child could have stood inside.

"Don't think you can escape," a soldier hollered after us. "Got a couple of guys waiting for you at the end of the tunnel. They'll kill you if you try anything."

"Nice to know," I shouted. "Always appreciate a warm welcome."

I'd taken the lead. Billy was just a kid, after all, but I'm not sure which of us was most frightened. As he followed, his breathing came in short, uneven huffs. I tried to control mine, but the deeper we crawled, the tighter my chest felt. Sunlight, which had streamed through the tunnel's entrance, could not reach this far, so the going was pitch-black, with only our hands guiding us as we edged forward. We pulled the shovels along.

A few weeks? How was I going to get out of this?

"Ouch," Billy said.

"You okay?" I asked.

"Yeah," he replied. "Landed on another sharp rock."

My palms and knees had met with a number of sharp rocks too. But the pain was nothing compared to the fear that welled in my gut. Of all the places for Emmeline's father to be, why underground? I tried not to imagine the tunnel caving in, its stones holding me captive, squeezing air from my lungs. I tried to imagine Emmeline's face, her wide green eyes, her sweet smile, but even her beauty was powerless against the fear that pounded my skull. With the enclosing silence, my chest tightened more.

"Do you think we're going to die?" Billy'd spoken so quietly, as if a million miles away.

"How old are you, Billy?"

"Eleven."

"Well, I'm eighteen and that's too young to die. That makes eleven much too young to die. So let's be determined to live. What do you say?"

"Okay."

Light drifted toward us and the tunnel widened. A pair of soldiers sat on stools, playing cards. They grabbed their swords and frowned at us. "Toss your shovels into the pit," one of them said.

Just as I'd feared, the tunnel stopped abruptly, a ladder's top rung the only thing that blocked our fall into nothingness. A chill sent my jaw shuddering. I took a long breath. *Steady now*, I told myself. I thought about trying to convince these soldiers that I was supposed to be back in Wolf's fight circle. But Billy clutched my arm, his trembling as fierce as a branch in a windstorm. I couldn't leave him alone.

"Climb," a soldier grunted.

I reached back and pulled the shovel from Billy's grip. "Watch out below!" I yelled, then dropped both shovels into the darkness. Two breaths passed before a *clang* reached our ears. No scream followed. That was the first good sign.

"I'm guessing you won't be lending us one of your lanterns," I said.

"You guessed right," a soldier said. "But I'd be happy to give you a push."

"Not necessary," I replied. "But thanks anyway."

Gripping the ladder, I reached around with my foot until it rested on a rung. Then I reached with the other foot until it found a lower rung. I took the first step. Breath. Then the next one. Keep breathing.

"Okay, Billy, your turn," I said, fighting the panic that scuttled in my chest like a trapped rat. The ladder wobbled as Billy stepped on.

We made our way, leaving the lantern light behind. Not even the cheese cellar at night was this dark. I willed my mind to take me back to my bedroom, to the image of Emmeline with her hair cascading across my pillows. To the sweet way she'd thanked the cow for protecting her at the river's edge. To the way she'd smiled when she first tasted the chocolate.

Just when I thought we'd be lost in the darkness forever, faint light drifted upward and my hands came into view. With each step the light grew, illuminating the ladder and the rock wall behind. Soon I could see Billy's face looking down at me. My foot hit something and with relief, I stepped onto solid ground.

We'd descended into a small cavern. A lantern flickered from a stone alcove. Water dripped nearby. Billy stood beside me. His face, blotched with dirt, was turned up at me, his eyes questioning our next move. I suppose that's how I used to look up at my older sister, before she'd gotten sick. Waiting for her leadership in all matters, from stealing Nan's biscuits to sneaking into town. "Come on," I said, grabbing the shovels.

Only one tunnel led from the cavern, and it was tall enough to walk through. Lanterns here and there guided our way, as did the distant sound of hammering. The hammering actually steadied my nerves. It meant that other people were down here—living people, breathing people. Maybe I wouldn't be buried alive.

Soon the tunnel opened into another cavern. Lanterns hung from nails that had been hammered into the stone wall. I raised my hand to shield my eyes, squinting against the sudden rush of bright light. Then my nightmare came true. "Watch out!" someone hollered. The hammering stopped, followed by the sound of falling rocks. I pushed Billy against a wall, covering both our heads with the shovels. Silence settled, then the same voice called, "Anyone hurt?"

A series of noes followed.

"That you, Billy?"

A young man walked toward us, red hair hanging past his shoulders, a red beard covering his neck. Billy rushed forward and wrapped his arms around the man's waist. "Wish I could say I'm happy to see you," the man said, patting Billy's back. "But I'm not. What are you doing here?"

"They brought me here, same as you," Billy said.

"Are you Billy's brother?" I asked.

"Aye. And who are you? You're not from the Flatlands."

"Owen Oak," I said. "From the Wanderlands."

Red-haired men, all holding shovels, picks, and hammers, gathered around us. I guessed there were forty or fifty of them. They all had a similar look—their homespun clothing tattered beyond repair, their faces gray with dirt, their red manes and beards matted. "I've come to find Emmeline's father," I said, my gaze traveling across their tired faces. "Emmeline Thistle's father." Murmurs arose and they parted slightly, allowing a man to make his way toward me.

"I'm Murl Thistle," he said. He was bone-thin and hunched in the shoulders. The resemblance was clear in the wide-set eyes, but nothing else about him reminded me of Emmeline. And though the eyes had the same shape and color, they lacked Emmeline's sparkle. His eyes, so dull and lifeless, belonged to a dead man. He clutched my shoulder with his long fingers. "Has something happened to Emmeline?"

I've never been much of a storyteller. I don't like the long-winded versions of things. But this was such a horrific story, it deserved respect. So Billy and I sat and the others settled around us. I told them of the rain that had pummeled the Flatlands and how the river had flooded. Billy confirmed, adding his own tragic story. I described how Emmeline had been carried into the Wanderlands and how my parents had cared for her. I spoke of their tax-collector who'd come by raft and who'd said that most of the families had made it to higher ground and safety. The men were comforted by these words, but I told the truth that I'd kept from Emmeline—that many bodies had washed downriver.

A man leaped to his feet. "We must get home!"

"What do you suggest?" another man asked desperately. "Everything we've tried has failed."

"There's no way to escape this place," another said. Murmurs of agreement filled the dank air.

"Wait," I said, waving my hands for silence. "You haven't heard the entire story. It's about Emmeline. She's wanted. She's the most wanted girl in all of Anglund."

"Emmeline?" Murl Thistle asked. "Wanted?"

"Yes. She can make chocolate."

Like Emmeline before them, none of the men knew what I was talking about when I said the word. I was about to explain when a quiet clearing of the throat drew everyone's attention.

All heads turned toward an elderly man as he struggled to his feet. The only hair on his head were the scraggily patches that grew on his ears. Loose skin hung on his neck, which jiggled when he spoke. "It has happened," he said, his voice raspy with mystery.

"What has happened?" I asked.

"The legend has come full circle."

Chapter Forty-one

The old man leaned on a shovel, his bony elbows sticking through holes in his shirt. "There has always been a legend about chocolate, but it was forbidden and the storytellers who used to tell it were killed long ago. It is dangerous to speak of it, even now, but I fear I'm the last to know."

"Speak it," a man urged. "There is no one here to punish you."

"What about the stranger?"

"I'm Emmeline's friend," I said. Surrounded by a sea of red hair, I was the misfit in this group. They had no reason to believe me, but I hoped they would. "I will not betray her."

"I've spent many days with him," Billy said. "We can trust him."

The men nodded, agreement rising among them. The old man's knees creaked as he steadied himself with his makeshift cane. "The legend says that we were once called the Kell, and we were first to make our homes in this land."

"Hold on a minute," I interrupted. "That can't be true. The books say you came as invaders."

"What books?" someone asked.

"All the books," I said. "All the schoolbooks, all the history books. They all say the same thing."

"We have no such books," the old man said. "We only have our story, and it goes back to the beginning when our people shared this land with no others but the animals. That is where the legend of chocolate begins, with the animals."

"Tell it," a man said.

"Our ancestors, the Kell, learned how to tame the wild horse and the wild boar. But they could not tame the wild wolf. One day, the queen of the wild cows came to the Kell village and spoke to the first chieftain. Said the cow queen, 'My kind can no longer live safely in the forest, for the wolf eats our young. If your people will let us live in your villages, we will freely give our milk. And when my life nears its end, I will give your people a magical spell—the sweetest spell of all.' "

"The chocolate," I whispered.

"The cow queen kept her word and just before she died, a magical spell was given to a Kell milkmaid, who then gave it to other milkmaids. The spell allowed them to make a special food from cow milk. It was eaten at feasts and weddings."

"That is why you do not eat cow meat," I realized.

"It has long been forbidden," the old man said. "In honor of the cow queen."

I didn't know what to believe. Perhaps the invading Kell had made up the story because they were embarrassed about their own history. Perhaps the story made them feel better about their powerlessness. Father had said that legends were half truth and half story. Honestly, I didn't care about the past. I didn't care who had been here first, and who had taken the land from whom. All I cared about was getting back to my family. Bringing Peddler to justice.

And seeing Emmeline again.

But my thoughts were scattered by the earsplitting clanging of a bell. Billy and I stuck our fingers in our ears and looked at each other with surprise. The men all got to their feet and stared up at the cavern's ceiling. The bell clanged again. "What's going on?" I asked Mister Thistle.

"They are summoning us to the surface," he said.

"Really?" I jumped to my feet. "But I thought I'd be down here a few weeks."

Leaving their tools behind, the men left the cavern and headed up the tunnel, toward the ladder. I would have been first in line, but Mister Thistle held me back, his hand pressing on my shoulder. "Where is my daughter?"

I hadn't mentioned the kidnapping. "King Elmer sent for her," I said, which sounded so much nicer. And it was true. "He wants her to make chocolate for him. But Emmeline wants to buy your freedom. I'm sure she'll make a deal with the king."

"She should forget about me," he said. "I deserve nothing from her."

Though I yearned to run through that tunnel and scramble up the ladder, I took a steadying breath and looked into Mister Thistle's weary eyes. "She loves you. I'm sure of it. She wants to bring you home."

"I don't know why she would love me. I cast her aside when she was born."

I had only one answer, and even though I didn't know Mister Thistle and didn't know his daughter very well, the answer felt true. "She loves you because you are her father. We forgive the mistakes of the people we love."

"She has her mother's heart," he said, tears pooling on his lower lids. I turned away from his sudden surge of emotion.

"Let's get out of here," I said.

But when we reached the ladder, the men were standing around. A voice bellowed from above, "Only the boy from Wander. Send him up and no one else."

Why did they want me?

Mister Thistle put a hand on my shoulder. "Good luck to you, lad."

When I finally reached the surface, the relief I'd expected didn't come. Below, the air had been cool and crisp. As I crawled into the sunlight, I inhaled a huge lungful of yellow particles, then broke into a fit of coughing.

"There he is!" Soldier Wolf grabbed my shirt sleeve and pulled me to my feet. He slapped my back, which sent me into another coughing fit. "Good thing you're leaving or you'd be getting wet lung right quick."

"Leaving?" I wiped spit from my lips. "You said I'd be down there for weeks."

"That was before I learned you could barefist fight," Wolf said. "Trying to keep a secret, were you? One-eyed Henry told me you were the champion of Wander. Then he reminded me that the king's tournament is just around the corner. I've been trying to figure a way to get into the king's good graces. If I bring two barefist champions to his tournament, I'm certain to be pardoned."

Henry had proven to have a brain in that seeping head of his after all. To enter the king's circle was the highest honor for a barefist fighter. Though I'd often imagined it, I knew my chances were slim at best. Mother would never have supported such a venture. But on that day, standing in the late afternoon glow of the mineral fields, I couldn't have asked for a better change of fate. Not only would I be getting out of this death trap, I'd be delivered straight to Londwin City, where Emmeline was sure to be.

"I'll fight as your champion," I said, "but I've got one condition."

Soldier Wolf's easygoing demeanor fell away as his face tightened. "What do you mean, *condition*?"

"I want to bring two dirt-scratchers with me."

"What for?"

"To get them out of here."

He folded his arms over his glistening chest. "You can bring one."

Billy wouldn't last long in this place, but for the time being he was better off with his brother. At least there was food and water here. There was nothing waiting for him in the Flatlands. "Agreed. I'll bring one."

"Why do you care about a dirt-scratcher?"

"He's a gift for a young lady. The man I want to bring is her father."

Wolf grinned. "You're in love with a dirt-scratcher girl?"

"No. Not *in love*. But I care about her. It would make her very happy."

"You say you're not in love, but look at you. I can see the longing in your eyes."

"That's yellow dust," I said.

He slapped my back again. "I agree to your condition. You can have your gift. I don't want it said that I kept a man from winning the woman he loves."

Chapter Forty-two

There were five chambermaids who kept my rooms tidy, laid out my clothes, brushed my hair, and filled my bath. Like a flock of birds they flitted around me, braiding my hair and winding it atop my head so it fit perfectly beneath my bonnet. Stuffing my fancy shoes with just the right amount of soft fabric to cradle my foot. At first it felt as if I had sisters, but they never spoke to me. I didn't know their names or where they'd come from. They smiled and did their work. But as soon as they stepped outside my rooms, they found their lost voices. The silence reminded me of those first days with Lara when I'd been desperate for conversation.

"Good morning," I said as I climbed out of bed. A maid slid a pair of slippers onto my feet while another draped a robe over my shoulders. I sat at a little table that had been set with breakfast. Tea was poured, a napkin placed on my lap, salt sprinkled onto my boiled eggs, a honey cake cut into bite-size pieces. While I ate, the chambermaids made the bed, fluffed the pillows, and put fresh flowers into the bedside vase, even though the old ones were perfectly nice.

Life at the palace was warm, comfortable, and delicious. How many days had passed since I'd been given these rooms? I'd lost track, distracted by luxuries I'd never imagined. But the happiness wouldn't be complete until Father joined me.

As soon as I finished morning meal, the chambermaids cleared the table and dressed me. Each day I was given a clean yellow dress and white apron with matching bonnet. And each day, soon after dressing, the Royal Secretary knocked on the door.

"Good morning," I said.

He always carried a bundle of parchment. And he always kept a white quill tucked behind his ear. "Good morning," he said, expressionless. His lips were stained purple to match his ruffled shirt. Each morning he escorted me from my rooms to the kitchens, which lay in the palace basement. We always took the same route—a narrow stairway where we never passed another person.

"Any news today?" I asked as I followed him down the stairs.

"It's a very long journey to the mineral fields," he replied. "But do not fret. The scroll has been sent. I saw to it personally. I'm sure the other dirt-scratchers will be on their way home very soon."

"And my father?" I asked, gripping the railing. Going downstairs was never easy for me. "Don't forget about my father."

"Yes, yes, of course. Your father." His pointed shoes clicked against the stairs. "I'm certain you will be reunited soon."

"Where will he stay? Can he have one of my rooms?"

"Her Majesty will choose a *suitable room* for your father."

It couldn't happen soon enough. Who could have ever imagined that a girl from the Flatlands would work in the palace? And live in four rooms? And have chambermaids? How proud my father would be of his unwanted daughter.

"Have you heard anything from the man who brought me here?" I never got the chance to say good-bye to Griffin.

"As I told you, your friend took his reward but left no message."

I knew Griffin had been eager to get back to the Flatlands. I understood his urge to leave right away, but I wished I could have thanked him for his help.

At the bottom of the staircase, the Royal Secretary pulled a ring of keys from his pocket and unlocked a door. Then we stepped into my churning room.

It was a simple room, with no windows. One door led to the narrow stairway, another door led to the kitchens, but I was not allowed to go there. A churning bucket, filled with fresh cream, waited next to a stool. There was a table of food—bread, cheese, honeycakes—anything I could possibly desire. This was my work, to sit there and churn. Every time a new batch of chocolate was ready, I rang a little bell and a kitchen boy came in and carried the bucket away.

"I will return for you at midday," the Royal Secretary said. "Remember, you are forbidden to leave this room." Then he locked the door and walked back up the staircase.

There I sat, the door to the staircase locked, the door to the kitchen bolted from the outside. Why did they feel the need to lock me in? Did the queen think I'd run away? I'd agreed to work for Their Majesties in exchange for all that I'd asked. I was here to stay. I'd provide a nice life for myself and my father. In time, I'd begin to call this place home.

That day's kitchen boy was new, and he smiled shyly at me after he'd unbolted the door to collect the first bucket. My arms began to ache as I finished churning the third bucket. Hopefully I'd get stronger with time. I rang the bell, then rang it again, but the kitchen boy did not appear. I waited. Where was he? That's when I noticed that the door to the kitchens was cracked open. He'd forgotten to bolt it. "Hello?" I called. "It's ready." The bucket needed to be delivered before the chocolate hardened. So I grabbed the handle and carried it out the door.

And I stepped into the vast underground world of the royal kitchens.

Though I knew I wasn't supposed to leave the churning room, I also knew that the chocolate was precious. Surely an exception would be made for me to leave under the circumstances. I passed a room filled with dead animals. Many had been skinned and were curing. A wild boar hung near a row of chickens. Partridges, unplucked, lay in a pile on a table. A cow's head sat at the table's end. I gasped and turned away from the barbarity. To think we Flatlanders were considered primitive. I still hadn't gotten used to the fact that the outside world ate the very creatures that had saved my life.

There was a room filled with vegetable and fruits. Another where servants ground grain into flour. There was a room with a great oven where the air sweltered. The cooks, red-faced and sweaty, stirred enormous pots. Kitchen boys ran back and forth with buckets of coal, feeding the roaring fire. Cauldrons bubbled, knives chopped.

No one took notice of me. I should have asked for help, but the scenery mesmerized me—I wanted to see more.

The kitchen floor began to tilt uphill until it reached ground level and opened onto a small courtyard. A wagon filled with potatoes drove into the courtyard, parking next to another wagon filled with cheese.

"You're not supposed to be out here," a voice said. I turned to find a familiar kitchen boy looking up at me. "You should go back."

"I have some chocolate," I said, holding out the bucket.

He took it, then hurried away. I was about to walk back to my little churning room when a soft sound caught my ears. *Mooooo.*

I waited until a wagon of apples passed by, then I walked across the kitchen courtyard to a fenced area. As I approached a chorus of mooing filled the air. These were not the brown woollies of the Oak farm, nor the short-haired cows of the Flatlands. The royal cows were pure white, with black noses and black tails. They greeted me in the gentle way of all cows, flicking their tails and pressing their nostrils against my outstretched palm. Three were being milked by milkmaids. Three others were being bathed by servants. How difficult it must have been to keep the soot off their white coats. Each cow wore a gold ribbon around its neck. The greenest alfalfa I'd ever seen filled their troughs.

"Hello," I said to them. "It's nice to meet you. My name's—"

A trumpet sounded. The milkmaids jumped to their feet and bowed their heads as King Elmer and Queen Beatrice entered the kitchen courtyard. Two servants swept a path across the soot-covered stones for Their Royal Majesties to follow. Another servant carried the royal crowns on pillows. I ducked behind a stack of alfalfa bales. Surely I'd get in trouble for leaving the churning room.

"If we need more coin, then we shall make more chocolate," the king said. He plucked a chocolate square from a golden box and popped it into his mouth. "Delicious."

"We'd like to increase production," the queen said. "The problem is, the dirt-scratcher girl has only two arms. She can't churn much more than she's already churning. I suppose she could get less sleep but we need to keep her healthy."

As they strode close to the alfalfa bales, the king turned his golden box upside down. "It's all gone!" he exclaimed. "Get me more!" He waddled off the carefully swept path. One of the sweepers followed, madly creating a new path.

The Royal Secretary slid alongside the queen, a paper bundle tucked under his arm. "If I may be so bold as to make a suggestion?" The queen nodded. "Is Your Majesty familiar with the phrase *less is more*?"

"Less is more?" The queen stopped walking. "Whatever do you mean?"

They spoke in hushed tones. I leaned around the bales, straining to hear.

"Would gold be as desired if it dripped from every tree?" the Royal Secretary asked.

A smile spread across the queen's powdered face. "Yes, of course. We will not make more. We will simply raise the price." She fiddled with the jewels that hung from her waist. "Send a box to the king of Franvia and to the Imperial Pope of Italialand. Include a price list for future shipments at triple what we discussed."

The Royal Secretary plucked the white feather from behind his ear and scribbled on a piece of parchment.

"No, wait!" the queen cried. "Tell them that we will be holding an auction. The highest bidder will receive a limited supply."

"Your brilliance shines like the sun," the Royal Secretary said.

"Make certain that every ambassador who attends the tournament receives a box of chocolate. That will be the best way to spread the word. We are going to be very rich," the queen said to her secretary.

Wasn't she already rich?

"Bring me more!" the king bellowed as he wandered over to the fence. Then he leaned close to one of the cows. "They tell me," he said in the cow's ear, "that the treasury is empty."

"Do not worry, my love," the queen said as she took her husband's puffy hand. "You've got the tournament to think about. I'll worry about the treasury. I'll get us lots and lots of pretty coin."

A kitchen boy ran up to the king and, after a little bow, handed him a new box of chocolates. The king shoved a piece in his mouth, the headed back to the palace. The queen and Royal Secretary followed. I took a deep breath, then hurried across the courtyard in the opposite direction. I retraced my steps, through the sweltering room of ovens, past the room of curing meat, and back to my little churning room where a bucket of cream waited for me. With a sigh of relief, I sat on the stool. I hadn't been caught. But what I'd heard made my thoughts spin. How could the king and queen of Anglund have no coin?

Just as I began churning, the door flew open. The scent of honeysuckle tickled my nose as Queen Beatrice stormed in. She towered over me, her hands on her hips. "What were you doing outside?" she demanded.

I rose slowly to my feet. Not wanting to get the kitchen boy into trouble, I said, "I needed to stretch my legs, Your Majesty."

"You are not supposed to leave this room, dirt-scratcher girl."

"I'm sorry," I said. The room felt smaller than it had a few moments ago, as if the walls were pressing in.

She ran a hand across her brow, patting a few stray hairs into place. Though she smiled sweetly at me, the rage in her eyes did not fade. "It is too dangerous for you to venture beyond this room. There are those who would try to take you from us. You must stay in here until the Royal Secretary delivers you back to your chambers."

"Who would try to take me?" I asked. "Surely no one would steal from the king."

"Don't be a fool. People steal from the king all the time. They cheat on their taxes. They hide their coin beneath their mattresses. It has become a national hobby to steal from the king."

As she opened the door and was about to leave, another question came to mind. "Your Majesty?" She stopped but did not turn to look at me. "If you have no coin, how did you pay my friend his five thousand coin reward?"

"That matter was taken care of. Now get back to work. We

need chocolate for the tournament. The ambassadors will be in attendance."

She glided through the kitchen, her sweeping servant running in front, clearing the floor of carrot tops and potato peelings. As I stood in the open doorway, two soldiers approached, then took their places at either side of the door. I should have felt better knowing that they'd been sent to protect me.

I thought about the Flatlander boy I'd seen sitting in the caged wagon—iron bars surrounding him as if he were an animal being taken to slaughter.

You should be happy, I scolded myself. I'd been given everything I could possibly desire. Beautiful rooms, delicious food, clean clothes. And my father would be joining me soon. He'd never again have to work the field. We'd never again know poverty.

But I'd never again know freedom.

Part Eight

Prince

Chapter Forty-three

I was eating supper when the Royal Secretary bustled in, a larger-than-usual stack of parchment under his arm. "You are called to the arena, immediately."

This was an interesting change in my routine because it meant that for the first time since being escorted to my rooms, I wasn't going to take the winding staircase that led to my churning room. Instead, I was going out, into the palace. I didn't care why I'd been summoned. The chance to get out was like the promise of a spring day after a long winter.

I'd been lounging in my nightfrock, so the chambermaids helped me get into a clean yellow dress. They tucked my hair into a bonnet.

"Make way for the Royal Secretary!" a soldier bellowed as we stepped into the hallway. When had they posted soldiers outside my chamber door? Lots of servants hurried about, carrying brooms and buckets, polish and rags. They stepped aside as we walked past, their gazes fixed on one thing—me. My, how things had changed. Not a single one of them stared at my limp. There were no sneers, no scorn. Their expressions were wide with admiration. Is this what it felt like to Griffin when all the girls gazed upon him?

It felt like sunshine.

"Secretary." A soldier approached. "There is a crowd gathering for the Bestowing of Coal, but there is no coal. The king has given no orders."

"Tell them to come back tomorrow," the secretary said.

"That is what I told them yesterday and the day before."

"Tell them!"

As the soldier marched away, someone else called out for the Royal Secretary. Two tax-collectors approached, their wide coats flapping as they walked, their floppy hats dripping over their foreheads. "We need to speak with you."

"Now is not the time." The Royal Secretary tried to dart around them, but they stood in the center of the hallway, blocking his way.

"There are uprisings and strikes. The king needs to know," said one.

"Citizens are refusing to pay the new water tax and my jail is full," said the other. "We have been threatened. We fear for our lives."

Water tax? How could the king tax something that flowed freely? I wondered.

"The tax-collectors' guild has sent us here to get instructions from the king. Leaders of the uprisings are being rounded up and sent to the mineral fields, but the king has yet to pay us for the transport of these offenders."

The Royal Secretary's face twitched, and I noticed, for the first time, the dark circles beneath his eyes that even the powder could not cover. "Wait in my office and I will try to get you an answer."

The men nodded and stepped aside. They whispered to each other as I hobbled past.

The arena was a gigantic round room with no roof. Because there'd been less burning in the city, patches of blue peeked through the gray sky. But how were the city folk heating their homes and cooking their food without coal?

Four levels of benches rose above the arena's dirt floor. Three thrones sat on the highest level. King Elmer slept in one throne, a plate perched on his belly. The queen, however, paced along a railing that separated the lowest row of benches from the dirt circle. She held a scroll.

"Your Majesties," the Royal Secretary announced as we entered. "I have brought the dirt-scratcher girl, as requested."

Queen Beatrice clapped her hands, and the soldiers who'd been standing guard at the entrance exited, as did the servants who'd been raking the floor. The queen waved me forward. I walked along the railing until I reached her. "Hello, Your Majesty," I said with a bow.

She looked past me. "What is wrong with you?" she asked her secretary. "Why are you twitching in that manner? And why is your collar limp?"

"Your Majesty, please forgive my disheveled appearance," the secretary said, fiddling with his ruffled collar. "There is much news to convey. There is citizen unrest. Uprisings. Strikes. Crowds have gathered outside the city walls."

"These are trivial matters," she said with a dismissive wave of her hand. "We have something much more pressing to deal with. We have important news." She pointed the scroll at me. "And it involves the girl."

"Is it about my father?" I asked, a flutter in my chest. "Is he here? When can I see him?"

The queen shoved the scroll at the secretary. He set his stack of parchment aside, then unrolled the scroll. "Your Majesty," he said with surprise. "Have you read this?"

"Indeed we have." She stroked a strand of blue stones that circled her powdered neck. "Go on. Tell the girl."

He cleared his throat. "It would seem that you have a proposal of marriage."

I almost laughed. "Me?"

"Yes. You. From the King of Germundy. He wishes to marry the Milkmaid." The Royal Secretary rolled the scroll and tucked it under his arm. "It would appear, Your Majesty, that while word has spread about the chocolate, word has also spread about the chocolate-maker herself, thanks to the wanted posters."

"Yes, so it would appear." The queen settled onto a bench, her silver dress cascading down her legs like water.

"I'm not going to marry him," I said worriedly. I didn't even know him. Had never even heard of him. But if ordered to marry a king, what could I possibly do?

"Be quiet. I need to think." The queen tapped her long fingernails on her knee. Up on the fourth level, the king snored loudly. After a long moment, the queen crooked her finger and her secretary leaned in close. "She is too valuable to give to the Germund king. No matter what he offers. We must triple the guard. Germund spies will try to kidnap her."

"I concur," the secretary said. "Shall I send a response to Germundy?"

"We must have a good reason," the queen said. "We cannot risk insulting a potential market. Those Germunds love sweets. And we suspect this is not the last proposal the dirt-scratcher girl will receive."

My name is Emmeline, I wanted to point out. They never called me by name. And they always talked about me as if I wasn't standing right there.

The queen continued. "How can we reject a sovereign leader? We will be at war before the year's end."

"Your Majesty could craft a reason why the girl cannot marry."

I was about to point out the reason I couldn't get married was because I didn't want to get married. Not to someone I didn't know. But the queen had turned her gaze to the sky. "What is he up to *now*?" she asked between clenched teeth.

Something floated downward, appearing as if by magic from a patch of blue. It was a large woven basket and it dangled from an enormous inflated balloon. I'd seen this contraption on the floor beneath the golden bridge when I'd first walked with the queen. A man leaned over the side of the basket, his hands cupped around his mouth. "Watch out below!"

While the Royal Secretary gathered his pile of parchment and scrambled up to the third level, the queen and I didn't budge an inch. The sight was so amazing I didn't want to miss a single moment as the basket landed in the middle of the dirt circle. It wobbled from side to side, tossing its two passengers about. With a drawn-out squeak, the balloon deflated, falling limp to the ground like a fainting woman. Except for the king's snoring, all was silent in the arena. Then the two men climbed out of the basket and strode toward us. They both wore simple white shirts and regular britches, not high-waisted ones like the secretary. They wore gloves, leather hats, and thick round spectacles. The lead man peeled off his spectacles and hat. After a quick bow, he took the queen's hand and kissed it. Then he nodded at the secretary and smiled at me.

I immediately liked his smile. It was lopsided and goofy. Laughter lay behind it.

"What is that thing?" the queen asked.

"It's a traveling balloon," he replied. He smiled at me again. The way his hair was tied back with a ribbon reminded me of Mister Oak. "It can easily fly across Anglund. With a few improvements, I believe we might be able to fly to other countries. What do you think?"

The queen stared angrily at the other man. He removed his spectacles and hat and bowed to the queen but said nothing. A thin mustache draped his upper lip.

"Mother?" the first man said. "Are you aware that a crowd has gathered outside the city wall? Our citizens are upset about the new taxes."

Mother? I gasped. I didn't know the king and queen had a son. I'd never heard anyone mention a prince. He had her same black hair and willowy build but was short like his father.

"I fear Father's safety may be in jeopardy if he doesn't address the crowd soon," the prince said.

"Nonsense. The people love their king," the queen said. The secretary and the prince exchanged a worried look. The queen turned her back to me and spoke in a low voice. "You spend too much time with your inventions. And far too much time with your *companion*. Your reputation is in ruins. There are wicked rumors about you two. You need to . . ." She froze. "You need to . . ." She whipped around and snapped her fingers. "Secretary!"

The Royal Secretary stumbled down the stairs until he stood at her elbow. "Yes, Your Majesty?"

"We have figured out a way to save our son's reputation and a way to keep the dirt-scratcher girl from the Germund king's marriage bed." Flecks of powder drifted onto her dress as she smiled. "Inform the King of Germundy that the Milkmaid is unavailable for marriage. You will repeat the same message to any future suitors."

"And the reason, Your Majesty?" the secretary asked, his quill poised and ready.

The queen glared at the mustached man. "Because she is already promised in marriage. To our son."

The prince and I may have had nothing in common, but at that moment we shared the same stunned expression.

Chapter Forty-four

His name was Prince Beauregard Borthwick Elmer of Anglund. He was nineteen years old, and I was to marry him as soon as arrangements could be made, whatever that meant.

Wasn't this every girl's dream? Even the Flatlander girls who'd spent their days and nights lost in dreams of Griffin Boar would have run Griffin over with a wagon to have a chance at marrying the prince of Anglund. Or any prince for that matter. This is what we were taught—to find a husband and then to have children. I'd always thought marriage to anyone but an unwanted was out of my reach. Yet here it was, offered to me on a golden platter. With a crown on the side.

My insides felt all tangled up as I sat at the edge of my bed. After they'd dressed me in my nightfrock, I'd told the chambermaids to leave so I could think without faces staring at me, watching my every move. If *arrangements* were being made, this could be one of my last nights alone. I slid off the bed and limped to the window, a pair of specially made slippers covering my feet. Night had fallen, cloaking the city in an inky blanket. Usually I'd be asleep by now, resting after a long day of churning. But how could I sleep? The only reason these men wanted to marry me was because of the chocolate. No one wanted me for myself. I wiped a hot, angry tear. No man had ever paid attention to the unnatural girl with the limp. Except for Owen.

How could I marry the prince when my heart still belonged to Owen?

Stop thinking about him. He's dead!

A creaking sound drew my attention from the window. My door was opening slowly, inch by inch. The Royal Secretary had warned me about the dangers of kidnapping. "The Germund spies once infiltrated the palace dressed as pigs," he'd said. "They are cunning. Do not leave your rooms." As the door continued to open, I grabbed a candlestick. Where were the soldiers who were supposed to protect me? I raised the candlestick above my head. That's when Prince Beauregard stepped into my room.

"Good, you're still awake," he said. "Hey, you're not going to hit me with that, are you?"

I set the candlestick in its place but said nothing. Why should I care that I was standing in my nightfrock? If the queen had her way, I'd be in the prince's bed soon enough.

"Your hair is beautiful," he said.

For a moment I panicked, my hand darting to my head. The queen wanted me to wear the bonnet at all times, but I always took it off at night, when I was alone. I glared at him.

"I see you're angry with me," the prince said. "Don't be angry with me. I have as little say in this matter as you." He cleared his throat. "So, what do I call you? My mother calls you dirt-scratcher girl and others call you the Milkmaid."

"Emmeline," I blurted. "My name is Emmeline."

He smiled and held out a small gold box. "I brought this for you. Go on, open it. I thought you might like to see the results of your hard work, Emmeline."

How could I resist? He was the first person in the palace to call me by name.

I peeled the wax seal from the box and opened the lid. Six perfect little chocolates sat inside, each shaped like a swan. The swans' wings were painted with delicate strokes of gold. "They're beautiful," I said.

"They will make my parents very rich. At least, that's my mother's plan." We stood almost the same height so it was easy to look into his eyes—green, like his mother's, but not one bit cold. "Mother is the brains behind everything around here. Father's mind isn't what it once was. All that barefist fighting in his youth scrambled things. His name is on everything but she runs the realm. He sleeps, she imposes taxes. He eats, she imposes taxes. Not a perfect relationship but it seems to work for them."

"But it doesn't work for the people," I said.

He raised his eyebrows. "No, it doesn't." He folded his hands behind his back. "What do you know about our troubles?"

"I know that there are too many taxes. My father could barely pay our land tax. The new potato tax took food from our table so we went hungry many nights."

He stood close enough for me to smell his sweat, which was light and musky. He didn't wear perfume like the other royals. Nor did he powder or paint his face. "I am sorry to hear that you were hungry. When I rule, life will be different."

"How will life be different?" I asked.

"My parents rarely leave the palace. They do not care what's going on outside these golden walls. They do not care about the people. They only care about surrounding themselves with new things. Expensive things. Golden, jeweled things purchased with the people's coin." He ran his hand over a golden vase. "The people pay an endless stream of taxes but get nothing in return. It is the sovereign's duty to provide for his people, not the other way round. When I am king, I will provide for the people by leading them into the future." He plucked one of the chocolate swans from the box and ate it. "What do you think of my traveling balloon?"

I couldn't hide my smile. "I loved it. Could you really fly all the way to another country?"

"Yes. One day. And one day that's how everyone will travel. That's the future. At least, that's the future I will bring to this backward kingdom. Who needs gold? We need innovation. New ideas. New ways to make life better for everyone." He grabbed another chocolate. "These are stupendous. You have an amazing talent, Emmeline. Want to go for a ride in the balloon?"

He was asking if I wanted to float through the air? I nodded so hard I almost jarred my neck. I threw a cloak around my shoulders and tucked my hair into a bonnet. None of the soldiers who stood guard at my door questioned the prince as he led me from my rooms.

“Why don’t you powder your face like the others?” I asked as I tied the bonnet’s ribbons.

“Makes me itch,” he said. “And all that perfume makes me sneeze. I hate it.”

“What am I supposed to call you?” I asked.

“Your Royal Majesty Prince Beauregard Borthwick Elmer of Anglund.” He’d lowered his voice in a serious way. But as I was about to ask him to repeat his name so I could memorize it, he laughed. “I’m kidding. Call me Beau.” He glanced down at my foot. “Do you need me to walk slower?”

“That would be nice,” I said. “Thank you.”

We didn’t go down to the arena as I’d expected. Instead, the prince led me up a steep flight of stairs and out onto a roof. I was glad I’d wrapped a cloak around my shoulders since the night breeze carried a chill.

The basket sat on the roof. The balloon was fully inflated and hovered over a smoking chimney. “We fill it with hot air,” Prince Beau explained. “That’s what makes it float.” The basket was attached to the balloon with ropes. The basket was deep, reaching up to my chest. I peered over its edge. Large stones lay inside, weighing it down. “These ropes will hold us?” I asked.

“They’ll hold.” The man with the mustache stepped out from behind the chimney. He wiped soot from his hands with a rag.

Prince Beau motioned me forward. “Emmeline, I’d like you to meet my friend and coinventor, the Baron of Lime.”

“You’re a baron?” I asked with surprise. I’d never met a baron so I’m not sure what I was expecting. Guess I’d figured they were old.

The Baron of Lime smiled and bowed. "Delighted to meet you, Emmeline." Then he squeezed the prince's shoulder. "Be careful," he said. "Do not land outside the city walls. The crowds are growing restless."

Prince Beau climbed into the basket. Since I was wearing my nightfrock, the baron lifted me and set me inside. "We should be able to see some stars tonight," the prince said. "The people are almost out of coal so the sky isn't as smoky as usual. We should get a good view."

As I clung to the side of the basket, Prince Beau handed the stones to the baron. As he handed over the last stone, the basket wobbled. I held my breath as we rose above the rooftop. My stomach fluttered as a strange weightless sensation gripped my insides. The baron waved and soon he and the rooftop disappeared in a haze. "We'll be out of this in a moment," the prince told me. "It's okay. You can breathe."

I took a long breath just as we hit a patch of clear air. The stars twinkled above like the candles in the throne room. Moonlight filled the basket. I'd spent many nights lying on the donkey shed roof, gazing at the stars. But here I was, floating among them. "It's beautiful."

"I thought we'd take a short flight, just across the city." He leaned against the side of the basket. "Don't be scared."

"I'm not," I lied. "I'm not scared of floating."

"I mean, don't be scared about our marriage. I will be a good husband. I won't try to control you or boss you around. I'll be busy with my work so you needn't worry about . . . What I mean to say is that there is no love between us so . . ." He looked away. "We will be friends but nothing more. I won't touch you in that way."

I should have been relieved at such a statement, but it felt like an insult. "You won't touch me? Because I'm a disgusting *dirt-scratcher*?"

His shoulders slumped. "No, Emmeline, that is not the reason. Any man would be happy to have you in his marriage bed."

"Any man but you?" I waited, my arms folded. He didn't look at me. "You're just like the rest of them. You think my people are stupid and dirty. You think I'm stupid and dirty. Don't pretend we're friends. How can we ever be friends if you feel that way?"

Our lovely ride had turned ugly. I pressed against the other side of the basket, as far away from the prince as I could get. Just when I'd thought that maybe I'd found someone to talk to, the truth was revealed. Until my father arrived, I was truly alone.

The blanket of haze drifted below us. Through its gaps I caught sight of the gray buildings and cobbled, sooty streets. Prince Beau rested his forearms on the basket's edge and stared into the night. My pride prickled like bee stings. Forget talking to him. And forget marrying him. There had to be a way out of this.

"Do you not wonder why there are no portraits of me?" he asked, breaking through my thoughts. "Do you not wonder why no one speaks of me?" Though I did wonder, I kept my back to him. "It's that way because my mother tries to keep me hidden. She hates the way I am."

I peered over my shoulder. "What's wrong with the way you are?"

"Well, first there's the constant reminder of our heritage." He pointed to his head. "Look carefully at my hair. What do you see?"

"It's black."

"Look closer. Look at the roots."

As I stepped closer, he bent his head and pointed at the part that lay in the center of his hair. Even in the faint moonlight I could see that the new growth was a lighter color. "You dye your hair?"

"My mother has ordered my hair dyed since birth. Because it's red. Just like yours."

Was this some kind of joke? "You're just trying to—"

"Emmeline, I'm serious. It's not as red as yours, but there are red streaks. Same with my mother's hair."

"Queen Beatrice has red hair?" Surely it was treason to say such a thing.

"My mother's bloodline goes all the way back to the first queen, Queen Margaret, who was a dirt-scratcher. Or, I guess in those days your people were called the Kell."

"Queen Margaret?" I frowned. "That's impossible. Queen Margaret fought the Kell chieftain. Queen Margaret had the magic of chocolate and the Kell chieftain took it away."

"That's the story that's taught to us in school. But it's not the truth. Queen Margaret's Royal Secretary wrote one version of the story for history, but he wrote the true story in his private diary. The diary is locked away in my mother's treasury. I've read it. Want to hear it?"

Did I want to hear it? I wanted to shake the words out of him. "Aye. Tell me. Please."

The prince tugged on a rope and released some air from the balloon. My stomach fluttered as we began our descent and floated back toward the palace. "The Kell were the first people to live in this land. They lived peacefully for many generations. They tamed many wild creatures, but not the wolf, who hunted everything including the wild cow. Tired of losing the calves to wolf attacks, the queen of the wild cows asked the Kell for protection. The legend says that the cows were so grateful to live on Kell farms that they freely gave their milk to the people. Many Kell women became milkmaids. Before she died of old age, the queen of the wild cows bequeathed a special gift to her personal milkmaid—a magic spell. When the magic spell flowed into the milkmaid she felt warm all over. Soon after, she discovered she could make chocolate."

"Wait, what was that?" I needed to hear it again. "She felt warm all over?"

"That's how the story goes."

Just like my last moments with Snow. "Go on," I urged.

"And this milkmaid passed the spell to other milkmaids so all the Kell could enjoy the chocolate. Margaret was one of those milkmaids."

"But I thought the magic spell was given to Margaret in a dream."

"Not according to the Royal Secretary's diary." He tugged the rope and released more air. "Margaret was different from the other Kell girls. She wanted more than a peasant's life. When the black-haired invaders came from beyond the Southern Sea, most of the Kell went into the forest to hide. But Margaret greeted the invaders with gifts of chocolate. Their king fell in love with her. He seduced her with promises of wealth and glory. He promised to make her his queen if she told him where her people were hiding. She agreed and turned against her own. There was a brutal massacre. Most of the Kell were murdered. But Margaret was safe with the southern king's army."

I shuddered. How many versions of this story existed?

"A scattering of the Kell survived, mostly young children, and they were sent to the Flatlands to live. Any survivors who possessed the magical spell were killed so only Margaret could now make the chocolate. The southern king made Margaret his queen and they began their long reign. The land of the Kell became known as Anglund. Queen Margaret became very popular and powerful. But the nightmares began to plague her. She was haunted by the massacre of her people. She couldn't get their screams out of her head. She changed her hair color. She ordered her Royal Secretary to change history so that future generations wouldn't know the truth." He paused. "She eventually went mad from the guilt of what she'd done. She locked herself in her rooms and never made chocolate again. Nor did anyone else. Until now."

I grabbed the basket's edge as we landed in the palace's courtyard, the very spot where I'd watched the Bestowing of Coal weeks ago. With a dramatic sigh, the balloon folded in on itself, just missing our heads as it collapsed. I felt lightheaded, but not from the landing. "If the Kell didn't do anything wrong, why does your mother dye her hair? Why doesn't she let the truth be known?"

"The truth doesn't matter to my mother. The Kell have no power. Everyone believes that they don't belong in this land. My mother dyes her hair because she's ashamed to be descended from them."

"And she dyes your hair for the same reason?"

Prince Beau nodded, then looked across the courtyard where the Baron of Lime stood waiting. "But that is not the only reason I shame her. Sometimes I think she wishes I'd never been born." He and the baron shared a long look.

The prince helped me from the basket, then led me back to my rooms. We were silent during our walk, the palace hallways echoing our footsteps.

"Are we really to be married?" I asked when we reached my door.

"I'm afraid so." He smiled halfheartedly. "Can you accept me for who I am? Can we simply be friends?"

I nodded. "Of course."

Back home I'd often thought that I'd get stuck marrying an unwanted. In a strange way, that was exactly what I was about to do.

Chapter Forty-five

I was a small boy when I last visited Londwin City so I could barely remember anything about the trip. But I remember this—I didn't arrived locked inside a cage!

"When are you going to let us out of this thing?" I complained.

"When we get to the king's arena and not a minute earlier," Soldier Wolf replied from the driver's seat. "I'm not risking you running off. Not when we've come this far. But I don't care about the dirt-scratcher. He can go whenever he wants. He's no use to me."

Mister Thistle rubbed his face and stared out between the bars. He didn't ask to leave. He knew his farm had been destroyed. He had nothing but his daughter and I'd promised a reunion. My promise was fed by pure, intangible hope. And a gut feeling that she'd be there. She had to be there. The king wanted her. I wanted her.

She'd be there.

Emmeline's father had said little during the journey from the mineral fields. He was a tortured man, twisted and knotted like a rope—the kind of man who wore his grief like a second skin. How could he have fathered such a beautiful daughter?

"What was Emmeline's mother like?" I asked.

He coughed a bit. We'd all been coughing, trying to hack out the last yellow remnants of hell from our lungs. With a deep sigh, Mister Thistle leaned against the bars and looked at me. "You ask a lot of questions about my daughter. What are your intentions?"

"My intentions?" I shifted my weight. "My intentions are pure, I assure you. I want to make certain she's safe."

One-eyed Henry snorted.

"You have something to say?" I asked. "If you have something to say, then say it."

"I got nothing to say." He glared at me. "Except when we get into that dirt circle, I'm going to knock your head off."

"Not if I knock yours off first."

"That's the spirit, boys!" Soldier Wolf hollered. "Beat the crud out of each other, and I'll be back in the king's favor for certain."

I wanted to punch Henry right then. I was sick of sitting in that cage. Sick of his oozing face. Yet he was the man who'd gotten us out of the mineral fields by reminding Wolf of the king's tournament. I stretched my legs, trying to get comfortable as the wagon wheels rumbled along. How long had I been away from home? Mother was probably crazy with worry. I closed my eyes, imagining riding my horse across the field toward the river. Emmeline was standing at the river's edge, waiting for me. Her hair blowing in the wind.

"She looks like her mother."

I opened my eyes. Mister Thistle was speaking so quietly I had to lean close to catch the words.

"My wife never forgave me for casting Emmeline aside. All our babes before Emmeline had been stillborn, and she'd grieved each one. She and Emmeline were like two vines, always wrapped around one another, always together."

"How'd she die?" I asked.

"Fever." He looked away. "It came fast. She was gone in two days' time." He drifted off in tortured thought.

As we neared Londwin City, we began to collect information. The road into the city was crowded with travelers, all eager to share their stories. The growing unrest over taxation had spread across the realm like a storm. Tax-collectors had been taken hostage, their treasuries looted. Villagers were taking up arms. Guilds were on strike. Citizens were making their way to the palace for answers. I searched the road for familiar faces but found none. Maybe things weren't so bad in Wander. But I needed to get home as soon as possible. If the Dairy Guild was on strike, then Father would be dealing with angry townsfolk.

"Has anyone heard about the Milkmaid?" I asked, calling between the bars at a group of passing merchants. One of them slowed his horse.

"She's with the king," he replied, brushing a stray leaf from the shoulder of his green jacket.

"Really?" I gripped the bars. "She's safe? She's unharmed?"

"No one has seen her, but word is she's making chocolate in the royal kitchens. The king is preparing to open trade with Germundy and Franvia."

"But those trade routes are closed," I said.

He gave me a quizzical look. "Why does a prisoner care about trade routes?"

"They're not prisoners," Soldier Wolf said. "They are champion fighters, destined for the king's arena."

"Did they catch Peddler?" I asked. "The man who kidnapped the Milkmaid. Did they catch him?"

"I know nothing about such matters," the merchant said. With a kick to his horse, he sped ahead to meet up with his companions.

She was alive and well! She was a short ride away. "Can't we go faster?" I called to Wolf.

"Anybody ever tell you that you talk too much?" Soldier Wolf grumbled. "We'll get there when we get there."

"She's safe," I said.

Mister Thistle stopped rubbing his face and met my gaze. He nodded, relief relaxing the creases around his eyes.

"Are you going to ask her to marry you?" one-eyed Henry asked.

It would be a waste of time to pretend I didn't know what he was talking about. I hadn't said anything about love, but even a lout like Henry had figured it out.

"I don't know what to do," I admitted. "She's making chocolate for the king. He's not going to let her go back to Wander with me."

"Then you'll have to stay with her," Soldier Wolf said, turning around on the driver's bench.

"Stay in Londwin City?" I'd never considered this. "And do what?"

"Whatever it takes," Wolf said. "If you've got the chance at love, boy, you've got to fight for it."

I was about to ask Mister Thistle what he thought when he suddenly hollered, "Stop!"

Red-haired people, dozens of them, sat alongside the road. Mostly women and children, and a few elderly men. Bone thin, they clung wearily to one another, staring at us with vacant expressions. One of the little girls held out her empty palm. "Let me out," Mister Thistle cried, gripping the bars. The cage shook.

"Let him out," I told Wolf.

As soon as Wolf unlocked the cage, Mister Thistle leaped to the ground and ran to his people. He knelt beside one of the elderly men and spoke in hushed tones. "Hurry up!" Wolf called. Mister Thistle ignored him. "You staying here? I ain't waiting around!"

"What's the matter with you?" I snapped at Wolf. "Can't you see they're starving? Give that girl some food."

Soldier Wolf looked over at the food bag. "You want to give up your rations?"

"Yes. Give them my rations."

"Mine too," one-eyed Henry said.

Wolf grabbed the bag and handed it to the girl, who peered up at him through ropes of tangled hair. She could have been Emmeline's younger sister. It didn't escape my notice that Wolf had handed over his rations too.

"What's going on?" I hollered.

As the girl passed out the rations of dried meat and fruit, Mister Thistle returned to the wagon. "It's just as you said," he told me. "The flood destroyed everything. All the food is spoiled. They've come here to ask the king for help. But the soldiers won't let them into the city."

"Then we'll tell the king," I said. "As soon as we get to the tournament, we'll make certain he knows."

"I'll stay here," Mister Thistle said. "They need menfolk to protect them. Tell Emmeline I will see her as soon as I can." I nodded. Then Mister Thistle leaned close to the bars and spoke directly to me. "You can ask Emmeline to marry you, but you'll still have to wait for the next husband market. That's how it's done with my people."

I guess that was his way of telling me he approved.

But would she?

Leaving the dirt-scratchers behind, Wolf drove the wagon toward the city gates. Londwin City's wall stood twice as tall as Wander's wall. Soldiers marched along the top. Beyond the wall, stone buildings towered as far as the eye could see, their lifeless chimneys pointing to the sky. My heartbeat doubled with anticipation. She was in there, somewhere. She'd be surprised to see me. I'd tell her how sorry I was that I didn't save her from Peddler. Then, if she didn't totally reject me, I'd tell her how I felt. How I'd felt since I first saw her lying on the riverbank. How I felt each time I saw her—dazed, stunned, an ache in my stomach. Those words were no good. Why was it so hard to describe a stupid feeling? Where was a book of poetry when I needed one?

Soldier Wolf pulled the horse to a stop. One-eyed Henry and I scooted to the front of the cage. Three messengers were arguing with a soldier. "I carry a scroll from the Baron of Highland for the king," one of the messengers declared. "It's urgent."

"I'm under strict orders not to let anyone into the city," the soldier replied. "King Elmer is preparing for his tournament and he wants no interruptions."

The messenger waved the scroll. "But I carry a proposal of marriage for the Milkmaid and it must be delivered immediately."

"Hey!" another messenger cried. "I carry the same proposal from the Baron of Lowland."

"As do I from the king's cousin, Lord Morgan," the third messenger said.

Wolf turned and frowned at me. "Looks like you'll have to get into line if you want to marry her." I gripped the bars so hard it felt as if my fingers would snap.

"Wait here," the soldier said. Then he walked through the gate to talk to another soldier. When he returned he addressed all the messengers. "You can all go home," he told them. "Your proposals aren't any good here."

The messengers waved their scrolls and objected, but the soldier silenced them with a shrill whistle. "I said they aren't any good because the Milkmaid has already accepted a proposal of marriage. She is to marry the Prince of Anglund."

My fingers released and my hands slid down the cage bars.

Chapter Forty-six

I might have been able to compete with a merchant or even a baron, since they were usually old, fat men. But I couldn't compete with a prince. I had no palace to offer, no kingdom. Just a dairy and a bunch of brown woolly cows. And my love.

Did the prince even love her? Surely he did. How could he not?

Did she love him?

I knew very little of the prince. People rarely spoke of him. Some said he dressed like a commoner and had no interest in politics. But he must have swooped in with his crown and treasures and servants, and she'd said aye to all of it. Of course she had. How could a girl who'd grown up with nothing say no to a prince? Even if she'd had feelings for me, which she probably never had, she'd be a fool to refuse such a proposal.

How different things might have been if I'd stopped Peddler from taking her!

"Tough luck," one-eyed Henry said as we drove through the

gates. The soldier, learning we were barefist fighters come for the tournament, had let us through.

"Shut up," I snapped.

"You shut up," he snapped right back.

Once we'd reached the tents, Soldier Wolf let us out of the cage. We signed our names to a list of fighters. "You try to escape now," Wolf said, "and you'll be hanged as traitors. You got that?" We both nodded. My gaze searched for signs of her. But there were no women in this crowd—only fighters and their promoters.

We claimed a pair of mattresses in the first tent and waited while Wolf went to do something. The tent was crowded with men. Some slept while others ate and shared fighting stories. I didn't want to lie there. My legs ached from the long journey. "Tell Wolf I've gone for a walk," I said. Henry grunted and wiped at his empty socket.

Just as I headed out the tent, a familiar voice called my name. "Owen? Owen Oak? Is that you?" Bartholomew Raisin scurried up to me, his pinprick eyes flashing with excitement. "Where have you been? We need to get you registered right away."

"I'm already registered," I said, actually happy to see him. He was the first person from Wander I'd run into since leaving.

He frowned. "I didn't register you. You're my champion. You're supposed to fight for me."

"Look, Raisin," I said, "stop yapping and listen to me. How are my parents?"

"Fine. Worried about you but they're fine." He looked around, then stepped closer, rubbing his puffy hands together. "Who are you fighting for? I'll buy you from him. I'll pay him well. You fight for me. That's how it's always been."

My gaze drifted over his head, searching for her. Servants dressed from head to toe in black were handing out loaves of bread and jugs of ale. I grabbed a jug and took a long drink, washing the remaining bitterness of the mineral fields from my mouth. But a new bitterness had taken its place. "I don't care who the hell I fight for," I told Bartholomew Raisin. "Make whatever arrangements you want."

I shoved past him and headed toward a gold-edged door from which the servants came and went. I'd promised Mister Thistle that I'd tell the king about the starving dirt-scratchers. And Emmeline needed to know that her father was just outside the city wall. No one stood guard at the door, but just as I was about to step inside, a man with a very white face stepped out.

"Who are you?" he asked. He'd painted his lips red. His collar reached so high it looked like his head had been placed there, like a snowball on top of a fence post. He carried a bundle of parchment.

"I need to get a message to the king," I told him.

"Indeed?" He pursed his lips. "I am the Royal Secretary. If you have a message, you may deliver it to me." I told him about the dirt-scratchers, but he didn't seem much interested. He tapped his long, pointed shoe. "Is there something else?"

"Yes. I need to see Emmeline."

"Who?"

"The Milkmaid."

He snorted. "The sudden interest in that dirt-scratcher girl is astounding. Away with you. Before I call the soldiers."

"But I must get a message to her," I insisted, my temper rising to the surface. "She needs to know that her father is here. He's with the other dirt-scratchers, just outside the city wall. Tell her that."

The secretary narrowed his eyes, a twitch pulling a corner of his mouth. "The father is here?"

"Yes."

"How very interesting." He pulled a quill from behind his ear and wrote something on a piece of parchment. Then he hurried off, darting between tents and disappearing from view. I had no faith he'd actually deliver the message. But I didn't have time to come up with another plan because Soldier Wolf ran up to me.

"You're in the first fight!" he cried, his face flushed. "Where's Henry?"

"Why am I first?"

"We were the last to arrive so we had no choice in the matter. The first slot was the only one unclaimed. It's not so good fighting first," he grumbled as we searched for Henry. "The first fight always gets the least attention."

I didn't care if I fought first or last. I'd come to see Emmeline. But that no longer seem likely.

After we found Henry, we entered the arena. The dirt circle was bigger than the one in Wander. The tiered benches were half-full. People mingled, greeting one another. Up on the top tier, three empty thrones waited. The people who sat closest to the thrones were an odd sort with powered faces and colored lips. The women had red circles painted on their cheeks and wore feathered hats. To my far right, a forest of green spread across the benches where merchants sat. To my left a cloud of floppy black hats hovered over the benches where the tax-collectors sat. No one paid us any attention. The air hummed with conversation.

"Get ready," Wolf told us. One-eyed Henry and I took off our shirts and boots. A boy, carrying a bucket of blue paint, painted the number 1 on Henry's chest, then painted number 2 on mine. Blue drops rolled past my navel. My heartbeat doubled, anticipation building in my gut the way it always did. I stretched my legs, still stiff from the cramped ride in the cage. I just wanted to get this over with. But if I knocked Henry off his feet, I'd be here for days, advancing to the next level, then the next. If I took a blow and threw the fight, I could leave. Get back home. Forget about Emmeline and her prince.

I'd do it. I'd throw the fight.

An official approached us—a burly man with flecks of his last meal in his thick beard. "You know the rules?" he asked.

I nodded, as did Henry.

"That's good." He folded his arms. "What do you want us to do with your bodies?"

I raised my eyebrows. "Pardon me?"

"One of you is going to die so I need to know what to do with you. We got the incinerator out back. But if you want your body sent home, then you'll need to pay a death tax and the gravedigger's fee."

"Look," I said calmly. "Henry, here, might be three times my size but he's not going to kill me. So don't worry about it."

The official glanced at Soldier Wolf. "No one told you?"

Wolf shrugged. "Told me what?"

The official smiled, his brown teeth like chunks of wood. "The rules were changed to make things more interesting. It'll be a fight to the death. No exceptions." He pulled a knife from his belt. "So if one of you doesn't kill the other, I'll step in and choose the loser."

One-eyed Henry and I shared a long, terrified look.

Chapter Forty-seven

The chambermaids held me down and poured black dye over my head. Fumes rose from the porcelain sink and stung my eyes. I trembled with humiliation. The queen watched, circling like a bird of prey. "There's nothing we can do about the foot. The surgeon said it's too late to straighten it. However, we can do something about the hair," she said. "You are no longer a dirt-scratcher. You are my son's future bride."

"I'm Emmeline," I insisted. "Emmeline Thistle. From the Flatlands."

She froze. "You are *not* from the Flatlands." She tapped her fingers on the side of the sink. "The Prince of Anglund cannot marry a commoner. Thus, from this moment hence, you are a princess from a distant land. No one can know your real identity."

She was going to rewrite history, just as Queen Margaret before her.

"I'm—" I sputtered, water trickling into my mouth. One of

the maids wrapped a towel around my head, another wiped my face dry. I pushed them away, stumbling backward. "I'm a Flatlander and I don't care who knows." The towel tumbled from my head.

"I care!" the queen roared, her eyes fiery with rage. The room fell into silence as our gazes locked. She'd made a huge mistake and I knew it. She knew it. She cleared her throat. "We care," she corrected. "*We* care."

"I know the truth," I whispered, my jaw trembling. "You have dirt-scratcher blood. So does your son." I held my ground, even as her face contorted with fury. "Your ancestor, Queen Margaret, was a *dirt-scratcher*."

The queen stomped her foot. "Out!" she ordered. The maids, their hands black with dye, scurried from the room. The two of us stood, glaring at each other. Droplets rolled down my face but I didn't wipe them away. "You speak treason," she said between clenched teeth.

"I know you dye your hair," I said. The queen took a step toward me. Though my heart nearly burst through my chest, I held my ground, balancing on the tip of my curled foot, trying to stand as straight as possible. "I know your true hair looks like mine."

"You are a fool to speak to us that way."

"Why don't you tell the people the truth?" I asked. "My people have a right to know that they were here first. They have a right to live outside the Flatlands. You share our blood. You should help us."

I'd gone too far. A gurgled sound arose in her throat. She lunged at me and grabbed my shoulders. Then she twisted me around to face a golden mirror. I gawked at the reflection that greeted me. The girl's hair hung in black ropes. Trails of black ran down the front of her dress. Tears welled in her eyes. *She isn't real*, I told myself. *She is part of a horrid dream. I do not know that girl.*

"You are no longer Emmeline. You are who we say you are," Queen Beatrice said with the icy cold of the River Time. "You do what we tell you to do." Then she released my shoulders and walked toward the door, her jeweled belt clinking with each precise step.

"That wasn't our agreement," I said. "I never agreed to be someone else." The queen kept walking, not a glitch to her steps. "I won't make chocolate for you. I'll stop. If you don't change my hair back, I'll stop."

"Then we will kill him," she said as she reached for the door's handle.

"Him?" I whispered.

"The boy who brought you here. We had him escorted to the dungeon."

My knees began to tremble. "You said you gave him the reward and he returned home."

"He's alive, that's his reward. And as long as you make the chocolate, he lives." The queen chuckled. "The only way I can keep you in your place is to possess something you love."

I clenched my fingers. "When your son rules, everything will be different."

"Rule? My son rule?" She opened the door. "Prince Beauregard is too weak to rule."

As she left the room, the chambermaids returned. I sat limply on a stool while they dried and combed my hair. It all made sense. That's why Griffin didn't wait to say good-bye. That's why he had simply disappeared. Everything had been a lie, right from the start.

"Griffin," I whispered.

Chapter Forty-eight

Henry and I stood in the dirt circle, our painted numbers now dry, though mine had begun to itch with sweat. The dirt was perfect, rock-free, soft beneath my twitching toes. The benches were almost full. I craned my neck and peered up at the sky. Even though Henry was a bumbling kind of brute, heavy on his feet, this could possibly be my last day. My last hour. My last moment.

I'd tried to run. As soon as I realized that Soldier Wolf had tricked us, that we had to fight to the death, I darted beneath the railing and had just about made it to the exit when three soldiers tackled me and dragged me back.

So there I stood, facing my opponent. His broad shoulders and wide chest blocked my view like a flesh-covered rampart. His sunken eyelid glistened. But there was no rage in his good eye, not like the other times we'd fought. "I'm sorry I've got to kill you," he said.

"Likewise," I told him. I'd never killed anyone. Death in the barefist fights happened. With the right angle and force, a jealous husband or hired assassin could easily snap a neck or crush a temple. But most men fought honorably within the dirt circle, the goal to knock the opponent off his feet for ten beats of the drum. Nothing more. But today it was kill or be killed. That was my choice.

What kind of cruddy choice was that?

"Think of it this way," Henry said with a shrug. "You can't have the girl you love. So what you got to live for? Might as well let me kill you."

"Thanks for the sentiment," I said. "That makes me feel much better."

"Good luck, Owen!" Bartholomew Raisin called from the pit where the fighters and their promoters sat. Standing on tiptoe, he leaned over the railing, his greedy eyes flashing with possibility. "I put fifty coin on you so you'd better win!"

"Wouldn't want to cause you any inconvenience!" I hollered back. How rude it would be of me to lighten Bartholomew's coin purse.

The bearded official stepped between us. "After the third beat of the drum you begin." He looked at one-eyed Henry, then looked pityingly at me. "If the pummeling gets too much to bear, just give me a signal and I'll cut your throat. Sometimes a swift death is best."

I swallowed hard. "That won't be necessary."

The official shrugged, then stepped back. A drummer, who sat in the pit, raised his baton, but a sudden blast of a horn interrupted his motion. Conversations immediately ceased and everyone stood, their heads turning toward a golden doorway on the upper level. "The king," the official said. Then he punched my arm. "On your knee for the king." One-eyed Henry and I copied the official as he knelt in the circle. A wave of turning heads rolled across the benches as the door opened.

King Elmer waddled in, a shrub of white hair sticking out the top of his crown. He breathed like a bulldog, wheezing and grunting with his strained movements. He headed toward his throne, then wedged himself between the armrests. Servants crowded around with trays of food and drink. I frowned. There sat the man responsible for squeezing Anglund in a vise with his unjust taxes. Had he been told about the starving dirt-scratchers? I had no way of knowing.

The horn sounded and Queen Beatrice entered. A tall, dark-haired woman, she moved with smooth steps as if her feet never touched the ground. Chains of glittering jewels dangled from her waist. She nodded and waved at the onlookers, then took her place on the other throne. One throne remained empty.

I waited, my breathing quick and shallow. Where was he? Where was the man who'd claimed Emmeline's heart? Would she be with him?

The arena was silent, everyone still facing the king who slurped ale from a golden goblet. The queen leaned over and whispered something in his ear. "What's that?" he bellowed.

"The fighters are waiting for your orders." She folded her hands in her lap, a tight smile plastered on her face.

"The fighters?" He shoved the goblet at a servant, then waved his hands. "I can't see a damn thing over those bloody hats!" The powder-faced people sat. The women removed their feathered hats. Then the king smiled. "Now I see. The fighters are ready. Hello, fighters!" He waved. The official jabbed me in the side with his elbow. I waved back. So did one-eyed Henry. Everyone in the audience waved too. The king waved again. The audience waved. Henry and I waved. I might have laughed if I hadn't been keenly aware of death hovering nearby.

My gaze darted here and there. Still no sight of her. Was she with him? Was he tall and handsome like his mother or was he a fat dullard like his father? She couldn't possibly love him, could she?

"Your Majesties," the official called, still on his knee. "The first fighters are ready."

King Elmer slapped his armrest. "Look at the size of number one. We wager he'll be victorious." He grabbed a skewer of meat and pointed it at me. "You there, number two. Since you are about to die, do you have a final request?"

Change the rules. Let me go. Give me a different opponent. All these requests ran through my head, but I knew that none would be granted. Henry and I were the entertainment for these lazy, soft-bellied fools who fed on the work of others. Who ate without toil. Who slept without exhaustion. They wanted a bloodbath to fill the moments between their naps and parties.

"Get on your feet when you address His Majesty," the official said with a shove.

I stood. King Elmer chewed, grease shining at the corners of his painted mouth. Queen Beatrice stroked a string of yellow beads, her gaze turned skyward. "Your Majesties," I said, boldly aiming my voice at the thrones. "I do have a final request."

The king stopped chewing. The strand of beads dropped from the queen's hands and she looked at me for the first time. Everyone sat forward in their seats.

"I want to see Emmeline, the Milkmaid," I called. "I need to tell her something."

"What's that?" the king hollered, a piece of meat flying from his mouth.

"He wants to marry her," one-eyed Henry bellowed.

"I want to talk to her," I said as I walked toward the railing. "She needs to know that her people are outside the city gates. The dirt-scratchers have no homes because the Flatlands flooded. They're starving and they've come here for help."

"Dirt-scratchers?" The word hissed around the arena, slipping from mouths pursed with disgust.

Queen Beatrice stood and held up her hands. The arena fell into silence. "Who are you?" she asked, her cold voice sliding over the heads of tax-collectors and merchants until it reached me.

"I'm Owen Oak, from Wander. I'm a dairyman's son."

"Well, Owen Oak, dairyman's son, we do not understand why you believe the Milkmaid would care about dirt-scratchers. The Milkmaid is not from the Flatlands. She is from a distant land, and her only concern is the making of chocolate and the pending marriage to our son, Prince Beauregard."

"Your Majesty," I said, not weighing the words before I spoke, for what did I have to lose? To kill or to be killed was my fate.

"Emmeline is from the Flatlands. I know this because I found her after she was washed downriver. Please, do not let her people starve. I have met many dirt-scratchers. They are good people. They are citizens of the realm. They need your help."

Stunned faces stared back at me from the tiered seats. Eyes widened, mouths hung open. The queen's face twisted into a grimace. "The Prince of Anglund would never marry a dirt-scratcher." She addressed the entire arena. "Dirt-scratchers have red hair. The Milkmaid has hair as black as mine. Everyone will see this at the Royal Wedding, which will take place tomorrow." People murmured in agreement.

Black hair?

The queen continued. "We have no interest in the welfare of dirt-scratchers. We will send them back to the Flatlands where they belong." More murmurs.

The king, who'd finished his skewer of meat, hollered, "Stop talking and fight! To the death!"

The crowd took up the call. "To the death. To the death." Cheers rose and feet stomped. The official motioned at the drummer, then stepped to the edge of the dirt circle. One-eyed Henry staggered to his feet. He raised his fists. The drum beat once, twice, thrice. I looked around one last time for Emmeline. She'd never know about her people. They'd die like dogs at the side of the road and she'd never know. Or maybe she didn't care anymore. Maybe a life with the prince was what she wanted. Maybe she'd dyed her hair so she could be one of them.

No. I didn't believe it.

Henry lunged at me. I ducked beneath his armpit. I could probably sidestep his blundering movements all day. Or until the official grew bored and slit one of our throats. Henry growled and lunged again. As I darted away, movement caught my eye. The golden door had opened and a young man walked out. Black-haired but with a normal, unpowdered face, he took the throne next to Queen Beatrice. I gritted my teeth, trying not to imagine him kissing Emmeline when . . . wham! Henry threw a punch to my right cheek.

The crowd cheered. I spat blood into the dirt. One-eyed Henry bent forward and charged me like a bull. That's when I decided what I had to do. Enough with this stupid fight. I turned and ran straight for the railing. The merchants who sat in the front row gasped as I leaped over the railing and ran up the steps toward the thrones. Rather than try to stop me, the powder-faced people shrank back, clinging to one another in fear. "Prince," I called as my feet hit the fourth tier. "Emmeline needs to know—"

Two soldiers grabbed my arms and twisted them behind my back, holding me in place. I didn't struggle. I was already a dead man. All I wanted was for Emmeline to know the truth.

The prince darted in front of his mother, guarding her with outstretched arms. He wore no weapon. A pair of strange spectacles hung around his neck. We locked gazes. "What did you say about Emmeline?" he asked.

"I need to tell her something. I'm her friend. My name is Owen." I winced as the soldiers tightened their grip. "I brought her father from the mineral fields. He's waiting outside the gates."

The prince took a step toward me. "Her father?"

"This boy is a madman, full of lies," the queen said, pushing the prince aside. "He claims that your future bride is a dirt-scratcher. He asks us to concern ourselves with dirt-scratchers who have gathered outside the city wall. We care not about such matters. We will order them back to the Flatlands."

"The Flatlands were destroyed," I said. "The people will die. They need food."

"Let them die," the queen said. "We care not. Take him away."

My gaze burned into the prince. "Tell her," I called as the soldiers dragged me toward the golden door. "Tell her about her father. Tell her about her people." The door opened and just before they shoved me through I cried, "Tell her that Owen Oak loves her."

Chapter Forty-nine

Prince Beau hurried into my room. He wore a long brown cloak. I lay curled on the bed, a ball of anger and shame. My hair had dried but the pillows were still damp. "Your mother lied to me," I said quietly.

The chambermaids were playing a game of cards. They scrambled to their feet and bowed like trained animals. "Out," he told them. As soon as we were alone, he slammed shut the door and tossed a second brown cloak onto the bed. "Put this on. I'm taking you outside."

"Outside?"

"Yes. There's something you need to see. It's important." He frowned at me. "I'm sorry she did that to your hair."

"She never gave Griffin his reward," I said as I grabbed the cloak and slid off the bed. I hadn't felt this much anger since my days with Peddler. I nearly broke the cord as I tied the cloak around my shoulders. "She promised to give him the reward but she stuck him in the dungeon. She said she'd kill him if I stopped making chocolate."

"It's worse than I ever imagined," the prince said as he stared out the window. "My mother has gone too far this time. She has lost her humanity."

"Where are we going?"

"Outside the walls."

"But I'm not supposed—"

"I'll say I ordered you to go."

I strained to keep up with the prince's determined pace. We took the narrow staircase that led to my churning room. No one questioned the prince as he led me through the kitchen labyrinth. The rooms and hallways were crowded with servants and cooks bustling here and there. The royal chefs shouted orders. "More salt!" "Baste the guinea hens!" "Brown the butter!" Baskets of carrots and cabbage were stacked one on top of the other. Cauldrons bubbled. A man unloaded a wagon of peacocks. Another led two pigs toward the slaughter room. "What's going on?" I asked.

"Our wedding is tomorrow," the prince said. "On the second day of tournament. All the ambassadors will be here. Mother decided to hold our wedding first thing in the morning, before the tournament begins."

"Tomorrow morning?" I didn't care if I sounded disgusted. I was. I hated the queen and wanted nothing to do with her plans. But I was as much her prisoner as Griffin.

"She will introduce you to the ambassadors and then she'll give them each a gift." He motioned me into the chocolate room.

Servants sat at a long table painting gold swans on the chocolate squares before setting them neatly into golden boxes. "These boxes will be given to each ambassador to take back to their kings and bishops. Once the outside world has tasted chocolate, the orders will pour in. With the profits, Mother will build a new palace. I've seen the design."

"Another palace?" I asked. He nodded. "And all the while, she'll hold Griffin hostage."

"My parents are holding the entire realm hostage," he said.

I followed him into a room lined with shelves of bread. His friend, the Baron of Lime, waited in the room, baskets in hand. One basket was filled with apples, the other with smoked turkey legs. The baron also wore a long brown cloak. The prince grabbed a crate and filled it with bread rolls. "Why do we need all this bread?"

"I'm taking you to see your people," he said.

"My people?"

"A group of dirt-scratchers are outside the city wall. They're starving. We're going to take this food to them, but we have to be sneaky." He and the baron tied their cloaks, then pulled the hoods over their heads. Prince Beau pulled my hood over my black hair. "If Mother finds out she'll punish me, probably by exiling the baron to the mineral fields."

The baron grumbled. "I'd like to see her try."

The peacock wagon lay empty, the driver carrying the last two birds toward the curing room. When the driver disappeared around a corner, the Baron of Lime set the baskets inside, then climbed onto the wagon's bench. Prince Beau placed the crate of bread into the wagon, then jumped in. He grabbed my hand and pulled me in beside him. The baron flicked the reins and drove the wagon through the kitchen courtyard, down an alleyway, and out onto a Londwin street.

My people were out there. They weren't supposed to leave the Flatlands. Would they be arrested? Or worse? As if sensing my impatience, the baron urged the horse into a gallop. We flew past lifeless stone buildings, soot rising in our wake. Though the chimneys had been asleep for weeks, soot still clung to everything—a powdery reminder of days gone by. The gargoyles no longer frightened me. I felt like one of them—stuck in this city for the rest of my life, as if I too were cemented to a rooftop.

Shouting filled the air as we neared the city gate—the sound of not one, but many voices calling the king's name.

To get the soldiers to open the gate, Prince Beau had to reveal his identity. But he pulled the hood over his head as soon as the gate opened. The gathered crowd was in an uproar, shaking fists and shouting, throwing stones at the wall. "Why are they here?" I asked, pulling my cloak tighter around my face.

"They've come to protest the taxes," the prince said as the wagon rolled through the gate. The crowd parted as the horse pushed through. Not far up the road, just as the shouting was beginning to fade in the distance, the baron yanked the reins. There, beneath a cluster of trees, sat a group of tattered people. My people.

I knew some of the women and children who'd once lived in Root, but many others I didn't know. My heart ached as I recognized the hollow cheeks and sagging skin of starvation. As the horse came to a stop, Prince Beau and I climbed out with the baskets of food. "Eat," the prince said. "It's free." But none of the Flatlanders moved, looking warily at him.

"It's okay," I told them. "We've brought food for you. You can eat." I pushed my hood away. The Flatlanders stared at me. Even though my accent sounded like theirs, distrust clung to their faces. "Please don't be afraid. I look different but I'm Emmeline. I'm from Root."

"Emmeline?" a woman said. It was Missus Trog, the grave-digger's wife. "Is that really you, Emmeline?"

"Aye." I carried the crate toward her, my limp speaking louder than words.

"Emmeline," they whispered, their faces relaxing. Even though I was an outcast amongst them, they trusted me over the prince and the baron. The women let go of the children, who flung themselves at the food. Prince Beau and the baron set the baskets on the ground. Every morsel was grabbed. The food wouldn't be enough, though. They'd die if I didn't figure out a way to help them. My gaze traveled over their faces. A boy with freckles, a young mother with her babe bundled on her back, an elderly woman with a missing tooth, a man with sharp shoulders . . .

Was I seeing things?

"Father?" He stood a few feet away. "Father?" I whispered.

He walked up to me, his face older than I remembered. "I thought I'd never see you again," he said.

Was he glad to see me? Honestly I couldn't tell. Or was it the same as always—my presence reminding him of the burden I'd brought to our family. "I wanted to find you," I started to explain. "I was trying . . ."

There was no hesitation. Before I could say another word he wrapped his arms around me. "I am happy you are safe." He had never embraced me in this way. The other Flatlanders stopped eating for a moment and watched. I tried to pull out of his hug. Surely his mind was sick from hunger. He'd never hugged me in private and to do so in front of our people would bring him shame.

"Father," I said, trying to remind him. "I know I look different, but I'm still Emmeline. They still think I'm unnatural."

"I don't care what they think." He held tight. "You are not my shame, Emmeline. That I cast you aside is my shame. That has always been my shame."

We stood like that for a long time, until our breathing settled and my tears stopped flowing. Until someone tugged on my skirt. Small green eyes stared up at me. "Thank you, Emmeline." The girl couldn't have been more than eight or nine. From her hollow features and sallow skin, it was clear that death had been hovering, waiting to snatch her.

"You're welcome," I said.

An older woman took the girl's hand. To my surprise, she did not pull the girl away from me. "We've had no food for days," the woman told me. "You have saved my daughter's life."

The others thanked me, including Missus Trog. Because exhaustion and fear had eaten away at them, maybe they no longer had the strength to despise me. But it genuinely felt as if my unnatural status had been vanquished by the simple act of bringing bread. In their desperate eyes, I was reborn.

"We will bring more," I said, glancing at Prince Beau. He nodded.

My father stepped away and looked down at his cracked boots. "Please forgive me, Emmeline. I haven't been as a father should be. Losing your mother was nearly too much to bear. I haven't felt alive since her death."

"I understand," I told him. "I know how it feels to lose someone you love." I took his callused hand. "Will you tell me about her? When we have more time?" He nodded.

While the Baron of Lime waited at the wagon, Prince Beau walked up to my father. "Mister Thistle?" he said, holding out his hand. "It's an honor to meet you. My name is Prince Beauregard."

Father did not offer his hand. "My people are not slaves," he said defiantly. I suddenly remembered this defiance. It had been a part of him when I was little, when he'd organized a revolt against taxes. Before Mother's death.

"Pardon me?" Prince Beau asked.

"My people are not slaves. We are citizens. You have no right taking us from our homes and enslaving us in the mineral fields."

"Slaves in the mineral fields?" Prince Beau frowned. "Well, I can guess who's behind that." He held out his chin and stared deep into my father's eyes. "For now, I can only offer you sustenance and apologize for my mother's actions. And promise that when I marry your daughter, she will be protected. I have no power yet, but when I'm king there will be no slavery in the realm." Over at the wall, the crowd's shouting grew louder. "We should get back to the palace before you are discovered missing."

I ran my hand over my blackened hair. "There is much I need to tell you," I said to my father. "But I must leave. We'll bring more food as soon as possible. And we'll figure out a way to help everyone." I had no idea how we'd do that, and the prince's uneasy look didn't give me much confidence. "In the meantime, don't tell anyone that you're my father," I warned, thinking of the queen's dungeon. She'd throw him into the same cell with Griffin. "Keep your name a secret until I can figure out how to fix things."

Prince Beau shuffled nervously, looking toward the looming city walls. "I really think—"

"You intend to marry my daughter?" my father asked, his head held high. I smiled. The way he'd interrupted, he could have been talking to our neighbor back in Root. It didn't seem to faze him that it was the prince of Anglund who stood before him.

"Yes," Prince Beau said. "Tomorrow. Before the second day of tournament."

"That is not possible." Father folded his arms. "Emmeline must bid for you at the next husband market."

"Husband market?" Prince Beau asked with a slight smile. "What's that?"

"It's our tradition," Father said. "It has always been our tradition. I tried to explain this to the other boy."

"What other boy?" I asked.

"The one who brought me here. The one who saved me from the mineral fields. Owen. Owen Oak."

I forgot how to breathe. The shouting in the distance faded and all I could hear was the beating of my heart in my ears.

Chapter Fifty

"Where is he?"

"He went to the tournament," my father said. "The king's tournament. He's going to fight."

I pulled my skirt to my knees and ran from the clearing, my lopsided stride carrying me past the wagon where the Baron of Lime waited to drive us back to the city. Owen. Owen was alive. Owen was behind those walls. In the arena. He'd saved my father. He was here!

I tried to run faster, my boots kicking up pebbles as I reached the road. The city gate seemed so far away. But someone grabbed my arm, pulling me to a stop. "Emmeline, where are you going?" the prince asked.

"Owen's alive," I said.

"Emmeline. Listen to me. There's something I must tell you."

"Please help me get back through the gate," I pleaded, my face twisted with happiness and panic. "I want to see him. I thought he was dead. But he's here. He's in the arena."

"That's what I need to tell you." Prince Beau held tight to my arm. "He was in the arena. He was one of the first fighters. But . . ."

"But what?"

"He said things. He spoke against the king. Mother had him sent to the dungeon."

I yanked my arm from his grip. "You knew Owen was in the dungeon? Why didn't you tell me?"

"I was going to tell you. No, that's a lie." He looked away. "I was going to have him released. Same with your other friend, that much is true. But I wasn't going to tell you because I was afraid you'd want to leave with them. If you marry me, Emmeline, you could solve a lot of problems for me."

"What do you mean?"

"My reputation is tenuous at best. The people don't know me. I've spent most of my life working on my inventions, shut away from public activities. Mother would rather leave the throne to one of my cousins. She thinks I'm weak, that I'm half a man because . . ."

"Because you love the baron."

He met my gaze with surprise. "Yes."

I stepped closer. "Do *you* think you're half a man?"

"No, of course not. I know what I'm capable of. I know the changes I want to bring to Anglund. The taxes must be fair. They must benefit the people with new roads and a better sewage system. And we must have progress. The last thing we need is a new palace."

"You don't need me by your side to accomplish that. As long as Anglund is your first love, the people won't care who you

choose as your private love." I turned and looked back at the city gate. *Owen.*

"Would you leave?" Prince Beau asked. "Would you leave if you could?"

"Aye."

"You'd give up a life with servants and jewels and a crown?"

"Aye. For freedom, aye."

"You would have freedom once I rule," he said. "You would not have to make the chocolate unless you wanted to. You could go wherever you wanted. You could . . ." Understanding filled his eyes. "Oh, I see. You are speaking of a different kind of freedom. You love him."

I nodded.

Prince Beau took my arm again, but this time with a gentle, guiding touch. "Then there is something else you need to know. He was thrown in the dungeon for treason. He's going to be executed after the tournament tomorrow."

"Executed?" My knees weakened, but the prince held me upright.

"I will still have him released," he said. "I will bribe the guards. Both of your friends will be free."

"Thank you."

I looked over his shoulder where my father and the Baron of Lime stood, the homeless Flatlanders gathered around. The Kell. The first people. My people.

"What do we do about them?" the prince asked as he followed my gaze. "Until I rule, I have no power to rebuild the Flatlands."

I struggled for an answer. It did not lie with the king, who was a buffoon, or with the queen, who'd prefer the Flatlanders to die. How had it come to this—that I was their only hope? Me. The girl they'd shunned. The girl with no purpose but to bring bad luck.

As the crowd continued to shout their protests outside the city wall, the answer came, unfurling itself like a flower in bloom. The link in our magic had been broken many generations ago, and I was about to fix it. I was about to change our world.

"The sweetest spell," I murmured.

And so, there on the road, with the unrest growing around us, the prince and I forged a plan.

Chapter Fifty-one

A trio of soldiers shoved me into a dungeon cell where I landed face-first in a pile of moldy straw. I scrambled to my feet as a thick wooden door closed behind me with a loud thud. A key turned in the lock. "Hey!" I shouted, my face pressed up to the door's barred window. "I'm a citizen. I demand to be heard. Send a scroll to my tax-collector. He'll vouch for me. Hey!" My voice echoed down the stone corridor. Laughter was the only reply as the soldiers strode away.

"You're wasting your time. They don't listen to reason."

A man stepped out of the shadows. It took a moment for my eyes to adjust to the dim light, which trickled in through slits set high in the wall. He stood tall and broad-chested. His shirt hung open and his pants had holes in the knees. Light settled on a newly grown beard and on the hair that covered his chest. The hair on his head was chopped as if with a dull knife. "You have red hair," I whispered.

"Aye, it's no secret. You don't have to whisper." His accent was exactly like Emmeline's. The forest grew in his eyes, just like it did in Emmeline's. "They know I'm a dirt-scratcher."

The air was rank with things I didn't want to discover. My gaze quickly swept the floor. Damp rotting straw, a bucket of crud, rat droppings—just like every dungeon in every story I'd ever read. How soon would the rats find my bare toes? Or my bare chest? How far underground were we? The walls began to close in and I struggled to find my voice. "Did they arrest you for leaving the Flatlands?" I asked as I pressed my spine against the door. "Did you leave because of the flood?"

"I didn't leave because of the flood. I left because . . ." He narrowed his eyes. "Why do you want to know these things? Who are you? Why do you have that number painted on your chest?"

"I'm a dairyman's son, from the town of Wander." The walls pressed closer. I turned around and yelled through the barred window. "Do you hear me out there? I demand to speak to someone! I have rights!"

"You're wasting your breath. They don't care. My name's Griffin, by the way."

I pounded my fists on the door. Surely I wouldn't be left here to rot. Bartholomew Raisin had witnessed the whole thing. He'd help me. He'd demand my release. "I broke no laws!" I hollered.

Griffin leaned against the wall. "I broke a few laws. I admit it. But that's not why I'm here. The king locked me away so he wouldn't have to pay the reward he'd promised. You heard of the Milkmaid?"

I stopped pounding. "Emmeline?"

"Aye. She's the one. I brought her to Londwin City and delivered her right to King Elmer's fat feet. He was supposed to give me the five thousand coin reward. But he threw me in here instead."

"*You* brought Emmeline to Londwin City?"

"She asked me to protect her." He stroked his furry chin. "Of course she wanted more from me than that. She's a woman, after all. She's going to bid on me at the next husband market."

"Bid on you?" Was this boasting or truth? "Emmeline wants to marry *you*?"

"Every girl in the Flatlands wants to marry me." He raised his eyebrows and looked at me as if I'd just crawled out from under a rock. As if I should have known that he was Mister Popular. Truth be told, his handsomeness shone even through the grime. Not that I usually paid attention to whether or not a man was handsome, but this guy was good-looking in a smack-you-in-the-face sort of way. It couldn't be ignored.

"I'm glad you're here," he said, slapping my back. "I'm thinking we'll have a good chance of escaping if we work together. That old guy in the corner's been no use at all. He's practically dead."

I didn't care about the old guy in the corner. Emmeline had traveled with this Griffin fellow so it was possible that they'd . . . "Wait a minute," I said. "Emmeline and you . . . ?" I cleared my throat. "*You're* in love with Emmeline?"

"She's in love with me," Griffin said. "No doubt about it. How could she not be?" He spread out his arms as if presenting himself to a panel of judges.

I measured myself against him. He stood at least a head taller, was nearly twice as wide, and then there was that whole "handsome" thing. His chest had probably grown to its size because it was inflated with confidence and arrogance, but didn't girls like that?

Griffin dropped his arms and smiled coyly. "Emmeline and I spent many a night together on the road. The least I can do is accept her bid. Besides, she's going to be the richest girl in the Flatlands and I deserve the richest girl."

Many a night? I was really starting to dislike this guy. "Look, buddy, I hate to break it to you, but Emmeline's marrying the prince of Anglund."

His smile fell. "Who?"

"The prince of Anglund."

"Never heard of him. But it doesn't matter because he's not from the Flatlands. Flatlanders marry Flatlanders. That's how it works."

"They *are* getting married," I said. "Queen Beatrice announced the marriage at the tournament." I pointed to the painted number on my own hairless chest. "I was there. I heard the queen tell everyone that Emmeline and the prince are getting married tomorrow."

Griffin scowled, then began to pace, his big boots kicking straw here and there. A rat darted from the straw, jumped over my bare feet, and squeezed through a space beneath the door. I cringed.

"I've got to get out of here," Griffin said. "I've got to talk to Emmeline."

I wanted the exact same thing. "We can take the soldiers," I said. "If we can get them to come into the cell, we can jump them. Do you have any kind of weapon?"

"No," Griffin said.

"I do," a weak voice said. "I have a knife."

"You have a knife?" Griffin lunged into the corner where someone lay in the shadows. Rustling sounded. "Why didn't you tell me you had a knife? Let me have it, old man!" More rustling sounds, a soft moan, and then Griffin returned to the light, a victorious smile on his face. "This will do," he said, holding out the blade. The handle was made from a brown woolly's horn. "Now we need a plan."

"Kill me," the old man said, his breath hissing like a teakettle. "If you kill me, then the soldiers will come and take away my dead body."

Wait a minute. I knew that voice! My heart leaped into my throat. Not caring what might be nesting beneath, I darted across the straw. He lay in a curled-up heap. I kicked his bone-thin leg. "Peddler, you bastard! Get up and face me like a man."

"You know him?" Griffin asked.

"He's the one who kidnapped Emmeline. He took her from my house. And he tried to kill me." I kicked him again. "Get up." Peddler groaned but didn't move.

"What was Emmeline doing at your house?" Griffin asked. "Hey, wait a minute. What's your name?"

Ignoring Griffin, I grabbed the tattered collar of Peddler's merchant coat and was about to pull him to his feet when he turned his weathered face toward me. "Go ahead and kill me, young Mister Oak. I have nothing to live for. My daughter is dead."

"I'm not interested in your lies," I said.

Slowly he sat up. His wispy hair, once covered in ground charcoal, was white again. He tilted his head back, exposing his wrinkled neck. "Do it. Break my neck. Kill me now."

I shuddered as his sour breath hit me. This was the moment I'd longed for. When I could bring him to justice. When I could take my revenge. My fingers twitched as I imagined wrapping them around his neck, which was as thin as a willow branch. I took a long breath . . .

. . . then relaxed my fingers. The urge to kill Peddler was gone. I'd carried a body's weight in hatred for him during this long journey. But now, knowing Emmeline was safe, I shed the hatred, feeling only disgust. "Your fate is in the king's hands now. I don't care if he hangs you or if he leaves you here to rot, but I'm definitely not going to relieve you of your misery."

Peddler slumped against the wall, his arms wrapped around his bony knees. "You have a right to hate me, Owen Oak. I shouldn't have taken Emmeline from you."

"Hold on." Griffin folded his arms and glared at me. "You're Owen. You?"

"Yes, I'm Owen. What of it?"

"She called out your name a few times in her sleep." He looked me up and down, not bothering to hide his surprise. "Why would she call out *your* name?"

"My name?" Was he serious? He looked serious, the way his eyebrows had knotted.

There I was, standing in the king's dungeon, surrounded by stink and filth, having learned that the woman I loved had spent *many a night* with the most handsome man in the kingdom and that she was also scheduled to marry a prince in the morning. I should have been nearly suicidal but that little piece of news—that she'd called out my name—gave me hope.

"In her sleep?" I couldn't believe it. "How did she say it? I mean, did she sound angry?"

He frowned. "I don't know how she said it."

"Come on, try to remember. Was it sad like this . . . *Owen*? Or was it kind of sweet like this . . . *Owen*? Or was it—"

"I don't remember." His glare could have burned me alive. "Doesn't matter how she said it, does it? Because I'm the one who protected her. You let her get kidnapped by an old man. But I brought her safely to the king. *I'm* the hero."

The truth stung. And because I had no good defense for losing to an old man, I went on the attack. "Some hero you are. You delivered her right into the prince's hands. And now you'll never marry her."

"Sounds like you two are in love with the same woman," Peddler mumbled from the corner. Griffin and I glared at each other.

"I was mistaken," Griffin said coldly. "She never called out your name. She thought you were dead."

"Emmeline thought I was dead? Why would she . . . ?" I whipped around. "What did you do, old man?" I darted into the corner and grabbed his arm. "Tell me!"

"I might have told her you were dead," he whimpered as I squeezed. "Okay, okay, I said you were dead."

His arm would surely snap if I squeezed any harder. "Why would you tell Emmeline that I was dead?"

"I didn't want her thinking you might rescue her. I was hoping she'd help me. I was trying to get coin for my daughter." He was weaving his lies again. "I kept my daughter, Lara, in a hidden place so no one would kill her. They kill lepers. They burn them alive. I wanted Emmeline to make me rich so I could buy Lara a nice house where she could live in secret." Pain clung to every inch of his face. "Where she could have nice things again. But the leprosy won." His shoulders shook as tears welled.

I released my grip. His grief was undeniable. The story was real!

He took a long, rattling breath. "Emmeline saw you lying on the ground after I stabbed you, so she believed me when I said you were dead. She shed many tears for you, Owen Oak."

Griffin snorted. "I doubt that."

"I've been searching for her all this time, yet she had no hope that I'd find her." The realization nearly sickened me. I pointed at Griffin. "That's why she turned to you. That's the only reason she turned to you. Because she thought I was dead."

"She turned to me because she's been in love with me her entire life, just like the other girls in Root." He gripped the knife.

Silence filled the cell. I steadied my breathing, pushing away the urge to knock the knife from his hands. The unfortunate fact was that I needed his help getting out of the cell. I couldn't take three soldiers on my own.

"I don't know if Emmeline loves you. I don't know if she loves me. But what I do know is that neither of us has a chance if we don't get out of here before she marries the prince."

"Aye," he said.

Peddler struggled to his feet, groaning as he leaned against the wall. "There is only one reason the queen is allowing her son to marry a dirt-scratcher and that is because of the chocolate. There is no love. You can be sure of that. You two must get out of here and tell Emmeline how you feel. Then she will have a chance for love."

"Why do you suddenly care about Emmeline's happiness?" I asked.

"Because Emmeline buried my daughter," Peddler said. "I went back and found the grave. No one buries a leper. But Emmeline did. She did that for Lara—my once-beautiful Lara. Even after what I'd done. Even after thinking I'd killed you. She paid my daughter great respect."

"What's the plan?" Griffin asked, pointing the knife at me. "Which one of us should use this?"

"I'm thinking," I said.

"You have to get the soldiers to enter the cell," Peddler said as he staggered toward us. "And there's only one way to do that."

"How—?"

With a sudden burst of energy, Peddler lunged at Griffin. He grabbed Griffin's outstretched arm with both of his withered hands, plunging the blade deep into his gut as he fell upon it. Shocked, Griffin released his grip on the knife and stepped away. Peddler collapsed onto the straw, blood spreading across the front of his coat.

I fell to my knees beside him. His words were garbled. "Dead body," he gasped. "The soldiers will come into the cell to collect a . . . dead . . . body."

Then he closed his eyes and took his final breath.

Part Nine

Emmeline

Chapter Fifty-two

By the time we got back inside the palace, darkness had fallen. The chambermaids, fearful of the queen's wrath, had kept my absence secret. They helped me into my nightfrock. Prince Beau took the blame, claiming he'd been escorting me through the royal gardens. Word was sent to the queen that I was in my bed, where I belonged. The prince took his leave, but we shared a knowing look. Tomorrow would be a big day.

I didn't sleep at all, picturing Owen in a cold, dreary, rat-infested dungeon. All this time I'd thought he was dead, but Peddler's knife hadn't killed him. Did he know I was to be married? Did he think I was marrying Prince Beau out of love? Would he even care? No words of love had ever passed between us.

But still, he'd come all this way to bring my father to me. Why would he do that if he didn't care?

Morning came, not quick enough. I was pacing the floor when faint sunlight crept between Londwin's buildings. *The plan would work*, I told myself. *It had to work.*

As the chambermaids dressed me for my wedding, I thought about what the prince had asked when we'd shaped our plan. Was I truly willing to give this up—the soft clean bed, the towels and warm baths, the soap and perfume, the endless banquet of food, the servants at my beck and call, the clothes and perfectly fitting shoes?

The dyed hair and fake marriage?

Aye. To be myself again. Aye.

The wedding gown was like spun clouds against my skin. It clung to my breasts and waist, falling in ribbons of white that brushed the floor as I walked. The chambermaids braided my black hair into dozens of twig-thin braids. I stepped away when they tried to powder my face. "No," I said. "No lip paint either." I wanted to look nothing like the monster who'd imprisoned me here.

The final touch was added—a wreath of white, thornless roses on my head. The Royal Secretary waited outside my chamber door. His collar stood higher than usual. Ruffles ran down both sleeves. "What's that?" I asked, pointing to a golden chair with long handles. Servants, dressed in wedding white, held the end of each handle.

"That is your chariot," the secretary said. He carried no pile of papers this morning—just a single scroll.

I sat in the chair. The seat wobbled as the servants carried me down the hallway, the secretary scurrying alongside. My thoughts were focused, not on the wedding ceremony, but on the interruption that the prince and I had planned. I had little control at this point. I'd done my part. The rest was up to him.

Just inside the throne hall, the chair came to a stop. I took a long look around. As before, when Griffin and I had been there together, it was filled with the odd painted people who surrounded the king and queen. Benches were set on both sides of the thrones. Seated on the benches were men who wore long, colorful robes. "Those are the ambassadors," the secretary whispered to me. "They are very important. Smile at them." Others filled the room. Men with large gold medallions around their necks. Women holding tiny dogs. Tax-collectors in their floppy hats, merchants in their green velvet coats. The candles sparkled above, musicians played from the balcony. A cloud of perfume choked the air.

People stepped aside, revealing the checkered pathway that led to the thrones. There sat King Elmer, his eyes closed, snoring. Queen Beatrice waited in her throne, a tense smile on her frozen face. Prince Beau stood at her side. His long white jacket also looked as soft as spun clouds. I started to get out of the chair. "The queen does not want you to walk," the Royal Secretary whispered.

"Why?"

He leaned in. "She does not wish anyone to see your disfigurement. It would bring her great shame. You are marrying her son, after all. You are never to walk in public again."

Everyone in the hall turned my way, cocking their heads to eavesdrop. Even the musicians slowed their music as they leaned over the railing to catch my words. "Never to walk again? That's ridiculous. How am I supposed to get around?"

"This chair will take you wherever you need to go." He fiddled with the scroll. "Of course, within the palace. You are to stay inside the palace at all times."

My glare shot down the checkered path, and I know the queen felt it because she winced. Ever so slightly, but she winced.

The Royal Secretary turned on his high heels. Facing the

thrones, he unrolled the scroll. The musicians ceased and the hall instantly quieted. The secretary cleared his throat, then read loud enough to wake the king. "Their Royal Majesties, King Elmer and Queen Beatrice, wish to thank all those who have gathered to witness this joyous occasion as the lineage of Their Royal Majesties is solidified through the union of Their son, Prince Beauregard Borthwick Elmer of Anglund, to a princess of a recently discovered but as yet unnamed island in the middle of the ocean."

I scowled. Who was going to believe that?

The crowd nodded and whispered, "Princess." The king sighed, rolling his eyes with boredom. But the queen fixed her gaze on me. This was her moment of glory over a peasant girl who would not only repair her son's reputation but also would make her the richest woman in the world. She smiled victoriously.

"We welcome you, Princess Sabina," the secretary announced. The crowd applauded.

What? They were changing my name too?

It was too much to bear. I pushed the Royal Secretary aside and jumped out of the chair, holding back a groan as I landed on my curled foot. Straightening my legs and holding my dyed head high, the wedding gown stretching with each deep breath, I met her gaze. The queen gripped her armrests, her smile gone. *She does not wish anyone to see your disfigurement. It would bring her great shame.*

I took a step, then another. The Royal Secretary gasped and tried to stop me but I shoved him away. Though this wasn't part of our plan, Prince Beau encouraged me with a nod. I walked down that checkered pathway, letting my body tip to the right, letting everyone see my *disfigurement*. The applause stopped. Everyone stared. When I reached the thrones, Prince Beau took my hand and guided me onto the stage. "You nervous?" he whispered.

"A little."

"Well, you don't look nervous. You look beautiful." He brushed a stray hair from my eyes, a gesture that didn't go unnoticed by the crowd. They nodded approvingly. The prince had such a kind, open face—a bit like Owen's. *Soon, Owen. You'll be freed from the dungeon soon.*

The Royal Secretary had followed me down the checkered pathway. He turned to the audience and continued reading from the scroll. "Their Royal Majesties, in accordance with tradition, will now bestow a gift to the honored ambassadors."

After a horn's blast, a line of servants entered, each carrying the golden boxes I'd seen in the chocolate room. A box was given to each of the robed ambassadors. The king opened his mouth but the queen shoved a box into his flabby hands, silencing whatever comment he was going to make. Then she stood and addressed the audience. "Honored guests, we are truly blessed that you have gathered with us today, not only to help King Elmer celebrate his renowned tournament, but also to witness our son's wedding. We have given you a small token to take back to your countries. But guard the contents carefully, for each of you has been given a treasured sweet, the likes of which you have never before tasted. Please open your boxes and enjoy."

The reaction was as it always was—pure delight. I remembered my first taste back in the Oaks' butter room, how nothing had ever melted on my tongue in such a way.

As soon as the ambassadors had consumed their gifts, they started asking questions. The queen held up a hand to quiet them. "You have just eaten a delicacy known as chocolate. We, the royal family of Anglund, are the only makers of chocolate in the world." Prince Beau and I shared a knowing look. "We know that you would like to have more, and therefore we will provide an additional box that you can take home to your sovereign leaders. But, honored guests, there is a limited supply of this delicacy. The secret ingredients are rare and expensive. That is why we will export our chocolate only to the kingdom that offers the highest bid."

"Only one kingdom?" an ambassador asked. The rest grumbled their disapproval.

"It is all we can spare," said the queen. She'd laid her trap. Now they'd fight until one of them fell right into it.

Except that the prince and I had also laid a trap. The time had come to reveal it. He squeezed my hand. I took a long breath. Was it fear or excitement that prickled the back of my neck? We risked the queen's wrath, which would terrify even the hardiest of men. But I'd learned, since my journey down that raging river, that the things we most desire are fraught with risk. Acceptance. Freedom. Love.

Prince Beau stepped to the edge of the stage and raised his hands. "Honored guests, may I please have your attention?"

Queen Beatrice smiled sweetly, but then spoke to her son in hushed tones. "We are not yet finished speaking."

"Mother, there is something I wish to show you."

Prince Beau nodded to the Baron of Lime, who was standing near the golden doors at the end of the hall. With a dramatic sweep of his arms, the baron opened the doors. Queen Beatrice gasped. The Royal Secretary dropped his scroll. The audience's faces froze in stunned awe.

For into the king and queen of Anglund's throne room stepped a dozen red-haired girls. Each carrying a churning bucket.

Chapter Fifty-three

Here's what had happened outside the city wall the night before my wedding, just after I'd learned that Owen was alive and in the queen's dungeon.

At that very moment, the story of chocolate filled my mind. Not the version told by a deranged queen who'd turned on her own people, but the true version written in a diary by the first Royal Secretary. The chocolate had been given to the Kell in gratitude. It had been a gift meant to be shared, passed from the first milkmaid to others. So there I was, just like the first milkmaid, holding the gift. I knew what I had to do.

I went back to the clearing where my people were gathered. They didn't know anything about chocolate. None of them had tasted it. Like Griffin and I, none had even heard of it. But they welcomed me to sit beside them and they thanked me once again for the food I'd brought.

"The food didn't belong to me. It was the prince who helped

you." I didn't know how to explain what I was about to do. "But there's something I've brought. Something that I'd like to give each of you."

I started with the smallest Flatlander girl, whose sunken eyes stared up at me with wonder. I took her hand and sat next to her. Then I closed my eyes, just as I had when I'd been crouching beside Snow, holding her as the river water flowed past. I'd asked Snow to stay with me forever and that's when the warmth had filled me. That's when the spell had entered my body. Holding the little girl's dirt-stained hand, I conjured this warmth, willed it to grow until it filled my insides. Then I guided it down my arm and out my fingertips. "I feel warm," the girl said.

I did this again and again, to every Flatlander girl and woman who'd come to Londwin City seeking help. Who'd journeyed to the outside world because they had nowhere else to go.

And so on that morning when I was supposed to wed Prince Beau, twelve Flatlander girls entered the throne room, carrying the buckets of cream that the prince had taken from the royal kitchens. The word *dirt-scratcher* slithered from painted lips as everyone gawked at the uninvited guests. "What is happening?" King Elmer asked after he'd eaten the last piece from his golden box. Queen Beatrice called out to her soldiers, but Prince Beau strode down the pathway and greeted the girls, leading them forward until they reached the thrones.

"Mother," Prince Beau announced, his usually soft voice surging with confidence. "Emmeline would like to present you and father with a gift on this joyous occasion."

"A gift?" King Elmer asked. "I love gifts. Hand it over. What are you waiting for?"

The breath that hissed from the queen's flared nostrils was so loud it could have been made of steam. "You mean Princess Sabina."

"No, Mother. I mean Emmeline. For that is her name." He took my hand and smiled at me. "Your turn," he said.

I should have been terrified, I suppose. Me, the nothing *dirt-scratcher* girl, facing the most powerful woman in the realm. The woman who could destroy everything and everyone I loved. But I wasn't terrified. I'd survived the flood, Peddler's torments, the leper beach, and the nightmare of believing that Owen was dead. I'd survived all those years on my own, all those years of believing that I was an unwanted, a mistake, a girl who should have died.

I filled my lungs with a steadying breath of the clotted, perfumed air and spoke the words I'd memorized last night. "For such appreciation do I feel for everything Their Royal Majesties have done for me, and because I know Their Royal Majesties love Anglund more than they love themselves, I give the gift of chocolate to all of Anglund in their names."

The Flatlander girls sat next to their buckets and began to churn. Their motion wasn't as graceful as mine, but they'd get the feel for it in time. Doubt did not exist at that moment. I knew the truth. That Queen Margaret had tried to keep the magic for herself, and her selfishness had killed her in the end. The magic of chocolate had made me famous and desired, but it had also imprisoned me. And it would continue to imprison me, and those I loved, if I kept the magic only to myself.

In setting myself free, I was setting us all free. Including the queen.

In each bucket, the cream turned from eggshell white to a lovely light brown. With a few more turns of the handles, it settled into its muddy hue. Whispers filled the hall. The crowd pushed forward, peering into the buckets. Queen Beatrice glared at me. "How?" She spat out the word. "How is this possible?"

I ignored her. Instead, I raised my voice so that it carried all the way to the back of the hall. "I do not come from some island in the middle of the ocean. I am not a princess. My name is Emmeline and I am from the Flatlands." More whispers. "These red-haired girls are also from the Flatlands. But we are not dirt-scratchers. We are Kell and we are citizens of Anglund. And we are the only people who can make chocolate."

The ambassadors leaned forward on their benches. Queen Beatrice tried to pull me away but Prince Beau stepped between us.

I continued. "The Flatlands have been destroyed by flood. My people need help rebuilding the main road. We need wagons and horses, livestock and timber. We need clothing and food. We will happily share the chocolate with all who wish to share with us in return."

"How dare you," the queen snapped. "How dare you cross us like this." She stomped off the stage and yanked a bucket from one of the girls' hands. "These dirt-scratchers are not allowed outside the Flatlands. Arrest them immediately."

"Do not arrest anyone," Prince Beau told the approaching soldiers. Then he pressed close to his mother, his voice quiet but dead serious. "You have violated our laws against slavery, Mother. I'm certain the nobles would be very interested to know about the mineral fields. As would the people who pay your taxes."

She raised her hand and I thought she might slap her son. But the hand lingered in the air for a moment, then retreated behind her back. "This was *your* idea?" She seemed surprised, as if a man who'd invented a flying balloon only had half a brain. "You would threaten your mother?"

He lowered his voice further. Only the Royal Secretary and I could catch the words. "I do not threaten. I'm simply trying to do what is right. You are destroying Anglund with your taxes and your greed."

The golden doors flew open again. "Your Majesties!" a soldier cried. The audience, who'd been standing frozen, trying to hear the exchange between the queen and Prince Beau, twisted around to face the door. "The people have stormed the gates! They have entered the city! They are armed and are demanding the king's head."

Color drained from the queen's painted lips. Trembling with rage, she fell back onto her throne, her hands gripping the armrests. The king, who'd taken a brief nap, fluttered his eyes and asked, "Has the tournament begun?"

Chaos erupted. Women and men screamed, feathered hats flew into the air, and little dogs yapped. The musicians jumped from the balcony and ran. Guests trampled one another as they tried to escape the throne room. The Royal Secretary tried to join the stampede, but Prince Beau grabbed his arm and held him in place. The king and queen sat on their thrones, their faces slack with disbelief and confusion. Prince Beau and I, and the Flatlander girls, remained calm, for we knew there were no crowds. We knew the soldier at the door was really the Baron of Lime in disguise.

"Mother, Father," Prince Beau said. "You are in danger. You must flee Londwin City immediately."

"They are approaching," the baron cried. "Make your escape. Now!"

Queen Beatrice was already out the back door by the time Prince Beau and I had helped the king from his throne.

The prince's flying balloon waited in the inner courtyard. Its basket bounced like an impatient child, as if eager to get to the sky. Once the king and queen were safely onboard, the Baron of Lime, still disguised as a soldier, climbed in and removed the first stone. "Where are we going?" the king asked.

"To the winter chalet," the prince answered. He'd dragged the Royal Secretary along and kept him close. "It is not too far for the balloon. You will be safe."

The baron emptied the last stone and the balloon quickly lifted.

"Good-bye, Father. Good-bye, Mother," Prince Beau called.

The king waved, his expression as confused as ever. The queen pointed at me. "We won't forget what you did!" she cried. "We'll never forget. *I'll* never forget!"

"Nor will I!" I yelled back.

The prince waited until the balloon had disappeared behind one of the palace's towers. Then he turned to the Royal Secretary, who stood empty-handed, his eyes bulging as if his high collar was cutting off all circulation to his head. "Deliver a proclamation to the crowds outside the city wall. Tell them I am in command. Let them know that all new taxes are immediately revoked. Then order the release of all those enslaved in the mineral fields. Send wagons to carry those men to their homes."

I wanted to hear the rest of the prince's proclamation, but there was one thing, and one thing only, on my mind. "Where's the dungeon?"

"They've already been released," Prince Beau said with a smile. "Even though we're not getting married, I still wanted to get you a wedding gift."

"Where—?"

"They're waiting for you at the palace gates."

Chapter Fifty-four

The crown of roses tumbled from my head. Why bother picking it up? I was no longer a royal bride.

My footsteps echoed as I ran through the empty throne room, through the golden door, and past the golden swans. It was at times like this, when my heart wanted to be somewhere but my body slowed me down, that I used to curse my curled foot. But if I'd learned anything over these months, it was that the foot was part of who I was. If I'd been born normal, I wouldn't have been left at the edge of the forest. I wouldn't have met Snow. If I'd been able to run as fast as everyone else, I might not have been swept downriver. I wouldn't be the girl I now was.

But there was no reason why I couldn't curse the stupid pointed wedding shoes. They tried their best to trip me as I turned down the hallway and hurried beneath the ceiling with its painted cloudscape. When walking along this same white marble floor with Griffin weeks earlier, I'd imagined I was being led into the everafter.

But the royal palace had turned out to be part of the real world—the unpredictable, crazy world where a peasant girl can be blessed with magic, rise to fame, and become a prince's bride.

Then give everything up and become a simple peasant girl once again.

Warm summer air wafted over me as I stumbled into the main courtyard, kicking up soot with my desperate steps. It felt ages ago that I'd watched the bestowing of coal in this very place. Gray, soot-stained tents now covered the grimy cobblestones. Men with numbers painted on their chests mingled around the tents. Sweaty men. Burly men. Growling, feisty, fight-loving men. Some punched bags of flour. Others punched one another as they got ready for the day's tournament. They didn't yet know that the tournament would be canceled, due to the fact that King Elmer was floating away. Most of the men stared at me as I stumbled past. In my white wedding gown I stood out like a single daisy in a field of ash.

"Emmeline!" It was Griffin. He strode right up and stood before me. The dark circles under his eyes and the beard made him look much older. He was covered in grime, his clothes torn, his hair filthy—he looked terrible, like he'd been locked in a dungeon.

"Griffin!" I threw my arms around his waist. "I'm so happy to see you. I didn't know about the dungeon. I thought she gave you the reward. I'm so sorry."

He hugged back. "I'm happy to see you too," he said quietly. Then he pulled away and looked down at me, confusion knotting his brow. "What are you doing out here? I thought you were getting married. And what have you done to your hair?"

"I didn't get married and my hair will be red again, but it will take a while." I looked up at him. "Are you okay?"

"I'm fine," he said, picking a piece of straw from his hair. "Wait, did you just say you didn't get married?" I nodded. "Why not? He's a prince."

"He's a very nice person but I don't love him. And he doesn't love me." I looked around. My legs twitching, my heart beating like a bird's, I couldn't stand still. Where was he? "Griffin, do you know—?"

"I have something to tell you, Emmeline." He gently squeezed my shoulders, holding me in place so he could look into my eyes. His hands were as big as bear paws. "I want you to know that if you bid on me at the next husband market, I will accept." He half-smiled. "What do you think?" A slight tremble ran through his fingers. His face flushed. Was Griffin Boar nervous? Was he was afraid I'd reject him?

A pair of fighters walked past, arguing about something. A cluster of kitchen boys handed out apples and meat pies. In the distance, a servant stood on a ladder, polishing the golden gate. "I shared the magic."

"Huh?"

"I shared the magic. I gave it to all the Flatlander girls and women who came to Londwin City looking for help. Now they can all make chocolate."

He let go of my shoulders and took a step back. "I see." I thought he'd walk away right then. Thought he'd tell me to "move out of his way" so he could go meet these other girls who were going to be rich. But he didn't. He cleared his throat and softened his voice. "Look, Emmeline, I still want . . . I mean, I still think that we should . . ." He rubbed his neck. "What I'm trying to say is that even though you're not perfect, there's something about you that I really like and I . . ." He folded his arms and frowned. "What are you doing?"

I was circling around him, my gaze scanning the crowded courtyard.

"You're looking for him, aren't you? You're looking for that Owen fellow."

"Aye, I am," I said. "Where is he? Is he okay?"

"You choose him over me, is that it?"

"Choose?" I circled again. "What do you mean? I didn't know I had a choice."

"Well, you do." Griffin Boar sighed. "He loves you."

I froze. The courtyard noise faded away and all I heard was my own breathing.

"Where is he?" I practically screamed as I grabbed Griffin's arm.

"He thought you'd gotten married," Griffin said. "He said he couldn't bear to stay and celebrate your wedding to another."

"He left?" Tears filled my eyes.

"Owen!" a voice called. A tent rustled and an enormous man stepped out, the number one painted on his chest. "I forgot to tell you something. Do you remember that fat promoter, the one from your village? He said you could ride home with him."

My entire body stiffened. I followed the man's one-eyed gaze across the cobblestones, past another tent, until it rested on a pair of soot-covered boots. Slowly, scared to death of disappointment, I lifted my gaze up a torn pant leg, up a bare chest, up a sun-colored neck, and onto the face that I'd seen in my dreams every single night since first seeing it in his bedroom.

I didn't need to call out his name because he was already looking at me. He'd seen me first.

Chapter Fifty-five

As it turned out, Peddler's dead body wasn't needed. The prince sent orders for us to be released. Peddler chose his death, so I suppose I shouldn't have felt sorry for him. He wanted to escape the misery he felt after losing his daughter. As I gave him once last glance, I tried to remember the man I once knew—the magical man with the pockets of treasures. But then I realized that Griffin was already heading up the dungeon stairs to chase after the woman I loved. I forgot all about Peddler.

By the time I reached fresh air, Griffin was long gone. If he found Emmeline first, my chances would be slim at best. He'd remind her that Flatlanders marry Flatlanders. He'd tell her he loved her. He'd do whatever it took to win her.

I asked around. Fighters, servants, and soldiers all told me that the royal wedding had already taken place. That I was too late. She'd never be mine. I'm not going to lie and say I wanted to impale myself on a knife the way Peddler had, but I can't remember a time

I'd ever felt so hopeless. A sudden chill possessed me, as if I'd fallen into the River Time.

But then, there she was. What was she doing in the courtyard amid the fighters' tents? Griffin stood next to her. They were talking. She was shaking her head. Then one-eyed Henry called my name and the next thing I knew, Emmeline was standing in front of me. What would I say now? Offer my congratulations? Pretend to be happy?

"Emmeline." I reached for her, then let my arms fall to my sides. She was married. I shouldn't touch her. But I wanted to whisk her off her feet and carry her from that courtyard. Take her home and pretend none of this had ever happened. Put her back into my bed and never leave her side.

"Owen," she said, her voice as warm as the courtyard's air. Though her hair had changed—black and hanging in thin braids—her eyes were the same deep green and they pulled me in. Were those tears at the corners? She grabbed my hands. "I thought you were dead." Her fingers trembled. I pressed my hands around hers, as tight as I could. "I thought Peddler had killed you."

"He missed my lung. I was lucky."

She smiled. "I'm so happy you're alive."

"I'm pretty happy about that too." I glanced at the dress, which clung to her body like cream. "Your wedding dress," I said, letting go of her hands. Unable to hide my disappointment, I winced. "You got married."

"No," she said. "No, no, no, no, no. There was no wedding."

"But everyone said—"

"We didn't get married," she insisted. "We're not getting married. I don't love him. And besides, he's promised to someone else."

My heartbeat doubled. One man down, one more to go. "What about Griffin? He said you were going to bid on him at the husband market. Is that true?"

"I don't love Griffin, either."

Emmeline and I both looked across the cobblestones where Griffin was sitting on a bench next to one of the fighters. He stared into a mirror as he shaved his face—his ridiculously handsome face.

I stuck my hands in my pockets. "Let me get this straight. You're not going to marry the prince of Anglund, who will one day be king, and you're not going to marry Griffin, the most popular guy in the Flatlands?"

Her eyes turned fiery. "What's so difficult to understand?" she snapped. "I don't love them."

We stared into each other's eyes. Why didn't I say anything? What was the matter with me? My feelings were practically seeping out of me but I couldn't put them into words. "I'm sorry," we both said.

"Why are *you* sorry?" I asked.

"Because it's my fault Peddler stabbed you. Your parents were so nice to me and you got hurt because of me. Because of the chocolate."

"Wait a minute." I frowned. "You have no reason to apologize. I should have saved you. I'm the one who blew it. If I'd saved you—"

"If you'd saved me I never would have learned the truth about the magic." She stepped closer. "I never would have learned the truth about my people."

I wasn't sure what she was talking about. All I could focus on was how close her face was. I wanted to take her chin in my hand. I wanted to kiss her. God, how I wanted to kiss her!

She reached out and touched the number two, still painted on my chest. Now was the time to tell her how I felt. Except that one-eyed Henry stood over by that tent, watching with a stupid grin on his face. And Griffin was watching us too, as were some of the fighters.

"Come on," I said. "There's no privacy here." I took her hand and led her through the golden gates and out onto the wide city boulevard. I knew not to walk too fast so she wouldn't have trouble keeping up. Unfortunately, the street was crowded, offering little privacy. The people of Londwin City were mingling with merchants and tax-collectors, with girls from the Flatlands and people with powdered faces. But this crowd wasn't acting like the one I'd seen outside the city wall. No one cried out in protest, no one waved weapons or shook fists. Smiles and laughter filled the air. Each Flatlander girl had a bucket at her feet and was handing out something to the delight of the crowd. "Are all those buckets filled with chocolate?" I asked. "You've been working hard."

"I didn't make any of it," Emmeline told me. "They made it. I shared the magic with each of them."

"Hi, Emmeline," one of the girls called. Emmeline waved back.

"You *shared* the magic?" Had I heard her correctly? "I didn't know you could do that."

"I didn't know either until I got here. The magic is a gift, Owen. It was a gift to my people. All of my people. It doesn't belong just to me." Sadness suddenly filled her eyes. "Are you disappointed?"

"Why would I be disappointed?"

"Because now that lots of girls can make chocolate, I won't be the richest girl in the kingdom. I won't be famous or important anymore."

"What are you talking about? Do you think I only care about the chocolate?" I couldn't bear one more second standing next to her. I pulled her close, pressing my chest against hers, and kissed her.

Chapter Fifty-six

Owen Oak kissed me.

He wrapped his arms around my waist and held me so close I could feel his heart pounding. Or was it my heart? I'm not sure but someone's heart was going to burst. But then I could only think about his lips, which were soft and pressed against mine. I'd never been kissed before. Warmth flowed over my entire body, the way it does when I make chocolate—only this was better. At that moment I didn't ask why. I didn't care why. It felt so good. We might have kissed forever if two merchants hadn't bumped into us on their way to get more chocolate.

"Emmeline," Owen said, his voice heavy as if he'd just woken from a nap. "I want to tell you something. I want to tell you how I feel."

"Wait," I said. Was this really happening? He'd kissed me and now he was looking at me with an expression both pained and happy. I knew that expression. I wore it every time I thought about how much I loved him.

"Wait," I repeated. "Before you say anything else, I need to do something." This was the moment I'd long dreaded—the moment when all of me had to be revealed. I walked to the edge of the boulevard and sat on a low wall that encircled a swan fountain. I pulled up the hem of my once pure-white dress, now stained with dungeon grime thanks to Griffin's and Owen's hugs. I began to unlace my right wedding shoe.

"What are you doing?" Owen asked.

"I need to show you."

He sat next to me. "Emmeline, you don't have to do this. I know all about your foot."

"I've spent my whole life hiding it. I want to show you." I took a long breath. Then, carefully, I pulled my foot from the shoe's velvet padding that had held it in place. Owen took the shoe and set it on the ground. My heart pounded as I unrolled the white knee-length stocking. I knew he'd seen my curled foot before, but this time it was my choice. As I pulled the stocking free, I watched from the corner of my eye for his reaction.

He didn't flinch, didn't grimace, didn't smile. He sighed, as if bored. "Is that all you got?" he asked. Then he pointed to a long wrinkled scar on his arm. "See that? That's where I leaned up against an ironsmith's furnace." He turned his back to me. "See that?" Another scar ran across his lower back. "I fell off my horse and landed on a rock." He turned back around. "See that? That's where Peddler stabbed me and it's going to leave another scar." A wound lay just below his ribs. "As you can see, I'm a mess."

Then he set his hand gently on my foot. Tears pooled in the

corners of my eyes. "If you think your foot is going to scare me away, Emmeline Thistle, you don't know me at all." He kissed me again.

I pulled away because he was smiling. "What's so funny?"

"I hear you've been calling out my name in your sleep."

"What?" I almost denied it, but then remembered that he and Griffin had been stuck in the dungeon together. Even so, I didn't want to deny my feelings—not anymore. "I missed you," I said.

"I missed you too."

He wrapped an arm around my shoulder, and we sat there as if it were perfectly normal for a Flatlander girl and a boy from Wander to be in love. It felt better than perfectly normal. It felt extraordinary!

Water trickled in the fountain behind us. The Flatlander girls were still handing out chocolate. People made room as a couple of wagons drove up the boulevard. The rest of the Flatlanders who had gathered outside the city wall now sat in the wagons' beds, my father among them. "Prince Beau is going to let us stay until the road's been repaired," he called out to me.

"That's good news," I called back. The wagon headed through the golden gates.

"Thank you for rescuing my father," I said to Owen.

"It was the least I could do," he said.

That's when I noticed Griffin. Freshly shaven and looking more like his old self, he leaned against the gate, talking to a woman I immediately recognized. The Baroness of Salt wore the same checkered cloak she'd worn when Griffin had pulled her from her carriage. Her blond hair, as golden as the gate itself, hung to her waist. She didn't seem angry at Griffin for stealing her carriage and horses. Quite the opposite, for she was smiling at him and laughing as he told her some story, probably about how he'd delivered the famous Milkmaid to the palace. A cluster of royal milkmaids stood nearby, watching him with awe. He was back where he belonged—the center of female attention.

"Look," Owen said. The royal cows walked through the golden gates and out into the boulevard, their golden neck ribbons sparkling. Kitchen boys ran after them, trying to turn them around, but the cows paid the boys no mind. They headed straight for me, calling to me with loud moos. Soon they were gathered around the fountain, drinking and flicking their tails. I pressed my palm against their muzzles as they greeted me. How wonderful, I realized for the first time, that the color of a cow's eyes is like melted chocolate.

"Come back to Wander with me," Owen said. "Stay with me."

"You don't care that I'm not the only one who can make chocolate?"

"Care? I think it's brilliant. Now I don't have to worry about you getting kidnapped again. You and your father can start a new life in Wander. We can be together." He whispered in my ear. "Your father said that the husband market is only once a year. Do I have to wait that long?"

"It's our tradition. And I think it's important that we Kell keep our traditions." I pushed a curly lock from his eyes. His brown eyes. Funny how I'd always found comfort in brown eyes, whether they belonged to a four-footed creature or a two-footed one.

"Must you keep all traditions? Even the one where Flatlanders only marry Flatlanders?"

"Well, maybe not *all* traditions." I smiled. "What makes you think I'd bid on you anyway?"

"Because you love me." He kissed my cheek. "And because I love you."

I laughed. "Guess I'll have to start saving my coin."

Acknowledgments

How is it possible that this is my fourth teen novel? Time has certainly flown since I wrote *Saving Juliet*. I had no idea when I started writing for teens that it would be such a fun journey. From the time-traveling adventures of an actress and pop star to a coffeehouse girl's encounter with an angel to a romance writer's daughter and her conversations with Cupid, and now this—a love story that centers around chocolate. Love *and* chocolate. What could be better than that?

I want to express my deepest gratitude to you, my readers, because you invite my stories into your busy lives, and for that I am honored. I can only hope that I live up to your expectations by whisking you away from this crazy world for a few hours and plunging you into a new world that is exciting, funny, and most important, entertaining. You amaze me every day with your love letters and enthusiasm.

Huge thanks to my first-draft readers and brainstormers for this book: Isabelle Ranson, Bob Ranson, Elsa Watson, Michael Bourret (who also doubles as my intrepid literary agent), and Emily Easton (who also doubles as my wise and patient editor). And thanks, once again, to Hot Shots Java in Poulsbo, Washington, for providing me with coffee, chocolate, and a great workplace.

Please visit me at www.suzanneselfors.com and keep sending those letters!